Burial
Rites

Burial Rites

Hannah Kent

PICADOR

First published 2013 in Picador by Pan Macmillan Australia Pty Limited, Sydney

First published in Great Britain 2013 by Picador
an imprint of Pan Macmillan, a division of Macmillan Publishers Limited
Pan Macmillan, 20 New Wharf Road, London N1 9RR
Basingstoke and Oxford
Associated companies throughout the world
www.panmacmillan.com

ISBN 978-1-4472-3316-9

Quotations from *The Icelandic Burial Hymn* and *The Way of the Cross* sourced
from the English translation originally published in 1913 in *The Passion-Hymns
of Iceland* by Charles V. Pilcher, London: Robert Scott, Roxburghe House.
The hymns were originally written by Hallgrimur Petursson.

Quotations from the *Laxdæla Saga* sourced from the translation by Magnús Magnússon,
first published in 1969 by Penguin Classics, London, and reproduced with the kind permission
of the publisher. The original author of the saga is unknown – it was written in 1245.

The line from the *Laxdæla Saga*, 'I was worst to the one I loved best', translated by the author.

1 3 5 7 9 8 6 4 2

A CIP catalogue record for this book is available from the British Library.

Map by Martin Lubikowski, ML Design, London
Printed and bound by CPI Group (UK) Ltd, Croydon, CR0 4YY

For my parents

A NOTE ON ICELANDIC NAMES

Icelanders have traditionally used a patronymic naming system, whereby a child's last name is derived from his or her father's first name, together with an affixation of -són or -dóttir. Agnes *Magnúsdóttir* is therefore literally translated as Agnes *Magnús's daughter*. Because of this system, blood members of an Icelandic family may all have different surnames.

A NOTE ON ICELANDIC PRONUNCIATION

For ease of pronunciation, not all Icelandic letters have been used in this printing. The consonants ð (Ð) and þ (Þ) have been replaced with 'd' and 'th' respectively.

The pronunciation of certain vowels are conditioned by accents:

á as the *ow* in *owl*
é as the *ye* in *yet*
í as the *ee* in *been*
ó as the *o* in *note*
ö as in the French *fleur*
ú as the *oo* in *moon*
ý as the *ee* in *been*
æ as the *i* in *wife*
au as in the French *oeil*
ei as the *ay* in *way*

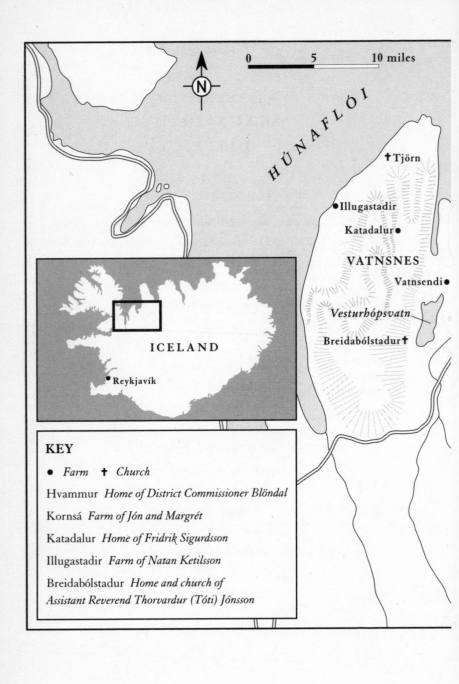

0 5 10 miles

HÚNAFLÓI

† Tjörn

● Illugastadir

Katadalur ●

VATNSNES

Vatnsendi ●

Vesturhópsvatn

Breidabólstadur †

ICELAND

● Reykjavík

KEY

● *Farm* † *Church*

Hvammur *Home of District Commissioner Blöndal*

Kornsá *Farm of Jón and Margrét*

Katadalur *Home of Fridrik Sigurdsson*

Illugastadir *Farm of Natan Ketilsson*

Breidabólstadur *Home and church of*
Assistant Reverend Thorvardur (Tóti) Jónsson

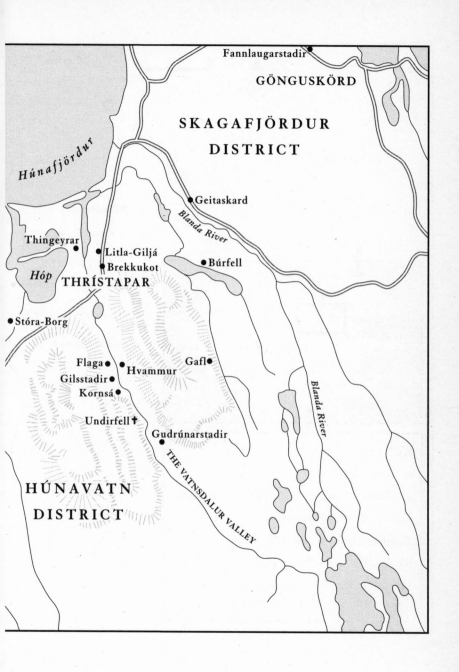

'I WAS WORST TO THE ONE I LOVED BEST.'
Laxdæla Saga

PROLOGUE

THEY SAID I MUST DIE. They said that I stole the breath from men, and now they must steal mine. I imagine, then, that we are all candle flames, greasy-bright, fluttering in the darkness and the howl of the wind, and in the stillness of the room I hear footsteps, awful coming footsteps, coming to blow me out and send my life up away from me in a grey wreath of smoke. I will vanish into the air and the night. They will blow us all out, one by one, until it is only their own light by which they see themselves. Where will I be then?

Sometimes I think I see it again, the farm, burning in the dark. Sometimes I can feel the ache of winter in my lungs, and I think I see the flames mirrored in the ocean, the water so strange, so flickered with light. There was a moment during that night when I looked back. I looked back to watch the fire, and if I lick my skin I can still taste the salt. The smoke.

It wasn't always so cold.

I hear footsteps.

CHAPTER ONE

Public Notice

THERE WILL BE AN AUCTION on the 24th of March 1828, at Illugastadir, for the valuables the farmer Natan Ketilsson has left behind. There is one cow, a few horses, a considerable amount of sheep, hay and furniture, a saddle, a bridle, and many dishes and plates. All this will be sold if a decent offer is presented. All valuables will be awarded to the highest bidder. If the auction is not possible due to bad weather, it will be cancelled and held the next day, weather allowing.

DISTRICT COMMISSIONER
Björn Blöndal

20th of March 1828

To the Very Reverend Jóhann Tómasson,

Thank you for your worthy letter from the 14th, where you wished to be informed of how we attended to the burial of Pétur Jónsson from Geitaskard, who is said to have been murdered and burned on the night between the 13th and the 14th of this month, with Natan Ketilsson. As my Reverend is aware, there was some deliberation over whether his bones should be buried in consecrated ground. His conviction and punishment for robbery, theft, and receiving stolen property was to follow after his prosecution in the Supreme Court. However, we have not had any letters from Denmark. The Land Court judge convicted Pétur on the 5th of February last year, and sentenced him to four years of hard labour in the Rasphus in Copenhagen, but at the time of his murder he was on 'free foot'. Therefore, in answer to your enquiry, his bones were buried with Christian rites, alongside Natan's, as he could not yet be thought of as belonging to those outside the Christian way. These people are expressly defined in the letter from His Majesty the King on the 30th of December 1740, which lists all persons who shall not be permitted Christian burial rites.

DISTRICT COMMISSIONER
Björn Blöndal

30th of May 1829

Rev. T. Jónsson
Breidabólstadur, Vesturhóp

To the Assistant Reverend Thorvardur Jónsson,

I trust this letter finds you well and thriving in your
administration of the Lord's work in Vesturhóp.

    Firstly, I wish to extend to you my congratulations, however
belatedly, for the successful completion of your studies in the
south of Iceland. Your parishioners say that you are a diligent
young man, and I approve of your decision to repair to the north
to begin your chaplaincy under the supervision of your father. It
is of considerable joy to me to know that there remain righteous
men willing to fulfil their duties to man and God.

    Secondly, I, in my capacity as District Commissioner,
write to you in request of service. As you will be aware, our
community has recently been darkened by the shadow of crime.
The Illugastadir murders, committed last year, have in their
heinousness emblematised the corruption and ungodliness of this
county. As District Commissioner for Húnavatn, I cannot abide
societal waywardness and, after the anticipated authorisation
from the Supreme Court in Copenhagen, I intend to execute the
Illugastadir murderers. It is with this event in mind that I ask for
your assistance, Assistant Reverend Thorvardur.

As you will recall, I related the event of the murders in a letter circulated to the clergy almost ten months ago, with orders that sermons of chastisement be delivered. Allow me to repeat what occurred, this time to provide you with a more invested consideration of the crime.

Last year, on the night between the 13th and 14th of March, three people committed a severe and loathsome act against two men, with whom you may be familiar: Natan Ketilsson and Pétur Jónsson. Pétur and Natan were found in the burnt ruins of Natan's farm, Illugastadir, and a closer examination of their corpses revealed wounds of a deliberately inflicted nature. This discovery led to an enquiry, and from there a trial ensued. On the 2nd of July last year the three persons charged with these murders – one man and two women – were found guilty in the District Court, presided over by myself, and sentenced to be beheaded: 'He that Smiteth a Man so that he Die, shall be surely put to Death.' The death sentences were upheld in the Land Court on the 27th of October last year, which met in Reykjavík. The case is currently being tried in Copenhagen's Supreme Court, and it is likely that my original judgment will stand there also. The name of the convicted man is Fridrik Sigurdsson, the son of the farmer at Katadalur. The women are workmaids, named Sigrídur Gudmundsdóttir and Agnes Magnúsdóttir.

These convicted persons are currently held in custody here in the north, and will be until the time of their execution. Fridrik Sigurdsson has been taken into Thingeyrar by Reverend Jóhann Tómasson, and Sigrídur Gudmundsdóttir was removed to Midhóp. Agnes Magnúsdóttir was to be kept until her execution at Stóra-Borg, but for reasons which I am not at liberty to state, will be moved to a new holding at Kornsá in the valley of Vatnsdalur next month. She is discontented with her current spiritual administrator, and has used one of her few remaining rights to request another priest. She has requested you, Assistant Reverend Thorvardur.

It is with some uncertainty that I approach you for this task. I am aware that your responsibilities have so far been confined to the spiritual education of your parish's youngest members, which is to say, of undoubted value, but it is of little political import. You may yourself admit that you are too pale in experience to know how to bring this condemned woman to the Lord and His infinite mercy, in which case I would not protest your disinclination. It is a weight that I would hesitate to bestow on the shoulders of experienced clergymen.

Should you, however, accept the responsibility of preparing Agnes Magnúsdóttir for her meeting with our Lord, you will be obliged to visit Kornsá regularly when the weather allows. You must administer God's word and inspire repentance and an acknowledgement of Justice. Please do not let flattery influence your decision, nor kinship, if any resides between you and the convicted. In all things, Reverend, if you cannot construct your own counsel, seek mine.

I await word of your response. Please provide my messenger with such.

DISTRICT COMMISSIONER
Björn Blöndal

ASSISTANT REVEREND THORVARDUR JÓNSSON WAS inside the small farmstead adjoined to the church of Breidaból-stadur, repairing the hearth with new stones, when he heard his father clear his throat in the doorway.

'There's a messenger from Hvammur outside, Tóti. He's asking for you.'

'For me?' In his surprise he let a rock slip out of his hand. It dropped to the packed earth floor, narrowly missing his foot. Reverend Jón sucked his teeth in annoyance, ducked his head under the doorframe and gently pushed Tóti out of the way.

'Yes, for you. He's waiting.'

The messenger was a servant, dressed in a worn coat. He gave Tóti a long look before speaking. 'Reverend Thorvardur Jónsson?'

'That's me. Greetings. Well, I'm an Assistant Reverend.'

The servant shrugged. 'I have a letter for you from the District Commissioner, the Honourable Björn Blöndal.' He pulled a small slip of paper out from the inside of his coat, and gave it to Tóti. 'I've orders to wait here while you read it.'

The letter was warm and damp from sitting inside the servant's clothes. Tóti broke the seal and, noting that it had been written that same day, sat on the chopping block outside the doorway and began to read.

When he finished Blöndal's letter, he looked up and noticed the servant watching him. 'Well?' the servant prompted, with a raised eyebrow.

'I beg your pardon?'

'Your response for the District Commissioner? I don't have all day.'

'May I talk with my father?'

The servant sighed. 'Go on then.'

He found his father in the badstofa, slowly smoothing the blankets upon his bed.

'Yes?'

'It's from the District Commissioner.' Tóti offered his father the unfolded letter and waited as he read it, unsure of what to do.

His father's face was impassive as he folded the letter and handed it back. He didn't say anything.

'What should I say?' Tóti asked, finally.

'That's your choice.'

'I don't know her.'

'No.'

'She's not in our parish?'

'No.'

'Why has she asked for me? I'm only an Assistant Reverend.'

His father turned back to his bed. 'Perhaps you ought to address that question to her.'

The servant was sitting on the chopping block, cleaning his nails with a knife. 'Well now. What response am I to give the District Commissioner from the *Assistant* Reverend?'

Tóti replied before he knew his decision. 'Tell Blöndal that I will meet with Agnes Magnúsdóttir.'

The servant's eyes widened. 'Is *that* what this is all about then?'

'I'm to be her spiritual advisor.'

The servant gaped at him, and then suddenly laughed. 'Good Lord,' he muttered. 'They pick a mouse to tame a cat.' And with that he mounted his horse and vanished behind the swell of hills, leaving Tóti standing still, holding the letter away from him as though it were about to catch fire.

STEINA JÓNSDÓTTIR WAS PILING DRIED dung in the yard outside her family's turf croft when she heard the rapid clop of horses' hooves. Rubbing mud off her skirts, she stood and peered around the side of the hovel to better see the riding track that ran through the valley. A man in a bright red coat was approaching. She watched him turn towards the farm and, fighting a flicker of panic at the realisation she would have to greet him, retreated back around the croft, where she hurriedly spat on her hands to clean them and wiped her nose on her sleeve. When she returned to the yard, the rider was waiting.

'Hello, young lady.' The man looked down at Steina and her filthy skirts with an air of bemusement. 'I see I have interrupted you at your chores.' Steina stared as he dismounted, gracefully swinging his leg over his horse. For a large man he landed lightly on his feet. 'Do you know who I am?' He looked at her for a glimmer of recognition.

Steina shook her head.

'I am the District Commissioner, Björn Audunsson Blöndal.' He gave her a little nod of his head and adjusted his coat, which, Steina noticed, was trimmed with silver buttons.

'You're from Hvammur,' she murmured.

Blöndal smiled patiently. 'Yes. I am your father's overseer. I have come to speak with him.'

'He's not home.'

Blöndal frowned. 'And your mother?'

'They're visiting folks down south in the valley.'

'I see.' He looked fixedly at the young woman, who squirmed and cast her eyes nervously to the fields. A smattering of freckles across her nose and forehead interrupted what was otherwise pale skin. Her eyes were brown and widely set, and there was a large gap between her front teeth. There was something rather ungainly about her, Blöndal decided. He noted the thick crescents of dirt under her fingernails.

'You'll have to come back later,' Steina finally suggested.

Blöndal tensed. 'May I at least come inside?'

'Oh. If you want. You can tie your horse there.' Steina bit her lip while Blöndal wound his reins through a post in the yard, and then she turned and almost ran inside.

Blöndal followed her, stooping under the low entrance to the croft. 'Will your father return this day?'

'No,' was the curt reply.

'How unfavourable,' Blöndal complained, stumbling in the dark passageway as Steina led him through to the badstofa. He had grown corpulent since his posting as District Commissioner and was accustomed to the more spacious dwelling provided for him and his family at Hvammur, built from imported wood. The hovels of the peasants and farmers had begun to repel him, with their cramped rooms constructed of turf that issued clouds of dust in the summer, irritating his lungs.

'Commissioner –'

'District Commissioner.'

'I'm sorry, District Commissioner. Mamma and Pabbi, I mean, Margrét and Jón, will return tomorrow. Or the next day. Depending on the weather.' Steina gestured towards the nearest end of the narrow room, where a grey woollen curtain served as a partition between the badstofa and a tiny parlour. 'Sit in there,' she said. 'I'll go find my sister.'

Lauga Jónsdóttir, Steina's younger sister, was weeding the meagre vegetable plot at a little distance from the croft. Bent over her task, she hadn't seen the District Commissioner arrive, but she heard her sister calling long before she came into sight.

'Lauga! Where are you? Lauga!'

Lauga rose to her feet and wiped her soiled hands on her apron. She didn't shout back to her sister, but waited patiently until Steina, running and tripping over her long skirts, spotted her.

'I've been looking everywhere for you!' Steina cried, out of breath.

'What on God's earth is wrong with you?'

'The Commissioner is here!'

'Who?'

'Blöndal!'

Lauga stared at her sister. 'District Commissioner Björn Blöndal? Wipe your nose, Steina, you're snotting.'

'He's sitting in the parlour.'

'Where?'

'You know, behind the curtain.'

'You left him there *by himself*?' Lauga's eyes grew wide.

Steina grimaced. 'Please come and talk to him.'

Lauga glared at her sister, then quickly untied her dirty apron and dropped it beside the lovage. 'I can't think of what goes through your head sometimes, Steina,' she muttered, as they walked quickly towards the croft. 'Leaving a man like Blöndal twiddling his thumbs in our badstofa.'

'In the parlour.'

'What difference does it make? I suppose you gave him the servants' whey to drink, too.'

Steina turned to her sister with a panicked expression. 'I didn't give him anything.'

'Steina!' Lauga broke into a little trot. 'He'll think us peasants!'

Steina watched her sister pick her way through the tussocks of grass. 'We *are* peasants,' she mumbled.

Lauga quickly washed her face and hands, and snatched a new apron from Kristín, the family's workmaid, who had hidden herself in the kitchen at the sound of a stranger's voice. Lauga found the District Commissioner seated at the little wooden table in the parlour, reading over a slip of paper. Expressing apologies for her sister's discourteous reception, she offered him a plate of cold, hashed mutton, which he took gladly, albeit with a slightly injured air. She quietly stood aside as he ate, watching his fleshy lips wrap about the meat. Perhaps her Pabbi was to be promoted from District Officer to an even greater title. Perhaps he would receive a uniform, or a stipend from the Danish Crown. There might be new dresses. A new home. More servants.

Blöndal scraped his knife across the plate.

'Would you like some skyr and cream, District Commissioner?' she asked, taking the empty dish.

Blöndal waved his hands in front of his chest as if to decline, then paused. 'Well, all right then. Thank you.'

Lauga blushed and turned to fetch the soft cheese.

'And I would not object to coffee,' he called after her as she ducked her head around the curtain.

'What does he want?' Steina asked, huddling by the fire in the kitchen. 'I can't hear anything except you, clomping up and down the corridor.'

Lauga shoved the dirty plate at her. 'He hasn't said anything yet. He wants skyr and coffee.'

Steina exchanged looks with Kristín, who rolled her eyes. 'We have no coffee,' Steina said quietly.

'Yes we do. I saw some in the pantry last week.'

Steina hesitated. 'I ... I drank it.'

'Steina! The coffee isn't for us! We save it for occasions!'

'Occasions? The Commissioner never visits.'

'The *District* Commissioner, Steina!'

'The servants are coming back from Reykjavík soon. We might have more then.'

'That's then. What are we going to do now?' Exasperated, Lauga pushed Kristín in the direction of the pantry. 'Skyr and cream! Hurry.'

'I wanted to know what it tasted like,' Steina offered.

'It's too late. Bring him some fresh milk instead. Bring everything in when it's ready. Actually no, let Kristín. You look like you've been rolling in the dirt with the horses.' Lauga shot a scathing look at the dung on Steina's clothes and walked back down the corridor.

Blöndal was waiting for her. 'Young lady. I suppose you are wondering at my occasioning your family with a visit.'

'My name is Sigurlaug. Or Lauga, if you like.'

'Quite. Sigurlaug.'

'Is it some business of my father's? He is –'

'Southbound, yes, I know. Your sister told me, and ... Oh look, here she is.'

Lauga turned and saw Steina emerging round the side of the partition, carrying the soft cheese, cream and berries in one grimy hand, and the milk in the other. Lauga gave her sister a vexed look as Steina accidentally dragged the edge of the curtain through the skyr. Fortunately the District Commissioner seemed oblivious.

'Sir,' Steina mumbled. She set the bowl and cup on the table in front of him, and then gave an awkward curtsey. 'May it do you good.'

'Thank you,' Blöndal replied. He sniffed the skyr appraisingly, then looked up at the two sisters. He smiled thinly. 'Who is the elder?'

Lauga nudged Steina to prompt her, but she remained silent, gaping at the brilliant red of the man's coat.

'I am younger, District Commissioner,' Lauga said eventually, smiling to show off her dimples. 'By one year. Steinvör is twenty-one this month.'

'Everyone calls me Steina.'

'You are both very pretty,' Blöndal said.

'Thank you, sir.' Lauga nudged Steina again.

'Thank you,' Steina mumbled.

'Both have your father's fair hair, though I see you have your mother's blue eyes,' he said, nodding at Lauga. He pushed the untouched bowl towards her and took up the milk. He sniffed it and set it down on the table again.

'Please, sir, eat,' Lauga said, motioning to the bowl.

'Thank you, but I am suddenly sated.' Blöndal reached into his coat pocket. 'Now, I would have preferred to discuss this with the master of the house, but as District Officer Jón isn't here and this cannot wait until his return, I see I must tell his daughters.' He took up his sheet of paper and unfolded it upon the table for them to read.

'I trust that you are familiar with the event that occurred at Illugastadir last year?' he asked.

Steina flinched. 'Do you mean the murders?'

Lauga nodded, her blue eyes wide with sudden solemnity. 'The trial was held at your home.'

Blöndal inclined his head. 'Yes. The murders of Natan Ketilsson the herbalist and Pétur Jónsson. As this most unfortunate and grievous tragedy occurred within the Húnavatn District, it was my responsibility to work with the magistrate and Land Court in Reykjavík to come to some sort of arrangement regarding the persons accused.'

Lauga picked up the paper and walked to the window to read by its light. 'So it is all over.'

'On the contrary. The three accused were last October found guilty of both murder and arson in the court of this country. The case has now proceeded to the *Supreme* Court in Copenhagen, Denmark. The King ...' and here Blöndal paused for effect '... The King himself must learn of the crime, and agree with *my* original sentence of execution. As you can read for yourself, they have each received a capital sentence. It is a victory for justice, as I am sure you will agree.'

Lauga nodded absently, still reading. 'They're not being sent to Denmark?'

Blöndal smiled, and swung back on the wooden chair, lifting the heels of his boots off the ground. 'No.'

Lauga looked up at him, puzzled. 'Then, sir, excuse my ignorance, but where are they to be ...?' Her voice trailed off.

Blöndal scraped back his chair and rose to stand next to her at the window, ignoring Steina. He peered out through the dried sheep's bladder that had been pulled across to serve as a pane, noticing a small vein twisted in its dull surface. He shuddered. His own house had glass windows.

'They shall be executed here,' he said finally. 'In Iceland. In the north of Iceland, to be exact. I and the magistrate who presided at Reykjavík decided it would be ...' He hesitated, deliberating. 'More economical.'

'Really?'

Blöndal frowned at Steina, who was eyeing him with suspicion. She reached over and plucked the slip of paper out of Lauga's hand.

'Yes, although I will not deny that the execution also brings with it an opportunity for our community to witness the consequences for grave misdemeanour. It requires careful handling. As you are aware, clever Sigurlaug, criminals of this stature are usually sent abroad for their punishment, where there are gaolhouses and the like. As it has been decided that the three will be executed in Iceland, in the same district in which they undertook their crime, we are in need of some sort of custodial holding until the date and place of execution have been agreed upon.

'As you well know, we have no factories, no public house in Húnavatn that we may use to accommodate prisoners.' Blöndal turned and eased himself back into the chair. 'This is why I decided that they should be placed on farms, homes of upright Christians, who would inspire repentance by good example, and who would benefit from the work these prisoners do as they await their judgment.'

Blöndal leaned across the table towards Steina, who stared at him, one hand over her mouth and the other clutching the letter. 'Icelanders,' he continued, 'who would be able to fulfil their duties as government officials by providing this accommodation.'

Lauga looked at the District Commissioner in bewilderment. 'Can't they be placed in holdings at Reykjavík?' she whispered.

'No. There are costs.' He waved his hand in the air.

Steina's eyes narrowed. 'You're putting them *here*? With us? Because the court in Reykjavík wants to avoid the cost of sending them abroad?'

'Steina,' Lauga warned.

'Your family will be compensated,' Blöndal said, frowning.

'What are we supposed to do? Chain them to our bedposts?'

Blöndal slowly rose to his full height. 'I have no choice,' he said, his voice suddenly low and dangerous. 'Your father's title comes with responsibility. I'm sure he would not question me. Kornsá has too few hands to work it, and there is the issue of your family's financial state.' He approached Steina, looking down at her small, dirty face in the dim light. 'Besides, Steinvör, I will not suffer you and your family to hold all three convicts. It is only one of the women.' He placed a heavy hand upon her shoulder, ignoring the way she recoiled. 'You're not afraid of your own sex now, are you?'

After Blöndal had left, Steina returned to the parlour and picked up the uneaten bowl of skyr. Cream had congealed at its rim. She shook with frustration and rage, and pressed the bowl hard into the table, biting her bottom lip. She screamed silently, willing the bowl to break, until the flood of anger passed. Then she returned to the kitchen.

THERE ARE TIMES WHEN I wonder whether I'm not already dead. This is no life; waiting in darkness, in silence, in a room so squalid I have forgotten the smell of fresh air. The chamber pot is so full of my waste that it threatens to spill if someone does not come and empty it soon.

When did they last come? It is all one long night now.

In the winter it was better. In the winter the Stóra-Borg folk were as imprisoned as I; we all shared the badstofa when the snow stormed the croft. They had lamps for the waking hours, and when the oil ran out, candles to keep the darkness at bay. Then spring came and they moved me to the storeroom. They left me alone without a light and there was no means to measure the hours, no way to mark the day from night. Now I keep company with only the fetters about my wrists, the dirt floor, a dismantled loom, abandoned in the corner, an old broken handspindle.

Perhaps it is already summer. I can hear the footsteps of servants patter along the corridor, the creak of a door as they go to and fro. Sometimes I hear the shrill, piping laughter of workmaids as they chat together outside, and I know that the weather has eased, that the wind has lost its teeth. And I close my eyes and I imagine the valley in the long days of summer, the sun warming the bones of the earth until the swans flock to the lake, and the clouds lifting to reveal the height of the sky: bright, bright blue, so bright you could weep.

✝

THREE DAYS AFTER BJÖRN BLÖNDAL visited the daughters of Kornsá, their father, the District Officer of Vatnsdalur, Jón Jónsson, and his wife Margrét, set out for home.

Jón, a slightly stooped, wiry man of fifty-five winters, with snow-blond hair and large ears that made him appear simple-minded, walked in front of their horse, leading it by the reins and stepping over the uneven ground with practised ease. His wife, sitting atop their black mare, was wearied by their journey, although she would not have admitted it. She sat with her chin slightly raised, her head propped up by a thin, tremulous neck. The glance of her hooded eyes skipped from farm to farm as they passed the small homesteads of the Vatnsdalur valley, closing only when she suffered fits of coughing. When these subsided she would lean over the horse to spit, then wipe her mouth with a corner of her shawl, muttering a short prayer. Her husband occasionally inclined his head towards her when she did so, as if vaguely concerned she might topple off the horse, but otherwise they continued travelling uninterrupted.

Margrét, having just exhausted herself with another racking bark, spat onto the grass and pressed her palms against her chest until she got her breath back. Her voice, when she spoke, was hoarse.

'See now, Jón, the folks of Ás have another cow.'

'Hmm?' Her husband was lost in his thoughts.

'I said,' Margrét remarked, clearing her throat, 'the folks of Ás have another cow.'

'Is that so?'

'I'm surprised you didn't notice it yourself.'

'Right.'

Margrét blinked against the dusty light, and made out the vague shape of the Kornsá croft in the distance ahead.

'Nearly home.'

Her husband grunted his agreement.

'Makes you think, doesn't it, Jón? We could do with another cow.'

'We could do with many more things.'

'Another cow would be nice though. The extra butter. We could afford another hand for harvest.'

'In good time, Margrét, love.'

'In good time I'll be dead.'

The words came out more bitterly than she intended. Jón didn't reply, only murmured to their horse to urge it onwards, and Margrét frowned at the back of his riding hat, willing him to turn around. When he kept plodding onwards, she took a deep breath and again peered towards Kornsá.

It was late afternoon and the light was fading across the hayfields, eased out of the sky by low clouds gathering in the east. Patches of old snow upon the mountain ridge looked by turns dull and grey, and then, as the clouds shifted, a startling white. Summer birds darted across the hayfields to catch the insects that quavered above them and the querulous bleats of sheep could be heard, as young boys drove them down the valley towards the farmsteads.

At Kornsá, Lauga and Steina stepped out of the croft to collect water from the mountain stream, Lauga rubbing her eyes in the sunlight and Steina absently swinging her bucket against her side in time with her step. They were not speaking.

The two sisters had worked the past few days in complete silence, only addressing one another to request the spade, or to ask which barrel of salted cod ought to be opened first. The silence, which began after a row following the District Commissioner's visit, had been streaked with anger and anxiety. The effort of speaking as little to each other as possible had exhausted them both. Lauga, frustrated by her elder sister's stubbornness and awkwardness, could not stop thinking of what her parents would say about Blöndal's visit. Steina's ungracious reaction to the news delivered by Blöndal could affect their social standing. Björn Blöndal was a powerful man, and would not like to be challenged by a stripling of a girl. Didn't Steina know how much their family relied on Blöndal? How they would only be doing their duty?

Steina was trying to avoid thinking about the murderess at all. The crime itself made her feel sick, and remembering the callous manner in which the Commissioner had forced the criminal upon them made her throat seize up with fury. Lauga was the youngest, she should not be the one telling her what she should and should not do. How was she to know the ins and outs of social niceties one was obliged to perform for fat men in red jackets? No. It was better to not think of it at all.

Steina let the weight of her bucket pull her shoulder down and gave a great yawn. Beside her, Lauga couldn't help but yawn too, and for a brief moment they caught each other's eye and an understanding of shared fatigue passed between them, until Lauga's curt reminder to cover her mouth made Steina glower and glare at the ground.

The gentle beams of afternoon light were warm on their faces as they moved towards the stream. There was no wind, and the valley was so still that the two women began to walk more slowly to keep with the pause in the air. They were nearing the rocky outcrop surrounding the brook when Lauga, twisting around to pull her skirt off a thorn bush, noticed a horse in the distance.

'Oh!' she gasped.

Steina turned. 'What is it now?'

Lauga nodded in the direction of the horse. 'It's Mamma and Pabbi,' she said breathlessly. 'They've returned.' She squinted through the haze of sunlight across the fields. 'Yes, it's them,' she said, as if to herself. Suddenly agitated, Lauga pushed her bucket at Steina and motioned for her to continue walking towards the stream. 'Fill these. You can manage both, can't you? It's better if I ... I'll go. To light the fire.' She shoved Steina on the shoulder, harder than she intended, then turned on her heel.

The brambles along the path caught at Lauga's stockings as she rushed back to the croft, overcome with relief. Now Pabbi could deal with the District Commissioner and Agnes Magnúsdóttir.

Pushing open the door to the farmhouse, Lauga made her way down the corridor and turned left into the kitchen. In the absence of her mistress, Kristín had taken the afternoon off to visit her family, but the hearth was still smoking from that morning's fire. Lauga quickly heaped it with dried dung, almost suffocating the flames that crept up in her rush. How would her father react to news of the District Commissioner's visit? How long would the prisoner be kept at Kornsá? She didn't even have the letter he had shown her; Steina had thrown it on the fire during their quarrel.

Still, Lauga thought, placing a pot on a hook above the flames, once Pabbi knew, he would take charge.

She stoked the hearth with a little air from the bellows, and then quickly trotted down the corridor to poke her head outside the door. Another thrill of panic ran down her spine. What *would* he do? She ducked her head back inside and went into the pantry to gather what she could for a broth. There was only a little barley left. They were still waiting for the farmhands to return from the merchants in the south.

Lauga stepped across the doorway, nearly tripping on the raised ledge, and went into the storeroom to fetch a little mutton for the pot. There was no point cutting down any smoked lamb at this time of year, but there was a slice or two of blood sausage left from the winter, very sour but good.

We'll eat together in the badstofa. I'll tell them then, Lauga decided. She heard the sounds of the horse's hooves in the dirt of the yard outside.

'*Komið þið sæl!*' Lauga stepped out of the croft, brushing the dust from the dung off her hands, and quickly smoothing her hair back under her cap. 'Good to see you both safely returned.'

Jón, her father, slowed the horse to a stop and gave her a smile from under his riding hat. He raised a bare hand in greeting and stepped forward to give her a quick, formal kiss.

'Little Lauga. How have you managed?' He turned to the horse to unload a few parcels fastened on its back.

'Hello, Mamma.'

Margrét glanced down at Lauga and gave her a warm look, although her lips barely moved. 'Hello, Sigurlaug,' she said.

'You look well.'

'I'm still alive,' she replied.

'Are you tired?'

Margrét ignored the question and slid awkwardly to the ground. Lauga embraced her mother shyly, then ran her hand over the mare's nose and felt the nostrils quiver, the hot, wet breath on her palm.

'Where's your sister?'

Lauga glanced at the outcrop where the stream was, but could see no movement. 'Fetching water for supper.'

Margrét raised her eyebrows. 'I thought she'd be here to welcome us.'

Lauga turned again to her father, who was placing the small

packages from the saddle on the ground. She took a deep breath. 'Pabbi, there is something I have to tell you later.'

He began to untie the stiff rope from about the mare. 'A death?'

'What?'

'Have we lost any animals?'

'Oh. Oh no, nothing like that,' Lauga answered, adding, 'Thank the Lord,' as an afterthought. She stepped closer to her father. 'I might need to tell you this alone,' she said in a low voice.

Her mother heard her. 'What you have to say can be told to the both of us, Lauga.'

'I don't want to distress you, Mamma.'

'Oh, I am often distressed,' Margrét said, suddenly smiling. 'It comes from having children and servants to look after.' Then, telling her husband to make sure he didn't set the remaining parcels down in puddles, Margrét picked up some packages and headed inside, Lauga following after her.

Jón had entered the badstofa and eased himself down next to his wife by the time Lauga brought in the bowls of broth.

'I thought a hot meal might be of comfort,' she said.

Jón looked up at Lauga, who was standing in front of him, holding the tray. 'May I change out of these clothes first?'

Lauga hesitated, and, setting the tray down on the bed beside her mother, dropped to her knees and began to untie the binds about Jón's shoes. 'There is something I have to tell you both.'

'Where's Kristín?' Margrét asked sharply, as Jón leant back on his elbows and let his daughter work the damp sock off his foot.

'Steina gave her half the day in holiday,' Lauga replied.

'And where is Steina?'

'Oh, I don't know. Here somewhere.' Lauga felt her stomach

twist in panic, aware of the scrutiny of her parents. 'Pabbi, District Commissioner Blöndal paid a visit when you were away,' she whispered.

Jón sat up a little and looked down at his daughter. 'The District Commissioner?' he repeated.

Margrét clenched her fists. 'What did he want?' she asked.

'He had a letter for you, Pabbi.'

Margrét stared down at Lauga. 'Why didn't he send a servant? Are you sure it was Blöndal?'

'Mamma, please.'

Jón was silent. 'Where is the letter?' he asked.

Lauga wriggled the shoe off his other foot and let it drop to the floor. Mud cracked off the leather.

'Steina burnt it.'

'Whatever for? Good Lord!'

'Mamma! It's all right. I know what it said. Pabbi, we are being forced to –'

'Pabbi!' Steina's voice rang down the corridor. 'You'll never guess who we have to keep locked up in our house!'

'Locked up?' Margrét twisted around to query her elder daughter, who had just bounced into the room. 'Oh, Steina, you're sopping.'

Steina looked down at her soaked apron and shrugged. 'I dropped the buckets and had to go back and fill them up again. Pabbi, Blöndal's forcing us to keep Agnes Magnúsdóttir in our *home*!'

'Agnes Magnúsdóttir?' Margrét turned to Lauga, horrified.

'Yes, the murderess, Mamma!' Steina exclaimed, untying her wet apron and carelessly flinging it onto the bed next to her. 'The one who killed Natan Ketilsson!'

'Steina! I was just about to explain to Pabbi –'

'And Pétur Jónsson, Mamma.'

'Steina!'

'Oh, Lauga, just because you wanted to tell them.'

'You ought not to interrupt –'

'Girls!' Jón stood up, his arms outstretched. 'Enough. Begin from the start, Lauga. What happened?'

Lauga hesitated, then told her parents everything she could remember about the District Commissioner's visit, her face growing flushed as she recited what she recalled reading in the letter.

Before she had finished, Jón began to dress again.

'Surely this is not something we are obliged to do!' Margrét tugged at her husband's sleeve, but Jón shrugged her off, refusing to look at his wife's distraught face.

'Jón,' Margrét murmured. She glanced over at her daughters, who both sat with their hands in their laps, watching their parents silently.

Jón pulled his boots back on, whipping the ties around his ankle. The leather squeaked as he pulled them tight.

'It's too late, Jón,' Margrét said. 'Are you going to Hvammur? They'll all be asleep.'

'Then I'll wake them.' He picked up his riding hat from its nail, took his wife by the shoulders and gently shifted her out of his way. Nodding farewell to his daughters, he strode out of the room, down the corridor and shut the door to the croft behind him.

'What shall we do, Mamma?' Lauga's small voice came from a dark corner of the room.

Margrét closed her eyes and took a deep breath.

Jón returned to Kornsá some hours later. Kristín, who had come back from her afternoon's holiday to a sound chastising from Margrét, was scowling reproachfully at Steina. Margrét paused at her knitting and was considering whether or not to make peace between the girls, when she heard the door to the croft creak open and the sound of her husband's heavy tread in the corridor.

Jón entered and immediately looked across at his wife. She clenched her jaw.

'Well?' Margrét ushered her husband to his bed.

Jón fumbled at the ties on his shoes.

'Please, Pabbi,' Lauga said, dropping to her knees. 'What did Blöndal say?' She jerked backwards as she pulled off his boots. 'Is she still to come here?'

Jón nodded. 'It's as Lauga said. Agnes Magnúsdóttir is to be moved from her holdings at Stóra-Borg and brought to us.'

'But why, Pabbi?' Lauga asked quietly. 'What did we do wrong?'

'We have done nothing wrong. I am a District Officer. She can't be placed with any family. She is a responsibility of the authorities, of which I am one.'

'Plenty of *authorities* at Stóra-Borg.' Margrét's tone was sour.

'She's to be moved nevertheless. There was an incident.'

'What happened?' Lauga asked.

Jón looked down at the fair face of his youngest child. 'I am sure it was nothing to worry about,' he said eventually.

Margrét gave a short laugh. 'Are we just going to yield to this? Like a dog rolling over?' Her voice dropped to a hiss. 'This Agnes is a *murderess*, Jón! We have our girls, our workmen. Even Kristín! We are responsible for others!'

Jón gave his wife a meaningful look. 'Blöndal means to compensate us, Margrét. There is remuneration for her custody.'

Margrét paused. When she spoke her voice was subdued. 'Perhaps we should send the girls away.'

'No, Mamma! I don't want to leave,' cried Steina.

'It would be for your own safety.'

Jón cleared his throat. 'The girls will be safe enough with you,

Margrét.' He sighed. 'There is another thing. Björn Blöndal has requested my presence at Hvammur on the night the woman arrives here.'

Margrét opened her mouth in dismay. 'You mean to make *me*
meet her?'

'Pabbi, you can't leave Mamma alone with her,' Lauga cried.

'She won't be alone. You will all be here. There will be officers
from Stóra-Borg. And a Reverend. Blöndal has organised it.'

'And what is so important at Hvammur that Blöndal requires
you there the very night he ushers a criminal into our home?'

'Margrét ...'

'No, I insist. This is unfair.'

'We are to discuss who shall be executioner.'

'Executioner!'

'All the District Officers will be present, including those from
Vatnsnes who will travel with the Stóra-Borg riders. We will sleep
there that night and return the next day.'

'And in the meantime I am left alone with the woman who killed
Natan Ketilsson.'

Jón looked at his wife calmly. 'You will have your daughters.'

Margrét began to say something further, but then thought better
of it. She gave her husband a hard look, took up her knitting and
began working the needles furiously.

Steina watched her mother and father from under lowered
brows, and picked up her dinner, feeling sick to her stomach. She
held the wooden bowl in her hands and examined the gobbets of
mutton swimming in the greasy broth. Slowly taking her spoon, she
lifted a piece to her lips and began to chew, her tongue locating a
lump of gristle within the flesh. She fought the instinct to spit it out
and ground it under her teeth, swallowing in silence.

AFTER THEY DECIDE I MUST leave, the Stóra-Borg men sometimes tie my legs together in the evening, as they do with the forelegs of horses, to ensure I will not run away. It seems that with each passing day I become more like an animal to them, another dull-eyed beast to feed with what can be scraped together and to be kept out of the weather. They leave me in the dark, deny me light and air, and when I must be moved, they bind and lead me where they will.

They never speak to me here. In winter, in the badstofa, I could always hear myself breathing, and I'd get scared to swallow for fear the whole room might hear it. The only sounds to keep a body company then were the rustling of Bible pages and whisperings. I'd catch my name on the lips of others, and I knew it wasn't in blessing. Now, when they are forced by law to read out the words of a letter or proclamation, they talk as if addressing someone behind my shoulder. They refuse to meet my eyes.

You, Agnes Magnúsdóttir, have been found guilty of accessory to murder. You, Agnes Magnúsdóttir have been found guilty of arson, and conspiracy to murder. You, Agnes Magnúsdóttir, have been sentenced to death. You, Agnes. *Agnes*.

They don't know me.

I remain quiet. I am determined to close myself to the world, to tighten my heart and hold on to what has not yet been stolen from me. I cannot let myself slip away. I will hold what I am inside, and keep my hands tight around all the things I have seen and heard, and felt. The poems composed as I washed and scythed and cooked until my hands were raw. The sagas I know by heart. I am sinking all I have left and going underwater. If I speak, it will be in bubbles of air. They will not be able to keep my words for themselves. They will see the whore, the madwoman, the murderess, the female dripping blood into the grass and laughing with her mouth choked with dirt. They will say 'Agnes' and see the spider, the witch caught in the webbing of her own fateful weaving. They might see the lamb circled by ravens, bleating for a lost mother. But they will not see me. I will not be there.

REVEREND THORVARDUR JÓNSSON SIGHED AS he left the church and entered the cool, damp air of the afternoon. Just over one month had passed since he had accepted Blöndal's offer to visit the condemned woman, and he had questioned his decision every day since. Each morning he had felt troubled, as though newly woken from a nightmare. Even as he had made his daily walk to the small church of Breidabólstadur to pray and sit awhile in the silence, his stomach had crowded with nerves, and his body had trembled as if exhausted by his mind's ambivalence. It had been no different today. As he had sat on the hard pew, gazing into his hands, he caught himself wishing that he were ill, gravely ill, so that he might be excused for not riding to Kornsá. His reluctance, and his willingness to sacrifice his own blessed health, horrified him.

It is too late now, he thought to himself as he walked through the rather pitiful garden within the churchyard. You have given your word to man and God, and there is no turning back.

Once, before his mother had died, the church plot had been full of small plants that threw purple blossoms over the edges of the graves in summer. His mother had said that the dead made the flowers sway, to greet the churchgoers after winter. But when she died, his father ripped out the wild flowers and the graves had lain bare ever since.

The door to the Breidabólstadur croft was ajar. As Tóti let himself in, the heavy warmth from the kitchen, and the smell of melting tallow from the candle in the corridor, made him feel nauseous.

His father was bent over the bubbling kettle, poking something with a knife.

'I ought to leave now, I think,' Tóti announced.

His father looked up from the boiling fish and nodded.

'I'm expected to arrive early in the evening to acquaint myself with the family at Kornsá, and be present when ... Well, when the criminal arrives.'

His father frowned. 'Go then, son.'

Tóti hesitated. 'Do you think I'm ready?'

Reverend Jón sighed and lifted the kettle off its hook over the coals. 'You know your own heart.'

'I've been praying in the church. I wonder what Mamma would have thought about it all.'

Tóti's father blinked slowly and looked away.

'What do *you* think, father?'

'A man must be true to his word.'

'Is it the right decision, though? I ... I don't want to displease you.'

'You should seek to please the Lord,' Reverend Jón muttered, trying to scoop his fish from the hot water with his knife.

'Will you pray for me, father?'

Tóti waited for a response, but none came. Perhaps he thinks *he* is better suited to meet murderesses, Tóti thought. Perhaps he is jealous she chose me. He watched his father lick a fragment of fish from where it had stuck to the blade. She chose *me*, he repeated to himself.

'Don't wake me when you return,' Reverend Jón called out as his son turned and left the room.

Tóti slipped a saddle over his horse and mounted. 'This is it, then,' he whispered quietly. He gently squeezed his knees to urge his horse forward, and looked back at the croft. Its thin wreath of kitchen smoke dissipated into the soft drizzle of the afternoon.

Travelling through the long grasses of the valley surrounding the church, the Assistant Reverend tried to think of what he should say. Should he be kind and welcoming, or stern and impenetrable, like Blöndal? As he rode, he rehearsed various tones of voice, different greetings. Perhaps he should wait until he saw the woman. Unexpectedly, a small thrill flickered through his body. She was only a workmaid, but she was a *murderess*. She had killed two men. Slaughtered them like animals. He silently mouthed the word to himself. Murderess. *Morðingi*. It slipped through his mouth like milk.

As he travelled over the north peninsula with its thin lip of ocean on the horizon, the clouds began to clear and the soft red light of the late June sun flooded the pass. Drops of water glittered brightly upon the ground, and the hills appeared pink and muted, shadows moving slowly across them as clouds drifted overhead. Small insects wound their way through the air, lit up like flecks of dust as they passed through the sunshine, and the sweet, damp smell of grass, almost ready to be harvested, lingered in the cool air of the valleys. The dread that Tóti had felt so firmly lining his stomach dissipated as he fell into a quiet appreciation of the countryside before him.

We are all God's children, he thought to himself. This woman is my sister in Jesus, and I, as her spiritual brother, must guide her home. He smiled and brought his horse to a *tölt*. 'I will save her,' he whispered.

CHAPTER TWO

3rd of May 1828
Undirfell, Vatnsdalur

The convict Agnes Magnúsdóttir was born at Flaga in the parish
of Undirfell in 1795. She was confirmed in 1809, at which age
she was written as having 'an excellent intellect, and strong
knowledge and understanding of Christianity'.

This is what is listed in the Undirfell Ministerial Book.

P. Bjarnason

THEY HAVE TAKEN ME FROM the room and put me in irons again. This time they sent an officer of the court, a young man with pocked skin and a nervous smile. He's a servant from Hvammur, I recognised his face. When his lips broke apart I could see that his teeth were rotting in his mouth. His breath was awful, but no worse than my own; I know I am rank. I am scabbed with dirt and the accumulated weeping of my body: blood, sweat, oil. I cannot think of when I last washed. My hair feels like a greased rope; I have tried to keep it plaited, but they have not allowed me ribbons, and I imagine that to the officer I looked like a monstrous creature. Perhaps that was why he smiled.

He took me from that awful room, and other men joined us as he led me through the unlit corridor. They were silent, but I felt them behind me; I felt their stares as though they were cold handgrips upon my neck. Then, after months in a room filled only with my own fetid breath and the stench from the chamber pot, I was taken through the corridors of Stóra-Borg into the muddy yard. And it was raining.

How can I say what it was like to breathe again? I felt newborn. I staggered in the light of the world and took deep gulps of fresh sea air. It was late in the day: the wet mouth of the afternoon was full on my face. My soul blossomed in that brief moment as they led me out of doors. I fell, my skirts in the mud, and I turned my face upwards as if in prayer. I could have wept from the relief of light.

A man reached down and pulled me from the ground as one wrests a thistle that takes root in a place it does not belong. It was then that I noticed the crowd that had gathered. At first I did not know why these people stood about, men and women alike, each still and staring at me in silence. Then I understood that it was not me they stared at. I understood that these people did not see *me*. I was two dead men. I was a burning farm. I was a knife. I was blood.

I didn't know what to do in front of these people. Then I saw Rósa, watching from a distance, clutching the hand of her little daughter. It was a comfort to see someone I recognised, and I smiled involuntarily. But the smile was wrong. It unlocked the crowd's fury. The servant women's faces twisted, and the silence was broken by a sudden, brief shriek from a child: *Fjandi*! Devil! It burst into the air like an explosion of water from a geyser. The smile dropped from my face.

At the sound of the insult, the crowd seemed to awaken. Someone gave a brittle laugh and the child was hushed and led away by an older woman. One by one, they all left to return indoors or to continue their chores, until I was alone with the officers in the drizzle, standing in stockings stiff with dried sweat, my heart burning under my filthy skin. When I looked back, I saw that Rósa had disappeared.

Now we are riding across Iceland's north, across this island washing in its waters, sulking in its ocean. Chasing our shadows across the mountains.

They have strapped me to the saddle like a corpse being taken to the burial ground. In their eyes I am already a dead woman, destined for the grave. My arms are tethered in front of me. As we ride this awful parade, the irons pinch my flesh until it bloodies in front of my eyes. I have come to expect harm now. Some of the watchmen at Stóra-Borg compassed my body with small violences, chronicled their hatred towards me, a mark here, bruises, blossoming like star clusters under the skin, black and yellow smoke trapped under the membrane. I suppose some of them had known Natan.

But now they take me east, and although I am tied like a lamb for slaughter, I'm grateful that I am returning to the valleys where rocks give way to grass, even if I will die there.

As the horses struggle through the tussocks, I wonder when they will kill me. I wonder where they will store me, cellar me like butter, like smoked meat. Like a corpse, waiting for the ground to unfreeze before they can pocket me in the earth like a stone.

They do not tell me these things. Instead, they set me in iron cuffs and lead me around, and like a cow I go where I am led, and there's no kicking or it's the knife. It's the rope and a grim end. I put my head down, go where they take me and hope it's not to the grave, not yet.

The flies are bad. They crawl on my face and into my eyes, and I feel the tiny ticking of their legs and wings. It's the sweat that draws them. These irons are too heavy for me to swat them away. They were built for a man, although they screw tight enough against my skin.

Still, it is a consolation to have movement, to have the warmth of a horse under my legs: to feel the life in something and to not be so cold. I've been half-frozen for so long, it is as though the winter has set up home in my marrow. Endless days of dark indoors and hateful glances are enough to set a rime on anyone's bones. So yes, it's better to be outside now. Even with the air full of flies it's better to be going somewhere than rotting slowly in a room like a body in a coffin.

Beyond the hum of insects and the rhythm of the horses at their walk, I hear a distant roar. Maybe it's the ocean – the constant thundering of waves hitting the sands of Thingeyrar. Or perhaps I am imagining it. The sea gets into your head. Like Natan used to say, once you let it in, it doesn't leave you alone. Like a woman, he said. The sea is a nag.

It was that first spring at Illugastadir. The light had arrived like a hunted thing, all wide-eyed and trembling. The sea was blank – Natan pushed the boat along its silvered skin, plunged his oars in its side.

'As quiet as a churchyard,' he had said, smiling, his arms heaving with the pull of water. I heard the creak of wood and the whispered cuss of the oars slapping the surface of the sea. 'Be good when I'm gone.'

Don't think of him.

How long have we been riding? An hour? Two? Time's as slippery as oil. But it can't have been more than two hours. I know these parts. I know we are now heading south, perhaps towards Vatnsdalur. Strange, how my heart grips to my ribs in an instant. How long has it been since I last saw this part of the country? A few years? More? Nothing has changed.

This is as close to home as I'll ever be now.

We are passing through the strange hills at the mouth of the valley and I hear the caw of ravens. Their dark shapes look like omens against the brilliant blue of the sky. All those nights at Stóra-Borg, in that damp, miserable bed, I imagined I was outside, feeding the ravens at Flaga. Cruel birds, ravens, but wise. And creatures should be loved for their wisdom if they cannot be loved for kindness. As a child, I watched the ravens gather on the roof of Undirfell church, hoping to learn who was going to die. I sat on the wall, waiting for one to shake out his feathers, waiting to see which direction his beak turned. It happened once. A raven settled upon the wooden gable and jerked his beak towards the farm of Bakki, and a little boy drowned later that week, found swollen and grey downriver. The raven had known.

Sigga was unschooled in nightmares and ghosts. One night, knitting together at Illugastadir, we heard a raven's shriek coming from the sea that chilled us to the core. I told her never to call out to, nor feed a raven at night. Birds heard cawing in the dark are spirits, I said, and they would murder you soon as look at you. I scared her, I'm sure, or she wouldn't have said the things she said later.

I wonder where Sigga might be now. Why they refused to keep her with me at Stóra-Borg. They took her away one morning when I was in irons, not telling me where she was held, although I asked more than once. 'Away from you,' they said, 'and that is enough.'

'Agnes Magnúsdóttir!'

The man riding beside me has a hard look on his face.

'Agnes Magnúsdóttir. I'm to inform you that you're to be held at Kornsá, until the time of your execution.' He is reading something. His eyes flicker down to his gloves. 'As a criminal condemned by the court of this land, you have forfeited your right to freedom.' He folds the piece of paper and slips it in his glove. 'You'd do well to wipe that scowl off your face. They're gentle people at Kornsá.'

Here, man. Here is your smile. Is it a good one? Do you see my lips crack? Do you see my teeth?

He passes my mare, and the back of his shirt is damp with sweat. Have they done it on purpose? Kornsá, of all places.

Yesterday, when I was shut up in the storeroom of Stóra-Borg, Kornsá would have seemed a heaven. A place of childhood, the river, the bright grass, the hillocks of turf oozing water in spring. But I see now that it will be a humiliation. People will know me in the valley. They will remember me as I was – as a baby, as a child, as a woman running from farm to farm – and then they will think of the murders and that child, that woman will be forgotten. I can't bear to look about me. I gaze at the horse's mane, at the lice crawling about the hair, and I don't know if they are from the mare or from me.

✝

REVEREND TÓTI STOOPED IN THE low doorway and squinted against the rosy hue of the midnight sun. At the lower end of the farm's northernmost field, he could see a trail of horses approaching. He searched for the woman among the riders. Against the golden flood of hay that surrounded them, the figures seemed small and black.

Margrét stepped out of the door and stood behind him.

'I hope they will leave some men behind, to make sure she doesn't kill us in our sleep.'

Tóti turned and looked at Margrét's hard face. She, too, was squinting to see the riders, and her forehead was puckered in creases. Her grey hair had been pulled into two taut braids and coiled, and she was wearing her best cap. Tóti noticed that she'd changed out of the dirty apron she'd received him in earlier that night.

'Will your daughters join us out here?'

'They're too tired to stand. I've sent them both to bed. Don't see why the criminal has to be brought in the middle of the night.'

'To avoid disturbing your neighbours, I should think,' he remarked, tactfully.

Margrét bit her lower lip, and a flush of colour spread across her cheeks.

'I do not like to share my home with the Devil's children,' she said, her voice lowering to a whisper. 'Reverend Tóti, we must make it known that we do not want her company. Let the woman be removed to an island if they won't keep her at Stóra-Borg.'

'We must all do our duty,' Tóti murmured, watching the trail turn and head up towards the home field. He took a snuff horn from his breast pocket and removed a small pinch. Delicately setting it on the hollow beside the knuckle of his left thumb, he bent his head and sniffed.

Margrét coughed and spat. 'Even if it means we are stuck like pigs in the night, Reverend Tóti? You are a man, a young man, yes, but a man of God. I don't think she would kill *you*. But us? My daughters? Lord, how will we sleep in peace?'

'They will leave an officer with you,' Tóti muttered, turning his attention to a lone rider who was now cantering towards them.

'They must. Or else I'm marching her back to Stóra-Borg myself.'

Margrét twisted her hands against her stomach, and turned her gaze to a small flock of ravens flying silently across the mountain range of Vatnsdalsfjall. They looked like ashes, whorling in the sky.

'Are you a man of traditions, Reverend Tóti?' Margrét asked.

Tóti turned to her, considering the question. 'If they be noble and Christian.'

'Do you know the right name for a flock of ravens?'

Tóti shook his head.

'A conspiracy, Reverend. A *conspiracy*.' Margrét raised an eyebrow, challenging him to disagree.

Tóti watched the ravens settle on the eaves of the cattle barn. 'Is that so, Mistress Margrét? I thought they were called an unkindness.'

Before Margrét had time to answer, the rider who was cantering towards them reached the edge of the home field.

'*Komið þið sæl og blessuð,*' he shouted.

'*Drottin blessi yður.* And may the Lord bless you,' they responded, in unison. Margrét and Tóti waited until the man had dismounted before they approached him. They exchanged formal, customary kisses. The man was damp with sweat and smelt strongly of horses.

'She's here,' he said breathlessly. 'I think you'll find her wearied by the journey.' He paused again, to remove his hat and run a hand through his damp hair. 'I do not think she will trouble you.'

Margrét snorted.

The man gave a cold smile. 'We've been ordered to stay here tonight to make sure of it. We'll camp by the home field.'

Margrét nodded solemnly. 'So long as you don't trample the grass. Would you like some milk? Whey and water?'

'Thank you,' the man replied. 'We'll reimburse you for your kindness.'

'No need.' Margrét pursed her lips. 'Just make sure the bitch stays away from the knives in my kitchen.'

The man sniggered and turned to follow Margrét into the turf home. Tóti grabbed his arm as he passed.

'The prisoner has requested that I speak with her. Where is she?'

The man pointed to a horse furthest from the croft. 'She's the one with the sour mouth. The younger maid remains in Midhóp. They say she's awaiting the result of an appeal.'

'An appeal? I thought they were doomed?'

'A lot of people Vatnsnes way hope Sigga will receive a pardon from the King. Too young and sweet to die.' The man pulled a face. 'Not like this one. She has a right temper when she fancies.'

'Is she awaiting an appeal?'

The man laughed. 'I don't like her chances. Blöndal's behind the youngest. They say she reminds him of his wife. This one ... Well, Blöndal wants to set an example.'

Tóti gazed down at the horses now gathered at the edge of the home field. The men had begun to dismount and attend to their packs. Only one figure remained mounted. He bent closer to the man.

'Is there a proper name? What should I call –?'

'Just Agnes,' the man interrupted. 'She'll answer to Agnes.'

WE'VE ARRIVED. THE MEN FROM Stóra-Borg are dismounting at a little distance from the crooked farmhouse of

Kornsá. Two figures stand outside the croft, a woman and a man, and the rider who announced my forfeited rights is walking up to them. No one is coming to unscrew my irons. Perhaps they have forgotten me. The woman ducks her head to go back indoors, coughing and spitting like a crone, but the man remains to talk with the Stóra-Borg officer.

To my left is laughter – two officers are pissing on the ground. I can smell it on the warm air. As usual, no one has noticed that I haven't eaten or had a sip of water all day; my lips are as split as firewood. I feel the same as when I was little and hungry, as though my bones are growing larger in my body, as if my skeleton is about to shiver out of me. I have stopped bleeding. I am no longer a woman.

One of the men is walking towards me, taking quick, long strides over the home field. Don't look at him.

'Hello, Agnes. My ... my name is Reverend Thorvardur Jónsson. I am the Assistant Reverend from Breidabólstadur in Vesturhóp.' He is out of breath.

Don't look up. It's him. It is the same voice.

He coughs, then bends as if to kiss me according to custom, but hesitates, stepping backwards and nearly tripping over a tussock. He surely smells the dried piss on my stockings.

'You asked for me?' His voice is uncertain.

I look up.

He doesn't recognise me. I don't know whether to be relieved or disappointed. His hair is as red as before, as red as the midnight sun. It looks as though his locks have soaked up the light as a skein of wool suffers the dye. But his face is older. It has thinned.

'You asked for me?' he says again. When I look him in the eye he glances away, then nervously wipes the sweat off his upper lip, leaving a trail of dark specks. Snuff? He doesn't want to be here.

My tongue has swollen in my mouth and it cannot be moved to form words. What would I say to him anyway, now that it has come to this? I pick at the scabs on my wrists where the irons chafe the skin, and blood bubbles up to the surface. He notices.

'Well. I must ... I'm glad to have met you, but ... it's late. You must be ... uh, I will call again soon.' He bows awkwardly, then turns and walks away, tripping in his haste. He goes before I can let him know I understand. I smear the fresh blood across my arm as I watch him stumble to his horse.

Now I am alone. I watch the ravens, and listen to the horses eat.

ONCE THE MEN FROM STÓRA-BORG had eaten and retired to their tents for the night, Margrét picked up the dirty wooden bowls and returned inside. She smoothed the blankets over her sleeping daughters, and walked slowly around the small room, bending down to pick up the strands of dry grass that had fallen from the turf layered between the rafters. She despaired at the dust in the room. The walls had once been panelled with Norwegian wood, but Jón had removed the boards to pay a debt owed to a farmer across the valley. Now the bare walls of turf collapsed their dirt and grass onto the beds in summer, and grew dank in winter, issuing moulds that dripped onto the woollen blankets and infested the lungs of the household. The home had begun to disintegrate, a hovel that had spread its own state of collapse to its inhabitants. Last year two servants had died from diseases wrought by the damp.

Margrét thought of her own cough, and instinctively raised a hand to her mouth. Ever since the news brought by the District Commissioner, her lungs had issued rot with increased regularity. She rose each morning with a weight upon her chest. Margrét could not tell whether it was dread of the criminal's arrival, or the night's accumulated dross in her lungs, but it made her think of the grave. Everything's collapsing inward, she thought.

One of the officers had gone to fetch Agnes from where they had left her tied with the horses. Margrét had only caught a distant glimpse of the woman when she had left the dim rooms of the farmhouse to bring the men their supper – a slight blur of blue, a smudge of skirt being hauled off a horse. Now her heart thumped. Soon the murderess would be in front of her. She would see the woman's face; feel her warmth in the small confines. What was to be done? How to behave in front of such a woman?

If only Jón were here, she thought. He could tell me what I should say to her. It takes a man, a good man, to know how to manage a woman who has made her bed among stones.

Margrét sat down and absently picked at the grass in her hand. She had managed the servants who had drifted through her husband's household for almost four decades, across as many farms, and yet she felt sluggish with her own uncertainty and apprehension. This woman, this Agnes, was not a servant, certainly no guest, and no pauper. She deserved no charity, and yet, she was condemned to die. Margrét shuddered. The light from the lamp played her shadow across the floorboards.

Dull footsteps sounded from the farmhouse doorway. Margrét stood quickly, the gathered grass fluttering to the ground as she released her clenched fists. The officer's voice boomed from the shadows of the corridor.

'Mistress Margrét of Kornsá? I have the prisoner. May we enter?'

Margrét took a deep breath and straightened her posture. 'This way,' she commanded.

The officer entered the badstofa first, smiling broadly at Margrét, who stood stiffly, her hands gripping the cloth of her apron. She glanced to where her daughters lay sleeping and felt the blood pulse in her throat.

There was a moment of silence as the officer blinked to accustom his eyes to the low light, and then, abruptly, he pulled the woman into the room.

Margrét was unprepared for the filth and wretchedness of the woman's appearance. The criminal wore what seemed to be a servant's common working dress of roughly woven wool, but one so badly stained and caked with dirt that the original blue dye was barely discernible under the brown grease that spread across the neckline and arms. A thick weight of dried mud pulled the fabric awkwardly from the woman's body. Her faded blue stockings were soaked through, sunk about the ankles, and one was torn, exposing a slice of pale skin. Her shoes, of sealskin it seemed, had split at the seam, but were so covered in mud that it was impossible to see how damaged they were. Her hair was uncovered by a cap and matted with grease. It hung in two dark braids down her back. Several strands had come loose and fell limply about the woman's neck. She looked as if she'd been dragged from Stóra-Borg, Margrét thought. The woman's face was hidden; she stared at the floor.

'Look at me.'

Agnes slowly raised her head. Margrét winced at the smear of dried blood across the woman's mouth, and the grime that lay in streaks across her forehead. There was a yellow bruise that spread from her chin down to the side of her neck. Agnes's eyes flickered from the ground to Margrét's own, and she felt unnerved by their intensity, their colour made lighter and sharper by the dirt on her face. Margrét turned to the officer.

'This woman has been beaten.' The officer searched Margrét's face for amusement, and, finding none, lowered his eyes. 'Where are her things?'

'Only the clothes on her back,' the officer said. 'The clerks took what she had to cover her vittles.'

Invigorated by a sudden curl of anger, Margrét pointed to the irons about the woman's wrists.

'Is it necessary to keep her bound like a lamb ripe for slaughter?' she asked him.

The officer shrugged and felt about him for a key. In a few deft twists he freed Agnes from the handcuffs. Her arms fell to her sides.

'You may go now,' Margrét told the officer. 'One of you may come in when I retire to sleep, but I want some time alone with her.'

The officer's eyes grew wide. 'Are you certain?' he asked. 'It's not safe.'

'As I said, I'll ask for you when I retire to bed. You may wait outside the doorway and I'll call out should there be need for it.'

The officer hesitated, then nodded and left with a salute. Margrét turned to Agnes, who stood, unmoving, in the middle of the room.

'You,' she said, 'you follow me.'

Margrét did not wish to touch the woman, but the lack of light indoors forced her to grip Agnes's arm in order to steer her into the right room. She could feel the bones in her wrist, crusted blood against her fingertips. The woman smelt like stale urine.

'This way.' Margrét walked slowly down to the kitchen, ducking her head under the low doorframe.

The kitchen was lit by the dying embers of the fire in the raised hearth of stones, and a small hole in the thatched turf ceiling that served as a chimney. It let through a weak, pink light that lay across the packed earth floor and illuminated the smoke that hung about the room. Margrét led Agnes inside, then turned and faced her.

'Take off your clothes. You need to wash if you're going to sleep in my blankets. I won't have you infesting this house with any more lice than already plague the place.'

Agnes's face was impassive. 'Where is the water?' she croaked.

Margrét hesitated, and then turned to a large kettle that sat upon the coals. Plunging her hand into it, she pulled out crockery that had been left to soak, and then heaved it onto the ground.

'There,' she said. 'And it's warm. Now hurry up, it's past midnight.'

Agnes looked at the kettle and then suddenly fell to the ground. At first Margrét thought she had fainted, then quickly realised her mistake. She watched as Agnes bent her head over the kettle's rim and scooped handfuls of greasy water into her mouth, gasping and drinking with the same urgency as an animal at a trough. Water ran down her chin and neck, dripping into the stiff folds of her dress. Without thinking, Margrét bent down and pushed Agnes's forehead from the kettle.

The woman fell back upon her elbows and let out a cry, water gurgling from her mouth. Margrét's heart lurched at the sound. Agnes's eyes were half-closed, her mouth open. She looked like those Margrét had seen driven out of their minds by drink, or by haunting, or by grief that sets in when deaths fall thickly in the home.

Agnes whimpered and rubbed the back of her hand across her mouth, then upon her dress. She pushed herself up from the ground and tried to stand.

'I'm thirsty.'

Margrét nodded, her heart still hammering in her chest. She swallowed hard.

'Ask for a cup, next time,' she said.

WHEN REVEREND TÓTI RETURNED TO his father's croft near the Breidabólstadur church, he was damp through with sweat.

He had ridden hard from Kornsá, digging his heels into his horse's flanks as the wind buffeted his face and brought the blood to his cheeks.

Slowing to a walk, he guided his cob, foam dripping from its mouth, to a stile near the croft's entrance. He dismounted with trembling legs. The wind had picked up, and as it pushed through the tight weave of his clothes, he felt his sweat-soaked skin grow cool and begin to itch. His jaw was clenched. His hands shook as they wound the reins through the stile.

Heavy clouds had blown in from the sea, and the light was fast disappearing, despite it not being long after summer solstice. Tóti pulled his damp collar up further about his neck and pushed his hat firmly down on his head. Giving his horse a pat on the rump, he started walking up the slow incline to the church. He felt like a wet rag wrung dry and left distorted upon the ground. These northern days, with their lingering fingers of light, the constant gloaming, unsettled him. He could not guess at the hour of the day as he could at the school in the south.

Rain began to fall and the gale grew stronger. It lashed at the tall grass, flattening the stalks to the ground before whipping them skywards again. The grass seemed silver in the darkening light.

Tóti took long strides up the hill, stretching his muscles as he walked, thinking about his meeting with the woman. *The* woman. The criminal. *Agnes*.

He had noticed, first, how, bound to the saddle, she had splayed her legs over the horse so that she would not slip. He had smelt her, then; the sharp pungency of a neglected body, of unwashed clothes and fresh sweat, dried blood and something else from between those spread legs. A stench peculiar to women. He blushed at the thought of it.

But it had not been her smell that had sickened him. She had looked like a new corpse, fresh dug from the grave. Wild black hair strung with grease, and the brown-grey of dirt sitting in the pores of her skin. Leprous colours.

He had wanted to turn away, flee at the sight of her. Like a coward.

Hunched against the smattering of rain and wind, Tóti inwardly chastised himself. What sort of man are you if you want to run at the sight of damaged flesh? What sort of priest will you be if you cannot withstand the appearance of suffering?

It had been a particularly vivid bruise upon her chin that had disturbed him the most. A ripe, yellow colour, like dried egg yolk. Tóti wondered at the force that might have birthed it. The rough hand of a man, gripping her under the throat. A rope binding her to fetters. A fall.

There are so many ways a person might take harm, Tóti thought. He reached the churchyard and fumbled with the gate.

It might have been an accident. She might have hurt herself.

The Reverend hurried down the stony path to the church, trying not to look at the shadowy graves and their wooden crosses. Drawing a crude key from his pocket, he let himself inside. He was relieved to close the wooden door behind him and shut out the low growl of the wind. Inside, it was perfectly still. The only sound was the light patter of rain on the church's solitary window, a hole covered with fish-skin.

Tóti pulled the hat off his head and ran a hand through his hair. The floorboards creaked as he walked to the pulpit. He stood for a moment, squinting up at the painted mural behind the altar. The Last Supper.

The mural was ugly: a vast table with a squat Jesus. Judas, lingering in the shadows, was troll-like, comical. The artist had been the son of a local merchant who had a Danish wife and connections within the government. After service one Sunday, Tóti had overheard the merchant speak with Reverend Jón, complaining about the flaking paint of the previous mural. The merchant had mentioned his son, the artistic talent that had secured the boy a scholarship in Copenhagen. If Reverend Jón would permit him to express his singular devotion to the parish, he would happily purchase all necessary materials and donate his son's labour without the church incurring expenses. Naturally, Tóti's father, being a man of economic mindfulness, had allowed the old picture to be painted over.

Tóti missed it. It had been a fine Old Testament illustration of Jacob wrestling with the angel, the man's face buried against the angel's shoulder, his fist full of holy feathers.

Tóti sighed and slowly sank to his knees. Placing his hat on the floor, he clasped his hands tightly to his chest and began to pray aloud.

'O Heavenly Father, forgive me my sins. Forgive me my weakness and fear. Help me to fight my cowardice. Strengthen my ability to withstand the sight of suffering, so that I might do Your work in relieving those who endure it.

'Lord, I pray for the soul of this woman who has committed a terrible sin. Please give me words so that I might inspire her to repent.

'I confess to fear. I do not know what to say to her. I do not feel at ease, Lord. Please guard my heart against the ... the *horror* this woman inspires in me.'

Tóti remained on his knees for some time. It was only the thought of his horse standing bridled in the rain and wind that caused him to finally rise and lock the church door behind him.

MÁRGRÉT WOKE EARLY THE NEXT day. The officer who had slept in the bed opposite to protect her from the criminal was snoring. The gargled breathing had entered her dreams and roused her.

Margrét turned in her bed to face the wall and dug the corners of her blanket into her ears, but the man's ragged snorting filled her head. Sleep was gone from her now. She lay on her back and looked across the unlit room to where the officer lay. His rough blond hair stuck up in oily tufts, and his mouth was open upon his pillow. Margrét noticed spots along the man's jaw.

So this is how they protect me against a murderess, she thought. They send a boy who sleeps soundly.

She cast an eye at the prisoner, lying in one of the servants' beds at the end of the room. The woman was lying still, asleep. Her daughters were also sleeping. Margrét sat up on her elbows to take a better look.

Agnes.

Margrét silently mouthed the word.

It seems wrong to call her by a Christian name, Margrét thought. What would they have called her in Stóra-Borg, she wondered. Prisoner? Accused? Condemned? Perhaps it was the absence of a name, the silence where a name should be, that they had summoned her by.

Margrét shivered and drew the blanket about her. Agnes's eyes were shut fast and her mouth was closed. The cap Margrét had given her had unfastened during the night, and had let loose her dark hair. It lay across the pillow like a stain.

Strange to finally see the woman after a month of anticipation, Margrét thought. A month of fear, too. A tight fear, like a fishing line, hooked upon something that must, inevitably, be dragged from the depths.

In the days and nights after Jón had returned from meeting with Blöndal, Margrét had tried to imagine how she would act towards the murderess, and what the woman might look like.

What sort of woman kills men?

The only murderesses Margrét had known were the women in the sagas, and even then, it was with words that they had killed men; orders given to servants to slay lovers or avenge the death of kin. Those women murdered from a distance and kept their fingers clean.

But these times are not saga times, Margrét had thought. This woman is not a saga woman. She's a landless workmaid raised on a porridge of moss and poverty.

Lying back down in her bed, Margrét thought of Hjördis, her favourite servant, now dead and buried in the churchyard at Undirfell. She tried to imagine Hjördis as a murderess. Tried to imagine Hjördis stabbing her as she slept, the same way Natan Ketilsson and Pétur Jónsson had died. Those slender fingers wrapped tightly around a hilt, the silent footsteps in the night.

It was impossible.

Lauga had asked Margrét whether she thought there would be an outward hint of the evil that drives a person to murder. Evidence of the Devil: a harelip, a snaggle tooth, a birthmark; some small outer defect. There must be a warning, some way of knowing, so that honest people could keep their guard. Margrét had said no, she thought it all superstition, but Lauga had remained unconvinced.

Margrét had instead wondered if the woman would be beautiful. She knew, like everyone else in the north, that the famous Natan Ketilsson had had a knack for discovering beauty. People had thought him a sorcerer.

Margrét's neighbour, Ingibjörg, had heard that it was Agnes who had caused Natan to break off his affair with Poet-Rósa. They had wondered if this meant the servant would be more beautiful than her. It was not so hard to believe a beautiful woman capable of murder, Margrét thought. As it says in the sagas, *Opt er flagð í fögru skinni*. A witch often has fair skin.

But this woman was neither ugly nor a beauty. Striking perhaps, but not the sort to inspire hungry glances from young men. She was very slender, elf-slender as the southerners would put it, and of an ordinary height. In the kitchen last night, Margrét had thought the woman's face rather long, had noted high cheekbones and a straight nose. Bruises aside, her skin was pale, and it seemed more so because of the darkness of her hair. Unusual hair. Rare for a woman to have hair like that in these parts, thought Margrét. So long, so dark in colour: an inky brown, almost black.

Margrét drew the covers up to her chin as the officer's snores continued their unceasing rumble. One would think an avalanche was approaching, she thought, annoyed. She felt tired, and her chest was heavy with mucus.

Images of the woman crowded behind Margrét's closed eyelids. The animal way Agnes had drunk from the kettle. Her inability to undress herself. The woman's hands had fumbled at the ties; her fingers had been swollen and would not bend. Margrét had been forced to help her, using her fingertips to crumble the dried mud off Agnes's dress so that the lacings could be undone. Within the confines of the small kitchen, smoky as it was, the stench from the clothes and from Agnes's sour body had been enough to make Margrét retch. She had held her breath as she pulled the fetid wool off Agnes's skin, and had turned her head away when the dress fell from those thin shoulders and dropped to the floor, raising motes of dried mud.

Margrét recalled Agnes's shoulderblades. Razor-sharp, they'd poked out from the rough cloth of her undergarment, which was yellowed around the neckline and stained a filthy brown under the armpits.

Margrét would have to burn all the woman's clothes before breakfast. She had left them in a corner of the kitchen last night, unwilling to bring them into the badstofa. Fleas had crawled through their weave.

Somehow, she had managed to wash off most of the grime and dirt from the criminal's body. Agnes had tried to wash herself, feebly running the damp rag over her limbs, but the grime had been so long upon her skin that it seemed ground into her pores. Eventually, Margrét, rolling up her sleeves and clenching her teeth, had snatched the rag off her and scrubbed Agnes until the cloth was soiled through. As she washed her, Margrét had – in spite of herself – looked for the blemishes Lauga had thought would be evident, a sign of the murderess. Only the woman's eyes had hinted at something. They seemed different, Margrét thought. Very blue and clear, but too light a shade to be considered pretty.

The woman's body was a terrain of abuse. Even Margrét, accustomed to wounds, to the inevitable maladies wrought by hard labour and accident, had been shocked.

Perhaps she'd scrubbed Agnes's skin too hard, Margrét thought, pushing her head under the pillow in an effort to shut out the gargled snores of the officer. Some of the woman's sores had broken and wept. The sight of fresh blood had given Margrét some secret satisfaction.

She had made Agnes soak her hair, also. The water from the kettle had been too full of silt and scum, so Margrét had requested an officer fetch more from the mountain stream. While they waited, she had dressed the woman's wounds with an ointment of sulphur and lard.

'This is Natan Ketilsson's own medicine,' she had said, casting an eye up to catch the woman's reaction. Agnes had said nothing, but Margrét thought she had seen the muscles in her neck tighten. 'God rest his soul,' Margrét had muttered.

With Agnes's hair washed as good as could be in the freezing water, and most of the weeping sores plugged with lard, Margrét had given her the undergarments and bedding of Hjördis. Hjördis had been wearing the underdress Agnes now slept in when she died.

Margrét suspected it did not make a difference if a mite of contagion lingered. Its new owner would be dead soon enough.

How strange to imagine that, in a short while, the woman who slept in a bed not ten feet from her would be underground.

Margrét sighed and sat up in bed again. Agnes still had not moved. The officer snored on. Margrét watched him as he pushed a hand into his groin and scratched it, audibly. She averted her eyes, amused and a little annoyed that this man was her only protection.

Might as well get up and begin preparing something for the officers' breakfast, she thought. Skyr perhaps. Or dried fish. She wondered whether she had enough butter to spare, and when the servants would return from Reykjavík with their supplies.

Loosening her nightcap, Margrét cast one last glance at the sleeping woman.

Her heart jumped into her mouth. In the dim recesses of the badstofa, Agnes lay on her side, calmly watching Margrét.

CHAPTER THREE

IT IS SAID OF THE CRIME that Fridrik Sigurdsson, with the assistance of Agnes Magnúsdóttir and Sigrídur Gudmundsdóttir, came inside Natan Ketilsson's home close to midnight, and stabbed and thrashed Natan and Pétur Jónsson, who was a guest there, to death with a knife and hammer. Then, due to the gushing and smearing of the bodies that was apparent, burnt them by setting fire to the farm so that their evil work would not be apparent. Fridrik came to commit this evil through hatred of Natan, and a desire to steal. The murder was eventually exposed. The District Commissioner was suspicious, and when the half-burnt bodies were revealed, he believed that those three had been a gang.

From the Supreme Court Trials of 1829.

I DID NOT DREAM IN the storeroom at Stóra-Borg. Curled up on the wooden slats with a mouldy horse-skin for warmth, sleep came to me like a thin tide of water. It would lap against my body but never submerge me in oblivion. There would be something to wake me – the sound of footsteps, or the scrape of the chamber pot on the floor as a maid came to empty it, the heady stink of piss. Sometimes, if I lay still with my eyes tightly closed and pushed every thought out of my mind, sleep would trickle back. My mind would shift in and out of consciousness, until the briefest chink of light crept into the room, and the servants shoved me a bit of dried fish. Some days I think that I haven't really slept since the fire, and that maybe sleeplessness is punishment from God. Or Blöndal, even: my dreams taken with my belongings to pay for my custody.

But last night, here at Kornsá, I dreamt of Natan. He was boiling herbs for a draught, and I was watching him and running my hands over the smithy's turf wall. It was summer, and the light was tinged with pink. The herbs for the draught had a strong perfume, and it surrounded me as I stood there. I breathed in the bittersweet scent, feeling a slow wave of happiness rise over me. I was finally gone from the valley. Natan turned and smiled. He was holding a glass beaker filled with scum he had collected off the brewing herbs, and steam was rising from it. He looked like a sorcerer in his black worsted stockings and the smoke rising from his hand. Natan stepped through the pool of sunlight and I opened my arms to him, laughing, feeling like I might die from love, but as I did the beaker slipped from his grasp and smashed on the floor and darkness poured into the room like oil.

I can't be sure if I have slept since that dream.

Natan is dead.

I wake every morning with a blow of grief to my heart.

The only thing for it is to push my mind back underwater, back to the dream, back to the golden moment that enveloped me before the beaker broke. Or to imagine Brekkukot, when Mamma was with me. If I concentrate I can see her sleeping in the bed opposite mine, and Jóas, little Jóas scratching at his fleabites. I will use my fingernail to crush them against my thumb.

But the memories I haul up are cold. I know what comes after Brekkukot. I know what happens to Mamma, and to Jóas.

When I open my eyes I see Margrét lying awake in her bed. She tosses and turns, and picks absently at her blanket. Her nightcap is a little loose, and I can see her grey hair scraped over her head and twisted into tight plaits, even as she rests. I can almost make out the contours of her skull.

Her face is a blotch, half-hidden by the blanket she has drawn about her. She's turned to study the sleeping officer lying in the cot opposite.

The officer is snoring and the farm mistress clicks her tongue in disapproval. I hear you, old woman. You've had enough already? Try a year of them and their hard hands, hard looks.

The dried seaweed in her pillow rustles as she turns her head. She sees me. She sucks in a quick breath and snatches a hand to her heart.

I should have been more careful. Never be caught staring at someone. They'll think you want something from them.

'You're awake. Good.' The farm mistress smoothes her hair

across her forehead, and regards me for a moment, unsure, perhaps, of how long I have been watching her.

'Get up,' she says.

I obey. The wooden slats are cool under my feet.

Margrét hands me a servant's garb of blue wool and we dress in silence. She keeps a nervous eye on the snoring officer. I pull the rough cloth down over my head, and look about the room. There are other people asleep in the beds. Servants, perhaps. There is no time to find out who they might be – Margrét leads me down the dank corridor of the cottage, pausing only to tug at a strip of turf that has come loose and hangs in threads across a beam.

'Falling to pieces,' she mutters.

She moves too fast for me to look into the other rooms of the croft. It's not a large dwelling, but I remember from my first time here a storeroom for barrels, and that little room there, with the buckets and pans and a milking tray, must be the dairy, or perhaps they have turned it into a pantry. We pass the kitchen. My clothes from Stóra-Borg lie heaped in one corner.

It is already a fine day outside. The grass is wet from a night rain, and the blades look bright in the light of the rising sun. There is a brisk wind and it blows ripples across the puddles in the yard. I notice the small things, now.

'As you can see,' Margrét begins, pausing when she trips on a piece of driftwood that has tumbled off the pile outside the croft. 'As you can see, there is a great amount of work that must be done about this place.'

This is the first thing she has said since bidding me dress. I say nothing and keep my eyes lowered. I notice that her skirt hem is stained from years of brushing the ground.

Margrét stands up straight and puts her hands on her hips, as though trying to make herself bigger. Her nails are bitten to the quick.

'I shall make no secret of my displeasure to you. I don't want you in my home. I don't want you near my children.'

Those sleeping bodies were her children.

'I have been forced to keep you here, and you …' She falters a little. 'You are forced to be kept.'

Our shoulders are tensed against the morning wind, which buffets our dresses against our legs. When I was little my foster-mamma, Inga, showed me how to spread the material of my skirt out against a gale and pretend I had wings. It was a feeling of flying. One day, she told me, the wind would pick me up and I would be blown along in its path, and everyone in the valley would look up and see my shift. I used to laugh at that.

'My husband Jón is at Hvammur, but he will return this morning. Our farmhands will be returning any day to begin the haymaking. It won't do to act up. I don't know what you did at Stóra-Borg, but let me tell you, you will have no opportunity to take advantage of us here.'

She knows nothing.

'Now.' She clasps her hands tightly against her waist. 'It is my understanding that you were in a serving position before …' She pauses.

Before what? Before Natan Ketilsson and Pétur Jónsson had their skulls hammered in?

'Yes, mistress.'

It alarms me to hear my voice aloud. It seems a lifetime ago that I spoke freely at all.

'A servant?' She hasn't heard me over the wind.

'Yes, a servant. Since I was fifteen. A hireling before that.'

She is relieved.

'You know how to spin and knit, and cook, and tend the animals?'

I could do it in my sleep.

'Can you wield a knife?'

My stomach drops. 'Pardon, mistress?'

'Can you cut hay? Can you wield a scythe? God knows how many servants have never cut grass in their lives, I understand it's not common practice these days for women to mow, but we are a farm of few hands and –'

'I can wield a scythe.'

'Good. Well, as far as I'm concerned, you shall work for your keep. Yes, you shall pay for my inconvenience. I have no use for a criminal, only a servant.'

Criminal. The word hangs in the air. Heavy, unmoved by the bluster of the wind.

I want to shake my head. That word does not belong to me, I want to say. It doesn't fit me or who I am. It's another word, and it belongs to another person.

But what is the use of protesting against language?

Margrét clears her throat.

'I will not tolerate violence. I won't take lazing. Any cheek, any step out of line, any idle, or thieving, or conniving hands and I will drive you out. I will drag you out of this farm by your hair if I have to. Are we clear?'

She does not wait for an answer. She knows I have no choice.

'I'll show you the stock,' she says, taking a deep breath. 'I'll milk the ewes and cow while you ...'

Her eyes slip from mine to the next farm along the valley. Something has caught her attention.

SNÆBJÖRN, THE FARMER FROM GILSSTADIR, walked up the slope of the valley. Next to him was one of his seven sons,

Páll, entrusted that summer with shepherding the sheep of Kornsá. Struggling to keep up was Snæbjörn's wife, Róslín, with two of her youngest daughters in tow.

'God help me,' Margrét muttered. 'Here comes the horde.' She suddenly gave a start and grabbed Agnes's arm. 'Go inside,' she whispered. She pulled Agnes back beside the croft and gave her an urgent push towards the door. 'Inside! Now.'

Agnes hesitated in the doorway, regarding Margrét, before disappearing into the darkness of the house.

'*Sæl og blessuð*,' Snæbjörn shouted. He was a stout, tall man with ruddy cheeks and dull blond hair that hung in his eyes. 'Fine weather!'

'Isn't it?' Margrét replied, tersely. She waited until he came closer. 'I see you and Páll have brought me a few visitors.'

Snæbjörn gave a sheepish grin. 'Róslín insisted on coming. Only, she's heard about your, er, unfortunate situation. Told me she wanted to make sure you were all right.'

'How kind of her,' she said, through clenched teeth.

Róslín had come within earshot. 'What fine weather!' she cried, like a child, throwing one arm in the air. 'Let's hope it holds out for haymaking. Good morning, Margrét!'

Snæbjörn's wife was pregnant with her eleventh child; her belly bulged in front of her, lifting the front of her dress and revealing swollen ankles, damp with morning dew. Her broad face was flushed with the exertion of the walk and she was panting, her breasts heaving over her round stomach.

'I thought I'd come along with Snæbjörn and Páll here, and pay you a visit.' Her five-year-old daughter staggered over a small tussock of grass and offered a covered plate to Margrét. 'Rye bread,' Róslín said. 'Thought you might like a little treat.'

'Thank you.'

'Oh, goodness me, I'm out of breath. Too old to be in this state, but they will keep coming.' Róslín cheerfully patted her belly.

'Indeed,' Margrét remarked, sourly.

Snæbjörn coughed and looked from Róslín to Margrét. 'Well, we two men had best get on with it. Is Jón about, Margrét?'

'At Hvammur.'

'Right then. Well, I'll get Páll to work and take a look at that scythe, if you don't mind me tinkering in the smithy.' He turned to his wife and daughters. 'Don't keep Margrét from her chores for too long, eh, Róslín?' He gave them both a brief smile then turned on his heel and began walking away in long, even strides, pushing the boy gently in front of him.

Róslín laughed as soon as he was out of earshot. 'Men, eh? Can't stand still. Go play with your sister, Sibba. Don't go far. Keep by us, now.' Róslín nudged her daughters out of the way and cast her eye around the farm as she spoke, as if looking for someone. Margrét shifted the plate of rye bread onto her hip. Its sweet fragrance combined with the hot, moist smell of Róslín made her feel ill. She fell into a fit of coughing that shook her body so hard Róslín had to grab the plate of bread before it toppled into the grass.

'There, now, Margrét. Breathe easy. Still not well?'

Margrét waited until the spasm passed, then spat a viscous clump into the grass. 'I'm well enough. It's just a winter cough.'

Róslín tittered. 'But it's high summer.'

'I'm fine,' Margrét snapped.

Róslín gave her a look of exaggerated pity. 'Of course, if you say so. But, actually, that's why I came today. I'm a little concerned for you.'

'Oh?' Margrét murmured. 'Whatever for?'

'Well, your bad chest, of course, but I've also heard a few rumours over the past weeks. All nonsense I'm sure, but still . . .' Róslín cocked her head to the side and her fat face broke into a dimpled smile. 'But here, I'm racing ahead of myself without even thinking to ask if you're busy.' She peered past Margrét's shoulder towards the croft, putting a hand to her forehead to shield her eyes from the sun. 'I hope I'm not interrupting. It looked like you were with another. A dark-haired woman. Visitor?' Róslín put on a face of polite indifference.

Margrét sighed, annoyed. 'You've good eyes, Róslín.'

'Oh. Ingibjörg perhaps?' Róslín asked, raising an eyebrow. 'I'll go, then, and leave you two friends in peace.'

Margrét fought the urge to roll her eyes. 'No.'

'Of course not, too early for a visit from her,' Róslín said, winking. 'A new servant? You need all the help you can get for haymaking.'

'Well, not quite –'

'A relative, then?' Róslín continued, taking a step closer.

Margrét sighed. She cleared her throat, realising that there was no way of avoiding Róslín's inquisition. 'The woman you saw has been placed with me by District Commissioner Björn Audunsson Blöndal.'

'Oh, really? How strange. Whatever for?'

'The woman is called Agnes Magnúsdóttir. She is one of the servants convicted of murdering Natan Ketilsson and Pétur Jónsson, and has been placed in custody with us until the date of her execution.' Margrét folded her arms firmly over her chest and looked down at Róslín defiantly.

Róslín exclaimed, and set the bread on the ground so that she could better demonstrate her horror.

'Agnes! As in Agnes and Fridrik? Natan Ketilsson's murderers!' She brought her hands to her flushed cheeks and stared at Margrét, wide-eyed. 'But, Margrét! This is the very reason I came! Ósk Jóhannsdóttir said she had spoken with Soffía Jónsdóttir, whose brother Jóhann is a farmhand at Hvammur, and she said that Blöndal had decided to take Agnes from Stóra-Borg, because they couldn't risk such an important family being slaughtered –'

Róslín stopped, realising her mistake. Margrét pursed her lips and glared at her.

'Oh, Margrét, I didn't mean …' Her round cheeks reddened.

'Yes, Róslín. It's true that Blöndal has placed the murderess with us, and that neither I, nor Jón, had any say in the matter. But the reasons for his decision are known only to Blöndal himself.'

Róslín nodded her head emphatically. 'Of course. Ósk *is* a terrible gossip.'

'Yes.'

Róslín kept nodding her head, then stepped forward and placed a hand on Margrét's shoulder. 'I'm so sorry for you, Margrét.'

'Whatever for?'

'Why, for having to keep a *murderess* under your family's roof! For being forced to look at her hideous face every day! For the fear it must inspire in you, for your own good self and your husband and poor daughters!'

Margrét sniffed. 'Her face is not so hideous,' she said, but Róslín wasn't listening.

'I actually know quite a lot about the case, Margrét, and let me warn you, I have heard fiendish things about the wicked three who robbed the good Natan Ketilsson and Pétur Jónsson of their lives!'

'Good is not a word I think many would choose for Natan and Pétur.'

'Oh! But they were good! They made mistakes, of course –'

'Pétur slit the throats of thirty sheep, Róslín. He was a thief.'

'But they were noble Icelanders all the same. Oh, and to think of Natan's family! His brother Gudmundur, and his wife and all their little children. They've gone to Illugastadir, you know, to mend the croft and Natan's workshop.'

'Róslín, if I have heard rightly, Natan spent more of his time in the beds of married women than in his Illugastadir workshop!'

Róslín was taken aback. 'Margrét?'

'It's just that ...' Margrét hesitated and turned around, looking towards the entrance of the croft. 'Nothing is simple,' she finally muttered.

'You don't believe they deserved to die?'

Margrét snorted. 'Of course not.'

Róslín regarded her cautiously. 'You do know she's guilty, don't you?'

'Yes, I know she's guilty.'

'Good. Then let me tell you, you'd be well advised to watch your back around ... What was her name again?'

'Agnes,' Margrét replied, softly. 'You know that, Róslín.'

'Yes, Agnes Magnúsdóttir, that's the one. Be careful. I know there's not much you can do, but ask the District Commissioner for a guard to watch her. Keep her hands tied! Folk are saying that Agnes is the worst of the three convicted. The boy, Fridrik, was under her sway, and she forced the other girl to keep watch, and tied her to the doorpost to make sure she wouldn't escape!' Róslín took a step forward and brought her face close to Margrét's. 'I've heard that it was she who stabbed Natan eighteen times. Over and over again!'

'Eighteen times, is that so?' Margrét murmured. She desperately wished Snæbjörn would come back to collect his wife.

'In the stomach and throat.' Róslín's face was flushed with excitement. 'And – oh, the Lord bless us – even in the face! I heard she plunged the knife into his *eye socket*. Pierced it like an egg yolk!' Róslín grasped Margrét tightly on the shoulder. 'If I were you I wouldn't sleep a wink with her in the same room! I'd rather sleep in the cowshed than risk it. Oh, Margrét, I can't believe the rumours are true! Murderers on our doorsteps! This parish has gone to the dogs. Worse than the things you hear about Reykjavík. And *her*, just now, standing in the very spot where my daughters play. It gives me the shivers. See, look at my arms – I am covered in gooseflesh! My poor Margrét, however shall you cope?'

'I'll manage,' Margrét said briskly, bending down to pick up the plate of rye bread.

'But will you? And where is Jón to protect you?'

'At Hvammur, with Blöndal. Like I said.'

'Margrét!' Róslín threw her hands into the air. 'It is wickedness for Blöndal to have you and the girls alone with this woman! I tell you what, *I* shall stay with you.'

'You will do no such thing, Róslín,' Margrét said firmly, 'but thank you for your concern. Now, I hate to set you on your way, but the sheep will not milk themselves.'

'Shall I help you?' Róslín asked. 'Here, let me take that bread and carry it inside for you.'

'Goodbye, Róslín.'

'Perhaps if I were to see her, I could gauge your danger. Our danger! What's to stop her from sneaking about at night?'

Margrét took Róslín by the elbow and turned her in the direction she had come from. 'Thank you for your visit, Róslín, and thank you for the rye bread. Watch your step, there.'

'But –'

'Goodbye, Róslín.'

Róslín cast a backward glance towards the croft, then attempted a smile and trudged heavily back down the slope towards Gilsstadir. Her little girls tottered after her. Margrét stood, gripping the plate of rye bread in front of her, and watched them leave, until they were nothing more than specks in the distance, then she squatted and coughed until her tongue was slippery. She spat wetly upon the grass. Then she slowly stood up, turned and walked back towards the croft.

✝

WHEN I COME INTO THE badstofa I see that the officer who was sleeping is gone. He must have joined his friends; I can hear men talking in a mixture of Danish and Icelandic outside the window. They must not have seen the farm mistress push me back inside. The two sleeping daughters have gone also. I'm alone.

I am alone.

There is no watchful eye, no guard at the door, no rope, no fetters, no locks, and I am all by myself, unbound. I am paralysed by the thought of it. Surely someone has an eye to a keyhole? Surely someone has pressed his body to a crack in the wall, is waiting to see what I will do, waiting to storm the room with a finger pointing like a knife at my throat.

But there is no one. *Not a soul.*

I stand in the centre of the room, and let my eyes adjust to the gloom. Yes, I am quite alone, and a tremble of exhilaration passes along my skin, like the tremor on the surface of a pot of water about to boil. In this minute I can do anything: I can examine the cottage, or lie down, or talk aloud, or sing. I can dance, or swear, or laugh and no one will know.

I could escape.

A bubble of fear passes up my spine. It's the feeling of standing on ice and suddenly hearing it crack under your weight – both thrilling and terrifying together. At Stóra-Borg I dreamt of escape. Of finding the key to my fetters and fleeing – I never thought of where I might go. There was never a chance. Yet here, now, I could slip out of the yard and run down the far end of the valley, away from the farms, to wait and escape under night into the highlands, where the sky will cover me with her rough, grey hand. I could flee to the heath. Show them that they cannot keep me locked up, that I am a thief of time and will steal the hours denied to me!

Specks of dust drift in the sunlight coming through the dried membrane fastened to the window. As I watch them, the thrill of escape is sucked away, like water down a geyser. I would only be trading one death sentence for another. Up in the highlands blizzards howl like the widows of fishermen and the wind blisters the skin off your face. Winter comes like a punch in the dark. The uninhabited places are as cruel as any executioner.

My knees are weak as I stumble to my bed. With my eyes closed, the silence of the room presses upon me like a hand.

When my heart slows, I look over to where the officer slept, the coverlet twisted and the worn mattress exposed. He ought to have replaced the bed board – he'll have bad luck. Perhaps if the bed is still warm, he is nearby. It feels intrusive to touch the bare mattress, but it's cold. He's gone. My bed is made. I run my hands over the thin blanket, worn smooth from use. How many other bodies have lain here before me? How many nightmares have been produced under this cloth?

The floor is boarded, but the walls and ceiling are not, and the turf is in need of repair; slabs of dried sod have slumped inwards and thinned, leaving fissures in the wall and the room prey to draughts. It will be cold in winter.

But I might be dead before then.

Quickly! Push that thought away.

Dead grass hangs from the ceiling like unwashed hair. A few carved ornaments have been arranged across the rafters, and a cross is nailed to the lintel over the entrance.

Do they sing hymns in the winter here? Maybe they recite the sagas instead – I prefer a story to a prayer. They whipped me for that at this farm, Kornsá, once, when I was young and fostered out to watch over the home field. The farmer Björn did not like that I knew the sagas better than him. You're better off keeping company with the sheep, Agnes. Books written by man, not God, are faithless friends and not for your kind.

I might have believed him were it not for my foster-mother Inga and the lessons she gave me, delivered in whispers as he dozed in the evening.

Near the entrance, close to the mistress's bed, is a grey woollen curtain that has been nailed to a slat. I suppose it serves as a door to the room beyond. The curtain falls short and in the gap above the floor the legs of a table are visible. They're slightly splintered, as though someone has gnawed at them.

The badstofa is almost as bare as all those years ago, although little planks have been nailed between the sloping rafters and the wall supports to serve as shelves. They hold the usual things – wooden canisters, sheep horns, a pipe, fishbones, mittens and knitting needles. There is a small painted trunk under one of the beds. An abandoned slipper wanting mending. The familiarity of day-to-day things can be comforting. I once had things like this. My white sack with the dried flowers in it. The stone Mamma gave me before she left. It will bring you good luck, Agnes. It is a magic stone. Put it under your tongue and you will be able to talk to the birds.

That stone sat in my mouth for days. If the birds understood my questions, they never cared to answer them.

Kornsá of Húnavatn District. I was delivered to its doorstep at six years old with a kiss and a stone from Mamma, and now I've been dragged here again at three and thirty winters because of two dead men and a fire. I've worked at more northern farms than should have been my share. But poverty scrapes these homes down until they all look the same, and they all have in common the absence of things that ought to be there. I might as well have been at one place all my life.

This is it, then. Kornsá, my last grim corner. The last bed, the last roof, the last floor. The last of everything brings lugs of pain, as though there will be nothing left, but smoke from fires abandoned. I must pretend that I am a servant still, and that these are my new quarters and I must think of all the chores I will do, and how I will make my mistress comment on the dexterity of my fingers. I used to think that if I worked hard I might one day be made a housemistress. But not here. Not at Kornsá.

Kornsá. It trips over and over itself in my head, so that I must very quietly say it aloud and feel the sound of it. I tell myself that it's just another farm, and I softly chant the names of all the places I have lived at. It's like an incantation: Flaga, Beinakelda, Litla-Giljá, Brekkukot, Kornsá, Gudrúnarstadir, Gilsstadir, Gafl, Fannlaugarstadir, Búrfell, Geitaskard, Illugastadir.

Of all the names, one is a mistake. One is a nightmare. The stair you miss in the darkness.

The name is everything that went wrong. Illugastadir, the farm by the sea, where the soft air rings with the clang of the smithy, and gulls caw, and seals roll over in their fat. Illugastadir, where the night is lit by fire, where smoke turns in the early morning to engulf the stars, and in ruins, always Illugastadir, cradling dead bodies in its cage of burnt beams.

Outside, the officers burst into laughter. One of them is talking about his rich cousin in Helgavatn.

'Let's stop and relieve him of his brandy!' one suggests.

'Yes! And his wife and daughters!' another shouts. They laugh again.

Will someone stay to make sure I don't run away? To make certain I don't light the lamps, in case I dash the flame upon the floor. To make sure I keep my hands clean, and my tongue still, and my legs together, and my eyes down.

I am the property of the Crown now.

I hope they all leave today.

As I strain to listen to the officers' conversation I notice that something has been hidden under the bed across from me, something shiny. It is a silver brooch, a strange thing to have in a room so stripped of luxury. Was it stolen? It wouldn't be so strange in this valley, where people can catch sheep and slice the marks from their ears before the flock scatters, and men grow their nails long to better pick up coins. There's many a thieving farmer and servant who has felt the law's whip in these parts. Even Natan bore the scars of his own youthful brush with the birch rod.

I pick up the brooch. It's unexpectedly heavy.

'Put it down.' A slender young woman is standing with her legs apart, her arms raised from her sides. 'That's mine.'

I drop the brooch and we both flinch as it hits the floor. The girl is fine-boned and small, with pale lashes striking against the dark blue of her eyes. Her head is covered with a scarf. There is a slight bump in her nose.

'Steina!' The girl hasn't moved, only regards me from the doorway. She is scared of me, I think.

Another girl steps through the doorway. She must be her sister, only she is taller, with brown eyes, and the skin over her nose is clouded with freckles. 'Róslín and her brood are –' She stops when she sees me.

'She was touching my confirmation gift.'

'I thought Mamma took her outside?'

'Me too.'

They stare. 'Mamma! Mamma! Come here!'

Margrét hobbles in, wiping her mouth. She sees the silver brooch on the floor by my feet and the blood drains from her face. Her mouth slips open.

'She was touching it, Mamma. I caught her.'

Margrét shuts her eyes and passes a hand over her lips as if in pain. I want to touch her on the arm. I want to reassure her. She comes towards me, furious now, and I hear the slap before I feel it. A neat crack. A tingling rush of pain.

'What did I tell you?' she cries. 'You will not touch a thing in this house!' She breathes heavily, her hand pointing at my face. 'Consider yourself lucky that I don't report this incident.'

'I'm not a thief,' I say.

'No, you're a murderess.' The blue-eyed girl spits the words out, dimples flashing in her cheeks. Her headscarf has slipped and a lock of white-blonde hair falls onto her forehead. Her face is flushed.

'Lauga,' Margrét warns, 'take Steina and go into the kitchen.' They leave. Margrét grabs my sleeve. 'Follow,' she says, dragging me out of the room. 'You can prove your penitence by working like a dog.'

REVEREND TÓTI WOKE IN THE early hours of the morning and could not return to sleep. Today he was expected at Kornsá again. Reluctantly rising and dressing, he walked out into the crisp clean air of the morning and started to complete chores about the farm and church. He rounded up the small flock of sheep belonging to his father and milked them with exaggerated care, whispering to them by name and running his fingers over their furred ears.

Mid-morning came and went, and the sun bled into the sky. Tóti fed and watered their cow, Ýsa, and then started to take the laundry off the stone church wall where his father had laid it out to dry.

'You don't need to do that,' Reverend Jón said, walking towards him from the croft.

'I don't mind,' Tóti said, smiling. He picked a grass seed out of a sock.

His father shrugged. 'Thought you'd be over Vatnsdalur way.'

Tóti grimaced.

'Why are you fussing with the laundry when you've her to see?'

Tóti paused, and looked at Reverend Jón, who was flapping a pair of trousers in the wind.

'I don't know what to say,' he said, then paused. 'What would you say to her?'

His father smacked his shoulder with his rough hand and glared at him. 'Get on,' he said. 'Who says you'll need to say anything? Go.'

✝

MARGRÉT TAKES ME ACROSS THE yard to show me the small plot of lovage and angelica, and then I assist her with the milking of the sheep. I suppose she does not trust me to be alone again. The small boy who arrived earlier has already rounded up the animals. Margrét points him out to me as Páll, but does not introduce us, and he does not come near me, although he stares, open-mouthed.

Then we burn my dress.

I made it two years ago. Sigga and I made one each, a working dress, blue and simple from the cloth Natan gave us.

If I had known that the dress I laboured over would be my only warmth in a room that reeked of sour skin. If I had known that the dress would one day be put on in the night, in a hurry, to be soaked with sweat as I ran through the witching hours to Stapar, screaming fit to raise the dead.

Margrét gives me a little warm milk from the pail, and then we go into the kitchen where her daughters are building up the fire with dung. They shrink back against the wall when I enter.

'Take the kettle off the hook, Steina,' Margrét says to the plain girl. Then she gathers my soiled clothes from the corner and throws them on the fire without ceremony.

'There.' She sounds satisfied.

We watch the woollen dress smoulder until our eyes water

from the smoke and Margrét coughs, and we are forced to go and work elsewhere while my clothes burn. The daughters go into the pantry.

That dress was my last possession. There is nothing in the world I now own; even the heat my body gives out is taken away by the summer breeze.

The herb plot of Kornsá is overgrown and wild, surrounded by a rough stone wall that has toppled to the ground at one end. Most of the plants have gone to seed, frostbitten roots rotting in the warmer weather, but there are tansies, and little bitter herbs I remember from Natan's workshop at Illugastadir, and the angelica smells sweetly.

We are weeding, finding the tufts of grass creeping about the healthier plants and pulling them from the soil. I relish the give of the roots and the gum on my fingers as the stalks burst, although my lungs ache. I have weakened. But I don't give myself away.

There is a pleasure to be had in squatting with my skirt bunched about me, and the smell of the smoke from the dung fire in my hair. Margrét works furiously and breathes heavily. What is she thinking? Her nails are black with soil, and she scrabbles in the dirt urgently. Her eyes are red-rimmed from the smoke in the kitchen. When she clears her throat I hear the rattle of phlegm.

'Go back to the croft and tell my daughters to come out to me,' she says suddenly. 'Then shovel ashes from the hearth and dig them into the dirt.'

The officers are saddling their horses in the yard when I return unaccompanied to the homestead. They're silent. 'Are you all right?' one of them calls to Margrét, and she reassures them with a wave of a soiled hand.

The door to the croft is open, probably to let the foul smoke out. I pick my feet up over the door ledge.

I find the daughters in the pantry, skimming yesterday's milk. The youngest sees me first and nudges her sister. They both take a few steps back.

'Your mother would like you to join her.' I give a small nod and step aside to let them past me. The younger slips out of the room immediately, her eyes never leaving mine.

The elder girl hesitates. What is her nickname? Steina. *Stone*. She gives me a peculiar look, and slowly sets down her paddle.

'I think I know you,' she says.

I say nothing.

'You were a servant here in this valley before, weren't you?'

I nod.

'I know you. I mean, we met once. You were leaving Gudrúnar-stadir just as we were moving there to take up the lease. We met on the road.'

When would that have been? May, 1819. How old could she have been then? No more than ten.

'We had a dog with us. A tan and white one. I remember you because he started barking and jumping up, and Pabbi pulled him off you, and then we shared our dinner.'

The girl looks at my face searchingly.

'You were the woman we met on the way to Gudrúnarstadir. Do you remember me? You plaited my sister's hair and gave us an egg each.'

Two small girls sucking eggs by the road, hems damp through with mud. The blur of a thin dog chasing his reflection in the water and the sky broken grey and wide. Three ravens flying in a line. A good omen.

'Steina!'

The walk from Gudrúnarstadir to Gilsstadir in a freezing spring. 1819. One hundred small whales come ashore near Thingeyrar. A bad omen.

'Steina!'

'Coming, Mamma!' Steina turns to me. 'I'm right, aren't I? That was you.'

I take a step towards her.

The farm mistress bursts in. 'Steina!' She looks at me, then her daughter. 'Out.' She grabs the girl's arm and yanks her from the room. 'The ashes. Now.'

Outside, the breeze picks up a handful of my dress's ashes from the pail and flings them against the blue of the sky. The grey flakes flutter and dip, and dissolve into the air. Is this happiness, this warmth against my chest? Like another's hand placed there?

I may be able to pretend I am my old self here.

'SHALL WE BEGIN WITH A prayer?' the Assistant Reverend Thorvardur Jónsson asked.

He and Agnes were sitting outside the entranceway to the croft, on a small heap of cut turf that had been prepared and stacked for reparations. The Reverend held his New Testament in one hand and a rather limp slice of buttered rye bread in the other, given to him by Margrét. Horsehair had settled on it from his clothes.

Agnes did not reply to the Reverend's question. She sat with her fingers in her lap, slightly hunched, gazing out at the line of departing officers. There were ashes in her hair. The wind had dropped and occasionally a shout or burst of laughter could be heard from the men, interrupting the soft tearing sounds of Margrét and her daughters ripping weeds from the plot. The elder kept raising her head to peer at the pastor and the criminal.

Tóti looked at the book he held in his hands, and cleared his throat.

'Do you think we ought to begin with a prayer?' he asked again, louder, thinking Agnes had not heard him.

'Begin what with a prayer?' she responded quietly.

'W-well,' Tóti stammered, caught off-guard. 'Your absolution.'

'My absolution?' Agnes repeated. She shook her head slightly.

Tóti quickly pushed the bread into his mouth, and chewed rapidly before swallowing in a loud gulp. He wiped his hands on his shirt, then thumbed the pages of his New Testament, rearranging himself on the turf. It was still wet from the night's rain and he could feel the moisture seeping into his trousers. A stupid place to sit, he thought. He should have remained inside.

'I received a letter from District Commissioner Blöndal just over a month ago, Agnes,' he said, pausing. 'Is it all right if I call you Agnes?'

'It's my name.'

'He informed me that you were unhappy with the Reverend at Stóra-Borg and wished for another churchman to spend time with you, before ... Before, well, before ...' Tóti's voice trailed off.

'Before I die?' Agnes suggested.

Tóti gave a little nod. 'He said you asked for me.'

Agnes took a deep breath. 'Reverend Thorvardur –'

'Call me Tóti. Everyone does,' he interrupted. He blushed, immediately regretting his familiarity.

Agnes paused, uncertain. 'Reverend Tóti, then. Why do you think the District Commissioner wants me to spend time with a churchman?'

'Well ... I suppose because, I mean, we want, Blöndal and the clergy, and I ... We want you to return to God.'

Agnes hardened her expression. 'I think I'll be returning to Him soon enough. By way of an axe-swing.'

'That's not what I ... I didn't mean it in that sense ...' Tóti sighed. It was going as badly as he had feared. 'You did ask for me though? Only I took the time to have a look in the ministerial book at Breidabólstadur, and you're not listed there.'

'No,' Agnes replied. 'I wouldn't be.'

'You've never been a parishioner of mine or my father's?'

'No.'

'Then why ask for me if we've never even met before?'

Agnes stared at him. 'You don't remember me, do you?'

Tóti was taken aback. There was certainly something familiar about the woman, but as his mind leafed through the images of women he had known or met – servants, mothers, wives, children – he couldn't place Agnes.

'I'm sorry,' he said.

Agnes shrugged her shoulders. 'You helped me once before.'

'Did I?'

'Over a river. On your horse.'

'Where was this?'

'Near Gönguskörd. I had been working at Fannlaugarstadir, and was leaving my work there.'

'Then you are from the Skagafjördur District?'

'No. I'm from this valley. Vatnsdalur. The Húnavatn District'

'And I helped you over a river?'

'Yes. The pass was flooded and you came by on your horse just as I was about to cross the water by foot.'

Tóti wondered. He had gone through Gönguskörd many times, but couldn't remember meeting a young woman. 'When was this?'

'Six or seven years ago. You were young.'

'Yes. I would have been,' Tóti said. There was a moment of silence. 'Was it because of that kindness that you ask for me now?' He looked closely at her face. She doesn't *look* like a criminal, he thought. Not since she's had a bath.

Agnes squinted and looked out over the valley. Her expression was inscrutable.

'Agnes ...' Tóti sighed. 'I'm only an Assistant Reverend. My training is incomplete. Perhaps you need a qualified clergyman, or one from your own district who knows you? Surely someone else has shown you kindness? Who was your Reverend here?'

Agnes tucked a strand of dark hair behind her ear. 'I haven't met many churchmen I care for, and certainly none that I would claim know me,' she said.

A few ravens swept through the valley, landing on the stone fence, and both Tóti and Agnes saw Margrét's head bob up from behind it. 'Nuisances!' she cried. A clod of dirt flew over the wall and the birds took off, cawing indignantly. Tóti looked at Agnes and smiled, but Agnes was stony-faced.

'They won't like that,' she murmured to herself.

'Well,' Tóti said, taking a deep breath. 'If you require a spiritual advisor, then I will consider it my duty to visit you. As District Commissioner Blöndal so desires, I will come to guide you in your prayers, so that you may walk towards what lies ahead of you with faith and dignity. I will take it as my responsibility to supply you with spiritual comfort and hope.'

Tóti fell silent. He had rehearsed this speech as he rode to the farm, and he was pleased that he'd managed to remember to say 'spiritual comfort'. It sounded paternalistic, and self-assured, as though he was in a lofty state of spiritual certainty: a state he felt he should be in, but had a vague, discomfiting sense that he was not.

Still, he wasn't used to talking so formally, and his hands sweated against the tissue-thin paper of the Testament. He carefully closed the book, making sure not to crease any pages, and wiped his palms on his thighs. Now would be a good time to quote scripture, as his father was wont to do, but all he could think of was his sudden yearning for his snuff horn.

'Perhaps I have made a mistake, Reverend.' Agnes's voice was measured, calm.

Tóti didn't know what to say. He looked at the bruises on her face and bit his lip.

'Perhaps it will be better if you stay at Breidabólstadur. I thank you but ... Do you really think ...?' She covered her mouth with her hands and shook her head.

'My dear child, don't cry!' he exclaimed, rising from the turf.

Agnes took her hands away. 'I'm not crying,' she said, flatly. 'I have made a mistake. You call me a child, Reverend Thorvardur, but you're little more than a child yourself. I'd forgotten how young you are.'

Tóti had no response for this. He regarded her for a moment, then nodded grimly and swiftly replaced his hat on his head. He bid her a good day.

Agnes watched him walk past the stone fence to farewell Margrét and the girls. The pastor and women stood together for a few minutes, chatting and looking over at her. Agnes tried to hear what they were saying, but the wind had picked up and it was blowing their words away from her. Only when Tóti raised his hat to Margrét and began to walk to the hitching post to retrieve his cob did Agnes hear Margrét call out: 'Easier to squeeze blood from a stone, I should think!'

✝

THE REST OF THE DAY passes in work – in weeding and tending
the pitiable herbs. I listen to the far-off bleats of sheep. The poor
things look thin and patchy with the winter wool newly pulled from
their backs. After the priest left, the daughters, Margrét and I ate a
dinner of dried fish and butter. I made sure I chewed each morsel
twenty times. Then we returned to the garden, and now I start to try
and mend the wall, pulling away the rocks that have shifted, sorting
them on the ground, then rebuilding it, locking the stones into place
and relishing the heavy mass of them in my hands.

I so often feel that I am barely here, that to feel weight is to be
reminded of my own existence.

Margrét and I work in silence; she speaks to me only when giving
me an order. It seems our minds are fixed on other things, and I think
of how strange it is that fortune has led me back to Kornsá, where
I lived as a child. Where I first learnt what it was to grieve. I think
about the paths that I have taken, and I think about the Reverend.

Thorvardur Jónsson who asks to be called Tóti like a farmer's
son. He seems too callow for his station. There is a softness about his
voice, and about his hands. They are not long and stained by tinctures
as Natan's were, or meaty like the hands of farm help, but small, and
thin and clean. He rested them upon his Bible as he spoke to me.

I have made a mistake. They condemn me to death and I ask for
a boy to coach me for it. A red-headed boy, who gobbles his buttered
bread and toddles to his horse with the seat of his pants wet, this is
the young man they hope will get me on my knees, full of prayer.
This is the young man I hope will be able to help me, although with
what and how I cannot think.

The only person who would understand how I feel is Natan. He
knew me as one knows the seasons, knows the tide. Knew me like
the smell of smoke, knew what I was, and what I wanted. And now
he is dead.

Perhaps I should say to him, poor boy, go back to the parsonage and back to your precious books. I was wrong: there is nothing you can do for me. God has had His chance to free me, and for reasons known to Him alone, He has pinned me to ill fortune, and although I have struggled, I am run through and through with disaster; I am knifed to the hilt with fate.

CHAPTER FOUR

To the Deputy Governor of North-East Iceland,

Thank you for Your Excellency's most illustrious letter from the 10th of January this year, concerning the charges of murder, arson and other crimes brought against the defendants Fridrik, Agnes and Sigrídur, for which they have been sentenced to death. In response to your letter, allow me to inform you that B. Henriksson, the blacksmith who was solicited to build the axe to be used for the execution, quoted the cost of five silver dollars of the realm for his work and materials, following my suggestions as to the make and size of the axe on the 30th of December last year. After receiving Your Excellency's letter however, I thought, in agreeance with Your Excellency, that it would be better to purchase a broader axe from Copenhagen for the same price, and that is why I since asked Simonsen the merchant to arrange that for me.

In this summer the man concerned, Simonsen, came to me with the axe, and although it has been made exactly as requested, I was surprised when I learnt from Simonsen that it had cost twenty-nine dollars of the realm. On examination of the bill, I found this sum to be correct, and was understandably forced to pay Herr Simonsen's invoice from the funds allotted to this case by Your Excellency.

Now, as I dare to explain to you the overdrawn state of these funds, I humbly ask if this expense should not, in fact, have been drawn from the monies budgeted for this case, which, amongst other items of expense, serve to pay for the custody of the prisoners. Also, I humbly enquire of Your Excellency what we are supposed to do with this axe after it has been used for the executions.

I am, Your Excellency, your most humble and obedient servant.

HÚNAVATN DISTRICT COMMISSIONER
Björn Blöndal

TÓTI HAD LEFT KORNSÁ WITH the full intention of writing to Blöndal and reneging on his promise to meet with Agnes. His second conversation with the criminal had been a failure; he hadn't even led a simple prayer. Yet, the thought that he would necessarily have to explain why he had changed his mind after only two visits filled him with dread and embarrassment, and he left off composing the letter. I will do it tomorrow, he promised himself with each new day at Breidabólstadur, but two weeks had passed, the peasants were readying themselves for the mid-July harvest, and he had not so much as picked up his quill.

One night Tóti was sitting with Reverend Jón, reading in silence, when his father lifted his grizzled head and asked him: 'Does the murderess pray?'

Tóti hesitated before replying. 'I'm not sure.'

'Hmmph,' Reverend Jón muttered. 'Make sure.' He squinted at his son out of gummy eyes until Tóti felt a blush flare over his cheeks and neck. 'You're a servant of the Lord. Don't disgrace yourself, boy,' he said, before returning to his scripture.

The next morning Tóti rose early to milk Ýsa. He pressed his forehead to the cow's warm flank, and listened to the even rhythm of the milk spurting into the wooden pail. Thoughts of Agnes sitting beside him sprang to his mind. His father knew that he wasn't visiting Agnes. He would be ashamed to know that his son could not shoulder the responsibility of one woman's atonement. But what to do with a woman who was not willing to atone? What had Agnes said? She hadn't met a churchman she cared for. She did not seem to be religious, and that stupid little speech he had composed about spiritual comfort – all those lofty words had fallen flat. What did she want from him, then? Why ask for him, if she didn't want to talk of God? Of death and heaven and hell, and the word of the Lord? Because he helped her over a river? It was unnerving. Why not enlist a friend or a relative to help her come to terms with her life's end?

Perhaps she didn't have a friend left in the world. Perhaps she wanted to talk of other things. Such as crossing the Gönguskörd pass in a waterlogged spring. Such as why she had left the Vatnsdalur valley to work further east, or why she doesn't care for clergymen. Tóti closed his eyes, and felt Ýsa shift her warm weight from one side to the other under his forehead, restless. To soothe her he recited Hallgrímur Pétursson: 'The pathway of Thy Passion to follow I desire, Out of my weakness fashion a character of fire.' He opened his eyes and recited the last line again.

By the time the pail was full, he had decided to return to Kornsá.

A morning mist lingered in the valley, obscuring Tóti's view of the mountains as he rode through the ghostly wreaths that hovered over the grass. He shivered from the cold and buried his hands into the warmth of his horse's mane. Today I will right things with Agnes, he thought.

By the time Tóti slowed his horse to a walk, up past the three strange hills of Thrístapar at the mouth of the valley, towards the green throat of Vatnsdalur, morning sunlight poured out over the cloud. It would be yet another clear day. Soon families and their servants would be dotted along the home fields, scythes in hand, spreading the cut grass out to dry and the smell of mown hay would overwhelm the valley. But now, so early in the morning, Tóti could see only the topmost caps of the mountains, their brown bulk still concealed by the band of slowly shifting fog. He heard a sudden shout and noticed Páll, the Kornsá shepherd boy, driving the sheep along the mountainside, obscured a little by the mist. Tóti urged his horse towards the bank of the river that wound through the valley and passed Kornsá at a distance, continuing on to the bowed croft of Undirfell.

A large, unshaven farmer appeared at the door.

'*Blessuð*. Greetings. I'm Haukur Jónsson.'

'*Saell*, Haukur. I'm Assistant Reverend Thorvardur Jónsson. Is the Reverend of Undirfell here?'

'Pétur Bjarnason? No, he doesn't take the tenancy here. He's not far though. Come in.'

Tóti followed the hulking shape of the farmer into the croft. The dwelling was larger than most he had seen. At least eight people were in the badstofa, dressing and talking amongst themselves. A young girl with large eyes held a screaming red-faced toddler on her lap, and two servant girls were trying to wrestle clothes onto a young boy who was more interested in his game of knuckles on the floor. At the sight of Tóti they stopped talking.

'Please, sit here,' said Haukur, gesturing to a space on a bed beside a very old woman whose withered face looked blankly into Tóti's own. 'That's Gudrún. She's blind. I'll fetch the Reverend for you if you don't mind waiting.'

'Thank you,' Tóti said.

The farmer left and a fresh-faced young woman soon bustled into the badstofa. 'Hello! So you are from Breidabólstadur? Can I offer you a drink? I'm Dagga.'

Tóti shook his head and Dagga swept the toddler out of the arms of the little girl and set her against her shoulder. 'Poor thing, she's been up all night screaming fit to wake the dead.'

'Is she not well?'

'My husband thinks it's gripe, but I worry it's worse. Do you know anything in the way of medicine, Reverend?'

'Me? Oh, no. No more than you'd know yourself, I'm sorry.'

'Never mind. 'Tis more the pity that Natan Ketilsson is dead, bless his soul.'

Tóti blinked at her. 'Excuse me?'

The girl in the corner piped up. 'He cured me of whooping cough.'

'Was he a friend of the family?' Tóti asked.

Dagga wrinkled her nose. 'No. Not a friend, but he was a useful man to send for when the children were ill or needed to be bled. When little Gulla there had the cough he stayed a night or two, mixing his herbs and looking in books of a foreign tongue. Odd fellow.'

'He was a sorcerer.' The old woman next to him had spoken. The family looked at her.

'He was a sorcerer,' she repeated. 'And he got what was coming to him.'

'Gudrún ...' Dagga smiled nervously at Tóti. 'We have a guest. You'll scare the children.'

'Natan Satan, that was his name. Nothing he did ever came from God.'

'Shush now, Gudrún. That's just a story.'

'What's this?' Tóti asked.

Dagga shifted the crying toddler onto her other hip. 'You've not heard it?'

Tóti shook his head. 'No, I've been at school in the south. At Bessastadir.'

Dagga raised her eyebrows. 'Well, it's just something folks say around the valley. There's people here who claim that Natan Ketilsson's mother had foresight – she dreamt things and they'd come to pass, see. Now, when she was pregnant with Natan she dreamt that a man came to her and told her she would have a boy. The dream man asked if she'd name the boy after him, and when she agreed, the man told her his name was Satan.'

'She took fright,' Gudrún interrupted, frowning. 'The priest changed it to Natan, and they thought that was decent. But we all knew that boy would never come to any good. He was a twin, but his brother never saw God's light – one for above, and one for below.' She slowly swivelled on the bed and brought her face close to Tóti's. 'He was never without money,' she whispered. 'He dealt with the Devil.'

'Or he was just a nimble-fingered herbalist, and the money came from charging a king's ransom,' Dagga suggested cheerfully. 'As I said, it's just something people say.'

Tóti nodded.

'Anyway, what brings you to Vatnsdalur, Reverend?'

'I'm Agnes Magnúsdóttir's priest.'

Dagga's smile dropped from her face. 'I heard she'd been brought to Kornsá.'

'Yes.' Tóti saw the two servant women exchange glances. Next to him Gudrún gave a hacking cough. He felt flecks of spittle land on his neck.

'The trial was held at Hvammur,' Dagga continued.

'Yes.'

'She's from this valley, you know.'

'That's why I'm here,' Tóti said. 'At Undirfell, I mean. I want to learn a little of her life from the ministerial book.'

The woman's expression soured. 'I could tell you a little of her life.' She hesitated, and then ordered the servants to take the children outside, waiting until they had left the room before speaking again. 'She always had it in her,' Dagga said in a low voice, casting a careful eye at Gudrún, who had slumped against the wall and seemed to be dozing off.

'What do you mean?' Tóti asked.

The woman pulled a face and leaned in closer. 'I hate to say it, but Agnes Magnúsdóttir never cared about anyone but herself, Reverend. She was always fixed on bettering herself. Wanted to get on above her station.'

'She was poor?'

'Bastard pauper with a conniving spirit like you'd never see in a proper maid.'

Tóti winced at the woman's words. 'You weren't friendly.'

Dagga laughed. 'No, not quite. Agnes was a different kind.'

'And what kind is that?'

Dagga hesitated. 'There's some folk who are contented with their lot and those they have for company, Reverend, and thank God for them too. But not her.'

'But you know her?'

The woman shifted her whimpering child onto her other hip. 'Never shared a badstofa, but know of her, Reverend. Know her as folks know everyone in this valley. There used to be a poem about her in these parts, when she was younger. Folks were fond of her then, and called her Búrfell-Agnes. But she bittered as she grew older. Couldn't keep a man, something about her. Couldn't settle. This valley is small and she had a reputation for a sharp tongue and loose skirts.'

Someone cleared his throat in the doorway. The farmer had returned with another man, who was yawning and scratching at the stubble on his neck.

'Reverend Thorvardur Jónsson, please meet Reverend Pétur Bjarnason.'

Undirfell church was a small house of worship with no more than six pews and only standing room at the back. Not large enough for all the farmers of the valley, thought Tóti, as Reverend Pétur absently pushed a pair of wire-rimmed glasses back up the bridge of his nose.

'Ah, here's the key.' The priest bent down to a chest by the altar and began to struggle with the lock. 'Now, you said you were staying at Kornsá?'

'No, just visiting,' Tóti said.

'Better you than me, I suppose. How is the family there?'

'I don't know them well.'

'No, I meant, how are they taking it – having the murderess?'

Tóti thought of Margrét's spiteful words the night Agnes arrived from Stóra-Borg. 'A little upset, perhaps.'

'They'll do their duty. A pleasant enough family. The younger daughter is quite a beauty. Those dimples. Conscientious and smart as a whip.'

'Lauga, isn't it?'

'Quite. Runs circles around her sister.' The priest heaved a large leather-bound book onto the altar. 'Here we are. Now, how old is she, my boy?'

Tóti stiffened with displeasure at being called a boy. 'I'm not sure. More than thirty years, I'd guess. You don't know her?'

The priest sniffed. 'I've only been here one winter myself.'

'That's a shame. I was hoping to learn something of her character from you.'

The priest scoffed. 'Surely Natan Ketilsson's dead body is a fair indication of her character.'

'Perhaps. But I'd like to know a little of her life before the incident at Illugastadir.'

Reverend Pétur Bjarnason looked down his nose at Tóti. 'You're awfully young to be her priest.'

Tóti blushed. 'She requested me.'

'Well, if there's anything worth knowing about her character it will be in the ministerial book.' Reverend Pétur carefully turned the yellow pages of scrawled handwriting. 'Here she is. 1795. Born to an Ingveldur Rafnsdóttir and Magnús Magnússon at the farm of Flaga. Unmarried. Illegitimate child. Born October 27th, and named the next day. What else did you want to know?'

'Her parents were unmarried?'

'That's what's written here. Says "the father lives at Stóridalur. Nothing else noteworthy." Now, what else do you want? Shall we look up her confirmation? It's in here. District Commissioner Blöndal had me write out the details for him a few months ago.' The priest sniffed and pushed his glasses back up his nose. 'Here's the notice. You can read it for yourself.' He stepped out of the way to let Tóti lean closer to the page.

'The 22nd of May, 1809,' read Tóti, aloud. 'Confirmed at fourteen with ...' He paused to count. 'Five others. But she would have been thirteen.'

'What's that?' The priest turned from where he had been looking out the window.

'It says she was fourteen. But in May she would have been thirteen.'

The priest shrugged. 'Thirteen, fourteen. What does it matter?'

Tóti shook his head. 'Nothing. Here, what does this say?'

The priest leaned over the book. Tóti caught a whiff of his breath. It smelt of brandy and fish.

'Let's see here. Three of these children – Grímur, Sveinbjörn and Agnes – have learnt all of the *Kverið*. Then, it goes on. You know, the usual comments.'

'She did well?'

'Says she had "an excellent intellect, and strong knowledge and understanding of Christianity". Shame she didn't end up following its teachings.'

Tóti ignored the last comment. 'An excellent intellect,' he repeated.

'That's what it says. Now, Reverend Thorvardur. Would you like to keep us out here in the cold looking up family trees for a while longer, or shall we return to Haukur's pretty little wife for some breakfast victuals and coffee, if any can be found?'

'REVEREND TÓTI!' MÁRGRÉT OPENED THE door not three seconds after the young man had rapped smartly on its surface. 'Nice of you to visit. We thought you might have gone back south. Come in.' She coughed and pushed the door open wider, and Tóti noticed that she was balancing a heavy sack on her hip.

'Here,' he offered, 'let me take that for you.'

'Don't fuss, don't fuss,' Margrét croaked, beckoning him down the corridor. 'I'm perfectly capable. The workhands have returned from Reykjavík.' She turned around to him with a thin smile.

'I see,' Tóti replied. 'From the merchants.'

Margrét nodded. 'Not too bad. No weevils in the flour, not like last year. Salt, and sugar, too.'

'I'm glad to hear it.'

'Would you like some coffee?'

'You've coffee?' Tóti was surprised.

'We sold all the woollen stuffs and some cured meat. Jón's out sharpening the scythes for harvest. Care for ten drops?' She directed him into the badstofa and pulled the curtain aside for him to step into the parlour. 'Wait here,' she said, hobbling out, the sack still on her hip.

Tóti sat down on the chair and began tracing his fingers along the grain in the wood of the table. He could hear Margrét break into a fit of coughing in the kitchen.

'Reverend Tóti?' a voice murmured from the other side of the curtain. Tóti got up and gingerly tugged the curtain across. Agnes peered around the gap and gave him a nod.

'Agnes. How are you?'

'I'm sorry. I just needed to get ...' She gestured towards a spool of wool that lay on the other chair in the room. Tóti stepped aside and lifted the curtain for her to enter.

'Stay, please,' he said. 'I've come to see you.'

Agnes picked up the spool. 'Margrét has asked me to –'

'Please. Sit, Agnes.' She obeyed, and sat down on the very edge of the chair.

'Here we are!' Margrét walked briskly back into the room bearing a tray of coffee and a plate with butter and rye bread. She suddenly noticed Agnes in the parlour.

'I hope you don't mind sparing Agnes for a moment,' Tóti said, standing up. 'Only I've come to speak with her.' Margrét stared at him. 'Blöndal's orders,' he joked, giving a weak smile.

Margrét pressed her lips together and nodded. 'Do as you like with her, Reverend Tóti. Take her off my hands.' She set the tray down on the table with a clunk and then turned and ripped the curtain across. Agnes and Tóti listened to her footsteps thump down the earthen floor of the corridor. A door slammed.

'Well, then.' Tóti sat down at the table and made a face at Agnes. 'Would you care for some coffee? There's only one cup, but I'm sure ...' Agnes shook her head. 'Please have the bread, then. I've just paid a visit to Undirfell and the housewife there stuffed me with skyr.' He pushed the plate over to Agnes and then poured himself a cup of coffee, shaking a little sugar into it from the stoppered bottle. Out of the corner of his eye he saw Agnes tear off some bread and slip it into her mouth. He smiled.

'It appears the servants did well with their master's trading in Reykjavík.' Tóti felt the hot coffee scald his tongue as he sipped it. His immediate reaction was to spit it out, but he was aware of Agnes's pale eyes watching him and forced the boiling liquid down his throat, choking a little.

'How do you like it here, Agnes?'

Agnes swallowed her bread and stared at him. Her face had filled out slightly, and the bruise on her neck had faded almost entirely.

'You look well.'

'They feed me better than at Stóra-Borg.'

'And you get along with the family?'

She hesitated. 'They tolerate me.'

'What do you think of Jón, the District Officer?'

'He refuses to speak to me.'

'And the daughters?'

Agnes said nothing, and Tóti continued. 'Lauga seems to be quite the favourite of the Reverend at Undirfell. He says she is supremely intelligent for a woman.'

'And her sister?'

Tóti took another sip of coffee, then paused. 'She's a good girl.'

'A good girl,' Agnes repeated.

'Yes. Have some more food.'

Agnes picked up the rest of the bread. She ate quickly, keeping her fingers close to her mouth and sucking them clean of butter when she finished. Tóti couldn't help but notice the greasy pink of her lips.

He forced his eyes to the coffee cup in front of him. 'I suppose you are wondering why I have returned.'

Agnes used her thumbnail to dig a crumb out of her teeth and was silent.

'You called me a child,' Tóti said.

'I offended you.' She seemed disinterested.

'I wasn't offended,' Tóti said, lying. 'But you're wrong, Agnes. Yes, I'm a young man, but I have spent three long years at the school of Bessastadir in the south, I speak Latin and Greek and Danish, and God has chosen me to shepherd you to redemption.'

Agnes looked at him, unblinking. 'No. I chose you, Reverend.'

'Then let me help you!'

The woman was silent for a moment. She continued picking at her teeth and then wiped her hands on her apron. 'If you are going to talk to me, talk in a common way. The Reverend at Stóra-Borg spoke like he was the Bishop himself. He expected me to weep at his feet. He wouldn't listen.'

'What did you want him to listen to?'

Agnes shook her head. 'Every time I said something they would change my words and throw it back to me like an insult, or an accusation.'

Tóti nodded. 'You would like me to speak to you in an ordinary way. And perhaps you would like me to listen to you?'

Agnes regarded him carefully, leaning forward in her chair so that Tóti suddenly noticed the curious colour of her eyes. The blue irises were as lightly coloured as ice, with ashy flecks about the pupil, but were contained by a thin circle of black.

'What do you want to hear?' she asked.

Tóti sat back in his chair. 'I spent this morning at the church of Undirfell. I went there to look for you in the ministerial book. You said you were from this valley.'

'Was I in there?'

'I found the record of your birth and confirmation.'

'So now you know how old I am.' She gave a cold smile.

'Perhaps you might tell me a little more of your history. Of your family.'

Agnes took a deep breath and began to wind the wool from the spool slowly about her fingers. 'I have no family.'

'That's impossible.'

She drew the wool tightly about her knuckles and the tips of her fingers grew darker from the trapped blood. 'You might have seen their names in that book of yours, Reverend, but I may as well have been listed as an orphan.'

'Why is that?'

There was a cough from outside the curtain, and a pair of fish-skin shoes could be seen shuffling under its hem.

'Come in,' Tóti announced. Agnes quickly unwound the wool from her fingers as the curtain was drawn to one side and Steina's freckled face peeped through.

'Sorry to disturb you, Reverend, but Mamma's asking for *her*.' She hastily gestured towards Agnes, who began to rise out of her chair.

'We are talking,' Tóti said.

'Sorry, Reverend. It's the harvest. I mean, it's high July, so it's haymaking today and onwards. Well, at least while the sun holds.'

'Steina, I've come all this –'

Agnes put a hand lightly on his shoulder and gave him a hard look that silenced him. He stared at her hand, her long, pale fingers, the pinking blister on her thumb. Noting his gaze, Agnes removed her hand as swiftly as she had placed it there. 'Come again tomorrow, Reverend. If you care to. We can talk as the dew dries from the hay.'

PERHAPS IT IS A SHAME that I have vowed to keep my past locked up within me. At Hvammur, during the trial, they plucked at my words like birds. Dreadful birds, dressed in red with breasts of silver buttons, and cocked heads and sharp mouths, looking for guilt like berries on a bush. They did not let me say what happened in my own way, but took my memories of Illugastadir, of Natan, and wrought them into something sinister; they wrested my statement of that night and made me seem malevolent. Everything I said was taken from me and altered until the story wasn't my own.

I thought they might believe me. When they beat the drum in that tiny room and Blöndal announced 'Guilty', the only thing I could think of was, if you move, you will crumble. If you breathe, you will collapse. They want to disappear you.

After the trial, the priest from Tjörn told me that I would burn if I did not cast my mind back over the sin of my life and pray for forgiveness. As though prayer could simply pluck sin out. But any woman knows that a thread, once woven, is fixed in place; the only way to smooth a mistake is to let it all unravel.

Natan did not believe in sin. He said that it is the flaw in the character that makes a person. Even nature defies her own rules for the sake of beauty, he said. For the sake of creation. To keep her own blood hot. You understand, Agnes.

He told me this after the two-headed lamb was born at Stapar. One of the servants had run to Illugastadir to tell of it, but by the time Natan and I arrived the lamb was dead. The farmer had killed it on sight because he thought it cursed. Natan asked to take the body so that he might dissect it and learn how it had been formed, but as he unburied the lamb, one of the women walked up to him and spat: 'Let the Devil take care of his own.' I watched as he laughed in her face.

We carried the strange thing to his workshop, and, covered with blood and dirt and sickened to the heart, I left Natan alone to butcher it. Sigga and I did not eat the scraps of meat he cut from it, and although he called us ungrateful, although he reminded us of the number of coins he'd exchanged for the twisted corpse, his appetite was not great either. We left the meat for fox bait. The twinned skull he kept in his workshop, the bone the colour of new cream.

I wonder if the Reverend sees me like that lamb. A curiosity. Cursed. How do men ever see women like me?

But the priest is hardly like a man at all. He is as fragile as a child without the bluster and idiocy of youth. I had remembered him as taller than he is. I hardly know what to think of him.

Perhaps he is merely a gifted liar. God knows I have met enough men to know that once weaned off the breast they begin to lie through their teeth.

I will have to think of what to say to him.

THE FOG HAD DISPERSED INTO the blue of the day, and the wet baubles on the grass had dried by the time the family of Kornsá gathered at the edge of the home field to begin cutting the hay. District Officer Jón stood to one side with the two male farmhands recently returned from Reykjavík – Bjarni and Gudmundur – both with long blond hair and beards, and Kristín, Margrét and Lauga to the other. They were all waiting silently for Steina and Agnes to join the circle. Steina stumbled along the yard, Agnes following her, tying a scarf over her braided hair.

'We're here,' Steina said cheerfully. Agnes nodded at Jón and Margrét. The farmhands glanced at her and then at each other.

Jón bowed his head. 'Our good Lord. We thank you for the good weather you have sent for our harvest. We pray that you see fit to preserve us in this time, to keep us from danger and accident, and to provide us with the hay we need to live. In Jesus' name, amen.'

The farmhands mumbled their amens, and picked up their long-handled scythes. They had been recently hammered and sharpened, and the iron blades shone brightly. Gudmundur, a short muscular man of twenty-eight, tested the edge of his scythe on the hair of his wrist, then, satisfied the edge was sufficiently honed, swiftly turned it the right way round and scraped it against the grass at his foot. He looked up and noticed Agnes watching him.

'Gudmundur and Bjarni,' the District Officer was saying. 'You'll be cutting with Kristín and ...' Jón hesitated, then briefly glanced at Agnes. The farmhands followed his look, and stared.

'You're giving her a scythe?' Bjarni asked casually, a sallow-looking man. He laughed nervously.

Margrét cleared her throat. 'Agnes and Kristín will be cutting with you three and Jón. Steina, Lauga and I will rake and turn.' She glared at Gudmundur, who was smirking at Bjarni, and spat on the ground near his feet.

'Give them scythes,' Jón said quietly, and Gudmundur dropped his own on the ground. He turned and picked up another two scythes and handed one to Kristín, who gave a confused curtsey, and then he reached forward to pass the other to Agnes. She extended her arm to take it, but Gudmundur refused to let go. For a brief moment they both stood there, clasping the handle of the scythe together, before Gudmundur suddenly released his hold. Agnes stumbled backwards and the scythe grazed her ankle. Bjarni stifled a laugh.

'Go fetch your rakes, girls,' Jón said, ignoring the grins of the farmhands and Lauga, who could not help but smile at Agnes's panicked glance at her leg.

'Are you hurt?' Steina whispered to Agnes as she walked past. Agnes shook her head, her jaw clenched. Margrét looked at her daughter and frowned.

I LET MY BODY FALL into a rhythm. I sway back and forth and let gravity bring the scythe down and through the grass, until I rock steadily. Until I feel that I am not moving myself, and that the sun is driving me. Until I am a puppet of the wind, and of the scythe, and of the long, slow strokes that propel my body forward. Until I couldn't stop if I wanted to.

It's a good feeling, not quite being in control. Of being gently swung back and forth, until I forget what it is to be still. Like being with Natan in those first months, when my heartbeat shuddered through me and I could have died, I was so happy to be desired. When the smell of him, of sulphur and crushed herbs, and horse-sweat and the smoke from his forge, made me dizzy with pleasure. With possibility.

I feel drunk with summer and sunlight. I want to seize fistfuls of sky and eat them. As the scythes run sharp fingers through the stalks, the cut grass makes a gasping sound.

Suddenly, I know that the servant, the one called Gudmundur, is watching me. He has arched his head around to leer. Perhaps he thinks I don't notice.

I was fourteen when men began to look at me like that. Hired on at Gudrúnarstadir, I arrived in March with my belongings in a white sack, and my head sore from tightly braided hair. My first proper employ. There was a young man hired on back then as well. A tall man, with bad skin and a way of watching the servant girls – Ingibjörg, Helga and me – that made us avoid him. I'd hear him touch himself at night – a hurried shuffling under the blanket, then a groan, or, sometimes, a whimper.

I let my body swing, I let my arms fall. I feel the muscles of my stomach contract and twist. The scythe rises, falls, rises, falls, catches the sun across its blade and flicks the light back into my eye – a bright wink of God. I watch you, the scythe says, rippling through the green sea, catching the sun, casting it back to me. The servant exhales, swings his scythe, stares in a low way at my bare arms. I flick the grass and the light through the air. I watch you, says the scythe.

AS PROMISED, REVEREND TÓTI RETURNED to Kornsá early the next morning, well before the sun had risen from its resting point above the horizon. His body ached from the first day of harvest at Breidabólstadur, and he relished the smack of cold air on his face and the fine fog of his mare's breath as they rode along the track to the Vatnsdalur valley. All the settlements of the district had begun their haymaking the previous day, and the sight of half-cleared fields, the grass gathered into cocks to stop the dew from damping the hay, contributed to a sense of order and prosperity. The lush north, they called it. Everywhere small birds hopped amongst the stubble, picking at the insects made vulnerable by the harvest, and coils of smoke lifted from the slanted roofs of the valley's crofts and cottages.

At the large farm of Hvammur where Tóti knew Björn Blöndal lived with his family and servants, on the other side of the river and within view from Kornsá, several chimneys could be seen giving off smoke. The flat wooden face of the adjoined turf huts boasted glass windows that glimmered brightly, even in the weak yellow light of morning. Like eyes, thought Tóti, feeling fanciful. He'd heard that much of the Illugastadir trial had been held in the guest room of the farm, which looked out onto the winding body of the river and its fringe of golden marsh grass.

I wonder what went through her mind, Tóti mused, peering at the farm from across the river. Sitting there in that room when they told her she had to die. Did she look out of the window and see the ice floe on the river? Possibly the world was too dark to see anything. Possibly they covered the windows with a curtain to block out the light.

District Officer Jón was outside his home with another man – a farmhand of some sort, thought Tóti – sharpening the scythes. Jón raised his whetstone in greeting and put his cap back on before walking over.

'Reverend Thorvardur. God bless you.'

'And you,' Tóti said cheerfully.

'You're here to see her.'

Tóti nodded. 'How do you find Agnes?'

Jón shrugged. 'Life goes on.'

'She's a good worker?'

'She's a good worker, but ...' He stopped.

Tóti smiled gently. 'It's only temporary, Jón.' He gave the man a reassuring clap on the back and turned to go into the house.

'Jón Thórdarson has offered to kill them,' Jón said suddenly.

Tóti turned around. 'Excuse me?'

'Jón Thórdarson. He came riding up to Hvammur a few weeks back, reckoned he'd play executioner to Fridrik, Sigga and Agnes. Said he'd swing the axe for a pound of tobacco.' He shook his head. 'A pound of tobacco.'

'What did Blöndal say?'

Jón grimaced. 'What do you think he said? Thórdarson's a nobody. He has someone else in mind, although there's some who are against it.'

Tóti glanced at the farmhand, who was slouching against the smithy wall, listening. 'Who would that be?' Tóti asked.

Jón shook his head, disgusted. It was the farmhand who spoke. 'Gudmundur Ketilsson,' he said, loudly. 'Natan's brother.'

'We can sit inside if you prefer,' Tóti said, nearly stumbling over the rocks next to the rushing stream by the Kornsá farm.

'I like to watch the water,' Agnes replied.

'Very well.' Tóti wiped the wet spray off a large rock and gestured for Agnes to sit down. He sat next to her.

The Kornsá stream offered a good view across the river. It was beautiful, but Tóti could think only of Jón's earlier words about the executioner. He stole a glance at Agnes's pale neck against the grey of the rock and imagined it slit.

'How was the harvest yesterday?' he asked, trying to clear his mind.

'It was very warm.'

'Good,' Tóti replied.

Agnes reached into her shawl and pulled out a bundle of wool and several thin knitting needles. 'You wanted to ask me about my family?'

Tóti cleared his throat and watched her fingers move as she began to knit. 'Yes. You were born at Flaga.'

Agnes inclined her head towards the farm in question, a slouched croft to the left of Kornsá's border. It was close enough that the voices of its servants, calling to one another outside, could be heard on the wind. 'The very one.'

'Your mother was unmarried.'

'You learnt that from the ministerial book?' Agnes gave a tight smile. 'The priests always make sure they write the important things down.'

'And your father, Magnús?'

'Magnús was unmarried too, if that's what you mean.'

Tóti hesitated. 'Who did you live with as a child, then?'

Agnes gazed about the valley. 'I've lived in most of these farms.'

'Your family moved about?'

'I don't have any family. My mother left me when I was six.'

'How did she die?' Tóti asked gently. He was taken aback when Agnes laughed.

'Does my life seem such a story of tragedy? No, she left me for others to deal with, but I suppose she's still alive. I wouldn't know. Someone told me she'd gone into the blue. Just upped and left one day. That was some years ago now.'

'What do you mean?'

'I don't know anything about my mother. I wouldn't recognise her if I saw her.'

'Because you were only six winters old when she left you?'

Agnes stopped knitting and looked Tóti squarely in the face. 'You have to understand, Reverend, that the only things I know about my mother are what other people have told me. Mainly what she did, which, you'll understand, they didn't approve of.'

'Could you tell me what you were told?'

Agnes shook her head. 'To know what a person has done, and to know who a person is, are very different things.'

Tóti persisted. 'But, Agnes, actions speak louder than words.'

'Actions lie,' Agnes retorted quickly. 'Sometimes people never stood a chance in the beginning, or they might have made a mistake. When people start saying things like she must be a bad mother because of that mistake …'

When Tóti said nothing in response she went on.

'It's not fair. People claim to know you through the things you've done, and not by sitting down and listening to you speak for yourself. No matter how much you try to live a godly life, if you make a mistake in this valley, it's never forgotten. No matter if you tried to do what was best. No matter if your innermost self whispers, "I am not as you say!" – how other people think of you determines who you are.'

Agnes stopped to take a breath. She had begun to raise her voice, and Tóti wondered what had provoked this sudden gush of words.

'That's what happened to my mother, Reverend,' Agnes continued. 'Who was she really? Probably not as people say she was, but she made mistakes and others made up their minds about her. People around here don't let you forget your misdeeds. They think them the only things worth writing down.'

Tóti thought for a moment. 'What was your mother's mistake?'

'I've been told she made many, Reverend. But at least one of those mistakes was me. She was unlucky.'

'What do you mean?'

'She did what any number of women do harmlessly in secret,' Agnes said bitterly. 'But she was one of the unfortunate few whose secrets are made visible to everyone.'

Tóti could feel the hot creep of a blush appear on his face. He looked down at his hands and tried to clear his throat.

Agnes looked at him. 'I've offended you again,' she said.

Tóti shook his head. 'I'm glad that you tell me of your past.'

'My past has offended your sensibilities.'

Tóti shifted his seat on the rock. 'What about your father?' he tried.

Agnes laughed. 'Which of them?' She stopped knitting to study him. 'What did your book say about my father?'

'That his name was Magnús Magnússon and that he was living at Stóridalur at the time of your birth.'

Agnes continued to knit, but Tóti noticed that she was clenching her jaw. 'If you spoke to certain people about these parts you might get a different story.'

'How is that?'

Agnes looked out across the river to the farms on the opposite side of the valley, silently counting the stitches on her needle with her finger. 'I suppose it doesn't matter if I'm honest with you or not,' she said coldly. 'I could say anything to you.'

'Indeed, I hope you will confide in me,' Tóti said, misunderstanding. He leaned closer in anticipation of what she would say.

'Your book at Undirfell ought to have said Jón Bjarnason, the farmer at Brekkukot. I've been told that he is my real father, and Magnús Magnússon is a hapless servant who didn't know better.'

Tóti was perplexed. 'Why would your mother name you Magnús's daughter if that were not the truth?'

Agnes turned to him, half-smiling. 'Have you no idea of how the world works, Reverend?' she asked. 'Jón of Brekkukot is a married man with enough legitimate children of his own. Oh, and plenty like me, you can be sure. But it seems a lesser crime to create a child with an unmarried man than one already bound in flesh and soul to another woman. So I suppose my mother picked a different sod to have the honour of fathering me.'

Tóti considered this for a moment. 'And you believe this because others told you so?'

'If I believed everything everyone had ever told me about my family I'd be a sight more miserable than I am now, Reverend. But it doesn't take an education in Copenhagen or down south to work out which bairns belong to which pabbis in these parts. Hard to keep a secret to yourself here.'

'Have you ever asked him?'

'Jón Bjarnason? And what would be the good of that?'

'To get the truth out of him, I suppose,' Tóti suggested. He was feeling disappointed with the conversation.

'No such thing as truth,' Agnes said, standing up.

Tóti stood up also and began rubbing the seat of his pants. 'There is truth in God,' he said, earnestly, recognising an opportunity to do his spiritual duty. 'John, chapter eight, verse thirty-two: "And ye . . . "'

'Shall know the truth, and the truth shall make you free. Yes, I know. I know,' Agnes said. She bundled her knitting things together and began to walk back down to the farm. 'Not in my case, Reverend Thorvardur,' she called to him. 'I've told the truth and you can see for yourself how it has served me.'

IT WON'T BE ANY GOOD for the Reverend to read ministerial books, or any book for that matter – what will he learn of me there? Only the things other men think important about me.

When the Reverend saw my name and birth in the church book, did he see only the writing and understand only the date? Or did he see the fog of that day, and hear the ravens cawing at the smell of blood? Did he imagine it as I have imagined it? My mother, weeping, holding me against the clammy warmth of her skin. Avoiding the looks of the Flaga women she worked for, knowing already that she'd have to leave and try to find work elsewhere. Knowing no farmer would hire a servant woman with a newborn.

If he wants to learn of my family he'll have a hard time of it. Two fathers and a mother who seem as blurry to me as strangers departing through a snowstorm. I have few clear memories of her.

One is the day she left me. Another is when I was young, watching her in the lamplight of a winter night. It's a silent memory, and one, like the others, I can't quite trust. Memories shift like loose snow in a wind, or are a chorale of ghosts all talking over one another. There is only ever a sense that what is real to me is not real to others, and to share a memory with someone is to risk sullying my belief in what has truly happened. Is the Reverend the person of my memory, or is he another altogether? Did I do that, or was it another? Magnús or Jón? It's the glaze of ice over the water, too fragile to trust.

Did my mother look down at her baby daughter and think: 'One day I will leave you'? Did she look at my scrunched face, hoping I would die, or did she silently urge me to stick to life like a burr? Perhaps she looked out to the valley, into the mist and stillness, and wondered what she could give me. A lie for a father. A head of dark hair. A hayrack to sleep in. A kiss. A stone, so that I might learn to understand the birds and never be lonely.

CHAPTER FIVE

**Poet-Rósa's poem to Agnes Magnúsdóttir,
June 1828**

*Undrast þarftu ei, baugabrú
þó beiskrar kennir þínu:
Hefir burtu hrífsað þú
helft af lífi mínu.*

Don't be surprised by the sorrow in my eyes
nor at the bitter pangs of pain that I feel:
For you have stolen with your scheming
he who gave my life meaning,
and thrown your life to the Devil to deal.

Agnes Magnúsdóttir's reply to Rósa,
June 1828

Er mín klára ósk til þín,
angurs tárum bundin:
Ýfðu ei sárin sollin mín,
solar báru hrundin.

Sorg ei minnar sálar herð!
Seka Drottin náðar,
af því Jésus eitt fyrir verð
okkur keypti báðar.

This is my only wish to you,
bound in anger and grief:
Do not scratch my bleeding wounds,
I'm full of disbelief.

My soul is filled with sorrow!
I seek grace from the Lord.
Remember, Jesus bought us both
and for the same accord.

'HOW IS IT TO HAVE her here, in this same room as you? I should find it difficult to sleep,' said Ingibjörg Pétursdóttir.

Margrét looked over to where the Kornsá mowers were cutting the grass closest to the river. 'Oh, I don't think she'd dare set a foot wrong.'

The two women were resting on the pile of stacked wood outside the Kornsá croft. Ingibjörg, a small, plain-looking woman from a nearby farm, had paid Margrét a visit, having heard that her friend's cough was preventing her from participating in the haymaking. While Ingibjörg had none of Margrét's acidity, or her forthrightness, the two women were fast friends, and often visited one other when the river that divided their farms was low enough to be forded.

'Róslín seems to think you'll all be strangled in your sleep.'

Margrét gave a brusque laugh. 'I can't help but think that's exactly what Róslín wants.'

'What do you mean?'

'It would give that well-oiled mouth something else to wag about.'

'Margrét ...' Ingibjörg warned.

'Oh, Inga. We both know having all those children has turned her head.'

'The littlest has croup.'

Margrét raised her eyebrows. 'Won't be long before they all have it, then. We'll hear them wailing at all hours of the night.'

'She's getting big, too.'

Margrét hesitated. 'Do you plan on helping with the birth? She's had that many you'd think she could do it herself.'

Ingibjörg sighed. 'I don't know. I have a bad feeling.'

Margrét studied her friend's grave expression. 'Did you have a dream?' she asked.

Ingibjörg opened her mouth as if to say something, and then shook herself, changing her mind. 'I'm sure it's nothing. Anyway, let's not be gloomy. Tell me about the murderess!'

Margrét laughed in spite of herself. 'There! You're as bad as Róslín.'

Ingibjörg smiled. 'How is she really, though? In character. Are you frightened of her?'

Margrét thought for a moment. 'She's nothing like how I imagined a murderess,' she said at last. 'She sleeps, she works, she eats. All in silence, though. Her lips might as well be sewn over for all she says to me. That young man, the Reverend Thorvardur, he's begun to visit her again over these last few weeks, and I know she talks to him, but he doesn't tell me what passes between them. Perhaps nothing.' Margrét glanced over to the field. 'I often wonder what she's thinking.'

Ingibjörg followed Margrét's gaze, and the two women looked together at the bent figure of Agnes amidst the hay, hacking at the grass with her scythe. The blade flashed brightly as she swung it.

'Who knows?' Ingibjörg murmured. 'I shudder to think of what goes on inside that dark head of hers.'

'The Reverend says her mother was Ingveldur Rafnsdóttir.'

Ingibjörg paused. 'Ingveldur Rafnsdóttir. I knew an Ingveldur once. A loose woman.'

'No doves come from ravens' eggs,' Margrét agreed. 'It's strange to think of Agnes being a daughter. I can't imagine my girls even thinking about something so wretched and sinful as murder.'

Ingibjörg nodded. 'And how are your girls?'

Margrét stood and dusted the dirt from her skirt. 'Oh, you know.' She started coughing again and Ingibjörg began to rub her back.

'Easy, now.'

'I'm fine,' Margrét croaked. 'You know, Steina thinks she knows her.'

Ingibjörg gave her friend a curious look.

'She thinks we met her on the way to Gudrúnarstadir, way back when.'

'Is Steina making up stories again?'

Margrét winced. 'Only the good Lord knows. I don't remember. Actually, I'm a bit worried about her. She *smiles* at Agnes.'

Ingibjörg laughed. 'Oh, Margrét! When did a smile ever get anyone into trouble?'

'Many a time, I should think!' Margrét snapped. 'Just look at Róslín. Anyway, it's other things, too. I've caught Steina asking questions of Agnes, and I've noticed she rushes to fetch her for errands and the like. Look – she's following her now, even while she's raking.' She pointed to Steina turning the hay near Agnes. 'I don't know, I just think of that poor girl Sigga, and I worry the same thing will happen to her.'

'Sigga? The other maid at Illugastadir?'

'What if Agnes has the same effect on Steina? Makes her go to the bad. Fills her head with wickedness.'

'You've just said that Agnes hardly says a word.'

'Yes, with me. But I can't help but feel it's another story with ... Oh, don't you mind.'

'And Lauga?' Ingibjörg asked thoughtfully.

Margrét tittered. 'Oh, Lauga hates having her here. We all do, but Lauga refuses to sleep in the next bed. Watches her like a hawk. Upbraids Steina for looking Agnes's way.'

Ingibjörg considered the shorter daughter, dutifully raking the hay into neat lines. Next to Lauga's windrows, Steina's rows looked as crooked as a child's handwriting.

'What does Jón say?'

Margrét snorted. 'What does Jón ever say? If I raise it, he starts on about his duty to Blöndal. I notice he's watchful, though. He asked me to keep the girls separate.'

'Hard to do on a farm.'

'Exactly. I can keep them as separate as Kristín keeps the milk and cream.'

'Oh dear.'

'Kristín's useless,' Margrét said, matter-of-factly.

'Just as well you've an extra pair of women's hands about the place, then,' Ingibjörg said practically. The two women fell into companionable silence.

I DREAMT OF THE EXECUTION block last night. I dreamt I was alone and crawling through the snow towards the dark stump. My hands and knees were numb from the ice, but I had no choice.

When I came upon the block, its surface was vast and smooth. I could smell the wood. It had none of the saltiness of driftwood, but was like bleeding sap, like blood. Sweeter, heavier.

In my dream I dragged myself up and held my head above it. It began to snow, and I thought to myself: 'This is the silence before the drop.' And then I wondered at the stump being there, the tree it might have been, when trees do not grow here. There is too much silence, I thought in my dream. Too many stones.

So I addressed the wood out loud. I said: 'I will water you as though you still lived.' And at this last word I woke.

The dream frightened me. Since the hay harvest I have slipped into something of my old life here, and I have forgotten to be angry. The dream reminded me of what will happen, of how fast the days are passing me by, and now, lying awake in a room full of strangers, gazing at the patterns of sticks and peat in the ceiling, I feel my heart turn over and over and over until I feel twisted in my gut.

I need to relieve myself. Trembling, I get out of bed and look about the floor for the pot. It's under one of the workhands' beds and nearly full, but there's no time to empty it. My stockings are loose and slide to my ankles without difficulty, and I squat and direct a hot stream of piss into the pail, feeling the splash of it against my thigh. Sweat breaks out on my forehead.

I hope no one will wake up and see me, and I'm so anxious to finish and tuck the pot out of sight that I yank up my stockings before I'm quite done. A warm trickle runs down the inside of my leg as I push the pail away.

Why am I trembling like this? My knees are as weak as a marrow jelly and it is a relief to lie down. My heart gibbers. Natan always believed dreams meant something. Strange, for a man who could so easily laugh at the word of God, to trust instead in the simmering darkness of his own sleeping hours. He built his church from wives' tales and the secret language of weather; saw the blinking eye of God in the habits of the sea, the swooping merlin, the gnashing teeth of his ewes. When he caught me knitting on the doorstep he accused me of lengthening the winter. 'Do not think nature is not watchful of us,' he warned me. 'She is as awake as you and I.' He smiled at me. Passed the smooth breadth of his palm over my forehead. 'And as secretive.'

I thought I could be a servant here. Over a month has passed at Korná and already I have forgotten what will become of me. The days of work have soothed me, have given my body cause for rest, so that I've slept deeply, below the surface of dreams stricken with portent. Until now.

It's true that I'm not one of them. All but the Reverend and Steina refuse to talk to me except in the briefest of ways. But how is that any different from before, when I was a low sort of workmaid, emptying the chamber pot as I will be asked to do in a few hours? Compared to Stóra-Borg this family has been kind.

But soon winter will come like a freak wave upon the shore – suddenly, with speed, obliterating the sun and warmth and leaving the land frozen to the core. Everything will be over so quickly. And the Reverend: how young he is, and how I still don't know what to say to him. I thought he could help me as he helped me over the river. But talking to him only reminds me of how everything in my life has worked against me, and how unloved I have been.

I expected him to understand me from the start. I want him to understand me, but I'm a fool to think we speak the same tongue. I may as well be talking to him with a stone in my mouth, trying to find a language that we both understand.

The Reverend will not arrive from Breidabólstadur for another few hours – it's still too early to rise. I fold my hands on top of the blanket and tell the strings of my heart to slacken, and think of what I will tell him.

Tóti wishes to hear about my family, but what I have told him has not been what he wants to hear. He must not be used to the gnarled family trees that grow in this valley, where the branches rope about one another, studded with thorns.

I haven't told him about Jóas, or Helga. He might be interested to hear I have siblings. I can imagine his questions: Where are they now? Why don't they visit you, Agnes?

Why, Reverend, I would say, the blood tie is not strong: they have different fathers apiece, and Helga is dead and buried. Jóas? Well, he's not a man who can be put to anything, even a visit to a doomed sister.

Oh, Jóas. I cannot reconcile the dull-eyed man to the sweet blur of boy I was once allowed to love.

We were lugged along in the arms of a common mother. Which farms? Countless badstofas belonging to other men and their red-eyed wives, kind or desperate enough to hire a woman with three mouths, two of which screamed at night in hunger because they did not know it was useless.

Beinakelda first. Until I was three, they tell me. Just Mamma and I. I remember nothing. It's all shadow.

Then Litla-Giljá. I don't remember the farm, but I remember the man. Illugi the Black, they called him, my brother's father. Sitting on the floor, rubbing my hands in the dirt, and then the man beside me, his eyes rolled back into his head and his body writhing on the ground like a landed fish, and all the women screaming to see the foam spurt from his mouth. Then, afterwards, the groans that came from his bed, and his sour-skinned wife pushing my face into her bony neck and saying, 'Pray for him. Pray for him.' Where was my mother? No doubt squatting over a chamber pot, searching for blood that would not come.

I remember the screaming. Illugi, healthy again, his great bear face roaring at his wife, who would not stop crying, and amidst them my Mamma in long skirts, throwing up on the ground.

Illugi died of that shaking sickness while he was fishing. They say he was drinking, then fell into a fit, upset the boat and drowned, tangled in his nets. Others say it was a fit punishment for a man who fished from elfish pools, but those were folks that had been at the wrong end of his drinking and fighting.

What would the Reverend make of all this?

Jóas Illugason, born at Brekkukot, the third farm. Five years old, I was allowed to hold the rag soaked in milk to his tiny salmon gums. The married folk there wanted to keep him and raise him with their own two children, and Mamma explained that I would be fostered to them too, that it would be for the best. For the next year we seven were a family, and I helped feed life into the small boy with hair as light as mine was dark. He smelt of snowmelt and fresh cream.

They must have changed their minds. One morning I was shaken awake by Mamma, who looked at me with swollen eyes. I asked why she was crying, but she said nothing. She climbed into bed with Jóas and me, and I fell asleep against the hot curve of her body, until the caw of the house ravens woke me and I saw my belongings bundled in a sack on the floor.

That morning we started on foot and returned to the valley through an ill-tempered day full of spasms of snow. I thought I would faint from hunger. We stopped in the yard of Kornsá and before I could finish the whey given to me by the woman there, Mamma whispered in my ear, pressed a stone into my mitten and left with Jóas on her back.

I tried to follow her. I screamed. I didn't want to be left behind. But as I ran I tripped and fell. When I got back on my feet my mother and brother had vanished, and all I could see were two ravens, their black feathers poisonous against the snow.

For a long time I thought those two birds were my Mamma and my brother. But they never answered my questions, even when I put the stone under my tongue. Years later I learnt that Mamma gave me a new half-sister, Helga, to the farmer at Kringla, and that Jóas was now a pauper, a child of the parish. But by that time I had convinced myself I no longer loved them. I thought I had found a better family, my foster-family: Inga and Björn, the tenants of Kornsá.

'HOW DID YOU SLEEP, AGNES?' Steina had found the woman out by the patch of lovage, where she was tossing the contents of the chamber pot in the ash pit.

'You'll get wet out here,' Agnes said, without looking at her. She had been using a rock to flick out the stickier contents of the pot, and was now wiping it against the grass. 'It's going to rain.'

'I don't mind. I thought I'd keep you company.' Steina lifted her shawl over her head. 'There, dry as a mouse.'

Agnes glanced at her and gave a small smile.

'Look, Agnes,' Steina said. She pointed out towards the mouth of the valley where a mass of low grey clouds was surging in from the north.

Agnes put her hand out to the sky. 'It's getting worse. It will be bad for the hay.'

'I know. Pabbi's cross. He snapped at Lauga for burning his breakfast and he never does that to her.'

Agnes turned to face Steina. 'Does he know you're out here with me?'

'I think so.'

'I think you should go back inside,' Agnes said.

'And do what? Have Lauga blame me for building the fire up too high? No thank you. I'm happier outside anyway.'

'Even in the rain?'

'Even in the rain.' Steina yawned and looked out at the field, its haycocks bundled into stacks to prevent the damp. 'All that work for nothing.'

'What do you mean for nothing? Come the next fine day we'll get on and then it will be finished.' Agnes glanced up at the croft. 'I think you ought to return to your mother,' she said.

'Oh, she doesn't mind.'

'She does. She doesn't like you being alone with me,' Agnes said carefully.

HANNAH KENT

'You've been here for weeks and weeks now.'

'Even so.' Agnes began to walk slowly down to the river and Steina turned to keep pace with her.

'Do you think the Reverend will come today?'

Agnes didn't respond.

'What does he talk to you about?'

'That's my business,' she snapped.

'What?'

'I said that it's my business. It has nothing to do with you or your family.'

Steina was taken aback, and paused in her step as Agnes marched on down the hill, holding the chamber pot stiffly at her side.

'Have I put you out of temper?' she asked.

Agnes stopped and turned to Steina. 'How could a young woman like you put me out of temper?'

Steina bristled. 'Because my family is holding you prisoner, and my father doesn't want anyone to speak with you.'

'He said that?' Agnes asked.

'He thinks we're better off leaving you to your chores.'

'He's right.'

Steina caught up to Agnes and gently took her arm. 'Lauga's scared of you, you know. She's been listening to Róslín and her lies. But I don't believe a word that gossip says. I remember you from before. I remember how kind you were, giving us your food like that.' Steina leaned in closer. 'I don't think you killed them,' she whispered. Agnes's body went rigid under her grip. 'Maybe I can help you,' Steina suggested quickly.

'How?' Agnes asked. 'Would you help me escape?'

Steina let go of her arm. 'I thought maybe a petition,' she murmured.

'A petition.'

Steina tried again. 'An appeal, then. You know, like the one they've got up for Sigga.'

Agnes's eyes flashed. 'What?'

'The appeal. Blöndal has got one up for the other one,' Steina stammered.

'The other who?'

'Sigga … you know, the other Illugastadir maid. Fridrik's sweetheart.'

Agnes's face had grown pale. She slowly placed the chamber pot on the wet grass, then stepped towards Steina. 'Blöndal has made an appeal for Sigrídur Gudmundsdóttir?' she asked gravely.

Steina nodded, a little afraid. She glanced down to the rock that Agnes still held in her hand. 'I heard Pabbi tell Mamma,' she explained. 'The District Officers were discussing it at Hvammur, with Blöndal. On the same day you arrived here.'

Agnes shook her head.

'I thought you knew,' Steina whispered.

Agnes's eyes slipped from Steina's and she swayed on her feet. 'Blöndal?' she muttered under her breath. Steina noticed that Agnes gripped the rock so hard her knuckles were white.

'I'm sorry I told you.'

Agnes staggered backwards, and then continued walking unsteadily towards the river.

'Maybe we can convince him to appeal to the King for you too!' Steina called after her. 'Tell them what really happened at Illugastadir!'

Agnes dropped to the ground by the riverbank, her skirts bulging around her. Steina, thinking she had fainted, ran towards her, but as she drew closer she saw that Agnes was staring blankly at the river. She was shivering. At that moment the dark clouds opened up, and the two women were engulfed in a sudden, freezing downpour.

'Agnes!' Steina called, wrapping her shawl more tightly about her head. 'Get up! We have to get out of the weather.' The sound of the rain drowned out her words.

Agnes didn't respond. She watched the drops hit the fast-flowing river, breaking the surface so that the mountains' reflection became wildly distorted. She still held the rock in her hand.

'Agnes!' Steina cried. 'I'm sorry! I thought you knew!' Her shawl was soaked, and she could feel her dress grow heavy with water. She hesitated by the riverbank, and then turned and began to run up the hill to the croft. The ground had become soggy, and she slipped in the mud. Halfway up the field she turned and saw that Agnes was still where she had left her. She called one more time, and then continued tripping up the muddy path to the farm.

'Goodness, Steina! Where on God's earth have you been?' Margrét rushed down the corridor to scold her eldest daughter, who slammed the croft door behind her. 'You look half drowned!'

'It's Agnes,' Steina gasped, dropping her sodden shawl to the ground.

'Did she hurt you? Oh my sweet Lord, protect us! I knew it.' Margrét wrapped her arms around her daughter, who was shaking with cold, and drew her towards her.

'No, Mamma!' Steina yelled, pushing her mother away. 'She needs help, she's by the river!'

'What happened?' Lauga had stepped out of the kitchen. 'Oh, Steina! You've muddied my shawl.'

'I don't care!' Steina shouted. She turned back to her mother. 'I told her about the appeal for Sigrídur Gudmundsdóttir and she went all strange and white and now she won't get up!'

Margrét turned to Lauga. 'What is she talking about?'

'Agnes!' Steina screeched. She wiped the rain off her face with her sleeve and began to run down the corridor. 'I need to tell Pabbi.'

Jón was in the badstofa, mending his shoes. 'Steina?' he asked, looking up from his work.

'Pabbi! Please, you have to go down to Agnes. I told her about the appeal Blöndal has for the other Illugastadir maid and she's gone mad.'

Jón immediately pushed the shoes from his lap and stood up. 'Where?' he asked in a low voice.

'By the river,' Steina said, fighting back tears. Jón pulled his boots out from under his bed and tied them on roughly.

'I'm sorry, Pabbi, I thought she knew! I wanted to help her.'

Jón stood up and gripped his daughter by the shoulders. His cheeks were pink with anger. 'I told you to stay away from her.' He glared at his daughter, then shoved her out of the way and left the room, calling for Gudmundur, who had been lying on his bed. The farmhand got up reluctantly. Steina sat down and began to cry.

A few moments later Lauga stepped into the badstofa with Kristín at her side.

'What did Pabbi say?' she asked quietly, then, seeing where Steina had sat, 'Oh! Get up, you're making my bed wet.'

'Leave me!' Steina screamed, causing Kristín to yelp and flee the room. 'Leave me alone!'

Lauga smirked and shook her head. 'You're in a temper, Steina. What were you trying to do out there? Make friends?'

'Go to hell, Lauga!'

Lauga's mouth dropped open. She glowered at her sister, as though about to cry, and then narrowed her eyes. 'You'd better watch yourself,' she hissed. 'If you continue this way you'll be as wicked as her.' She turned to walk away, but stopped. 'I'll pray for you,' she sniffed, and then left the room. Steina put her head in her hands and cried.

I SIT AND WAIT UPON my bed as Margrét, Jón and their daughters talk about me behind the grey curtain in the parlour. Although Margrét speaks in hissed whispers I catch the words as they slither through the gap between this room and the next. My hands shake and I can feel my heart throbbing. It's as though I have just run for my life. It's the same feeling as in court, when I felt outside of everything.

I could have been a pauper; I could have been their servant, until those words! Sigga! Illugastadir! They anchor me to a memory that snatches the breath out of me. They are the magic words, the curse that turns me into a monster, and now I am Agnes of Illugastadir, Agnes of the fire, Agnes of the dead bodies with the blood, not burnt, still clinging to the clothes I made for him. They will free Sigga but they will not free me because I am Agnes – bloody, knowing Agnes. And I am so scared, I thought it could work, I thought I could pretend, but I see it will not, I will never, I cannot escape this, I cannot escape.

THE LETTER WAS SMALL, AND written in bunched cursive on a tiny piece of paper, the lines overlapping in the author's attempt to conserve space. Tóti took it into the badstofa to read, where he had been eating his midday meal.

'Blöndal again?' his father asked, without looking up from his meat.

'No,' Tóti said, casting his eyes quickly over the message: *Come quickly, it is Agnes Magnúsdóttir. I do not like to tell Blöndal. Your brother in Christ, Jón Jónsson.* 'It's from Kornsá.'

'Don't they know it's raining? And a Sunday,' the elder priest muttered.

Tóti sat down at the table and observed his father. Crumbs of dried porridge were visible in his beard. 'I ought to go,' he said.

Reverend Jón breathed out heavily. 'It's a Sunday,' he repeated.

'Yes, the Lord's day,' Tóti said. 'For the Lord's work,' he added.

Reverend Jón pulled a piece of gristle from his mouth, examined it, and then began chewing again.

'Father?'

'I hope Blöndal knows how you slave to his will.'

'The Lord's will,' Tóti said gently. 'Thank you, Father. I'll return tonight. Or tomorrow, if the weather is bad.'

Tóti was drenched to the bone by the time he reached the pass leading to the Vatnsdalur valley. He saw the messenger who had delivered him the note riding ahead and spurred his mare onwards to catch up with him.

'Hello there,' Tóti shouted, peering through the thick glaze of rain.

The man turned in his saddle and Tóti recognised him as one of the Kornsá servants. He was wearing fishing skins to keep himself dry. 'So you've come!' he shouted back. 'That's two of us riding in this miserable weather.'

'Bad for the hay,' Tóti said, by way of conversation.

'You don't need to tell me twice,' the man snorted. 'I'm Gudmundur.' He raised his hand. 'And you're the Reverend that's been trying to save our murderess.'

'Well, I –'

'A grisly business,' the man interrupted. 'She gives me the shivers.'

'How do you mean?'

The farmhand laughed. 'She's wild.'

Tóti spurred his cob to keep pace. 'What has happened? That note –'

'Oh, she had a fit. Fought off Jón and me, scratching and clawing, screaming all the while, soaked like, lying in the mud like a madwoman. See this?' He pointed to a bruise on his temple. 'That's her handiwork. I tried to lift her and she tries to stone my brains out. Howling things about Blöndal. Same act they say she put on at Stóra-Borg, what got her shifted.'

'Are you sure?' Agnes seemed so self-contained to Tóti.

'I thought she'd kill me then and there.'

'What upset her?'

The man sniffed and wiped his nose with a gloved finger. 'Damned if I know. One of the girls said something. Mentioned the other servant girl they caught. Sigga.'

Tóti turned and looked at the puddles in the path before them. He felt ill.

'Not bad looking,' Gudmundur said, turning to Tóti with a glint in his eye.

'Pardon?'

'Agnes. Nice hair, and that,' the servant said. 'But too tall for me. Needs to be a head or so shorter, you know.' He winked at Tóti and laughed.

Tóti pulled his riding hat more firmly over his head. The rain lightened for a minute, and then resumed falling as they turned into the valley, sheets of grey sweeping over the curved earth before them, and water falling over the rocky precipices of the mountains.

Agnes was in bed when Tóti entered the badstofa. Kristín, the workmaid, brought a stool for him, and the youngest daughter began to fuss over his wet clothes. As Lauga stooped to untie his boots, Tóti peered across to the unlit corner where Agnes sat. She was awfully still.

Lauga pulled away his remaining boot with a sudden jerk that nearly knocked him off the stool. 'I'll leave you, then,' she muttered, and walked out of the room, holding the boots at arm's length in front of her.

Tóti made his way to Agnes in his damp socks. She slouched against the wooden post by her bed, and as he grew closer he saw that she had been handcuffed.

'Agnes?'

Agnes opened her eyes and looked up at him blankly.

Tóti sat down on the edge of her bed. Her skin appeared ashen in the low light and her lip was split and bloody.

'What happened?' he asked gently. 'Why have they put you in irons again?'

Agnes looked down at her wrists, as if surprised to see them there. She swallowed hard. 'Sigga is to have an appeal. Blöndal is appealing to the King to reduce the sentence he gave her.' Her voice cracked. 'They pity her.'

Tóti sat back and nodded. 'I knew.'

Agnes was aghast. 'You knew?'

'They pity you too,' he added, wanting to comfort her.

'You're wrong,' she hissed. 'They don't *pity* me; they hate me. All of them. Blöndal especially. What about Fridrik? Are they appealing his sentence, too?'

'I don't believe so.'

Agnes's eyes glistened in the shadow. Tóti thought she might be crying, but when she leaned closer he saw that her eyes were dry.

'I'll tell you something, Reverend Tóti. All my life people have thought I was too clever. Too clever by half, they'd say. And you know what, Reverend? That's *exactly* why they don't pity me. Because they think I'm too smart, too knowing to get caught up in this by accident. But Sigga is dumb and pretty and young, and that is why they don't want to see her die.' She leant back against the post, her eyes narrowed.

'I'm sure that's not true,' Tóti said, trying to soothe her.

'If I was young and simple-minded, do you think everyone would be pointing the finger at me? No. They'd blame it on Fridrik, saying he overpowered us. Forced us to kill Natan because he wanted his money. That Fridrik desired a little of what Natan had is no great secret. But they see I've got a head on my shoulders, and believe a thinking woman cannot be trusted. Believe there's no room for innocence. And like it or not, Reverend, *that* is the truth of it.'

'I thought you didn't believe in truth,' dared Tóti.

Agnes lifted her head off the post and stared at him, her eyes paler than ever. She grimaced. 'I have a question for you, speaking of truth. You say God speaks the truth?'

'Always.'

'And God said, "Thou shalt not kill"?'

'Yes,' Tóti said, carefully.

'Then Blöndal and the rest are going against God. They're hypocrites. They say they're carrying out God's law, but they're only doing the will of men!'

'Agnes –'

'I try to love God, Reverend. I do. But I cannot love these men. I ... I hate them.' She said the last three words slowly, through clenched teeth, gripping the chain that connected the irons about her wrists.

There was a knock from the entrance to the badstofa and Margrét entered with her daughters and Kristín.

'Excuse me, Reverend. Don't mind us. We'll work and talk amongst ourselves.'

Tóti nodded grimly. 'How goes the harvest?'

Margrét huffed. 'All this wet August weather ...' She returned to her knitting.

Tóti looked at Agnes, who gave him a bleak smile.

'They're even more scared of me now,' she whispered.

Tóti thought. He turned to the group of women. 'Margrét? Is it not possible for these irons to be removed?'

Margrét glanced at Agnes's wrists, and put down her needles. She left the room and returned with a key shortly after. She unlocked the irons.

'I'll just set them here, Reverend,' she said stiffly, lifting the cuffs onto the shelf above the bed. 'In case you need them.'

Tóti waited until Margrét had returned to the other end of the room and then looked at Agnes. 'You mustn't act like that again,' he said in a low voice.

'I was not myself,' she said.

'You say they hate you? Don't give them further reason.'

She nodded. 'I'm glad you're here.' There was a moment before she spoke again. 'I had a dream last night.'

'A good one, I hope.'

She shook her head.

'What did you dream of?'

'Dying.'

Tóti swallowed. 'Are you afraid? Would you like me to pray for you?'

'Do what you like, Reverend.'

'Then, let's pray.' He glanced at the group of women before taking up Agnes's cold, clammy hand.

'Lord God, we pray to you this evening with sad hearts. Give us strength to bear the burdens we must carry, and the courage to face our fates.' Tóti paused and looked at Agnes. He was aware that the other women were listening.

'Lord,' he continued, 'I thank you for the family of Kornsá, who have opened their home and hearts to Agnes and I.' He heard Margrét clear her throat. 'I pray for them. I pray they have compassion and forgiveness. Be with us always, O Lord, in the name of the Father and of the Son, and of the Holy Spirit.'

Tóti squeezed Agnes's hand. She looked at him, her expression inscrutable.

'Do you think it's my *fate* to be here?'

Tóti thought a moment. 'We author our own fates.'

'So it has nothing to do with God then?'

'It's beyond our knowing,' Tóti said. He gently placed her hand back on the blanket. The feel of her cold skin unsettled him.

'I am quite alone,' Agnes said, almost matter-of-factly.

'God is with you. I am here. Your parents are alive.'

Agnes shook her head. 'They may as well be dead.'

Tóti cast a quick look at the women knitting. Lauga had snatched Steina's half-finished sock from her lap and was ripping back the wool to amend an error.

'Have you no loved one I might summon?' he whispered to Agnes. 'Someone from the old days?'

'I have a half-brother, but only sweet Jesus knows what badstofa he's darkening at the moment. A half-sister, too. Helga. She's dead. A niece. Dead. Everyone's dead.'

'What about friends? Did any friends visit you at Stóra-Borg?'

Agnes smiled bitterly. 'The only visitor at Stóra-Borg was Rósa Gudmundsdóttir of Vatnsendi. I don't think she'd describe herself as my friend.'

'Poet-Rósa.'

'The one and only.'

'They say she speaks in lines of verse.'

Agnes took a deep breath. 'She came to me in Stóra-Borg with a poem.'

'A gift?'

Agnes sat up and leant closer. 'No, Reverend,' she said plainly. 'An accusation.'

'What did she accuse you of?'

'Of making her life meaningless.' Agnes sniffed. 'Amongst other things. It wasn't her finest poem.'

'She must have been upset.'

'Rósa blamed me when Natan died.'

'She loved Natan.'

Agnes stopped and glared at Tóti. 'She was a married woman,' she exclaimed, a tremor of anger in her voice. 'He wasn't hers to love!'

Tóti noticed the other women had stopped knitting. They were watching Agnes, her last sentence having carried loudly across the room. He rose to fetch the spare stool beside Kristín.

'I'm afraid we're disturbing you,' he said to them.

'Are you sure you don't want to use the irons,' Lauga asked nervously.

'I think we are better off without them.' He returned to Agnes's side. 'Perhaps we should speak of something else.' He was anxious that she should remain calm in front of the Kornsá family.

'Did they hear?' she whispered.

'Let's talk about your past,' Tóti suggested. 'Tell me more about your half-siblings.'

'I barely knew them. I was five when my brother was born, and nine when I heard about Helga. She died when I was twenty-one. I only saw her a few times.'

'And you're not close to your brother?'

'We were separated when he was only one winter old.'

'When your mother left you?'

'Yes.'

'Do you remember her from before then?'

'She gave me a stone.'

Tóti shot her a questioning look.

'To put under my tongue,' Agnes explained. 'It's a superstition.' She frowned. 'Blöndal's clerks took it.'

Tóti was aware of Kristín rising to light a few candles – the bad weather had made the room quite gloomy, and the day was rapidly dying. In front of him, he could only see the pale lengths of Agnes's bare arms above the blankets. Her face was shadowed.

'Do you think they will let me knit?' whispered Agnes, inclining her head towards the women. 'I would like to do something while I talk to you. I can't stand being still.'

'Margrét?' Tóti called. 'Have you any work for Agnes?'

Margrét paused, and then reached over and plucked Steina's knitting from her hands. 'Here,' she said. 'It's full of holes. It wants unravelling.' She ignored the look of embarrassment on Steina's face.

'I feel sorry for her,' Agnes said, slowly pulling out lines of crimped wool.

'Steina?'

'She said she wants to get up a petition for me.'

Tóti was hesitant. He watched Agnes nimbly wind the loose wool into a ball, and said nothing.

'Do you think it possible, Reverend Tóti? To organise an appeal to the King?'

'I don't know, Agnes.'

'Would you ask Blöndal? He would listen to you, and Steina might speak to District Officer Jón.'

Tóti cleared his throat thinking of Blöndal's patronising tones. 'I promise to do what I can. Now, why don't you talk to me.'

'About my childhood again?'

'If you will.'

'Well,' Agnes said, wriggling up higher on the bed so that she could knit more freely. 'What shall I tell you?'

'Tell me what you remember.'

'You won't find it of interest.'

'Why do you think that?'

'You're a priest,' Agnes said firmly.

'I'd like to hear of your life,' Tóti gently replied.

Agnes turned around to see if the women were listening. 'I have told you that I have lived in most of the farms of this valley.'

'Yes,' Tóti agreed, nodding.

'At first as a foster-child, then as a pauper.'

'That's a horrible pity.'

Agnes set her mouth in a hard line. 'It's common enough.'

'To whom were you fostered?'

'To a family that lived where we sit now. My foster-parents were called Inga and Björn, and they rented the Kornsá cottage back then. Until Inga died.'

'And you were left to the parish?'

'Yes,' Agnes nodded. 'It's the way of things. Most good people are soon enough underground.'

'I'm sorry to hear that.'

'There's no need to be sorry, Reverend, unless of course you killed her.' Agnes glanced at him, and Tóti noticed a brief smile flicker across her face. 'I was eight when Inga died. Her body never took to the manufacture of children. Five babes died without drawing breath before my foster-brother was born. The seventh carried her to heaven.'

Agnes sniffed, and began to carefully thread back through the loose stitches. Tóti listened to the light clicking of the bone needles and cast a surreptitious look at Agnes's hands, moving quickly about the wool. Her fingers were long and thin, and he was astounded at the speed with which they worked. He fought off an irrational desire to touch them.

'Eight winters old,' he repeated. 'And do you remember her death very well?'

Agnes stopped knitting and looked around at the women again. They had fallen silent and were listening. 'Do I remember?' she repeated, a little louder. 'I wish I could forget it.' She unhooked her index finger from the thread of wool and brought it to her forehead. 'In here,' she said, 'I can turn to that day as though it were a page in a book. It's written so deeply upon my mind I can almost taste the ink.'

Agnes gazed straight at Tóti, her finger still against her forehead. He was unnerved by the glitter in her eyes, her bloody lip, and wondered if the news of Sigga's appeal had, in fact, made her a little mad.

'What happened?' he asked.

CHAPTER SIX

IN THIS YEAR 1828, ON the 29th of March, we, the clerks stationed at Stapar at Vatnsnes – transcribing District Commissioner Blöndal's oral description – write up the value of the possessions of prisoners Agnes Magnúsdóttir and Sigrídur Gudmundsdóttir, both workmaids at Illugastadir. The following assets, ascertained as belonging to the aforementioned individuals, have the following value:

AGNES MAGNÚSDÓTTIR	RBL.	RBSK
1. A women's shawl of blue plain-woven wool.	—	48
2. An old blue skirt with a blue bodice of plain-woven wool, with a red collar and eight silver buttons.	1	64
3. A blue shirt of plain-woven wool with a green collar, bordered with six tin decorations.	—	20
4. An old blue hat and the remains of another black one, burnt.	—	10
5. Two long black skirts.	—	20
6. An old shift of faded blue.	—	80
7. A striped apron of Icelandic weaving.	—	10

8. One measure of white, plain-woven wool.	—	*16*
9. An evangelical book: no. 33–38.	—	*16*
10. Four measures of green material with a 'sarte' border, damaged.	—	*10*
11. One small glass and one cup.	—	*16*
12. One lod of indigo and approximately two pages of paper.	—	*20*
13. Two knitting needles and one pair of old scissors.	—	*6*
14. Seven copper and two silver buttons, approximately twenty other buttons and some hook and eye of copper.	—	*24*
15. A white sack with useless odds and ends in it.	—	*20*
16. Two pairs of socks, one blue, the other white, and a yellowed inner sole.	—	*12*
17. A needle case, thimble and one pair of white gloves.	—	*8*
18. One small box, one small wooden dinner bowl and several little boxes.	—	*20*

SIGRÍDUR GUDMUNDSDÓTTIR	RBL	RBSK
1. Two yellowed shawls, damaged.	—	*80*
2. A blue skirt of plain-woven wool, of poor quality.	—	*40*
3. A blue skirt with a damaged bodice.	—	*24*
4. An old thin, striped cloth.	—	*24*
5. An old blue hat with a green silk top, damaged.	—	*8*
6. A little nightdress with a twin of green silk.	—	*10*

7. One sheep, currently located at Illugastadir,
   and hay.   2   —

We stamp and certify that the above assets comprise the total
belongings of the aforementioned prisoners.

WITNESSED BY:

J. Sigurdsson, G. Gudmundsson

THIS IS WHAT I TELL the Reverend.

Death happened, and in the usual way that it happens, and yet, not like anything else at all.

It started with the northern lights. That winter was so cold that I woke every morning with a fine dust of ice on my blanket, from my breath freezing and falling as I slept. I was living at Kornsá then and had been for two or three years. Kjartan, my foster-brother, was three. I was only five years older.

One night the two of us were working in the badstofa with Inga. Back then I called her Mamma, because she was as much to me. She saw I had an aptitude for learning, and taught me as best she could. Her husband, Björn, I tried to call Pabbi also, but he didn't like it. He didn't like me reading or writing either, and was not averse to whipping the learning out of me if he caught me at it. Vulgar for a girl, he said. Inga was sly; she waited until he was asleep and then woke me, and then we would read the psalms together. She taught me the sagas. During *kvöldvaka* she'd tell them by heart, and when Björn fell asleep she'd make me recite the stories back to her. Björn never knew that his wife betrayed his orders for my sake, and I doubt he ever understood why his wife loved the sagas as she did. He humoured her saga stories with the air of a man humouring the unfathomable whim of a child. Who knows how they had come to foster me. Perhaps they were kin of Mamma's. More likely they needed an extra pair of hands.

This night Björn had gone outside to feed the cattle, and when he returned from tending them, he was in a good mood.

'Look at you all, squinting by the lamp, when outside the sky is on fire.' He was laughing. 'Come see the lights,' he said.

So I put my spinning aside and took Kjartan's hand and led him outside. Mamma-Inga was in the family way, so she didn't follow us, but waved us out and continued her embroidering. She was making me a new coverlet for my bed, but she never got to finish it, and to this day I don't know what happened to it. I think perhaps Björn burnt it. He burnt a lot of her things, later.

But on this night, Kjartan and I stepped out into the chill air, our feet crunching the snow upon the ground, and we soon understood why Björn had summoned us. The whole sky was overrun with colour as I'd never seen it before. Great curtains of light moved as if blown by a wind, billowing above us. Björn was right – it looked as though the night sky was slowly burning. There were smears of violet that swelled against the darkness of the night and the stars that were littered across it. The lights ebbed, like waves, then were suddenly interrupted by new streaks of violent green that plunged through the sky as if falling from a great height.

'Look, Agnes,' my foster-father said, and he turned me by the shoulders so that I might see how the brilliance of the northern lights threw the mountain ridge into sharp relief. Despite the lateness of the hour I could see the familiar, crooked horizon.

'See if you can't touch them,' Björn said then, and I dropped my shawl on the snow so that I could raise my arms to the sky.

'You know what this means,' Björn said. 'This means there will be a storm. The northern lights always herald bad weather.'

At noon the following day the wind began to whip around the croft, stirring up the snow that had fallen overnight, and dashing it against the dried skins we'd stretched across the windows to keep out the cold. It was a sinister sound – the wind hurling ice at our home.

Inga wasn't feeling well that morning and had remained in bed, so I prepared our meal. I was in the kitchen, setting the kettle upon the hearth, when Björn came in from the storehouse.

'Where is Inga?' he asked me.

'In the badstofa,' I told him. I watched Björn take off his cap and shake the ice into the hearth. The water spat on the hot stones.

'The fire's too smoky,' Björn said, frowning, then left me to my chore.

When I'd boiled some moss into porridge, I took it into the badstofa. It was quite dark in the room and, once I'd served Björn his meal, I ran to the storehouse to fetch some more oil for the lamp. The storehouse was near the door to the croft and as I approached it I could hear the wind howling, louder and louder, and I knew that a storm was fast approaching.

I'm not sure why I opened the door to look outside. I suppose I was curious. But some strange compulsion took me and I unlocked the latch to peek out at the weather.

It was an evil sight. Dark clouds bore down upon the mountain range and under their smoky-blackness, a grey swarm of snow swirled as far as you could see. The wind was fierce, and a great, icy gust of it suddenly blew against the door so hard that it knocked me off my feet. The candle on the corridor wall went out in an instant, and from within the croft Björn shouted what the Devil I thought I was doing, letting the blizzard into his home.

I heaved against the door to shut it, but the wind was too strong. My hands stiffened with the cold rush of air. It was as though the wind was some form of ghoul demanding to enter. Then, all of a sudden, the wind dropped, and the door slammed shut. As though the spirit had finally entered and closed the door behind it.

I returned to the badstofa with oil and filled the lamps. Björn was angry at me for letting the cold air in, with Inga in such a delicate state.

The blizzard hurled itself upon our croft that afternoon, and raged for three days. On the second, Inga began to have her baby.

It was too soon.

Late that night, amidst the sound emitted by the wind and snow and ice, Inga began to have terrible pains. I believe she was afraid that this baby, too, would arrive before its time.

When Björn realised that the baby was coming, he sent Jón, their workman, to his brother's farm for his sister-in-law and their servant woman. My foster-father bade Jón tell the women what was happening, so that they might at least give their advice, if they couldn't return with him.

Jón protested that the blizzard was too forceful, and that he couldn't be expected to perform such a task, but Björn was a demanding man. So Jón dressed himself in thick garments and went outside, but he returned soon after, covered in ice and snow, and told my foster-father that he couldn't see two steps in front of him, and that he wouldn't be made to walk farther than the barn when the weather promised only death. Yet, Björn made him try again, and when Jón returned, half-frozen with cold, telling him he could scarcely stand in the wind, and had not made it more than six feet, my foster-father took him by the collar of his jacket and pushed him outside. I think then, when he opened the door, he saw just how dangerous the weather was, for when Jón returned inside a few minutes later, shaking with cold and anger, Björn said nothing, but let Jón undress and get into bed to revive himself.

I'm sure Björn was scared then, too.

Inga had remained in her bed and was now groaning with pain, as white as milk and overcome with a shuddering that left her covered in sweat. Björn carried her from the badstofa to the apartment in the loft – there used to be a loft in this cottage – so she might be afforded some privacy, but when he lifted her, her nightgown and the linen of her bed were soaked with water, and I cried out in surprise. I thought she had wet herself.

'Don't move her, Björn!' I called, but he ignored me and lifted my foster-mother up the stairs, asking me to boil water and bring him some wadmal. I did as he asked, taking the new woven stuff I myself had made. I asked if I might see Mamma, but he told me to go and look after Kjartan, so I returned to the badstofa.

Kjartan must have realised that something ill was afoot, for he was whimpering when I returned. As I sat back on our bed, he clambered across and in my own fear and need for comfort, I pulled him onto my lap, and we sat waiting for Björn to tell us what to do, listening to the storm.

We waited for a long time. Kjartan fell asleep against my neck, so I laid him down in our bed and tried to card some wool, separating the tangles into thin wisps between my paddles, and picking out the little burrs. But my fingers were shaking. All the while I could hear Inga in the loft, crying out. I reminded myself that the crying was normal, and that soon I'd have a new foster-brother or sister to love.

After some hours Björn stepped down from the loft. He entered the badstofa, and I saw that he was holding a small parcel. It was the baby. Björn's face was ashen, and he held out the wee thing and made me take it into my arms. Then he left the room and returned to the loft to see to his wife.

I was excited to hold the baby. It was very small and light, and didn't move much, but it was mewling, and it rumpled its eyes and mouth, and its face was very red and awful looking. I unwrapped it and saw that it was a girl.

Kjartan had awoken by this time. It had become chill inside; the wind was getting in through some crack, and a draught suddenly blew out most of the tallow candles we had lit and put on the table.

Only one candle remained and, in its flickering light, our shadows danced out across the wall, and Kjartan started to cry. He closed his eyes and buried his head into my shoulder.

Because it had become so cold, I tried to tuck the baby in its blanket in my shawl, and then used my pillow to hold it close to my chest. But we didn't have down pillows, only seaweed, and they did not give off much warmth. But the baby had stopped crying, and I thought that maybe it wasn't too cold, and would be all right. I used my fingers to wipe a little of the thick fluid off the baby's head, and then Kjartan and I gave it a kiss.

We sat on the bed together for a long time. Hours passed. Days could have slipped by for all I knew. It remained gloomy and cold, and the storm raged endlessly. I had told Kjartan to go and pull off the blankets from his parents' bed, and we'd draped them around us, huddling together for warmth. Inga's moans came unceasingly from the loft. It was a sound someone might make if they were asleep and having a terrible nightmare: a low, awful language without words, just sounds. And the wind was blowing so hard all the while, that sometimes I couldn't tell if it was Inga crying out, or the wind, making the candle gutter in its candlestick.

I had put an arm around Kjartan, and used the other to bring the baby close to my chest, and I told them both to try to listen to my heartbeat so that they would forget the snowstorm.

I think we fell asleep. I say I think, because I don't remember waking, but I do remember suddenly seeing Björn standing in the badstofa. The last candle had snuffed out, and in the dimness of the room I could just see him standing very still, his head hanging down.

'Inga is dead,' he said. The words fell heavily in the room. 'My wife is dead.'

'Björn,' I said, 'the baby is here. Take the baby,' and I moved it out from under the blankets and offered it to him.

He wouldn't take it. 'The baby is dead too,' he said.

I looked down at what I held in my hands, and I saw that the baby had become still, and that it wasn't warm any more. The blankets were only warm because I had pressed them to my own body. I started to cry. Kjartan saw the baby's little blue face, with the dried blood still clinging to its cheek, and he saw that it didn't move, and he began to whimper. Björn watched us. I became upset, and I put the baby on the bed, and threw myself down on the floor with my face in my hands. I was wailing, and I cried out, 'I want to die too!'

'Maybe you will,' Björn replied. That was all he said to comfort me. 'Maybe you will die too.'

I lay on the floor for a long time, screaming. I remember the wooden boards – the very same ones here by our feet now – were wet and smeared with my tears and the mess from my nose. I was angry at Björn, sitting on his bed in the darkness, with his head in his hands and not crying, not screaming, not telling me to get up and stop my tantrum. He was as frozen as the ground outside. And so I screamed and rolled on the floor until my eyes were swollen and my hands stung from slapping the wood. I howled like the blizzard outside, until I remembered Inga in the loft, and then I got up and ran out of the room, tripping on my skirts and falling on my knees. I climbed the stairs to the loft and ran inside.

In our loft there was a little window in the roof, above the beams. We normally stuffed the hole with cloth to keep out the rain and snow, but it had fallen out, and let in a little blue light, although the blizzard still stormed outside. It was extremely cold in the room. My breath floated out from me in a soft cloud. A great deal of snow had blown in, and it had melted into a large puddle on the floor, and I saw that puddle first, how it threw back the light admitted by the window, so that it was bright on the floor, like a looking glass. And then I saw Inga.

In the blue light of the room her blood looked purple. She lay on a narrow mattress of hay, over the woven wadmal I had given Björn earlier, except that the cloth was no longer white, but stained with blood. Her eyes were open and they reflected the light in moist glints that made me think she was still alive. I bent down to her and cried out 'Mamma!' and put my hand on her shoulder, but when I touched her I knew that she was dead. Her body had stiffened, and she was cold to touch.

Her blood was everywhere. Her nightgown seemed black with it, all over her legs and the bed, but her bare shoulders were smeared in it too, and I noticed her hands, which lay beside her, palms upturned, were covered in it, just like when she'd make sausage, letting the blood clot and straining it through linen. Her face was white, too white in the dim room, and her hair had slipped from her cap and was stiff over her forehead.

I won't forget the smell. That room was filled with the smell of her blood, and the sharp, clean scent of the snow on the floorboards. It made me feel sick to breathe it in.

Inga's nightgown was bunched about her waist, and so I pulled it, stiff with dried blood as it was, back down over her legs so that her body was not so naked. Then I kissed her slack mouth. Finally, I pulled off her cap and pushed my face into her hair. It was the only part of her that still smelt of my foster-mother and not the blood. I lay my body down next to hers and covered my face in her long hair, and breathed her in, for how many minutes I don't know, until Jón pushed aside the curtain to the loft and picked me up, and carried me back downstairs to bed.

And when I next woke the blizzard had stopped.

This is what I tell the Reverend. I try to tell the story in the best way I know how. I let the words come as I knit, and I snatch little looks at the Reverend's face, to see if he is moved.

I can feel the others listening. I can feel Steina and Margrét and Kristín and Lauga stretching their ears towards us in the shadowy corner, eating up this story like fresh butter and bread. Margrét and Lauga maybe thinking that it served me right, perhaps feeling sorry for me. Steina thinking I am like her – miserable, ignored. At fault.

But because I know the others are listening, I can't ask the Reverend what I want to ask. I can't say, Reverend, do you think that I'm here because when I was a child I said I wanted to die? Because, when I said it, I meant it. I pronounced it like a prayer. *I hope I die.* Did I author my own fate, then?

I want to ask the Reverend if he thinks I killed the baby. Did I hold her too tightly? But there is no right way to ask this question, and I don't want to put more thoughts into these women's heads. There are some things they should not hear.

It seems everyone I love is taken from me and buried in the ground, while I remain alone.

Good thing, then, that there is no one left to love. No one left to bury.

'WHAT HAPPENED THEN?' TÓTI ASKED. He realised that he had hardly breathed during Agnes's story.

'It's strange,' Agnes said, using her little finger to wind the wool about the needle head. 'Most of the time when I think of when I was younger, everything is unclear. As though I were looking at things through smoked glass. But Inga's death, and everything that came after it … I almost feel that it was yesterday.'

Across the room, a chair scraped. Margrét gave a muffled cough.

'I remember that after Inga died Jón was sent to fetch Björn's relatives,' Agnes continued. 'I can remember lying in my bed, watching my foster-father sit on the stool Inga had used for her spindle work. He was too big for its seat. Kjartan was in bed with me, and he was sleeping all hot and heavy on my shoulder. The wind had dropped and it was suddenly very quiet.

'We eventually heard the clink of harness from the yard outside. Then Björn slowly rose to his feet and stepped towards my bed. He scooped my brother up with one arm so I could sit, and he told me to take the dead baby, wrap its face in a blanket and put it in the storeroom.

'The baby seemed lighter dead than alive. I held it out from me and walked down the corridor in my stockings.

'It was very chill in the storeroom. I could see the fog of my breath before me, and my forehead ached from cold. I covered the baby's face with a corner of the cloth it was wrapped in and laid it upon a sack of dried cod heads. When I stepped back into the corridor, a blast of freezing air hit the side of my face, and I turned to see the door open, the faces of Björn's brother, sister-in-law and their servant appearing from the murk outside. Their cheeks were wet and shiny from sleet.

'I remember Uncle Ragnar and Jón carefully carrying Inga down from the loft while Björn was outside, attending to the sheep. It was my job to make sure they didn't bump her head against the rungs of the ladder. They brought her into the badstofa and set her on the stripped bed. Aunt Rósa was in the kitchen heating some water, and when I asked her what she was doing, she said she was going to clean my poor foster-mamma's body. She wouldn't let me watch. She let Kjartan play by her feet, and she ordered me to go upstairs to the loft and help her servant, Gudbjörg.

'When I climbed the ladder I saw Gudbjörg scrubbing blood off the floorboards. The smell made me feel sick and I started to cry. Gudbjörg took me into her arms. "She's gone to God now, Agnes. She's safe."

'I sat on the floor with Gudbjörg's shawl about me and watched the fat of her arms wobble as she knelt and scrubbed the boards. Gudbjörg wrung out the pinked water from the rag over and over again. She kept shaking her head, and sometimes she stopped to wipe her eyes.

'I told Gudbjörg what Björn had said when I'd screamed that I wanted to die; that he had told me maybe I'd be next. Gudbjörg shushed me and said that Björn wasn't himself, and didn't mean it.

'I told her how Björn had given me the baby to look after, and that I had held it tightly and that it had died in my arms, and I didn't even notice.

'Gudbjörg rocked me like I was a baby myself. She said that the child wasn't meant for this earth, and that it wasn't my fault it didn't live. She told me that I was brave and that God would watch over me.'

'Do you know where Gudbjörg is today?' Tóti interrupted.

Agnes looked up from her knitting. 'Dead,' she said, unwaveringly. She pulled at the ball of wool to loose more thread.

'When Ragnar, Kjartan and Björn returned from the barn, Rósa called Gudbjörg and me down from the loft and we all sat in the badstofa around the bed where Inga lay. She looked clean, but still. Eerie still, as when the wind drops and the grass doesn't move, and you feel left behind.

'Uncle Ragnar produced a flask of brandy and silently passed it around. That was the first time I tasted liquor, and I didn't much care for it, but Jón had left on my foster-father's horse to fetch the Reverend, and there was nothing to do but wait and drink. The hours creaked past, and I felt sick from the brandy and the bones in my legs grew stiff from sitting.

'Jón didn't return with the priest until late that night. I let them in. The Reverend forgot to knock the snow off his boots.

'Gudbjörg, Aunt Rósa and I served the men food and they ate it off their laps, Inga on the bed in front of them. Aunt Rósa had lit a candle and placed it near Inga's head, and I kept checking to see that it hadn't fallen over; I was worried her hair would catch alight.

'Once the men had eaten their food, the women took Kjartan and me to the kitchen while the Reverend spoke with the men. I tried to listen to what they were saying, but Aunt Rósa took my arm and pulled Kjartan onto her lap, and she started telling a story to distract us. She only stopped when Uncle Ragnar and Jón walked past the open doorway, carrying Inga's body between them. They'd covered her face with a piece of cloth. I wanted to know where they were taking her and got up to follow, but Aunt Rósa tightened her grip around my arm and yanked me towards her. Gudbjörg quickly told me that the Reverend had said there was no chance of a burial until spring: the ground in the churchyard was frozen solid, and they were going to keep my poor foster-mother in the storehouse until the ground thawed and someone could dig a grave. We went to the doorway to watch them put Inga away.

'The Reverend was following Björn down the corridor. I heard him say: "At least it leaves you plenty of time to make the coffins." Then he suggested that they put her in the barn.

'"Too warm," my foster-father replied.

'Uncle Ragnar and Jón laid Inga next to the dead baby in the storehouse. At first they put her down on a bag of salt, then Uncle Ragnar pointed out that the salt might be needed sooner than we could bury Inga, so they swapped the salt for dried fish, and I could hear the thin, dried bones of the cod snap in the sack, under the weight of her body.'

'When did they bury her?' Tóti asked. He suddenly felt claustrophobic sitting in the badstofa, surrounded by the muffled clicks of knitting needles and the rasp and squeak of wool.

'Oh, not for a long time,' Agnes said. 'Inga and the baby were in the storehouse until the end of winter. Every time I had to fetch more lamp oil, or help Jón roll a barrel out to the pantry, I saw their bodies lying in the corner, bundled upon the sacks of dried fish.

'Kjartan didn't understand what had happened to his mamma. I suppose he forgot about the baby, but he always cried for Inga, sitting on the floor in the badstofa and howling like a dog. His pabbi ignored him, but when Uncle Ragnar visited, Kjartan received a cuff about the ears. He soon stopped crying.

'Uncle Ragnar always seemed to be at Kornsá – talking with Björn in the badstofa, or bringing him brandy. Björn had grown more silent since the blizzard. When I served him his dinner he no longer thanked me, just picked up his spoon and began to eat.

'And then one day I was told Björn didn't want me any more. It must have been early spring, I was in a bad temper, and had refused to eat any dinner. My foster-father hadn't said anything, not even a sharp word to tell me off for wasting food. He was spending all his time with the animals, which had begun to die from the cold, and I was frustrated that he loved them and Kjartan more than me.

'Winter had turned and on this day there was a little light, so when I left the table I decided to go outside. No one stopped me. I stormed down the corridor and picked up the shovel that stood within the doorway, and began to dig out a path from the croft, relishing the feel of snow flecks upon my hot cheeks. Once I had cleared a way out, I threw the shovel aside and began to dig in the snow with my hands, taking huge armfuls and throwing them as far as I could. I worked until I had dug quite a large hole. When I paused to catch my breath, I looked up and noticed a black smudge in the distance: it was Uncle Ragnar on another of his visits. He greeted me and asked what I was doing covered in snow. I explained that I had begun to dig a grave for Mamma. Uncle Ragnar frowned and told me I shouldn't call her

Mamma, and wasn't I ashamed of myself, thinking to bury her near the doorstep where everyone would tread on her, and not in the holy ground of a churchyard.

'"Wouldn't it be better to keep her warm in the storeroom until she can sleep in peace in consecrated ground?" he asked me.

'I shook my head. "The storeroom is as cold as a witch's tit," I told him.

'Uncle Ragnar said: "Watch your mouth, Agnes. Ugly words show an ugly mind."

'That night he told me that Björn was going to give up the lease for Kornsá and go to Reykjavík to work at the fishing stations. The winter had killed my foster-mother and her baby, as well as over half of Björn's flock, and without a wife, and with nothing to pay the wages of another farmhand, Björn couldn't afford to keep me. Kjartan went to live with his aunt and uncle, and when the weather warmed I was thrown on the mercy of the parish.'

'And that is how you came to be an urchin,' Tóti said.

Agnes nodded, pausing in her knitting to stretch her fingers. She rested the sock on her lap and looked up at him through the darkness. 'That is how I came to be a pauper. Left to the mercy of others, whether they had any or no.'

I HAVE WOKEN EARLY, AND the badstofa is still heavy with shadows. I thought someone was bent low to my ear and whispering, Agnes, Agnes. The whisper severed me from my dreams, but there is no one here, and a cold dread suddenly drips through my heart.

I could have sworn someone was calling me.

I lie still and try to listen to the others breathe, so as to discern whether another is awake. Reverend Tóti is in the bed closest to me, having decided to sleep at Kornsá because of the lateness of the hour. But I know it wasn't him who woke me. A priest would not wake a prisoner by whispering in her ear like a lover.

Minutes pass. Why is there so much darkness in the room? I can't see my hands, although I hold them above my eyes. The gloom encroaches upon my mind, and my heart flutters like a bird held fast in a fist. Even when I force my eyes shut, the darkness is still there, and now, too, there are awful tremors of flickering light. Are my eyes open or shut? Perhaps it was a ghost who woke me – how can I explain these lights appearing in the murk before me? They're like flames peeling off a wall, and Natan's face is before me, his mouth wide in screaming, and his teeth bloody and shining, and his burning body dropping flakes of charred skin on my blankets. Everything smells of whale fat and Fridrik's knife is deep in Natan's belly, and a scream jerks from my chest as if it had been pulled from my gut by a rope.

The lights vanish. Was I dreaming? It seems as if no time has passed.

'Reverend Tóti?' I whisper.

He turns over in his sleep.

'Reverend? May I light a lamp?'

The Reverend does not wake easily – he lolls like a man addicted to drink. I shove him harder than I'd like. He's embarrassed, I think, to wake and see me in my underthings.

'What is it?'

'I had another dream.'

'What?'

'May I light a lamp?'

'The light of Jesus is enough for any true Christian.' His voice is sluggish with sleep.

'Please, Reverend.'

He has not heard me. He begins to snore.

I return to my bed then, uncomforted. I can smell smoke.

My Mamma is dead. Inga is dead.

She is lying in rags in the storehouse while the snow and ice clamp their jaws about the earth and forbid the digging of holes, the digging of graves.

So cold she has to wait to be buried.

So lonely I make friends with the ravens that prey on lambs.

I close my eyes and I am creeping down the corridor with the flickering light of my lamp and I am shaking, terrified. I hear the wind howl into the night outside and I think I can hear my foster-mother claw at the storehouse door where she is bundled and waiting to be nailed in the box and buried come spring. I stop walking and I listen hard, and under the wind I think I hear scratching, and then my name – Agnes, Agnes, calling to me. It is Inga calling me to let her out. I'm not dead, I have returned, I am come alive, I need to be let out of the storehouse, not kept like butchered meat, drying in the stale air. Kept with salt and whey and flour crawling with Danish weevils.

I stand still and I shake, scared. Then, Mamma, Mamma! I take a step to the storehouse and push open the door – there is no lock. I push open the door and I hold out the thin light of my lamp, and I see the lump of her body on the floor, her head resting upon a sack of dried fish-heads, and I weep because it is worse to know that she is really dead. Oh, my foster-mother is dead and my own mother is gone. And I sit on the floor, my legs buckled with the pure, ripe grief of an orphan, and the wind cries for me because my tongue cannot. It screams and screams and I sit on the packed earth floor, hard with cold, and smell the fish-heads, sickening, lacing the bland scent of winter with its stench of salt and dried bone.

CHAPTER SEVEN

THE MURDERER FRIDRIK SIGURDSSON was born at
Katadalur here in the parish of Tjörn on the 6th of May 1810,
and was confirmed by my predecessor here in this parish,
Reverend Sæmundur Oddson, in 1823. He was described
then as being in possession of 'a good intellect', and a good
knowledge and understanding of the catechism. However, his
behaviour did not answer to this knowledge and education. He
girdled himself in blatant disobedience of his parents, so that
they complained to me in the autumn of 1825. It was through
speaking with them that I learnt of his greatly unbending
character.

How his upbringing has been obtained I cannot sufficiently
attest to with certainty – I have not, except for four years, been
a priest in this parish. However, such is my opinion that he has
been raised with too much freedom.

The testimony of the Reverend Jóhann Tómasson.

5th of September 1829

Rev. T. Jónsson
Breidabólstadur, Vesturhóp

To the (Assistant) Reverend Thorvardur Jónsson,

I write to enquire about your progress with the criminal, Agnes Magnúsdóttir. I recently met with Reverend Jóhann Tómasson of the parish of Tjörn, who deemed it so good as to supply me with a report concerning the spiritual advancement and improved behaviour of the criminal Fridrik Sigurdsson, whom he is supervising. I consider it necessary to meet with you also. Once you, similarly, give me an account of what has and continues to transpire between you and the criminal, I might comprehend to what degree religious instruction is collectively bettering the condemned.

Please present yourself to Hvammur next week to give an account of your transactions with the criminal, and what counsel you have hitherto supplied.

DISTRICT COMMISSIONER
Björn Blöndal

'THANK YOU FOR COMING, ASSISTANT Reverend Thorvardur,' Björn Blöndal said, stepping out of the farm door of Hvammur. He had dressed in his official regalia, his red jacket open to reveal a clean, cream shirt. Tóti, who had only met the District Commissioner on a few occasions, mostly when he was a boy travelling with his father, paused in awe at the spectacle of his uniform, and his rather imposing figure.

'Greetings, District Commissioner Blöndal.'

Tóti dismounted and gave the reins of his horse to a servant man. Hvammur, he noticed, was crawling with people, all going about their chores in the wide yard before the house. A man was gutting trout, caught that morning from the river, on a rock to his left, and two women were spreading clothes out to dry in what slender sun the day afforded. He noticed another servant, a young woman wearing the national headdress of cap and tassel, leading a huddle of four or five children outdoors.

'Hello,' they called brightly, nodding their heads in Tóti's direction.

'You have a pleasant home,' Tóti said, smiling, walking up to meet Blöndal.

'Indeed. Welcome, Reverend. I trust your journey was not too arduous. Please, come inside, and mind your step.'

An older servant woman led Tóti through the labyrinth of corridors to a small guest room. Blöndal followed closely behind and watched in the doorway as she sat Tóti down on an upholstered chair and deftly removed his riding hat and coat.

'Have you been here before?' Blöndal asked, as he waited. Tóti realised that he had been gaping at his surroundings.

'Only as a boy,' Tóti blushed. 'This is a very fine quarter. I see you have several etchings.'

Blöndal sniffed and removed his plumed hat, brushing the feather absently. 'Yes,' he said, matter-of-factly. 'We're very fortunate here to enjoy the luxuries usually only afforded to those on the mainland. Although it is my wish that, within the century, more Icelanders will come to know the benefits of glass windows, wooden panelling, iron stoves, and so forth. I am of the opinion that a drier home allows better circulation of air, and is therefore better for the health.'

'I am sure you are right,' Tóti said, looking at the servant busy untying his laces. She glanced at him without smiling.

'Come, Karitas, leave him alone now,' Blöndal said. 'Reverend Thorvardur, if you will follow me to my office.'

'Thank you, Karitas.'

The servant stood up, holding his shoes, and looked at him as though she was about to say something.

'Karitas. Leave.'

Blöndal waited until the woman had stepped out of the room, before gesturing for Tóti to follow him. 'Down this way, if you please, Reverend. My rooms are in a remote quarter of the building. It keeps the roar of the servants from becoming more than a mild disturbance.'

Tóti followed Blöndal down a long corridor, over which more servants and children ran, going into other rooms. Tóti marvelled at the size of the house – it was like no other he had seen.

'In here please, Reverend.'

Blöndal pushed open a door to a light-filled study. The pale blue walls were lined with two solid bookshelves, filled with leather-bound spines. A large writing desk sat in the middle of the room, its surface gleaming in the sunlight that entered through a tiny curtained window near the peak of the gable.

'It's beautiful,' Tóti gasped.

'Sit down, Reverend,' Blöndal said, pulling out a cushioned chair. Tóti sat as directed.

'Here we are then.' Blöndal ran his large hands over the smooth surface of the desk. 'Shall we begin?'

'Of course, District Commissioner,' Tóti said, nervously. The grandeur of the office made him uncomfortable. He had not known that people in the north lived like this.

'My men said that the condemned was brought to Kornsá without incident.'

'That's my understanding, also,' Tóti said. 'And I am pleased to report that Agnes has settled into her new custodial holdings at Kornsá.'

'I see. You call her by her Christian name.'

'She prefers it, District Commissioner.'

Blöndal leaned back in his chair. 'Continue.'

'Well, the prisoner has hitherto been included in all aspects of the household's haymaking,' Tóti continued. 'And I have been informed by District Officer Jón Jónsson that she labours with a humble demeanour, as befits her reduced state.'

'They do not keep her in irons?'

'It is not usual practice.'

'I see. And her domestic duties?'

'She attends them with utmost diligence. The prisoner seems quite content to spend days of ill weather knitting.'

'Remind them to be wary of supplying her with tools.'

'They are watchful, District Commissioner.'

'Good.' Blöndal pushed his chair back and, opening a drawer in his desk, carefully drew out a sheet of light green paper and a penknife. He then turned and picked up a glass jar stuffed with long, white swan feathers from a corner of a bookshelf. 'I always send the women to collect these,' Blöndal said, momentarily distracted. 'In late summer. It's best to get them when the birds moult. No need to pluck them out.' He offered Tóti the jar holding the clutch of feathers.

'Oh no, I couldn't.' Tóti shook his head.

'I insist,' Blöndal boomed. 'A true man is distinguishable from all others by his writing implements.'

'Thank you.' Tóti gingerly took a feather.

'A provider, the swan,' Blöndal said. 'The skin of the feet makes excellent purses.'

Tóti absently brushed the light edge of the feather against his hand.

'And the eggs are tolerable. If boiled.' Blöndal neatly swept up the slivers of quill from the desk, and then unscrewed a small bottle of ink. 'Now, if you will, a brief summation of your religious administrations to the criminal.'

'Of course.' Tóti was aware of sweat creeping out on his palms. 'During the harvest I visited the criminal intermittently, being, as you will understand, occupied with the harvest at Breidabólstadur.'

'In which ways did you prepare for your communication with the condemned?'

'I ... I would be lying if I said that, at first, my responsibility towards her immortal soul did not weigh heavily upon me.'

'I was worried of as much,' Blöndal said grimly. He made a note on the paper in front of him.

'I thought that the only recourse to her absolution would be through prayer and admonishment,' Tóti said. 'I spent several days in consideration of the verses, psalms, and other literature I thought might bring her to the feet of God.'

'And what did you select?'

'Passages from the New Testament.'

'Which chapters?'

'Uh ...' Tóti was unnerved by the rapidity of Blöndal's questions. 'John. Corinthians,' he stammered.

Blöndal looked askance at Tóti and continued writing.

'I tried to talk to her about the importance of prayer. She asked that I leave.'

Blöndal smiled. 'I'm not surprised. She struck me as especially godless during the trial.'

'Oh no. She seems very well versed in Christian literature.'

'As is the Devil, I am sure,' Blöndal rejoined. 'Reverend Jóhann has set Fridrik Sigurdsson to reading the Passion Hymns. Revelations, also. It is more inciting.'

'Perhaps. However ...' Tóti sat up straighter in his chair. 'It's become apparent to me that the condemned requires means other than religious rebuke to acquaint herself with death and prepare for her meeting with the Lord.'

Blöndal frowned. 'By what means have you been *acquainting* the condemned with God, Reverend?'

Tóti cleared his throat and gently set the feather on the desk in front of him.

'I fear that you may find it unorthodox.'

'Pray, tell me and we shall ascertain whether your fear is reasonable.'

Tóti paused. 'I have come upon the conviction that it is not the stern voice of a priest delivering the threat of brimstone, but the gentle and enquiring tones of a friend that will best draw the curtain to her soul, District Commissioner.'

Blöndal stared at him. 'The gentle tones of a *friend*. I hope I am mistaken in thinking you are serious.'

Tóti reddened. 'I am afraid you're not mistaken, sir. All attempts to press the condemned with sermons had adverse effect. Instead, I, I ... I encourage her to speak of her past. Rather than address her, I allow her to speak to me. I provide her with a final audience to her life's lonely narrative.'

'Do you pray with her?'

'I pray *for* her.'

'Does she pray for herself?'

'I find it impossible to believe she does not, in private. She is to die, sir.'

'Yes, Reverend. She *is* to die.' Blöndal slowly set down his quill and pursed his lips together. 'She is to die, and for good reason.'

There was a knock on the door. 'Ah,' said Blöndal, looking up. 'Sæunn. Come in.'

A nervous-looking young maid entered the room, bearing a tray.

'On the desk, if you will,' Blöndal said, watching as the girl placed coffee, cheese, butter, smoked meat and flat bread in front of him. 'Eat, if you are hungry.' Blöndal immediately began heaping slices of mutton onto his plate.

'Thank you, I am not,' Tóti said. He watched the District Commissioner push a large mouthful of bread and cheese into his mouth. He chewed slowly, swallowed, and pulled out a handkerchief to wipe his fingers.

'Assistant Reverend Thorvardur. You might be forgiven for thinking that friendship will direct this murderess to the way of truth and repentance. You are young and inexperienced. I bear some blame for this.' The District Commissioner slowly leaned forward and rested his elbows on the desk.

'Let me be forthright with you. Last year, in March, Agnes Magnúsdóttir hid Fridrik Sigurdsson in the cowshed at Illugastadir. Natan Ketilsson had returned from the farm Geitaskard with a worker there, Pétur Jónsson –'

'Forgive me, District Commissioner, but I believe I know what is thought to –'

'I think you do not know enough,' Blöndal interrupted. 'Natan had returned home after visiting Geitaskard to attend to Worm Beck, the District Officer there. Worm was very ill. Natan returned to Illugastadir to consult his books, and – as I understand it – fetch additional medicines, and Pétur accompanied him. It was late, Reverend. They decided to sleep the night at Natan's home and return in the morning.

'That evening Fridrik arrived in secret from Katadalur and Agnes hid him in the cowshed. They had planned to kill Natan and steal his money all winter, and that is what they did. Agnes waited until the men were asleep before summoning Fridrik. It was a cold-blooded attack on two defenceless men.'

Blöndal paused to gauge the impact of his words upon Tóti.

'Fridrik confessed to their murder, Reverend. He confessed that he took a hammer and a new-sharpened knife into the badstofa and killed Pétur first, crushing his skull with one blow of the hammer. He either believed it was Natan, or wished to be rid of a witness – I do not know. But he then certainly attempted to kill Natan. In his confession Fridrik said that he raised the hammer and aimed the blow at Natan's skull, but missed. He said he heard the crunch of bone, and, Reverend, examination of the remains revealed that Natan's arm was indeed broken.

'Fridrik told me that Natan then woke, and thought, in what was likely a stupor of pain, that he was at Geitaskard and that it was his friend Worm before him.

'He said: "Natan saw Agnes and me in the room and he started begging for us to stop, but we continued until he was dead." Note his words, Reverend. "Agnes and me." Fridrik said that Natan was killed with the knife.'

'Agnes did not kill them, then.'

'That she was in the room cannot be disputed, Reverend.'

'But she did not handle the weapon.'

Blöndal settled back in his chair and placed his fingertips together. He smiled. 'When Fridrik confessed to the murders, he was unrepentant, Reverend. He thought he had done the will of God. He thought it was justice for past wrongs committed by Natan, and claimed both murders as his own. I am of the opinion that it was not quite as he said.'

'You think Agnes killed Natan.'

'She had incentive to, Reverend. More incentives than Fridrik.' Blöndal daubed his finger against the crumbs remaining on his plate. 'I believe Fridrik killed Pétur. The man was killed with one blow, and a hammer is a heavy tool to wield.

'Fridrik said Natan woke and saw what it was they were doing to him. I believe that he lost his nerve, Reverend. How easy it is to forget that Fridrik was only seventeen on this night. A boy. A thug, certainly – it is well established that he and Natan were enemies of a kind. But think, Reverend ...' Blöndal leaned closer. 'Think of how it must be to kill a man for his money. Imagine if he begged you for his life? If he promised to pay you whatever ransom asked, no authorities notified, if you would only let him live?'

Tóti's throat was dry. 'I cannot imagine such a thing.'

'I must,' Blöndal said. 'And I have. I am of the opinion that, on seeing Natan wake and beg for his life, Fridrik lost his nerve and faltered. He wanted money, and it would undoubtedly have been offered to him in those moments.' His voice was low. 'I am of the opinion that Agnes picked up the knife and killed Natan.'

'But Fridrik did not say that.'

'Natan was stabbed to death. Fridrik was a farmer's son; he knew how to kill animals with a knife. The throat is slit.' Blöndal reached over his desk and jabbed a finger in Tóti's throat. 'From here ...' He dragged the nail across Tóti's skin. 'To here. Natan did not have his throat cut. He was stabbed in the belly. This indicates motives more sordid than theft.'

'Why not Sigga?' Tóti asked in a small voice.

Blöndal shook his head. 'The maid of sixteen who burst into tears as soon as I summoned her? Sigga didn't even attempt to lie – she is too simple-minded, too young to know how. She told me everything. How Agnes hated Natan, how Agnes was jealous of his attentions to her. Sigga is not bright, but she saw that much.'

'But women may be jealous and not murder, District Commissioner.'

'Murder is unusual, I'll concede that, Reverend. But Agnes was twice the age of Sigga. She had travelled to Illugastadir from this valley – a not inconsiderable distance – where she had spent all her life. Why? Surely not just for employment – she had sufficient opportunities here. There was something else, surely, that made her go to work for Natan Ketilsson.'

'I'm sure I don't understand, District Commissioner,' Tóti said.

Blöndal sniffed. 'Excuse me for speaking plainly, Reverend – Agnes believed that she deserved more. A hand in marriage, I would expect. Natan was an indiscreet man – his bastards litter this valley.'

'And he broke his promise?'

Blöndal shrugged. 'Who said he promised her anything? As far as I can see, Agnes was under the impression that she had successfully seduced him. But Sigga testified that Natan preferred her ... attentions.'

'This was spoken of in the trial?'

'A coarse matter. But murder trials are composed of coarse matters.'

'You believe Agnes planned to kill Natan because she was spurned.'

'Reverend. We have a seventeen-year-old common thief armed with a hammer, a sixteen-year-old maid afraid for her life, and a spinster woman whose unrequited affections erupted into bitter hatred. One of them plunged a knife into Natan Ketilsson.'

Tóti's head spun. He focused on the white feather resting on the edge of the desk before him.

'I cannot believe it,' he said, finally.

Blöndal sighed. 'You will not find proof of innocence in Agnes's stories of her life, Reverend. She is a woman loose with her emotions, and looser with her morals. Like many older servant women she is practised in deception, and I do not doubt that she has manufactured a life story in such a way so as to prick your sympathy. I would not believe a word she says. She lied to my face in this very room.'

'She seems sincere,' Tóti said.

'I can tell you that she is not. You *must* apply the Lord's word to her as a whip to a hard-mouthed horse. You will not get anywhere otherwise.'

Tóti swallowed. He thought of Agnes, her thin pale body in the shadowy corners of Kornsá, describing the death of her foster-mother.

'I will invest all my energies into her redemption, District Commissioner.'

'Allow me to redirect you, Reverend. Let me tell you of the work Reverend Jóhann Tómasson has done upon Fridrik.'

'The priest from Tjörn.'

'Yes. I first met Fridrik Sigurdsson in person on the day I went to arrest him. This was in March of last year, shortly after I heard news of the fire at Illugastadir and saw for myself the remains of Natan and Pétur.

'I rode to his family's home, Katadalur, with a few of my men, and we went to the back of the cottage so as to surprise him. When I knocked on the farm door, Fridrik himself opened the hatch and I immediately set my men upon him. They put him in irons. That young man was furious, exhibiting behaviour and language of the most foul and degenerate variety. He struggled with my men, and when I warned him not to attempt escape, he shouted, plain enough for all to hear, that he regretted not having brought his gun outside with him, for it would become me to have a bullet through my forehead.

'I had my men bring Fridrik here, to Hvammur, and I proceeded to question him, as I had done previously with Agnes and Sigrídur, who told me of his involvement. He was stubborn, and remained silent. It was not until I arranged for Reverend Jóhann Tómasson to speak with him that he confessed to having, with the aid of the two women, murdered the men. Fridrik was not repentant or remorseful as a man accused of killing in a passionate state might be. He repeatedly uttered his conviction that what he had done to Natan was necessary and just. Reverend Jóhann suggested to me that his criminal behaviour was a direct consequence of his having been badly brought up, and indeed, after seeing Fridrik's mother's hysterics when we arrested her son, I have come to share his opinion. What other factor could incite a mere boy of seventeen winters to thrash a man to death with a hammer?

'Fridrik Sigurdsson was a boy raised in a household careless with morality and Christian teaching, Reverend. Slothfulness, greed, and rude, callow inclinations bred in him a weak spirit, and a longing for worldly gain. After recording his confession, I was of the unwavering opinion that his was an intransigent character. His appearance excited in me strong suspicions of that order – he is freckle-faced and – I beg your pardon, Reverend – red-headed, a sign of a treacherous nature. When I set him in custody with Birni Olsen at Thingeyrar I had little hope for his reformation. However, Reverend Jóhann and Olsen fortunately possessed more hope for the boy than I entertained, and set to work upon his soul with the religious fervour that makes both men so necessary to this community. Reverend Jóhann confided to me that, through the combination of prayer, daily religious reprehension, and the good, moral example set by Olsen and his family, Fridrik has come to repent of his crime and see the error of his ways. He talks openly and honestly of his misdeeds and acknowledges that his impending execution is right given the horrific nature of the crime committed by his hands. He recognises it as "God's justice". Now, what do you say to this?'

Tóti swallowed. 'I commend both Reverend Jóhann and Herr Birni Olsen for their achievement.'

'As do I,' Blöndal said. 'Does Agnes Magnúsdóttir repent of her crime in a similar manner?'

Tóti hesitated. 'She does not speak of it.'

'And that is because she is reticent, secretive and guilty.'

Tóti was silent for a moment. He wanted nothing more than to run from the room and join the rest of the household of Hvammur, whose chatter slipped under the door of Blöndal's office.

'I am not a cruel man, Assistant Reverend Thorvardur. But I am God-fearing, and it is apparent to me that this District is overrun with criminals of the worst kind. Thieves, thugs, and now murderers. During the years that have passed since my appointment as District Commissioner, I have seen the moral boundaries that have kept the people here safe from depravity and vice disintegrate. It is a political and spiritual embarrassment, and it is my responsibility to see to it that the criminals in this District, who have gone so long unpunished, are given their justice in the eyes of their peers.'

Tóti nodded, and slowly picked up the swan feather. The down near its base clung to his damp fingers. 'You mean to make an example of her,' he said quietly.

'I mean to deliver God's justice here on earth,' Blöndal said, frowning. 'I mean to honour the authorities who have appointed me by fulfilling my duty as lawkeeper.'

Tóti hesitated. 'I hear that you have appointed Gudmundur Ketilsson as executioner,' he said.

Blöndal sighed and leaned back in his chair. 'I've never known tongues to wag faster than they do in this valley.'

'Is it true that you've asked the brother of the murdered man?'

'I do not have to explain my decisions to you, Reverend. I am not accountable to parish priests. I am accountable to Denmark. To the King.'

'I did not say I disapproved.'

'Your opinion is writ large upon your face, Reverend.' Blöndal picked up his pen again. 'But we are not here to discuss my performance. We are here to discuss yours, and I must say that I am disappointed with it.'

'What will you have me do?'

'Return to God's word. Forget Agnes's. She has nothing that you need to hear, unless it is a confession.'

Reverend Tóti left Björn Blöndal's study with a pounding head. He could not stop thinking of Agnes's pale face, her low voice in the dark, and the image of red-headed Fridrik, raising a hammer above a sleeping man. Had she been lying to him? He fought off a compulsion to cross himself in the corridor, in front of the busy huddle of female servants lugging pails of milk and pots of waste. He pulled on his shoes against the wall.

It was a relief to be outside. It had grown cloudy and dim, but the cold air, and the strong smell of fish drying on racks near the cowshed, seemed sympathetic to his confusion. He thought of Blöndal's greasy finger against his throat. The crunch of bone. Natan Ketilsson begging for his life. He wanted to be sick.

'Reverend!' Someone was calling him. He turned around and saw Karitas, Blöndal's servant, running hurriedly after him. 'You left your coat, sir.'

Tóti smiled and extended an arm to take the garment, but the woman did not let go of it. She pulled Tóti closer and whispered to him, looking at the ground.

'I need to speak with you.'

Tóti was surprised. 'Excuse me?'

'Shh,' hissed the woman. She glanced over to the servant men gutting the fish on the stone. 'Come with me. To the stable.'

Tóti nodded and, taking his coat, stumbled towards the large cowshed. It was dark inside, and smelt strongly of manure, although the stalls had already been cleaned. It was empty – all the animals had been taken out to pasture.

He turned around and saw Karitas silhouetted against the open doorway.

'I don't mean to be secretive, but ...' She stepped closer, and Tóti saw that she was distressed.

'I didn't mean to grab at you like that, but I didn't think I'd have another opportunity.' Karitas gestured towards a milking stool and Tóti sat down.

'You are the Reverend attending Agnes Magnúsdóttir?'

'Yes,' Tóti said, curious.

'I worked at Illugastadir. With Natan Ketilsson. I left in 1827, just before Agnes arrived to work there also. She came to take my position as housekeeper. Well, that is what Natan told me.'

'I see. And what did you want to tell me?'

Karitas paused, as if trying to find the right words. '"The treachery of a friend is worse than that of a foe,"' she said eventually.

'I don't understand.'

'It's from Gisli Sursson's Saga.' Karitas swivelled to the open doorway, checking to see if anyone was coming. 'He broke his word to her,' she whispered.

'His word?'

'Natan promised Agnes my position, sir. Only, before she arrived, he decided that Sigga should have it.'

Tóti was confused. He absently stroked the feather Blöndal had given him. He still held it in his hand.

'Sigga was young – fifteen or sixteen, Reverend. Natan knew it would embarrass Agnes to be under her authority.'

'I'm afraid I don't understand what you mean, Karitas. Why would Natan promise Agnes a position and then give it to an inexperienced girl half her age?'

Karitas shrugged. 'Did you ever meet Natan, Reverend?'

'No, never. Although I gather that many here in the valley knew him.' He smiled. 'I've been hearing some rather mixed opinions. Some say he was a sorcerer, another a good doctor.'

Karitas did not return his smile.

'But you are of the mind that he deceived Agnes?'

Karitas scuffed her slipper against the straw on the ground. 'It's only ... Folks here have blacked her name, and that does not rest well with me.'

Tóti hesitated. 'Why are you telling me this, Karitas?'

The woman bent closer. 'I left Illugastadir because I couldn't bear Natan any more. He ... he *toyed* with people.' She leant closer still, her lip trembling. 'It was as though he did it to amuse himself. I never knew where I stood with him. He'd tell me one thing and do another.

And if I had a mind to ask for leave to church-go, well.' The woman looked askance at Tóti. 'I'm a good Christian woman, Reverend, and I swear that I have never heard a man spout such disbelief.' Karitas pulled a face and looked back towards the doorway. 'You won't tell Blöndal I've spoken with you?'

'Of course not. But I don't see what good it does to tell me this about Natan. I can see that opinion is divided about him, but even still, mischief-makers, even if they are non-believers, don't deserve to be stabbed in the middle of the night.'

Karitas was taken aback. 'Mischief-maker?' She gave him a look. 'Has Agnes said anything about Natan?'

'No. She doesn't talk of him.'

'What has Blöndal said?' She jerked her head in the direction of the farmhouse.

'I have heard very little to trust from anyone besides superstitious talk of his being named for the Devil.'

Karitas gave a weak smile. 'Yes, they say that. Blöndal wouldn't speak badly of him anyway. Natan healed his wife.'

'I didn't know she was ill.'

'Deathly. He paid plenty for him too. But it worked. Natan Ketilsson fetched his wife from heaven's gate.'

Tóti suddenly felt angry. He stood up and brushed his trousers clean of straw and dust. 'I should go.'

'So you won't tell Blöndal I spoke with you?'

'No.' Tóti attempted a smile. 'Karitas, I wish you well. God keep you.'

'Reverend, you must ask Agnes about Natan. I think they knew each other better than they knew themselves.'

Tóti turned from the doorway, puzzled. 'Would you visit her in person?'

Karitas gave a hoarse laugh. 'Blöndal would have me gutted

and hung out to dry. Besides, I had already left when she arrived at Illugastadir. I'd had enough.'

'I see.' Tóti looked at her for a moment, then swiftly brought a hand to the brim of his hat. 'God bless you.' He left to collect his horse from the yard and, once seated, turned to wave goodbye to Karitas, who stood at the entrance to the cowshed. She did not wave back.

HARVEST HAS BEEN BROUGHT IN and everyone is longing to finally open their mouths for food and talk and drink after all those weeks of gritted teeth. I assist Margrét in the kitchen, cooking mutton for guests that have started to arrive for harvest celebration. There isn't much time for private thoughts. The daughters are not here – sent away to the mountain heath with Kristín to collect berries and moss – and now it is up to Margrét and me to pour and blend the whey and water, churn the butter, serve the men, and ensure all the drying laundry is taken from the yard before any of the neighbours see our underthings. It was a surprise to suddenly realise that the girls were gone; I suppose I have grown used to Lauga's rolling eyes, like some disgruntled calf, and Steina following me like a shadow. 'I know you,' she said to me before she left. 'We are alike.'

I am nothing like Steina. She is unhappy too, yes, but she is not like me. When I was her age, I was working for my butter at Gudrúnarstadir, helping with the five children there – each as thin and faint as tidemarks – and cleaning, and cooking, and serving until I thought I'd collapse. Always up to my elbows in something – brine, or milk, or smoke, or dung, or blood. When Indridi was born, the youngest of the Gudrúnarstadir clan, I was there beside his poor mother, holding her hand and cutting the knotted cord. What has Steina seen of the world? When I was her age I was alone, keeping an eye ajar at night to prevent a foul-mouthed servant from lifting my shift when he thought I was asleep. Not that he was always so secretive. He grabbed me by the creek one morning, twisted my arms behind my back and pushed me down, so that my face splashed against the water, and I worried I would drown while he fumbled with his trousers. Has Steina had to struggle under the weight of a servant man like that? Has Steina ever had to decide whether to let a farmer up under her skirts and face the wrath of his wife, who will force her to do the shit-work, or to deny him and find herself homeless in the snow and fog with all doors barred against her?

That babe, that thistle-headed child Indridi I saw into the world, they buried him a few years after I cut him free. He was old enough to talk. Old enough to know he was hungry. What does Steina know of dead children? She is not like me. She knows only the tree of life. She has not seen its twisted roots pawing stones and coffins.

I left Gudrúnarstadir after Indridi died, the farmer and his wife, their remaining huddle of children, splintered with starvation. They gave me kisses, a letter of recommendation and two eggs for the journey to Gilsstadir. I gave the eggs to a pair of fair-headed girls I met on my way.

I could almost laugh. To think those round-cheeked lasses throwing clumps of dirt for their dog to chase are now my custodians here at Kornsá.

Lauga kicked up a terrible fuss when Jón told them they must miss the harvest party and go berrying. She's a tremendous sulker and reminds me a little of Sigga, only smarter. Jón spoke with her and Steina last night when he thought I was asleep. 'She must meet her God, and in an ugly way,' he said. 'Our family way of life must continue. We must keep you safe from her.' He does not want them to pity me. He does not want them to draw close, and so he has sent them away for a time, while the weather permits. A reprieve from my presence.

Margrét says that the guests will eat outside today, for it is a fine September morning and it will do us good to take what we can of the sunshine, for soon winter will be upon us. Already the mountain grass is fading to the colour of smoked meat, and the evenings smell of burning fish oil from lamps newly lit. At Illugastadir there will soon be a prickle of frost over the seaweed thrown upon the shore. The seals will be banked upon the tongues of rock, watching winter descend from the mountain. There will be the call and whoop of men on horseback, rounding up the sheep, and then there will come the slaughter.

'Greetings to all at Kornsá!' There is a call from the farm entrance, and Margrét looks up, alarmed. 'Stay here,' she says. She bustles out. There is the rise and fall of a woman's voice, and then a large, pregnant woman enters the room, surrounded by a swarm of white-blond children with runny noses. Another woman, a thin grey lady, follows her. I look up from the hearth, where I am stirring the soup, and see that the fat woman is staring at me, her hand over her mouth. The children gape at me also.

'Róslín, Ingibjörg, this is Agnes Magnúsdóttir,' Margrét sighs.

I curtsey, aware that I must look a sight. The steam has made my hair stick to my damp forehead and blood is on my apron from the meat.

'Out! Children, outside now!' The little flock of children leave, one emitting a violent sneeze. They seem disappointed.

Not so their mother. The Róslín woman turns to Margrét and grabs her by the shoulder.

'You invite us all with *her* here!'

'Where else would she be?' Margrét glances over at the other woman, Ingibjörg, and I see a glimmer of conspiracy in their eyes.

'At Hvammur for the day! Locked up in the storeroom!' Róslín shouts. Her face is flushed; she's enjoying her tantrum.

'You are working yourself into a frenzy, Róslín. You'll bring about your time.'

I glance down to the woman's swollen belly. She looks full-term.

'It's a girl,' I say, without thinking.

The three women stare at me.

'What did she say?' Róslín whispers, looking horrified.

Margrét gives a small cough. 'What did you say, Agnes?'

I feel uneasy all of a sudden. 'Your baby will be a girl. It is the shape of it. The way your belly protrudes.'

Ingibjörg observes me, interested.

'Witch!' Róslín cries. 'Tell her to stop looking at me.' She storms out of the room.

'How do you guess at that?' Ingibjörg asks. Her voice is gentle.

'Rósa Gudmundsdóttir told me. She is a midwife in the west.'

Margrét nods slowly. 'Poet-Rósa. I did not know you were friends.'

The meat is cooked. I place the spoon on the top of a barrel and use both hands to lift the pot from the hook. 'We aren't,' I say.

Ingibjörg picks up a small dish of butter by my side and nods towards Margrét.

'I hope your mistress will let you come outside for a time,' she says, smiling. 'You ought to feel the sun on your face.'

She and Margrét leave, but her words hang in the room behind her. You ought to feel the sun on your face. 'Before you die,' I cannot not help but add, aloud, to the rustle of the embers.

The guests arrive on foot and horseback, the women bearing food and the men coyly slipping small bottles of brandy from out of their vests and coats. I see them as I place dishes on the tables, but for the most part Margrét keeps me busy in the kitchen, out of sight of the neighbours. They look sideways at me and fall silent as I set jugs of milk down, pats of fresh butter.

I don't want to be out here. There will be people I know, perhaps farmers I have worked for, servants I have shared quarters with. My forehead aches from the tightness of my plaits, and I suddenly long to untie them, to walk about with my hair unbraided, to lie on my back in the sun.

☦

TÓTI FOUND AGNES IN THE dairy, churning the butter.

'Not joining the party, Agnes?' he asked quietly.

She didn't turn around. 'I am better use in here,' she said, continuing to raise the plunger and push it through the cream. Tóti thought it was a good sound, the dull splash of the churn.

'I hope you don't mind me interrupting you.'

'No. But if you don't mind, I won't stop until the butter takes.'

Tóti leant against the doorframe as Agnes continued to raise and drop the plunger. After a moment he became aware of Agnes's breath, fast and hard in the small room. It seemed intimate somehow; the rhythm of the plunger and the sound of quickened breathing. He felt himself blushing. Eventually a thud could be heard inside the small barrel, and Agnes stopped and deftly strained the butter from the buttermilk. Tóti blinked as Agnes washed it then formed and slapped the paddle, skilfully forcing out the remaining liquid, and thought of what Blöndal had said. *Someone plunged the knife into Natan Ketilsson's belly.*

Once the butter had been shaped and covered with a cloth, Tóti suggested that they go outside to take the air. Agnes looked nervous, but after fetching some knitting from the badstofa, followed Tóti outside. They sat down on the turf pile by the croft and looked across at the group of adults and children, the farmers getting steadily drunker on their brandy, and the women gossiping in tight clusters of dark clothes. Several were taking turns to hold a baby, clucking into its face. It broke into a wail.

'I have been to Blöndal,' Tóti said eventually.

Agnes blanched. 'What did he want?'

'He thinks I should spend more time engaging you in prayers and sermons, and less time letting you speak.'

'Blöndal likes only one thing better than religious chastisement, and that is the sound of his own voice.' Agnes's words were crabbed.

'Is it true Blöndal hired Natan to heal his wife?'

Agnes gave him a wary look. 'Yes,' she said slowly. 'Yes, that's true. Natan visited Hvammur some years back to give her poultices and bleed her.'

Tóti nodded. 'Blöndal also told me a little about Fridrik. Apparently he is doing very well under the guardianship of Birni Olsen and the counsel of Reverend Jóhann.' He looked at Agnes to measure her reaction. She narrowed her eyes.

'Will they get up an appeal for him too?' she asked.

'He did not say.' Tóti cleared his throat. 'Agnes, a servant called Karitas sends her regards. She asked if you had spoken to me about Natan.'

Agnes stopped knitting and clenched her jaw.

'Karitas?' Her voice cracked.

'She asked to speak with me after I had met with Blöndal. She wanted to tell me about Natan.'

'And what did she say about him?'

Tóti rummaged for his snuff horn, poured a little on his hand and snorted it. 'She said that she could not bear working for him. She said that he toyed with people.'

Agnes said nothing.

'I have met others here in this valley who say he was a sorcerer, that he got his name from Satan,' Tóti said.

'That's a very popular story. And plenty believe it too.'

'Do you believe it?'

Agnes smoothed the length of the unfinished stocking out across her knees. 'I don't know,' she said finally. 'Natan believed in dreams. His mother had foresight and her dreams often came true. His family is famous for it. He made me tell him my dreams and put a lot of store by them.'

Agnes stopped running her palm over the stocking and looked up. 'Reverend,' she said quietly. 'If I tell you something, will you promise to believe me?'

Tóti felt his heart leap in his chest. 'What is it you want to tell me, Agnes?'

'Remember when you first visited me here, and you asked me why I had chosen you to be my priest, and I told you that it was because of an act of kindness, because you had helped me across the river?' Agnes cast a wary glance out to the group of people on the edge of the field. 'I wasn't lying,' she continued. 'We did meet then. But what I didn't tell you was that we had met before.'

Tóti raised his eyebrows. 'I'm sorry, Agnes. I don't remember.'

'You wouldn't have. We met in a dream.' She stared at Tóti, as if worried he would laugh.

'A dream?' The Reverend was struck again by the contrast of her dark lashes against the lightness of her eyes. She is unlike anyone else, he thought.

Satisfied that he wasn't going to laugh, Agnes resumed her knitting. 'When I was sixteen years old I dreamt that I was walking barefoot in a lava field. It was covered with snow and I was lost and scared – I didn't know where I was, and there was no one to be seen. In every direction there was nothing but rock and snow, and great chasms and cracks in the ground. My feet were bleeding, but I had to keep going – I didn't know where, but I was walking as fast as I could. Just when I thought I would die from fear, a young man appeared. He was bareheaded, but wore a priest's collar, and he gave me his hand. We kept going in the same direction as before – we didn't know where else to go – and even though I was still terrified, I had his hand in mine, and it was a comfort.

'Then suddenly, in my dream, I felt the ground give way beneath my feet, and my hand was wrenched out of the young man's, and I fell into a chasm. I remember looking up as I fell into the darkness, and seeing the ground close back up over my head. It shut out the light and the face of the man who had appeared. I was dropped into the earth, buried in silence, and it was unbearable, and then I woke.'

Tóti felt his mouth go dry. 'Was I that man?' he asked.

Agnes nodded. She had tears in her eyes. 'It terrified me when I saw you then, at Gönguskörd. I recognised you from my dream, and I knew then that you were bound to my life in some way, and it worried me.' Agnes wiped her nose on her sleeve. 'After we parted I found out your name. I heard that you were to be a priest like your father, and that you were going south to the school there, and I knew then that my dream was real, and that we would meet for a third time. Even Natan believed that everything comes in threes.'

'But you are not down a chasm, and it is not yet dark,' Tóti said.

'Not yet,' Agnes replied quietly, swallowing hard. 'Anyway. It wasn't the darkness in the chasm that scared me. It was the silence.'

Tóti was thoughtful. 'There is a lot in this world and the next that we don't understand. But just because we don't understand doesn't mean we have to be afraid. We can be sure of so little in this life, Agnes. And it *is* frightening. I would be lying if I said I wasn't frightened by what I did not know. But we have God, Agnes, and more than that, we have His love and He takes our fear away.'

'I can't feel sure of anything like that.'

Tóti reached over and tentatively took up her hand. 'Trust me, Agnes. I'm here, as I was in your dream. You can feel my hand in yours,' he added.

Tóti pressed her slender fingers, her knuckles. He was aware of her smell, the sweet scent of fresh buttermilk, and a sourness also. Of skin? Of the dairy? He fought off a sudden compulsion to put her fingers in his mouth.

Unaware of his thoughts, Agnes smiled and patted his knee with her free palm. 'I am sure that you will make a fine priest after all,' she said.

Tóti stroked the skin on the back of her hand. 'You know,' he said, 'Blöndal nearly didn't let me come to you.' He felt conspiratorial.

'Of course he didn't.'

'When I saw him today I was worried he would forbid me from seeing you.'

'And did he?'

Tóti shook his head. 'He said I must preach to you.'

Agnes gently pulled her hand out of his grasp, and he reluctantly released her. He watched her resume her knitting.

'Why don't you tell me about Natan,' he asked, a little peevish.

Agnes glanced at the people before them. 'Do you think they need more food brought out?'

'Margrét would have called you.' Tóti wiped his sweaty palms against his trousers. 'Go on, Agnes. Blöndal isn't here.'

'And thank the Lord for that.' Agnes took a deep breath. 'What do you want me to tell you about Natan? You know that he was my employer at Illugastadir. You've obviously heard enough about his character from people around here. What else do you want to know?'

'When did you meet him?'

'I met Natan Ketilsson when I was working at Geitaskard.'

'Where is that?'

'In Langidalur. It was my sixth farm as a workmaid. It's run by Worm Beck. He was good to me. I'd been working at Fannlaugarstadir, in the east, then Búrfell. That is when we first met, Reverend, when I was on my way towards Búrfell and you took me across the river. I'd gone because I'd heard that Magnús Magnússon, the man named as my father, was working there, and I thought I might go stay with him.

'I didn't stay there long. Magnús was kind, but when I reminded him I was named Magnúsdóttir for him, he flew into a rage and said that my mother had damaged his good name, and would he ever see the end of the trouble women had brought him. I didn't like to stay after that. Magnús fixed me a bed and let me stay with everyone there, but from time to time I'd see him looking at me with a queer expression and I knew it was because he saw my mother's likeness. He gave me some money before I left. It was the first time I ever held money in my life.

'I decided to go to Geitaskard. I set off quite early in the morning on foot, and was following the white river Blanda downstream, when I saw a group of men coming from an eastern mountain pass. They fell in with me and my companions, other servants mostly, and we introduced ourselves, and if one of them wasn't my own little brother, now all grown up! We hadn't even recognised each other. Jóas was overcome. He pressed my hand and called me sister, and the others mocked him when they saw tears in his eyes. I was happy to find Jóas too, but I noticed he had the lick of brandy about him, and his dress was slovenly. He told me that he was a servant, but he carried no letter of recommendation, and he had the nervous look of vagrants you see about these parts. Something told me he was not doing well for himself, and I was heartsore to see it. We talked all the way to Geitaskard that morning, and I learnt that Jóas's childhood hadn't been any brighter than mine. Mamma had left him soon after she lugged me down to Kornsá, and he told me he'd been thrown up and down the valley like a hot coal. He didn't know where Ingveldur was, and he said that she could be in hell for all he cared. So that was the two of us, paupers both, only he looked the worse for it. He couldn't read or write, and when I offered to teach him he was put out of temper and told me not to show off.

'Jóas and his friends, a greasy lot with nary a clean face between them, told me they were headed to Geitaskard to see what odd jobs they could pick up, it being a large farm. Jóas hadn't organised himself a position like I had, but I vouched for him in front of Worm, and he was taken on, too. Those were kinder days, having family about me like that, even though we hardly knew each other, and a good farm to work on. There was plenty of food at Geitaskard, not like Gudrúnarstadir or Gafl, or even Gilsstadir. There were times at those farms when I had no choice but to give the bairns tallow candles to eat, and myself a bit of boiled leather. The servants at Geitaskard always minded themselves too. With all those cows and horses, and butter and grass, and thick servings of meat to line your stomach, it wasn't hard to be good. I fell in with one of the other servants there, María Jónsdóttir. I never had many friends, but she had been a pauper as well, and I suppose we understood one another in a way.

'Jóas seemed to like Geitaskard, which I was glad to see. But I didn't care for his friends. They seemed a gang, and were slouch-faced, weedy sort of men, with stained trousers and nits in their hair. Jóas had scratched his scalp raw. Worm got rid of some of the men after no more than a week – he'd caught them sleeping behind the cowshed – and the rest didn't last long either. I don't know whether it was because he was a better sort of man, or if it was because he had me there with him, but Jóas let me clean him up and comb the nits out of his hair, and he worked hard. At nights, when we had time to ourselves, we'd talk. He told me he'd heard stories about me, that he'd asked around and heard I'd gone to work at Gudrúnarstadir. He said he'd tried to find me there, but I'd left when he arrived, and they couldn't remember where I'd gone. I didn't let him see it, but I wept over that, the thought of my brother trying to find me. He'd had a child, as well. A little girl, whose mamma was a workmaid. But he told me that the baby was stillborn, and the maid did not care for him. I told him about Helga, our poor dead sister, and he said he'd gone to her funeral and that the farmer Jónas, Helga's father, gave him a little bit of money on account of Jóas being abandoned by a whore. Jóas insisted that our Mamma was no good, and that she could go to hell for leaving two children to the mercy of the parish, which was no kind of mercy at all, and he called her many other things besides. He spoke of Mamma as Magnús had, and we quarrelled about it one night, and when I woke up Jóas couldn't be found. He'd taken the money that Magnús had given me. I haven't seen him since.'

There was a loud cackle of laughter from the gathering on the bottom field. Tóti saw that two of the men had let out the cow and the others were trying in vain to herd it back into the field.

'I'd been saving that money,' Agnes continued. 'For when I got married; to pay the licences and help my husband buy a plot of land so we could be decent and independent.'

'Had you a fiancé?' Tóti asked.

Agnes smiled. 'Oh, there was a servant at Geitaskard. Daníel Gudmundsson. He was fond of me, and he told everyone that we were engaged to be wed. He said so in the trials, but I don't see how he could have been serious. Neither of us had a coin to our name. I let him think what he fancied, so long as it meant that he was kind to me.

'Daníel worked at Illugastadir when I was there, too. He was at the trials, first as a witness, then Blöndal decided he must have known what was to happen, and he was sentenced to time in the Rasphus in Copenhagen.'

'Did he know what was going to happen?' Tóti asked.

Agnes looked up from her needles and regarded him coolly.

'If anyone knew what was going to happen do you think I'd be sitting here, talking to you? Do you think any of those others, Daníel, Fridrik's family, would be strapped over a barrel being whipped to within an inch of their lives if they knew what was going to happen?'

There was a moment of silence.

Agnes took a deep breath. 'After Jóas left, the best thing about working at Geitaskard was María. I never had many friends growing up; I'd been bundled along from farm to farm. To anyone who needed to do their parish duty, or who wanted a girl-stripling to watch over the grass, or sheep, or kettles. I used to keep to myself anyhow. I preferred to read than talk with the others.' Agnes looked up. 'Do you like reading?' she asked Tóti.

'Very much.'

Agnes gave a wide smile, and for the first time Tóti remembered the servant girl he had helped over the river. Her eyes were bright, and her lips parted to reveal even teeth; she suddenly looked younger, altered. He was aware of his own chest rising and falling. She is quite beautiful, he thought.

'Me too,' she said, her voice dropping to a whisper. 'I like the sagas best. As they say, *blíndur er bóklaus maður*. Blind is a man without a book.'

Tóti felt something rise in him, a cry, or a laugh. He gazed at Agnes, at the afternoon sun lighting the tips of her eyelashes, and wondered at Blöndal's words. *Agnes killed Natan because she was spurned*. He saw the sentence written in his mind.

'When I was a girl, I used to be hired out to watch over fields. Sometimes those farms had books.' She gestured to the rocky hills behind them. 'I used to take them and read up over Kornsá Hill. I could fall asleep there, and have some peace from the farm, and from the chores. Though sometimes I'd be caught and punished.'

'Your confirmation said that you were well-read.'

Agnes straightened her back. 'I liked confirmation; the Holy Communion and everyone looking at you as you walked up the aisle and knelt before the priest. The farmers and their wives couldn't tell me not to read when they knew I was preparing for confirmation. I could go to the church and study with the Reverend there, if he had time. I was given a white dress, and there were pancakes afterwards.'

'What about poetry?'

Agnes looked sceptical. 'What about it?'

'Do you like it? Do you compose?'

'I don't brag about my poems. Not like Rósa. Everyone knows hers.' She shrugged.

'That is because they are beautiful.'

Agnes went quiet. 'Natan loved that about Rósa. He loved the way she knew how to build things with words. She invented her own language to say what everyone else could only feel.'

'I hear Natan was a poet, too.' Tóti pretended nonchalance. 'Did you two speak in poems to each other, as Rósa and Natan did?'

'Not like Rósa, no. But we spoke to each other in a kind of poetry.' Agnes looked out over the field. 'I met Natan on a day like this.'

'A harvest celebration?'

She nodded. 'At Geitaskard. I was serving with María. We were bringing out food and drink, and taking our time about it too. María knew everything there was to know about a person, and I remember that she'd been pointing out the swollen belly of one of the farmer's servants and saying some things that perhaps weren't kind, but she had me laughing till I couldn't breathe. Then she grasped me by the elbow and dragged me to the cowshed, and told me that she'd just seen Natan Ketilsson arrive on horseback.

'I already knew about Natan, of course. He was famous for all sorts of things, depending on who you spoke to. Everyone found out about his affair with Rósa. Everyone knew her children were Natan's, not Ólaf's. Natan travelled all through the north. As a young man he went about letting blood and then he went to Copenhagen, and everyone said he came back a sorcerer. They also said that he became friends with Blöndal, who was studying there at the time, and that is why he never got caught for what he did later. Everyone thought Natan was a thief, and it's true that he was whipped for it when he was younger. No one could account for his having so much money when they saw for themselves how little they put in his palm. Some swore that he got others to steal animals for him. He had a lot of enemies. But whether those folks were wronged or just jealous is hard to say. Stories have a way of boiling over, and Natan himself liked to keep people guessing.'

'What was your opinion of Natan then?'

'Oh, I had none to speak of, then. I'd never met him before, though his brother Ketil had once tried to woo me. In the cowshed María told me that Natan had finally left Rósa and taken up a farm for himself. A lot of people were talking about it on account of Rósa being well-liked, and sorry to see her heartbroken, though she was married. María told me that Worm was a great friend of Natan's, and had helped him buy Illugastadir, a farm right by the sea with plenty of seals and eider ducks and driftwood too, if you could haul it from the shore. She said Natan had started giving himself some airs, calling himself Lyngdal, not Ketilsson, though neither of us could work out why – it was a strange sort of name to have, not Icelandic in the slightest. María thought it was probably to make himself out to be a Dane, and I wondered that he was allowed to change his name at all. María told me that men might do as they please, and that they are all Adams, naming everything under the sun.

'We brushed ourselves down and María bit her lips to make them redder. Then we walked out of the cowshed, pretending to see if any of the dishes had been emptied.

'It was then that I saw Natan for the first time. I thought he'd be a big man, a handsome, upright fellow with long hair, like those men servant girls usually go giddy over. But Natan was not handsome. The man I saw talking with Worm was not tall and he was quite thin in the face – he never *looked* strong. His hair was reddish-brown, and his nose was too big for his face. I thought he looked like a fox with his chestnut hair and beady little eyes, and told María so. She burst out laughing, and said no wonder some northerners thought he was a shapeshifter.

'Natan noticed us then. It was obvious that we had made a joke at his expense, but he didn't seem to mind. He made some comment to Worm and began walking towards us.

'I remember that he was smiling, as though he knew us already. I suppose he liked the attention. "Good afternoon, girls," he said. He wasn't much taller than I was, but his voice was deep. He said: "May I have the pleasure of learning your names?" and I answered for the both of us.

'Natan smiled and made a bow, and it was then that I noticed his hands. They were very white, like a woman's hands, and his fingers were as slender as birch twigs, and as lengthy. No wonder they called him "long-fingers". He said he was pleased to meet us both, and wasn't it a fine day? He started to ask us if we were enjoying the celebration, but I interrupted him, and said that he hadn't yet given us his name. María scoffed, but Natan always liked those who had a tongue in their heads, as he told me later. He said his name was Natan Lyngdal. There was a glitter in his eye.

'María asked if he wasn't actually Ketilsson, and Natan replied that yes, indeed he was also Ketilsson, and that he had a great many more names besides, though not all of them were fit for our delicate ears. He was easy in his address, Reverend. He always knew what to say to people; what would make them feel good. And what would cut the deepest.

'We didn't speak for long. Worm summoned Natan, and he made his farewell, but not before he murmured that he hoped he would see more of us at a later time when he was not so called upon.'

Reverend Tóti ran a finger around his gums, dislodging a dreg or two of tobacco. He wiped his fingertip on his trousers, and couldn't help but notice the small, unremarkable shape of his own pink hands. He felt a snag of envy in his chest.

'When did you see Natan again, after that?'

Agnes paused to count her stitches before casting off. 'Oh, that same day,' she said. 'María and I were kept busy all afternoon, running errands for Worm's wife, and keeping the children from underfoot, but we were given the evening to celebrate the harvest in our own way. It was a fine delicate sort of twilight, and all the servants sat outside to watch the night fall down. One of the hands was telling a story of the hidden people, when a cough was heard and we saw Natan standing behind our group in the shadows. He apologised for sneaking up on us, but told us he was fond of stories, and would we humour a stranger by allowing him to join our festivities? One of the servant men said that Natan Ketilsson was hardly a stranger, especially amongst the women, and most laughed. But one or two of the men and also a number of the workmaids looked away.

'María made room for Natan next to her. I was on the outer of the group, not being as popular on account of my having a certain way of talking to people, but Natan walked right past María and sat down next to me. "Now, we are all ready," he said, and he looked over to the man who had been speaking, and he invited him to continue his tale. We all sat into the night telling stories and looking at the stars, until it was time to sleep and that was that.'

'Why do you think Natan chose to sit next to you?'

Agnes shrugged. 'He told me afterwards that he'd been watching me all day, and could not read me. I misunderstood him at first, and said, well, no wonder, for I was a woman, not a book. And he laughed, and said that no, he could read people too, although some seemed to be in a script he couldn't comprehend.' Agnes gave a slight smile. 'Make what you will of that, Reverend. But that is what he said.'

THE REVEREND IS SURELY WONDERING at what we were to one another. I watch him and know that he is thinking of Natan and I, letting the thought roll through his mind, savouring it, like a child sucking the marrow out of a bone. He might as well be sucking a stone.

Natan.

How can I truly recall the first moment of meeting him, when the hand I felt press my own was merely a hand? It is impossible to think of Natan as the stranger he was, once, to me. I can picture the way he looked, and recall the weather, and the play of light across his stubbled face, but that virgin moment is impossible to recapture. I cannot remember not knowing Natan. I cannot think of what it was not to love him. To look at him and realise I had found what I had not known I was hungering for. A hunger so deep, so capable of driving me into the night, that it terrified me.

I did not lie to the Reverend. That night of stars and stories, and the warm pressure of his hand on mine, happened as I told him. But I did not tell Tóti what followed when the servants went to bed. I did not tell him that María went with them too, sending me a reproachful glance. I did not say that we were left alone, and that Natan urged me to stay with him in the half-light. To talk, he said. Only to talk.

'Tell me who you are, Agnes. Here, let me take your hand so that I might learn a little of you.'

The swift warmth of his fingers tracing the length of my open palm.

'These are calluses, so you are a hard worker. But your fingers are strong. You not only work hard, but you do your work well. I can see why Worm hired you. See this? You have a hollow palm. Like my own, here, can you feel how it is unfilled?'

The soft depression, the ghost creases in his skin, the suggestion of bones.

'Do you know what it means, to have a hollow palm? It means there is something secretive about us. This empty space can be filled with bad luck if we're not careful. If we expose the hollow to the world and all its darkness, all its misfortune.'

'But how can one help the shape of one's hand?' I was laughing.

'By covering it with another's, Agnes.'

The weight of his fingers on mine, like a bird landing on a branch. It was the drop of the match. I did not see that we were surrounded by tinder until I felt it burst into flames.

CHAPTER EIGHT

**Poet-Rósa's poem to Natan Ketilsson,
c. 1827**

Ó, hve sæla eg áleit mig, –
engin mun því trúande, –
þá fjekk eg líða fyrir þig
forsmán vina, en hinna spje.

Sá minn þanki sannur er, –
þó svik þín banni nýting arðs –
Ó, hve hefir orðið þjer
eitruð rosin Kiðjaskarðs!

Oh, how happy I believed I was –
no one could have known how free –
even when I suffered for you,
when everyone was mocking me.

Traitor, look at your misfortune –
these are my thoughts, they're true –
Oh, how this rose of Kidjaskard
has gone and poisoned you!

AUTUMN FELL UPON THE VALLEY like a gasp. Margrét, lying awake in the extended gloom of the October morning, her lungs mossy with mucus, wondered at how the light had grown slow in coming; how it seemed to stagger through the window, as though weary from travelling such a long way. Already it seemed a struggle to rise. She'd wake in the chill night with Jón pressing his toes against her legs to warm them, and the farmhands were coming in from feeding the cow and horses with their noses and cheeks pink with the ice in the air. Her daughters had said that there was a frost every morning of their berrying trip, and snow had fallen during the round-up. Margrét had not gone, not trusting her lungs to last the long walk up over the mountain to find and herd the sheep from their summer pasture, but she'd sent everyone else. Except Agnes. She could not let her walk over the mountain. Not that she would flee. Agnes wasn't stupid. She knew this valley, and she knew what little escape it offered. She'd be seen. Everyone knew who she was.

The round-up had been a day of disquiet. The farmhands had left first, before light, riding horses up beyond the Vididals mountain with other men of the valley, and some of the women of the district had followed on foot not long after. Margrét had stayed behind with Agnes to prepare the meal for their return. As soon as it had grown light that day, Margrét had felt uneasy. The sky had dawned grey and foreboding, and she had known something would happen. It was the way the clouds had crouched too close to the ground. The smell of iron in the air. All morning she'd been thinking of the people who had been lost on the mountains. Only the year before a maidservant had gone missing in a sudden snowstorm during round-up, and they hadn't found her bones until the next spring, miles away from where she'd last been seen. Worry pressed on Margrét's mind to the point where she found herself talking to Agnes just for the relief of expressing concern. Together they listed the people they had known who had died on the mountains. A bleak conversation to have, thought Margrét, but there was some comfort in talking about death aloud, as though in naming things, you could prevent them from happening. Perhaps that was why Agnes spoke more to the Reverend than he to her, she thought.

She'd been right, of course; something had happened. Soon after midday, with no one yet returned from the mountain, there had come a rapid knocking on the farm door, and Ingibjörg had burst in. 'It's Róslín,' she had said.

The farm at Gilsstadir was overrun with children. Margrét had noticed that despite the chaos, the smoking kitchen filled with burning pots and kettles left to boil over, Róslín's horde of children seemed bored at the fact of their mother's labour. After the three women had entered, Róslín had staggered to the badstofa, pale and sweating. Something was wrong, she kept repeating. Of course, she was horrified to see Agnes standing quietly in the doorway, but as Ingibjörg had calmly pointed out, where else was Margrét supposed to put her?

The baby had been wayward. It was Agnes who had told them that, suddenly stepping forward to place her hands on Róslín's belly. Róslín had screamed, had demanded the others get Agnes off her, but neither Margrét nor Ingibjörg had moved. Even as Róslín batted at her hands and scratched her arms, Agnes had continued to gently press her thin fingers against the swollen round.

It's in breech, she had said. Róslín had groaned then, and stopped fighting. Agnes had not moved either, but told Róslín to lie down on the floor, and remained by her side throughout the ordeal. Margrét remembered how Agnes had not taken her hands off the woman. Throughout the whole birth she had stroked Róslín with those slender palms of hers, soothing her, telling the children to get out of the way, to fetch cloth, to boil water. She had one of them run back to Kornsá to fetch some of the wild angelica collected by the girls on their berrying trip. 'It's in a tray of sand in the pantry,' she had said, and Margrét had wondered at how Agnes seemed so familiar with her home. 'Don't bruise the root. Run back with a little handful.' She'd asked Ingibjörg to make a tea of the root, told her it would let it come more easily. When the hot liquid was brought to her lips, Róslín clenched her jaw, refused to drink it.

'It's not poison, Róslín,' Margrét had said. 'Save us the tantrum.' There had been a moment then. A shared look with Agnes. A quick, taut smile.

The baby had come in breech, like Agnes said. Legs first, bloody toes peeping through, then the body, and finally, the head, with the cord wound about its arm and neck. But it was alive, and that was all Róslín needed to know.

Agnes had refused to deliver it. She had asked Ingibjörg to help it into the world, and would not touch it, even later, when Róslín had fallen asleep, and the sound of the herded, bleating sheep began to resound throughout the valley. Margrét had thought it strange – the way Agnes would not cradle the newborn. What is it she had said? 'It ought to live.' As though it would die if Agnes took it into her arms.

There had been double cause to celebrate that evening. Snæbjörn was elated, plied with rum and brandy by the other farmers, so that when he climbed into the sorting pen to drag his sheep into his family's hold, he staggered and slipped in the mud, and received a sharp butt to the head from a ram. Margrét heard Páll tell the story to his recovering mother, brightly recalling how Snæbjörn had to be dragged out to lie on the grass while the others sorted the rest of the animals.

They hadn't eaten until late. Margrét's daughters had rescued what they could of the neglected cooking and served it to the ravenous workhands that night. 'It was snowing a little,' Steina said, after they had heard about Róslín's childbirth. She glanced over at Agnes. 'It must have been a good sign.'

'I did very little,' Agnes said. 'Ingibjörg delivered it.'

'No,' Margrét had corrected. 'That tea of angelica root – where did you learn such a thing?'

'It's common knowledge,' Agnes had murmured.

'Probably Natan,' Lauga suggested sourly.

Margrét wondered at how, even for an hour, Agnes had seemed part of the family. She'd found herself speaking with Agnes the following day, asking her about what dyes she was used to making, and they'd gone on like mistress and servant, until Lauga had come into the room and complained that she was sick of Agnes staring at her clothes and belongings. Lauga knew as well as Margrét that if Agnes were a thief, they would have noticed something missing by now. Not even the silver brooch had shifted from its place in the dust underneath the bed. Margrét briefly wondered if Lauga was jealous of Agnes, before putting the thought out of her mind. Why on earth would Lauga be envious of a woman who would be dead before the weather turned again? Yet, there was an intensity to her revulsion that seemed fired by something more than resentment.

Gently extracting her legs from under her husband's heavy weight, Margrét got out of bed, padded quietly to the window and peered through the dried skin. There was sleet outside. What a nuisance, she thought. Though the rams and milking sheep had been put to pasture in the cropped home field, the yearling lambs were still penned in. They were to begin the slaughter today.

Margrét thought back to when Agnes had first arrived at Kornsá. Some part of her had relished the tension between her family and the criminal, was greedy for it, even. It had unified them; made her feel closer to her daughters, her husband. But now she realised that their silence had shifted into something more natural and untroubled. Margrét worried at this. She was too used to Agnes's presence on the farm. Perhaps it was the usefulness of an extra pair of hands about the place. Having another woman's help had already eased the pain in her back, and her cough did not seem to interrupt her breath as frequently as it had done. She avoided thinking about what would happen when the day of execution was announced. No, it was better to not think of it at all, and if she was feeling more comfortable around the woman then it was because it was easier to get the work done. No point looking over one's shoulder when the task at hand was before you.

THERE IS AN URGENCY THAT comes with slaughter. The weather is bad, there is ice in the rain, and the wind is like a wolf nipping at your heels, reminding you that winter is coming. I feel as low as the dense snow clouds that are gathering.

No one wants to work into the night, and so we are all wrapped in layers, waiting outside in the October half-light, for the servants and Jón to catch the first sheep. They have kept aside as many animals as they think will keep us during the winter. Have they kept me amongst their number of mouths to feed? I fight an impulse to offer myself up to Jón and his knife. Why not kill me here, now, on an unremarkable day? It is the waiting that cripples. The sheep scavenge for what grass hasn't been blistered brown by the weather. Do these dumb animals know their fate? Rounded up and separated, they only have to wait one icy night in fear. I have been in the killing pen for months.

Gudmundur catches the first sheep, kneeling on it to fix its head still. I don't like him, but he is efficient – the throat is slit through to the spinal cord, and he is so quick with the pail that hardly a drop is spilled. Only a few minutes and all the blood is let. I step forward to take the pail from him, but he ignores me and hands it to Lauga. Never mind. Ignore him, too. I wait for a pail of blood from Jón, who has heaved his slaughtered ewe over the pen to better catch the red flow. There is always more blood than expected, and it always leaps in a direction unpredicted. Some of the blood spills onto the muddy ground, and into the grey wool of the animal, but soon the pail is full.

I return inside where Margrét has banked up the fire with dung and peat. My eyes water from the smoke, and Margrét coughs in the haze, but as she reminds me, we'll have no cause for complaint when we eat the smoked meat we'll string up over the rafters. I put my blood down and return outside.

We wait until the sheep are skinned. Bjarni's ewe is still bleeding out – he lacks the technique for good slaughter. Gudmundur is nimble with a knife, however. He reminds me of Fridrik, who came to help with the killing at Illugastadir before he and Natan dropped all pretence of friendship. Fridrik always seemed a little too keen to rip the animal apart – a little too quick with the blade. Jón is slower, but more careful. He begins skinning from the back hocks, and breaks the joint in the hind legs without any sinew left to cut. Gudmundur skins as much as he can down the shoulders, but struggles to pull the skin off the brisket, and Jón asks Bjarni to help him. Together they haul the sheep onto the wall, where the rest of the skin is punched out from the carcass and finally pulled off. Bjarni has made a mess of it. I wish I could step in to show him how it's done. Imagine their faces if I stepped forward and requested a knife.

We take the pluck of heart, lungs and oesophagus, and the intestines and the stomach, as the carcass is gutted.

That autumn at Illugastadir, Natan nicked the gall bladder of a sheep. The bitter liquid spilled onto the meat, and Fridrik howled with laughter. 'You pretend to be a doctor,' he said to Natan. Strange, how these moments come back to me now.

With the offal in our pails, we leave the men to cut the flesh into portions and hang it, and return to the kitchen. Some of the smoke has cleared now, and the fire is high. Margrét has set a pot of water upon the hearth to boil, and all of us begin work on the sausage. Even Lauga helps by straining the blood through a cloth. She flinches as flecks hit her face as it slops. I go outside to collect the stomachs for the sausage, and when I return the air inside the croft is thick with the animal smell of boiling fat and kidneys, frying for the men's breakfast. Margrét has placed some suet into another pot and covered it with water to simmer. Kristín, Margrét, Steina and I stitch the stomachs into bags, leaving a small hole for the stuffing. When Lauga has finished straining the blood I stir in the rest of the suet and the rye flour, and I suggest we stir in some lichen as well, as we used to do at Geitaskard. When Margrét agrees, and sends Lauga down to the storeroom to get it, I feel a swell of happiness murmur throughout my heart. This is my life as it used to be: up to my elbows in the guts of things, working towards a kind of survival. The girls chatter and laugh as they stuff the bags with the bloody mix. I can forget who I am.

The suet renders quickly. Three of us drag the pot from the fire to leave it to cool, until we can break the lid of tallow hiding the liquid beneath.

The men come in to eat the kidneys, stinking of shit and wet wool. I think the servants look at us women, dropping bags of blood sausage into a pot of boiling water in the smoky, warm kitchen, with envy. When I serve Jón his food he looks me in the eyes for the first time. 'Thank you, Agnes,' he says quietly. It is because of Róslín's baby – I am sure of it. He sees me differently now.

The men have finished eating, and they leave to fetch the first cuts of meat. I start to measure out the saltpetre and mix it with salt. It reminds me of when I used to help Natan in his workshop: measuring out sulphur, dried leaves, crushed seeds. I have been thinking of Illugastadir a lot today. The slaughter in the only autumn I ever spent there. I enjoyed putting provisions aside for the winter. Things we would eat later, that would sustain Natan on his long trips. He stood against the kitchen doorframe as I mixed the meal through the blood that day, reading to me from the sagas, and telling me of his time in Copenhagen, where the *blodpølse* was spiced and speckled with a type of dried fruit. Then Fridrik and Sigga burst into the room giggling together, with pails of guts from the slaughter yard, snow in their hair, and Natan left me for his workshop.

My fingers sting as I press layer after layer of salted meat into the wooden drum. A pink crust crackles in between my fingers, and my back aches from bending into the barrel. Steina watches me, asking how much water to sprinkle over each layer, remarks on the way her fingertips pucker from the salt. She licks her skin, wrinkles her nose at the taste. 'I don't see why we can't store it all in whey. Salt is so expensive,' she says.

'It suits the foreign tongue,' I reply. This barrel is to be traded for goods. The fattier meat we will store in whey, will keep for the family.

'Is salt fetched from the sea?'

'Why do you ask me so many questions, Steina?'

The girl pauses, her cheeks pink. 'Because you give me answers,' she mumbles.

Next are the bones, and the heads. I ask Lauga to empty the tallow pot of gristle and water, but she pretends she cannot hear me and keeps her eyes fixed ahead of her. Kristín goes instead. When Steina sidles up to me again, smiling shyly, wondering if there is anything I need doing, I ask her to fill the emptied pot with the bones that cannot be used for anything else. Salt. Barley. Water. Steina and I haul the pot next to the poaching blood sausage, for the marrow to leach into the simmering water, for the salt and heat to prise away all the tenderness from the carcass. She claps her hands when we fix the slopping pot upon the hook and immediately begins to throw more fuel on the fire.

'Not too much, Steina,' I say. 'Don't cover the coals.'

The sheep-heads I hold close to the embers of the hearth to singe away all the hair. The burning wool does not catch, but shrivels at the lick of flame, and I feel my nostrils flare in the rising stink of it.

Oh, God. The smell.

The badstofa in Illugastadir. The whale fat smeared on the wood and the beds, and then the flame from the lamp smoking on the greasy, woollen blankets. Burning hair.

I can't do it; I need fresh air. Oh God!

Don't let them see how it upsets you. I give the heads to Steina, let her do it. I need fresh air. I tell Steina it is the smoke.

Outside the drizzle settles on my face like a blessing. But the stench of scorched wool and burnt hair remains in my nostrils, acrid, sickening me to my core.

It is Margrét who finds me, squatting in the dark with my head on my knees. I wait for her to berate me. What are you doing, Agnes? Get inside. Do as you're told. How dare you leave Steina to do it all herself. She's burnt the meat beyond recognition.

But Margrét remains silent. She eases herself down next to me and I hear her knees crack.

'How quickly the light leaves now.' Is that all she is going to say?

She's right. The blue eventide seems to have crept up from the dark intestine of the river in front of us.

The smell of things always seems stronger at night, and sitting here I am aware of the odour of the kitchen on Margrét. Blood sausage. Smoke. Brine. She is breathing heavily, and in the silence of the evening I can hear a catch in her lungs; the grip of something upon her breath.

'I needed some air,' I say.

Margrét gives a sigh, clears her throat. 'No one ever died from fresh air.'

We sit and listen to the faint rush of the river. The drizzle ceases. Snow begins to fall.

'Let's see what those girls are doing now,' Margrét says eventually. 'I won't be surprised if Steina has strung herself up on the rafters, instead of the meat. We might discover her smoked through.'

A soft thud sounds from the smithy. The men must be spreading the sheepskins out to dry.

'Come, Agnes. You'll catch your death.'

Looking down, I see that Margrét has extended her hand. I take it, and the feel of her skin is like paper. We go inside.

THE FIRE IN THE KITCHEN had collapsed into a pile of whispering embers, and night had fallen thick upon the spilt blood in the stocks outside, by the time Lauga, with swollen fingers, tied the last wet bag of sausage to a string to hang and dry. Steina, her apron covered in smears from offal and blood, leaned against the doorframe and watched her sister.

'It's snowing outside,' she said.

Lauga shrugged.

'Everyone's gone to bed.' She sniffed. 'Smells nice in here, don't you think?'

'I don't know when killing ever smelt nice.' Lauga bent down and picked up the pails that had held the sheep entrails.

'Oh, leave them to dry out. We'll set to washing them in the morning.' Steina walked over to her sister and pulled a stool out in front of the fire. 'Did you see how Agnes set the meat in store? I've never seen anyone work so fast.'

Lauga stacked the pails against the wall and sat down beside Steina, holding her hands out to the hot ashes. 'She's probably poisoned the whole barrel.'

Steina pulled a face. 'She wouldn't do such a thing. Not to us.' She sucked a corner of her apron and began to sponge at the stains covering her hands. 'I wonder what gave her that funny turn.'

'What turn?'

'Agnes and I were sitting here, as we are now, tending to the heads, and all of a sudden she throws them in my lap, and off she goes, muttering to herself. Mamma followed her out, and I saw the two of them sitting there, talking. Then they came back inside.'

Lauga frowned and stood up.

'It's funny,' Steina continued. 'For all she says, I think Mamma holds a fondness for her now.'

'Steina,' Lauga warned.

'She'd never say as much, but –'

'Steina! In heaven's name, must you always talk about Agnes?'

Steina looked up at her sister, surprised. 'What's wrong with talking about Agnes?'

Lauga scoffed. 'What's wrong? Am I the only person who sees her for who she is?' Her voice dropped to a hissed whisper. 'You talk about her as if she's nothing. As if she's a servant.'

'Oh, Lauga. I wish you'd –'

'You wish I'd do what? What! *Make friends* like the rest of you?'

Steina gaped at her sister, open-mouthed. Lauga suddenly walked to the back of the kitchen and pressed her hands, clenched in two fists, against her forehead.

'Lauga?'

Her sister didn't turn around, but slowly picked up the soiled buckets. 'I'm going to go wash these.' Her voice was unsteady. 'You should go to bed, Steina.'

'Lauga?' Steina rose and took a few steps towards her. 'What's the matter?'

'Nothing. Just go to bed, Steina. Leave me alone.'

'Not until you tell me what I've done to upset you.'

Lauga shook her head, her face contorting. 'I thought it would be different,' she said finally. 'When Blöndal came, I thought we might not suffer her too much because there'd be officers. I thought we would keep her locked up! I didn't think she'd always be with us, talking to the Reverend in our badstofa. Now I see that even *Mamma* is talking to her in a familiar way! No one seems to care that everyone in the valley gives us strange looks now.'

'They don't. No one minds us.'

Lauga narrowed her eyes and dropped the buckets by her feet. 'Oh, they do, Steina. You don't see it, but we're all marked now. And it does us no favours that they see us talking to her, giving her plenty to eat. We'll never be married.'

'You don't know that.' Steina eased herself down on the stool by the hearth. 'It's not forever,' she said finally.

'I can't wait till she's gone.'

'How can you say such a thing?'

Lauga gave a shuddering breath. 'Everyone sees the Reverend gadding about Agnes like some besotted boy, and even Pabbi nods and says good morning to her now, ever since she witched Róslín's baby from her. And you, Steina!' Lauga turned to her sister, her face incredulous. 'You treat her like a sister more than you do me!'

'That's not true.'

'It is. You follow her around. You help her. You want her to *like* you.'

Steina took a deep breath. 'I ... It's only that I remember her from years ago. And I can't stop thinking that she wasn't always like this. She was our age, once. She has a mother and father, like us.'

'No,' hissed Lauga. 'Not like us. She's nothing like us. She's come here and no one even sees how everything has changed. And not for the better, either.' She bent down and picked up the bloody pails and stalked out of the room.

IT HAD BEGUN TO SNOW most days in the north. Breidabólstadur was clouded in a thick fog and a cold that refused to lift, even as the October sun brought what little light it could into the world. Despite the weather, Tóti was reluctant to stay at home with his father. He felt that some invisible membrane between Agnes and him had been broken. She had begun, finally, to speak of Natan, and the thought that she might draw him closer still, might trust him enough to speak of what had happened at Illugastadir, set something quickening in him.

As he carefully wrapped his shivering body in as many layers of woollen clothing as could be found in his trunk, Tóti thought again of their first meeting. He could vaguely recall the rushing water of Gönguskörd, the roar it made as the melting spring waters plunged across the pass. Could see the wet gravel shining under the sun. And ahead of him, bending by the edge of the water and unrolling her stockings, a dark-haired woman preparing to cross the current.

Tóti pulled on his gloves in the badstofa of Breidabólstadur and searched his mind for her face as he'd first seen it that day. The woman had squinted against the sun as she'd looked up at him, unsmiling. Her hair had been damp against her forehead and neck from walking. A white sack lay on the river stones beside her.

Then, the warmth of her body against his chest as they forded the foamy waters on his mare. The smell of sweat and wild grass issuing from the back of her neck. The thought of it ran through him like a fever.

'What's got you in such a hurry?'

Tóti looked up and saw his father regarding him from across the room.

'They're expecting me at Kornsá.'

Reverend Jón looked thoughtful. 'You spend a great deal of time there,' he mused.

'There is a great deal of work to be done.'

'I hear the District Officer has two daughters.'

'Yes. Sigurlaug and Steinvör.'

His father narrowed his eyes. 'Beauties, are they?'

Tóti looked puzzled. 'I'm sure some think so.' He turned to leave the room. 'Don't wait into the night for me.'

'Son!' Reverend Jón took a few steps towards the door and gave Tóti his New Testament. 'You forgot this.'

Tóti blushed, snatched the little book and thrust it in his coat.

Outside the Breidabólstadur croft, the cold stung Tóti's cheeks and set his ears aching. He struggled to breathe as he saddled his sleepy mare and turned her towards Kornsá. Even as the fog gave way to snow, shaking down flakes that tangled in his cob's mane, and Tóti felt his limbs grow sore from so long in the sharp air, he cast his mind back, again and again, to the woman he met by the Gönguskörd pass, and the memory warmed him to the bone.

'After the harvest celebration, I did not see Natan again for some time. Then one day I was in an outbuilding, cutting hung meat from a rafter. I was on the ladder, the knife in my hand, and I had paused to watch the blue November light outside. Then suddenly he was there, leaning in the doorway.'

Agnes shifted her position on the bed to get the most of the lamplight. Tóti glanced over at the rest of the Kornsá family, seated at the other end of the badstofa. Tóti suspected they were listening but Agnes seemed oblivious. It was as though she could not stop talking, even if she wanted to.

'I was so surprised to see him that I nearly fell off the ladder. The meat would have dropped in the dirt had Natan not caught it. He said he'd come to visit Worm, and that he'd been at Hvammur to heal Blöndal's wife, and did not see the point of returning home when there was nothing but work and the seals to greet him. That's what he said, anyway.

'I think I asked him how he liked Illugastadir, and he told me he was in need of more servants to help with the work. Natan said he had a workmaid but he told me she was soft in the head. Besides, she was very young, and Karitas, his housekeeper, was leaving for the Vatnsdalur valley next Flitting Days.

'We talked for some time then. I remember I asked him about his hollow palms, it being something we had spoken of on his first visit, and he laughed and said that they would soon be filled with money if Blöndal cared to see his wife alive at the end of winter.

'Then we walked back to the homestead, and some of the other servants working in the yard saw us. María was taking the ashes out, and when she saw Natan she stopped and stared. There is my friend, I said, but Natan ignored her. He began talking, saying how it was going to snow, he could feel it in his bones, and who was that? He was pointing at Sheepkiller-Pétur.'

'The other dead man?' Tóti asked.

Agnes inclined her head. 'His name was Pétur Jónsson. He'd been sent to stay at Geitaskard for the winter after being accused of the animal killings a few years ago. He was a strange sort of man. I didn't like him much. He had a habit of laughing when there was nothing to laugh at, and he would tell us servants about his nightmares, which made a lot of us uneasy.'

'Did he have foresight, too?'

Agnes hesitated, and glanced around at the others in the badstofa. When she spoke again it was in a hushed tone. 'Lots of people remember one dream Pétur told about at Geitaskard. He had it more than once, and it always gave me gooseflesh. He dreamt that he was walking in a valley when three of the sheep he had killed with Jón Arnarson came running up to him. He said that the flock was led by one of the ewes he had killed, and when the sheep reached him she vomited blood, splashing him. He laughed at this dream, but afterwards there were a number of people who saw something in it.'

'A prophecy? Did you tell Natan about Pétur's dream?'

'Yes. And then Natan told me about some of the strange dreams he'd had over his life. But they're not important now.'

'I know about Natan's dreams,' a breathless voice said from across the room. Agnes and Tóti looked around and saw Lauga observing them, a queer expression on her face.

'Lauga,' Margrét warned.

'Róslín told me about them, Mamma. I think you'd find them of interest.'

'We don't want to hear such things,' Jón said, slowly rising to his feet.

'No. Let her tell us about Natan Ketilsson's dreams,' Steina protested. 'If Lauga thinks she knows about them, I'm sure we'd all like to hear. Agnes included.'

Jón was thoughtful. 'Let Reverend Thorvardur speak with his charge without your interference.'

'My interference!' Lauga laughed and threw her knitting on her bed. 'How about *her* interference! She's in *our* home! Always breathing over my shoulder in the kitchen! Speaking lies in our badstofa!' Lauga turned to her parents. 'Mamma, Pabbi, forgive me, but you told Steina and I to close our ears to this woman. And now you let her spin stories not five feet away from us? "Oh, pity me, I'm a pauper!"'

'We can hardly send her and Reverend Tóti out into the snow,' Steina reasoned.

'Well then, Pabbi, if one of us may tell fairy stories at night, why not all of us?'

Margrét was stony-faced. 'Pick up your knitting, Lauga.'

'Yes, pick up your knitting, Lauga,' Steina scoffed.

'Enough of the both of you,' Margrét barked. 'Reverend Tóti, you should know that we cannot help but hear –'

'What did Róslín tell you about Natan's dreams, Lauga?' Agnes interrupted. She had stopped knitting and was looking at the sisters intently.

Everyone fell silent.

'Well,' Lauga murmured, clearing her throat. She threw a glance of uncertainty at Agnes, then looked over to her father, who lowered his eyes. 'Róslín said that Natan told lots of people about a dream he had where an evil spirit was stabbing him in the belly. And he had another where he dreamt he was in a graveyard. She told me that, in this dream, he saw a body, or a corpse or something in an open grave, and three lizards were eating it. Then a man appeared at his side, and when Natan asked him whose corpse it was, the man replied: "Do you not know your own body?"'

'Sweet Jesus,' Kristín murmured.

'What happened then?' Bjarni asked, from his bed.

Lauga shrugged. 'I suppose he woke up. But Róslín said that he told a lot of people about that dream, and they all agree that's what happened. She heard it from Ósk, who heard it from her brother, who heard it from Natan himself.'

Eyes shifted to Agnes. The woman looked thoughtful, and then swung her legs over the side of the bed to better face them all.

'He told me that he'd dreamt he saw his body in an open grave, and he saw his soul standing at the other end. Then his body called out to his soul, and sang the psalm from Bishop Stein.' Her voice cracked in the silence.

No one said anything. Tóti eventually cleared his throat.

'Agnes. Would you like to go on with your story? You were talking about Pétur.'

'Can I come closer to the lamplight?'

Jón glanced at Margrét, then at the rest of his family, and shook his head.

Margrét winced. 'Jón,' she whispered in a low voice. 'What harm can it do now?'

Tóti noticed him dart his eyes towards his daughters.

Margrét sighed. 'It's best if we all keep our place,' she said to Agnes. 'You've light enough for storytelling.'

A brief flicker of anger passed over Agnes's face, but when she resumed speaking it was in a soft voice.

'Pétur was infamous in Langidalur, and also in Vatnsdalur, as you'd know. No one trusts a man who has killed so many animals. I was surprised that Natan didn't recognise Pétur, back then at

Geitaskard, because I'd guessed that Natan knew all manner of men, and so I told him that Pétur was a criminal in custody, and that he had slit the throats of more than thirty sheep, and for the fun of it too, and that he might be sent to Copenhagen. Natan gave the man a long look, but said nothing more of it.'

'Perhaps he wanted to recruit him to steal some sheep,' Lauga said sharply.

'Perhaps,' Agnes returned, from her dark corner. She turned back to Tóti. 'That day I took Natan to Worm, and then joined María in the home field. When I told her that Natan had surprised me in the storeroom she asked me what he had wanted. I told her that he had come to Geitaskard to visit Worm. María took me by the hand then, and told me to be careful.'

'Why?' Kristín asked. Gudmundur guffawed from the shadows.

Agnes ignored them. 'I told her that I was a grown woman, with a head of my own. María said that that was what worried her.'

'Reverend,' Jón said suddenly. 'Perhaps it is best you speak together away from the family.'

'What's wrong with it, Pabbi? I want to hear what happened,' Steina said.

'Get into bed, Steina.'

'Excuse me, Jón,' Tóti interrupted. 'With respect, I am here to listen to Agnes tell me whatever she finds in her heart to tell me. As your wife and daughter have made abundantly clear, our close proximity means that our discussion cannot help but be heard by your family and servants.'

'Your discussion?' Gudmundur frowned. 'You let her talk to you as though she's telling a bedtime story.'

Before Tóti could think of what to say, Margrét interrupted.

'Shut your mouth, Gudmundur. Let Agnes talk to the Reverend. What difference does it make anyway, my Jón? Both of them know what happened, and what they didn't know before, Róslín has evidently poured into their ears since.'

'You have nothing to fear,' Tóti said.

'I hope that is the case,' Jón replied. He pinched his lips together and resumed fulling his sock.

Tóti turned to Agnes. 'Your friend. Why did she say this to you?'

'I thought she was jealous. She had so wanted to meet Natan in the first place. The thing was, we knew that he was in need of a housekeeper.'

'And what of that?' Tóti asked.

'A new position with a man never short of money? A better position, where you could be more than just a servant? Run a home and a farm and do as you please with no farm mistress to answer to?' Agnes glanced at Margrét.

'Go on, Agnes,' Margrét muttered.

'News of an opportunity like that doesn't stay hidden, Reverend. All the girls at Geitaskard knew that Natan Ketilsson was unmarried, in need of a housekeeper, and maybe more besides, and María was as keen to better herself as I was, Reverend.' She looked over to the others. 'I wanted Karitas's position more than anything. I didn't do myself any dishonour.'

Gudmundur snorted, and Agnes's eyes flashed.

'The truth is that Natan and I became friends because we were fond of speaking with one another. He came to Geitaskard every few weeks, and we would talk.' She glared at Lauga. 'He offered me friendship, and I was pleased to have it, for I had precious few friends about me. María soon ignored me, and the more Natan saw of me, the less inclined everyone else was to be friendly. But they were just servants.' She spat these words towards the farmhands slouching in the corner of the badstofa. 'Natan was a clever man, a doctor, and he knew arithmetic, and he was generous with his money. He healed more than one cough among the Geitaskard workmen that autumn, and were they grateful? Not at all. They knew he was oftentimes only visiting to see me, and they punished me for it. What fault was that of mine? When I told them that Natan had finally asked me to work for him at Illugastadir, I thought they might be pleased for me. But they accused me of bragging, and thinking myself better than the pauper I really was. And that winter brought a new kind of loneliness, and I was grateful for the diversion Natan brought. I was pleased I was leaving Geitaskard. My brother had gone. María had spurned me. I had nothing to keep me there.'

Agnes fell silent, and knitted furiously. Tóti noticed that Lauga and Gudmundur were exchanging small, furtive glances. There were several moments of uncomfortable silence, broken only by the click of knitting needles, and a muffled giggle from Kristín. Eventually, as the wind gathered force outside, Jón stood and suggested they go to sleep. Tóti, suddenly weary, took the offer of a spare bed. A malaise had crept over him while Agnes had told of Natan, and his throat felt tight and painful. As the lamp was extinguished, he wondered if he was right in letting her speak.

SOMETIMES, AFTER TALKING TO THE Reverend, my mouth aches. My tongue feels so tired; it slumps in my mouth like a dead bird, all damp feathers, in between the stones of my teeth.

What did I say to him? What did the others make of what I said? It doesn't matter. No one could understand what it was like to know Natan. In those early visits it was as though we were building something sacred. We'd place words carefully together, piling them upon one another, leaving no spaces. We each created towers, two beacons, the like of which are built along roads to guide the way when the weather comes down. We saw one another through the fog, the suffocating repetition of life.

At Geitaskard we walked in the evenings upon the snow, and it squeaked under our tread. Once, when I slipped on the ice, I grasped his arm and he lost his balance. We fell together, laughing, and on the ground he pushed me back so that we gazed up at the hazard of stars above us. He named the constellations for me.

'Do you think that's where we go when we die?' I asked.

'I don't believe in heaven,' Natan said.

I was shocked. 'How can you not believe in heaven?'

'It's a lie. Man has created God out of fear of dying.'

'How can you say such a thing?'

He turned his head, ice crystals caught in his hair. 'Agnes. Don't pretend you disagree. This is all there is and you know it. Life, here, in our veins. There is the snow, and the sky, and the stars and the things they tell us, and that's all. Everyone else – they're blind. They don't know if they're living or dead.'

'They're not so bad.'

'Agnes. You pretend you don't understand me, but you do. We're the same kind.' Natan propped himself up on his elbows and the moonlight poured over his face. 'We're better than this.' He nodded towards the farmhouse. 'This life of mud and struggle. Accepting everything as it is.' He leaned closer and then he kissed me, gently. 'You don't belong in this valley, Agnes. You're different. You're not scared of everything.'

I laughed. 'I'm certainly not scared of you.'

Natan smiled. 'I've got a question for you.'

My heart throbbed. 'Oh yes? What's that?'

He lay back down on the snow. 'What's the name for the space between stars?'

'No such name.'

'Make one up.'

I thought about it. 'The soul asylum.'

'That's another way of saying heaven, Agnes.'

'No, Natan. It's not.'

It was only later that I suffocated under the weight of his arguments, and his darker thoughts articulated. It was only later that our tongues produced landslides, that we became caught in the cracks between what we said and what we meant, until we could not find each other, did not trust the words in our own mouths.

That night we went to the cowshed. I filled the hollow of his hands with my mouth, my breasts; I met his body against my own. His hands bunched the cloth of my skirt and lifted it up, and I felt the cool air address my skin. I was worried we would be discovered; worried they would call me a whore. Then there was the first touch of skin on skin, and that was the gunshot, the freefall. The bands of my stockings were loose about my knees as the softness of his hair caressed my neck.

I craved his weight, then. I craved the breath of him: the quickening inhalation and the warm pressure of his mouth. His smell, the slippery buck of his body, he was nothing like the others. I arched my neck until my face was wet with the drifting damp. I could feel him, the heat of him, the very quick of him. He groaned and the sound lingered in the air like a cloud of ash over a volcano.

I wanted to weep afterwards. It was too real. I felt too much to see it for what it was.

Natan smiled as he tucked his shirt in. His tousled hair was lit at the ends with tiny drops of water. He smoothed my cheek, asked me if he'd hurt me, if I had bled. Laughed when I told him no. Was he relieved? Annoyed?

'You don't have to go so soon.'

'Get up out of the straw, Agnes. Go to bed.'

'Will you come back?'

He came back. He returned to me again and again throughout that long winter. There were nights shivering in the powdery snow and evenings in the cowshed while the others slept. And though the snow smothered the valley and the milk froze in the dairy, my soul thawed. A fire raged in the wake of his lips, while the wind shrieked outside. When everything froze we met in the storeroom, with a constellation of drying meat above our heads. The smell of straw soaked us in the perfume of summer. I remember feeling too full with blood. The famous Natan Ketilsson, a man who could bleed the sap of sickness from the limbs of the ill, who had been with the famous Poet-Rósa, who had heard the bells of Copenhagen, and taught himself Latin – an extraordinary man, a saga man – had chosen me. For the first time in my life, someone *saw* me, and I loved him because he made me feel I was enough.

To think of how I slid my hand in through the folds of my skirt to find and press the bruises he left there, feeling the start of pain across my skin. Bruises as echoes of his touch, proof of his hands on mine, his hips against mine: the exultant exhalation, the clamber of our limbs in the dark. Throughout a dull-eyed cycle of work, nights slept alone, waking to nothing but chores, chores, those hidden bruises suggested something more – an end to the stifling ordinariness of existence.

I hated it when they faded. They were all I had of his to keep for myself until he came again. All those weeks, all those nights, I was rotted through with hunger. In the cowshed, my head hard against the floor, Natan broke the very yolk of my soul. I concealed my true feelings from the servants. All that willpower to contain that which I wanted to cry into the wind, and scratch into the dirt, and burn into the grass.

We had agreed that I would come live with him. He would haul me out of the valley, out of the husk of my miserable, loveless life, and everything would be new. He would give me springtime.

And all that while, there was Sigga.

CHAPTER NINE

Handar-vagna-Freyjum fljóð
Flytur sagnir ljóða.
Kennd við Magnús, blessað blóð,
Búrfells-Agnes góða.

Leading the way for women
A poet, named for Magnús.
His blessed blood flows in her veins:
The good Búrfell-Agnes.

Anonymous, c. 1825.

'**HAVE YOU EVER BEEN TO** Illugastadir, Reverend?'

Tóti shook his head. 'I don't have much need to travel north of Breidabólstadur.'

The next day had broken in the embrace of more wet and snowy weather, and Margrét had persuaded Tóti to delay his return home until the skies cleared. He was relieved. His dreams had been troubled, and he had woken with an aching head.

With the sheep rounded up, slaughter done, and the hay brought home, the household of Kornsá was spending the day indoors, attending to spinning, knitting and rope-making.

Agnes was sitting on her bed, trying to find stitches Steina had lost on a mitten. 'Illugastadir is almost on the edge of the world,' she said, inclining her head, as though to point out where the farm stood. 'I didn't know the way, and everyone had been telling me how lonely it would be, how it was nothing like the valley, where there are folk you know wherever you look. But I wanted to work for Natan.'

'When did you go there?'

'As soon as I was able. The Flitting Days, at the end of May.'

'What year was this?' Tóti asked.

'1827. I saw through Yuletide and the new year at Geitaskard, and then waited for the Golden Plover to arrive and sing the snow away. I packed up my possessions, and set off on foot. There were lots of servants moving up and down the valley, but no one was going to Vatnsnes, and no one was headed to Illugastadir. As I started walking northwards on the peninsula a fog came down and I was worried I would be lost. But I could hear the sea in the distance, and I knew I was going in the right direction. When the fog cleared I saw that I wasn't far from the church of Tjörn. I asked to sleep the night there and the next day the priest gave me directions to Illugastadir.

'It didn't take me long to reach the farm from Tjörn. That morning was the first time I had ever seen sea so wide and far. The wind was coming from the north, blowing spray off the waves that scudded against the shore, and there were hundreds of seabirds screaming in circles above the surface. I could even see the west fjords over the grey swell of water. Like a shadow of themselves.

'It made an impression. The priest from Tjörn had told me to watch for a croft by a rocky bay, and I soon came across this very place. There was a little boat upon the shore, and bedclothes tied to fish-drying racks, which were waving madly about in the wind. At the time I took it as a good sign; I thought it seemed that they were waving to me in welcome.

'I hadn't gone very far down the slope when someone appeared out of the croft, and started to trip up the hill. As the figure grew closer I saw that it was a young girl, no more than fifteen winters old. She was waving at me, and seemed exhilarated. When I came within speaking distance she cried out a welcome, and ran towards me. She seemed even younger as she drew closer, Reverend. She had a snub-nose and very red lips, and her hair was fair and tangled in the wind. She was too pretty for a peasant girl, and I remember wondering whether she was some daughter of Natan's. Her clothes were too fine for her to be a servant.

'The girl took my sack of belongings and kissed me. She asked if I was Agnes Magnúsdóttir, and she introduced herself as Sigrídur, but said that everyone called her Sigga.'

'This was the girl-servant Natan had mentioned to you at Geitaskard?'

Agnes nodded. 'Sigga exclaimed she'd been expecting me all week, and was I hungry, and had I come very far, and wasn't I frightened of highwaymen or outlaws, walking alone on the mountain paths. She spoke so fast that I barely had time to provide her with answers, and before I knew it she had ushered me inside and showed me my bed, which she had only made up that morning. The badstofa was very small, with only four bunks, and no space to speak of. There was a tiny window over one of the beds, but I supposed that Sigga had taken that bunk for herself. Illugastadir was more cramped and dirtier than I'd imagined. But I reassured myself that it was better to be mistress of a croft than a servant in the home of the governor. Sigga said that she would give me some time to arrange my things about my bed, and went and made coffee for us. When I told her she needn't go to any expense, that whey and water would be plenty, she smiled and assured me that Natan was fond of coffee and that they drank it at all hours. It seemed a great luxury to me.

'I waited until Sigga had left the room before looking at my surroundings. Only two beds were made up – hers and mine – and I wondered where Natan slept, and if there was a loft I hadn't noticed.

'When Sigga returned, I asked her where Natan was. I'd expected him to be there to greet me. Sigga looked embarrassed and blushed, and said that Natan was out.

'It was a Sunday, so I asked if Natan was at church, but Sigga shook her head. Natan was not a church-going man. She said that he was the only man she'd ever known who refused to read the evening blessings, and said that if I had a book of psalms I should hide it under my pillow otherwise Natan might kindle the hearth with it.

No, Natan was fox-hunting on the mountain, she said, but she would show me the farm in his place.

'I can't remember what my first impression of the farm was, Reverend. I was tired from my journey and overwhelmed from seeing so much water on the horizon. But I can certainly tell you what Illugastadir is like after spending a year or so trapped upon that corner of God's earth.'

'I should like to hear you describe it,' Tóti prompted.

'It's not much more than the base of the mountain, and the shore of the sea. It's a long line of rocky ground, with one or two smooth fields where winter fodder is grown, and all the rest is wild grass, growing around the stones. The shore is of pebbles, and huge tangles of seaweed float in the bay and look like the hair of the drowned. Driftwood appears overnight like magic, and eider ducks nest upon nearby banks of rocks near seal colonies. On a clear day it's beautiful, and on others it's as miserable as grave-digging in the rain. Sea fog plagues the place, and the nearest farm is Stapar, which is a fair distance away.

'There are several stony skerries of land that reach a little way out into the fjord, and on one of these is Natan's workshop. You have to walk out over a narrow bed of rocks to reach it. I remember thinking it was a strange place to build a workshop, away from the croft and surrounded by water, but Natan planned it thus. Even the window of the cottage looked inland, rather than out to sea, because Natan wanted to observe who might be travelling along the mountain. He had some enemies.

'Sigga said that she didn't know where the key to his workshop was kept, but that the little hut was where he had his smithy, and where he made his medicines, and that he probably kept a lot of money in there. She told me this with a wild sort of giggle, and I remember thinking her as daft as Natan had told me she was.

'Sigga told me that Natan went seal-clubbing, and there'd be seal leather shoes if I wanted them, and that they had eiderdown mattresses just like all the District Commissioners of Iceland, and that I would sleep like the dead, they were so soft. Sigga said she'd grown up at Stóra-Borg, but that her mother was no longer living, and she was new to service and had not been a housekeeper before, but that Natan had spoken highly of me and she hoped I would teach her.

'I was surprised to hear her call herself a housekeeper. I said: "Oh, you are the mistress here? Did you take Karitas's position?" And she nodded and said yes, she'd been working as a simple maidservant before, but when Karitas gave her notice Natan had asked her to be his housekeeper. She *thanked* me then for coming to be *her* servant, and she took me by the arm and said that we must get along well, for Natan was often away, and she grew lonely.

'I thought there must have been a mistake. I thought that perhaps Natan had only asked her to be his housemistress until I arrived, or perhaps she was a liar. I didn't think that Natan would lie to me.

'We had some coffee then, and I told Sigga a little of where I'd worked before. I was careful to mention the number of farms I had lived in and Sigga seemed quite impressed, and kept saying how pleased she was to have me at Illugastadir to help her, and would I teach her how to make such a patterned shawl as I was wearing, so that all in all, I grew more easy.

'Soon our conversation turned to Natan again, and Sigga said that she expected him after dinner. But he didn't come home until it was late.'

'Did you ask him about your position then?' Tóti asked.

Agnes shook her head. 'I was asleep when he came in.'

PERHAPS IT WAS THAT FIRST morning at Illugastadir when I understood the nature of things. Perhaps not.

I woke late to the plaintive shrieks of the gulls and stepped outside to see Natan walking down to the stream. Down by the shore, his bedclothes still flapped in the breeze. I thought, then, he had only returned that morning.

Even when Sigga later told me he had returned at midnight with two fox pelts slung over his shoulder, I did not think to ask what bed he had passed the rest of the night in.

✝

'I WAS SO PLEASED TO see Natan that morning that I forgot to ask him why Sigga thought herself the mistress of Illugastadir. It wasn't until later that day, when I was following Natan across the rocks to his workshop, that I raised the matter with him.

'I didn't want to seem rude, so I only asked, very casually, how he liked having Sigga as a housekeeper. But Natan, as always, saw through my questioning. He stopped and raised his eyebrows.

'"She's not my housekeeper," he said.

'I was relieved to hear him say so, but explained that when I arrived Sigga had told me she'd taken Karitas's position.

'Natan laughed and shook his head, and reminded me that he'd warned of how young and simple she was. And then he opened the lock to his workshop, and we stepped inside. I'd never seen a room like it. There was the usual anvil, bellows and so on, but also big bunches of dried flowers and herbs along the walls, and jars filled with liquids, some cloudy, some light. There was a large pail of what looked like fat, and needles and scalpels and a glass jar that held a small animal, all pale and puckered like a boiled stomach.'

'How horrible,' Steina murmured from the other side of the badstofa. Agnes looked up from the mitten, as though she had forgotten the family was there.

A sudden knocking could be heard from the farm entrance.

'Lauga,' Margrét said. 'Will you go and see who that is?' Her daughter went to answer the door. She soon returned with an old man brushing snow off his shoulders. It was the Reverend Pétur Bjarnason from Undirfell.

'Greetings to all in God's name,' the man grumbled, wiping his glasses on his inner shirt. He was breathing heavily from his walk in the ice and wind. 'I've come to enter you all into the soul register of Undirfell's parish,' the man intoned. 'Oh, hello, Assistant Reverend Thorvardur. Still in the valley, I see. Oh, of course. Blöndal's got you ...'

'This is Agnes,' Tóti interrupted. Agnes stepped forward.

'I am Agnes Jónsdóttir,' she said. 'And I am a prisoner.'

Margrét immediately stood up in surprise, looking over to Jón, who sat on their bed, his mouth open in horror.

'What?! She isn't our –' Lauga began, but Tóti cut her off.

'Agnes Jónsdóttir is my spiritual charge. As I told you before.' He was aware of the family gaping at him, stunned that he would agree to such a name. There was a long moment of awkward silence.

'Duly noted.' Reverend Pétur sat down on a stool under the flickering lamp, and took a heavy book out from under his coat. 'And how is the family of Kornsá? Slaughter finished?'

Margrét stared at Tóti strangely, then slowly sat back down. 'Uh, yes. Just the manure to spread over the *tún*, and then we'll be making woollen goods for trade.'

The old priest nodded. 'An industrious family. District Officer Jón, if you could please speak with me first?'

The priest conversed with each family member, one by one, examining their reading skills and ability to recite catechisms. He also asked them questions to ascertain the characters of those they lived with. After all the servants had had their time with the priest,

Agnes was summoned. Tóti tried to listen to their conversation, but Kristín, relieved her reading test was over, had collapsed into giggles with Bjarni, and he couldn't hear anything over their laughter. The priest did not take long with Agnes, but soon gave her a nod.

'I thank you all for your time. Perhaps I'll see you at a service soon,' Reverend Pétur said.

'Won't you stay for coffee?' Lauga asked, curtseying prettily.

'Thank you, my dear, but I have the rest of the valley to see, and this weather's only going to get worse.' He set his hat atop his head and carefully bundled the book back inside his thick coat.

'I'll see you out,' Tóti said, before Lauga could offer.

In the corridor, Tóti asked the priest what he had recorded about Agnes.

'Why do you want to know?' the man asked, curious.

'She's my charge,' he said. 'It is my responsibility to know how she behaves. How well she reads. I am invested in her welfare.'

'Very well.' The priest took the ministerial book out of his coat again and flicked to the new pages. 'You may read it for yourself.'

Tóti brought the book over to a candle bracketed into the wall of the corridor and squinted in its dim light until he made out the words: Agnes Jónsdóttir. A condemned person. *Sakapersona*. 34 years old.

'She reads very well,' the priest offered, as he waited for Tóti to finish.

'What is this you have written about her character?' He could hardly make out the words, his eyes swimming in the gloom.

'Oh, that says *blendin*, Reverend. Mixed.'

'And how did you arrive at that answer?'

'It was the opinion of the District Officer. And his wife.'

'What was your opinion of Agnes, Reverend?'

The old man tucked the book back into his coat and shrugged. 'Very well-spoken. Educated, I should think. Surprising, considering her illegitimacy. Well brought up. But when I spoke to the District Officer, he said her behaviour was ... Unpredictable. He mentioned hysterics.'

'Agnes is facing a death sentence,' Tóti said.

'I'm aware,' the priest retorted, opening the door. 'Good day, Reverend Thorvardur. I wish you the best.'

'And I you,' Tóti mumbled, as the door slammed in his face.

✝

AGNES JÓNSDÓTTIR. I NEVER THOUGHT it could be that easy to name yourself. The daughter of Jón Bjarnasson of Brekkukot, not the servant Magnús Magnússon. Let everyone know whose bastard I truly am.

Agnes Jónsdóttir. She sounds like the woman I should have been. A housekeeper in a croft that overlooks the valley, with a husband by her side, and a kip of children to help sing home the sheep at twilight. To teach and frighten with stories of ghosts. To love. She could even be the sister of Sigurlaug and Steinvör Jónsdóttir. Margrét's daughter. Born blessed under a marriage. Born into a family that would not be ripped apart by poverty.

Agnes Jónsdóttir would not have been so foolish as to love a man who spent his life opening veins, mouths, legs. A man who was paid to draw blood. She would have been a grandmother. She would have had a host of faces to gather round her bed as she lay dying. She would have been assured of a place in heaven. She would have believed in heaven.

It is almost impossible to believe I was happy at Illugastadir, but I must have been, once. I was happy that first day, when Natan and I stayed in his workshop all afternoon. He showed me the two fox pelts. They were drying inside, the sea air too damp that morning for them to hang with the fish.

He took my hands and ran them over the white fox fur.

'Feel that? These will fetch a pretty penny at Reykjavík this summer.'

He told me how he caught the foxes up in the mountains. 'The trick is to find and catch a fox kit,' he said. 'The kit must then be made to cry out to its parents, otherwise it's near impossible to lure them out of their hole. They're wily things. Cunning. They smell you coming.'

'And how do you make a fox kit cry?'

'I break its front legs. They cannot escape then. The parents hear it mewling and come running out of their den, and they're easily caught. They won't leave one of their own.'

'What do you do with the kit after you kill its parents?'

'Some hunters leave it there to die. They are no use for market – the skins are too small.'

'What do you do?'

'I stove their heads in with a rock.'

'That is the only decent thing to do.'

'Yes. To leave them is cruelty.'

He showed me his books. He thought I might like them. 'Sigga does not care for words,' he said. 'She is a terrible reader. It's like trying to make a cow talk.'

I ran my fingers over the sheets of paper and tried to read the new words they offered.

'Cutaneous diseases.' He corrected my awkward tongue. 'Cochlearia officinalis.'

'Say it again.'

'Cetraria islandica. Angelica archangelica. Achilla millefolium. Rumex digynus.'

It was a language I didn't understand, so I stopped his laughs with kisses, and felt his tongue press lightly against my own. What did all these words mean? Were they the names of the things in his workshop? In the jars and bottles and clay pots? Natan kissed my neck and my thoughts were lost in a rising swarm of lust. He lifted me onto the table, and we fumbled with our clothes before he pushed himself inside me, before I knew what we were doing, before I was ready. I gasped. I felt the papers beneath me, and imagined the words lifting from the page and sinking into my skin. My legs were tight around him, and I felt the cold sea air grasp me about the throat.

Later, I stood naked, my hips pressed against the edge of his table. Natan's books lay in front of me, the papers were wrinkled, showed eddies of our love.

'Look at all this illness, Natan. Books and books of disease and horror.'

'Agnes.'

He said my name softly, letting the 's' carry over his tongue, as though tasting it.

'Natan. If there is so much illness in the world ... if there is so much that can go wrong with a person, how is it that any of us remain alive?'

Sigga must have known about us. Those first nights at Illugastadir we waited until she fell asleep. I'd hear Natan's careful tread on the floorboards of the badstofa, and feel the gentle tug of blankets. I tried so hard to be quiet. We knotted ourselves together as though we should never become undone, but the first bar of morning light that came through the window severed our trysts as though it were a knife.

He always returned to his own bed before Sigga awoke.

AGNES SEEMED TO BE LOST in thought. It wasn't until Tóti gently put a hand on her shoulder that she gave a start and noticed he had come back into the room.

'I'm sorry to startle you,' he said.

'Oh no,' Agnes replied, a little breathlessly. 'I was only counting stitches.'

'Shall we continue?' he asked.

'What was I saying?'

'You were telling me about your first day at Illugastadir.'

'Oh, yes. Natan was glad to see me, and made sure I was settled, and he told me stories about the folk and farms about the place. Nothing very remarkable occurred in those first few weeks. I worked every day with Sigga from dawn to dusk, and we'd spend each night together telling stories, or laughing at one thing or another. All in all, my time at Illugastadir for the first few months was a happy one. Sigga told me that it was unusual for Natan to spend as much time at home as he had been doing, and I thought it was my company that kept him with us. He spent most days out in his workshop, preferring to tinker and mend tools than actually tend the farm. He would rather hire men to come and see to the grass, or horses, than do it himself. Not that he was lazy. He showed me how he let blood, and told me about all the diseases that could befall a person. I think he was glad to have someone interested in his work; Sigga was pretty, and good at laundry, and she had a deft hand with a gutting knife and cleaned the fish we caught, but she did not care for what Natan called the things of the intellect. I was allowed to read as much as I wanted, and to discover something of the study of science. Do you know, Reverend, that it is necessary for someone with spots on their legs and bleeding gums to eat cabbages?'

Tóti smiled. 'No, I didn't.'

'I thought he was making fun at first, but I saw with my own eyes how something as simple as a tea made from leaves, or a poultice from lard and sulphur, or gum squeezed out of roots, or even a cabbage, could heal a person.

'I thought it was sheer good fortune, moving to Illugastadir. Natan made me new shoes from sealskin, and gave me a shawl, and there were as many duck eggs as you could fit in your stomach. When he did leave the farm, he always returned with gifts for Sigga and me. That was why I had thought Sigga his daughter when I first saw her. Natan kept her well dressed, and when I arrived, he gave me gifts too. Lace, and silk, and a little handkerchief he said had come all the way from France. It seemed a luxurious existence, despite the isolation, despite the close, cramped quarters. We did not often have visitors. But I had Natan, and Sigga wasn't too insufferable.' Agnes lowered her voice. 'Have you seen her, Reverend? Has she been granted her appeal?'

Tóti shook his head slowly. 'I don't know yet.'

Agnes was thoughtful. 'She has probably changed. She's probably as pious as they come now. But at Illugastadir she had a saucy little manner when it suited her. She was forever speculating about folks, and Natan would ask her who she thought should marry whom, and what their children would look like and so forth. It was harmless sport for him; he found her simplicity amusing. I didn't even mind it when Sigga kept calling herself the housekeeper, or ordered me to do the tasks she ought to have been doing herself – emptying the chamber pot, mucking out the cowshed, drying the fish Natan caught. She was, like Natan said, only a child, with a child's way of thinking.

'Fridrik Sigurdsson visited Illugastadir soon after I arrived. I'd never met him before, but Sigga had told me about him, and she'd said that he and Natan were acquaintances of sorts. She was always as pink as a skinned lamb when she spoke of him. But Fridrik unsettled me. There was something off-balance in Fridrik. And Natan, too. They both got into moods and the feel of a room would fall from high spirits to a glowering in an instant. It was contagious, too. With them you'd feel every small injustice done against you like a thorn in your side. Fridrik, I thought, was a daring sort of boy, desperate to prove himself a man. He was easily offended. I suppose he thought the world against him, and raged at it. I did not like that in him, the way he looked for a reason to anger. He liked to fight. Liked to keep his knuckles bruised.

'Natan was different. He did not think he had to prove himself to anyone. But superstitious signs troubled him. And, what I admired in him, his way of seeing the world, and yearning for knowledge, and his easy way with those he liked, had a darker underbelly. It was a matter of enjoying the bright skies all the more, so as to endure the sloughs when they came.'

Agnes paused as Tóti grimaced, stroking his neck with his hand. 'Does something trouble you?' she asked.

The Reverend cleared his throat. 'The air is rather close in here, is all,' he said. 'Go on. I'll fetch some water in a little while.'

'You look pale.'

'It is only a slight chill from going to and fro in the weather.'

'Perhaps you ought not return to Breidabólstadur tonight.'

Tóti shook his head, smiling. 'I've felt worse,' he said. 'I didn't mean to interrupt you. Please go on.'

Agnes gave him a careful look, and then nodded. 'Well, then. The first time I met Fridrik Sigurdsson I was hauling water from the stream. I heard a shout, and saw a red-headed young man and his horse trotting along the mountain path. There was a woman also. Natan peered out of his workshop window at the noise, and didn't waste time stepping out and locking the door behind him. Not many folks visited Illugastadir, and Natan seemed to prefer it that way.

'Natan introduced the boy as Fridrik, and Fridrik told me he was the son of the farmer Sigurdur at Katadalur, a farm just up over the mountain. He said he'd been away for the winter, and then he introduced his companion, Thórunn, a servant woman with very bad teeth, who grinned at everyone. I noticed that Sigga was anxious when she first saw Thórunn. To tell you the truth, Reverend, I didn't like either of the pair on first meeting. I thought Fridrik a braggart and a show-off. He talked aimlessly, speaking of how he was going to make his father a rich man, and he'd fought three men in Vesturhóp and given them all black eyes and worse. All the dull lies you'd expect to hear from a boy of that age. I don't know why Natan bothered to listen to Fridrik's boasting – he didn't often care to hear that sort of thing, although he wasn't shy about trumpeting his own good fortune. But I supposed that he was a mentor to Fridrik, as he told me he was trying to be to Sigga.

'That day Natan invited Fridrik and Thórunn inside. I was not particularly interested in my new neighbours, but I gathered that Fridrik's family was quite poor. He gobbled down his fish like a starveling. I thought him an odd friend for Natan.

'When Fridrik left, Thórunn trailing like a puppy after him, Natan disappeared. When I found him again, I asked him where he'd been, and he smiled and said that he'd gone to check his belongings. When I asked him why, he told me that Fridrik had long fingers, and only ever called on him to try and discover where he kept his money.

'I asked Natan why on earth he let Fridrik step foot inside his house if that was the case, and Natan laughed and said he never kept his money in the croft anyway, and besides, he liked the game of it. Theirs was not a true friendship, but a strange rivalry with one another, borne out of boredom. Fridrik thought Natan rich and wanted to take a little of what he had, and Natan encouraged him for his own private amusement, knowing all the while that Fridrik would never find his money. At the time I told Natan I thought it dangerous to provoke a man like that, but Natan laughed and said Fridrik was hardly a man, only a foolhardy boy. But it troubled me. I argued that Fridrik was twice his size, and could easily overpower him if it came to it. Natan did not like that. We had our first row, then.'

'What did Natan say?'

'Oh, he grabbed me by the arm and pulled me outside and told me to never speak of him in that way in front of Sigga. I said that I'd only told the truth, and hadn't meant to embarrass him, and that Sigga only thought the best of him, as did I. This appeased him a little, but I was frightened at the way his mood changed so quickly. I learnt later that he was as changeable as the ocean, and God help you if you saw his expression shift and darken. One day he might call you friend, and the next threaten to throw you into the night if you so much as dropped a pail of water on the ground. As folks say, for every mountain there is a valley.'

'Perhaps if you'd known that you would never have agreed to be his servant?' Tóti suggested.

Agnes paused, and then shook her head. 'I wanted to leave Vatnsdalur,' she said quietly.

'Tell me about what Sigga is like,' Tóti suggested gently.

'Well, that night, after Fridrik's visit, Sigga began speaking of marriage. I asked her if she did not find Fridrik Sigurdsson a most attractive man with such inviting prospects. I was making fun, of course. Fridrik is freckled, and ginger-haired and as mottled as a sausage, and his family are so poor you might call them barrel-lickers. But when I asked Sigga this, her cheeks turned as bright as new blood, and she asked me if I thought Fridrik was engaged to that Thórunn. It was then that I knew she held some hope for him.

'I continued teasing Sigga. "Do you know how much hard work it is to get married?" I asked her. Sigga said: "The work can't be harder than this," and I laughed and told her I didn't mean farm work, but the work a maid like her had to do just for the privilege of giving her life away. I reminded her that the priest must give his permission, the District Officer must give his permission, the District Commissioner must also be on side, and then, Natan must be kept happy, for everyone looks to the master for the final word.

'"You need more than one man to say I do," I told her. Sigga took this news very badly. She grew pale when I mentioned that Natan must approve of any engagement, and didn't say anything more about the subject, not even when I tried to cheer her up by telling her what Natan had told me; about his little game with Fridrik.

'"Do you really think Fridrik is a thief?" she asked, and I said no, I was sure he was a most upstanding fellow.

'Natan laughed heartily when I told him about Sigga's reaction to the news that he would have to approve any wedding she had in mind. He said that it was a good thing she knew it. I told him that I thought Sigga was soft on Fridrik, and mentioned concern that Natan thought him a thief. Natan said that that is what happens when you put two creatures in a pen together, and we didn't speak any more of it at the time.

'This all happened around lambing season. The weather was clear, and Natan took the chance to earn money by travelling about the north, calling in on folks and selling his medicines. It happened that Natan was away when the lambing began at Illugastadir. When Sigga and I went outside to feed the cow, we saw that one of the ewes was birthing. Neither of us was strong enough to properly swing any lambs that might come out motionless, and we were worried that Natan would return in a few weeks and find his number of sheep not as high as expected. I told Sigga to run to a neighbour and ask for the loan of a workman, even though Natan had said to not let anyone onto his farm. Sigga fetched Fridrik.

'I was worried to admit him at first, given Natan's warning, but we needed the help and by the time he arrived more ewes had gone into labour. He was a true farmer's son, helping us pull the lambs, and swinging them about to get them breathing. When we discovered that one ewe had teats too thick to feed her young, Fridrik fashioned a teat from odds and ends we had about the place and let us feed them ourselves. I liked him a little better after that, but I still wouldn't let him sleep in the house. I made up a bed for him in the cowshed.

'Fridrik stayed with us for a week during lambing. I made sure he did not set a finger on anything in the house, for I noticed that Fridrik seemed fixed on naming the price of everything. He would calculate the worth of the lambs born, their mothers, the cow we had there, the land, even the silk ribbon Sigga wore in her hair. I put it down to his being brought up poor. Still, I kept my eyes close on his back, especially when I happened upon him digging holes by the front door of the croft. When I asked him what he was doing, he laughed and said it was naught, only he'd asked Natan to keep some money for him, and wouldn't it happen but that Natan had forgotten where it was buried and he'd never seen it again. I knew him to be lying. Fridrik Sigurdsson didn't have a coin to his name, and I knew Fridrik had been looking for Natan's money.

'Sigga seemed blind to the conniving character of the boy, though. That spring I noticed her dote on Fridrik, fetching him this and that as he worked outside and giggling at his stories of fist fights and daredevilry. In the evenings she'd often go out to the cowshed to bring him a little milk and wish him goodnight, and she'd take her time about it too. As I said, she's a pretty little thing, and I expect Fridrik soon forgot brown-toothed Thórunn. He's a keen rider, and used to flog his pony to death in an effort to impress Sigga. Even when that good horse threw him for the way he switched its hide all bloody, Sigga fetched him a supper and sat by his side as he wolfed it, sponging his swollen temple and stooping to kiss it better when she thought I could not see.

'When Natan came back he saw that most of the ewes had given birth, and he praised us for doing the job so well. Sigga told him that we couldn't have done it without Fridrik, and Natan asked us why in the Devil's name we'd let that thieving boy upon the place when he wasn't home to watch him. Sigga began to cry – she didn't have the stomach for quarrels – and when Natan continued to rail at her for thoughtlessness, I stepped in and claimed it was my idea to fetch him.

'I told Natan that I understood Illugastadir was not his only responsibility, but that without another man he could hardly expect Sigga and I to manage certain tasks. I told him that neither of us were strong enough to swing the lambs, and that we struggled to do a great many things besides. I told him that for all he had a grudge against Fridrik, that boy had saved a great number of his livestock, and we'd been careful not to let him sleep indoors. I didn't tell him that Fridrik had been scratching in the front yard for money.

'Eventually Natan calmed, and things returned to normal at Illugastadir. He said that he would ride to Geitaskard and hire Daníel Gudmundsson for harvest. He said that he wanted another man with us in his absence, but that he did not want it to be Fridrik.'

CHAPTER TEN

13th April 1828

RÓSA GUDMUNDSDÓTTIR FROM VATNSENDI was asked to appear at court. She declined to give any information about the case, but she said that Agnes came sometime that winter to her and spoke well about her master Natan. The baby that had been in foster care at Illugastadir is now at home with Rósa, being her daughter. She said that the baby is now three years old. She did not think that the baby had been harmed in any way by the murder, but remarked that the baby always says Natan is 'up in the hills'. This is what the baby was told after the murder occurred. Rósa said that there is nothing unusual she can say about Agnes or Sigrídur as she doesn't know them well. She said that Natan left Vatnsendi in the summer of 1825 after having stayed there with her and her husband for two years. She said that she knows Natan had at that point a considerable amount of money. She had taken 50 spesiurs from him for safekeeping.

The spring after Natan left, Fridrik from Katadalur came to Vatnsendi, and called her out for a private conversation in the cowshed. Rósa then said that he started to express how he desired her, and asked her to allow him to stay the night and come to her bed. She said that she rejected Fridrik, walked away from him and asked her husband not to allow him to stay inside even though he later requested it again. After that, she said her husband, Ólaf, came to her and told her that Fridrik had asked to see the storeroom so he could look for the money he thought Rósa kept for Natan. He said that Natan had told him he could take the money if he ever managed to sleep at Rósa's place. Fridrik offered her husband two or four spesiurs and told Ólaf that his mother had had a dream where the money was stored under a barrel in the storeroom. Rósa said that she told her husband Natan's stored money was absolutely not in the storeroom and Fridrik could look there for as long as he liked. After that her husband went out and, though she and her workmaid were sleeping, Fridrik went into the storeroom, ripped everything out of the barrel but didn't find anything. She said he remarked that 'his mother ought to dream better'. He said he had found a heavy object he couldn't move, and was going to come back after he had received better information from his mother about where he should look. But he did not come back.

After this Fridrik was thought to hate Natan because he couldn't find the money. Rósa said that she gave Natan the money she had stored for him the spring after Fridrik came, but said that she had not heard from him for a long time. She also remarked that while Natan lived with her he would often keep his money buried in the ground inside or outside the farm. No further evidence or information was possible to get from this woman, and she furthermore refused to confirm that what is recorded here is correct.

Anonymous clerk, 1828.

TÓTI WOKE IN THE UNLIT badstofa of Breidabólstadur, struggling to breathe. Pushing himself to a sitting position, he felt a feverish rush of blood to his head, and his arms trembled and gave way. He tried to cough; his tongue stuck to the roof of his mouth.

Across the room his father lay sleeping, his snores catching, his breath pausing for a few stricken seconds, then resuming in a rumbled exhalation. Why is he still sleeping, thought Tóti. It must be morning. I need a sip of water.

Fighting his light-headedness, Tóti tried to move his legs to the floor, setting his bare feet gently upon the boards. I must have had a nightmare, he thought, feeling his heart flutter in his chest. I'll fetch some water.

The pantry air was deliciously cool on his clammy skin. Perhaps I ought to sleep in here, thought Tóti, sinking to the ground. It is so hot in the badstofa, someone has lit a fire beneath us.

He woke again at the touch of his father's rough hands lifting him under his armpits.

'Are you trying to catch yourself a cold? Sleepwalking like a madman.'

'Mother?'

There was a pause. 'No, son. It's me.'

Reverend Jón stumbled back, and then managed to haul his son up against his side. 'Now walk,' he commanded, bending down to pick up his candle. 'Are you still asleep?'

Tóti shook his head. 'No, no. I'm not asleep. I felt queer and wanted some water. I think I drifted off there.'

He grasped his father's offered arm and together they stumbled back to the badstofa. 'Sit yourself down on your bed now,' his father said. He took a few steps back, watching as Tóti swayed uneasily on his feet. His eyes were unusually bright, his hair slick with sweat in the candlelight.

'You've exhausted yourself, son. It's all your travelling to Kornsá in this unfit weather. It's addled you.'

Tóti looked up at him. 'Father?'

Reverend Jón caught him as he fell.

THE DAYS ARE DWINDLING NOW. There is time enough for everything; too much time, and so the family of Kornsá have gone to church to kill the miserable hours that creak about on a Sunday morning. The mountains are covered in snow and the water in the cowshed iced over last night. Jón sent Bjarni out to crack it with a hammer, and now it is just we three, Bjarni, Jón and me, waiting until the others return.

I wonder where the Reverend is? I have not seen him in many days. I thought he might come for my birthday, seeing as he knew of it from the ministerial book, but the day came and went and I dared not say anything to the family. The November days are now crawling past, and still he does not come, with no letter, no message to sustain me. Steina asked me if I thought the weather might be keeping him away: there was a blizzard a week ago that almost snowed us in. Perhaps he is too taken up by pastoral duties, and is travelling around his own parish with the soul registers, writing countless names down so that history will not forget them. Or perhaps he has had enough of my stories; perhaps I have said something and he is now convinced I am guilty, that I must be abandoned and punished. I am too godless. I am distracting him from his dedication to Christian thinking. I make him doubt his belief in a loving Lord. Perhaps Blöndal has summoned him again, told him to stop listening to me. Either way, it seems cruel to leave me without warning, without an assurance that he'll come back. Without his visits the days seem longer, even as the light flees this country like a whipped dog. I've less and less to do, and the waiting for him keeps me on a knife-edge. Every boot knocking off snow, every cough in the corridor makes me think he has come again. But it is never him. Only the servants, returning from feeding the stock in the evenings. Only Margrét, spitting into her handkerchief.

This waiting makes me want to be sick. Why not now? Why not pick up the axe and do the deed here, on the farm. Bjarni could do it. Or Gudmundur. Any of the men. God knows they'd probably like to push my face into the snow and take my head off without ceremony, without priest or judge. If they're going to kill me, why not kill me now and be done with it?

It must be Blöndal. He means to cripple me with waiting before stretching my neck out. He wants me to break; he takes away the only comfort I have left in this world because he is a barbarian. He takes Tóti, and makes me watch time pass. A cruel gift, to give me so much time to farewell everything. Why won't they tell me when I have to die? It could be tomorrow – and the Reverend is not here to help. Why won't he come?

I am sick with finality. It is like a punch in the heart, the fact of my sentence alongside the ordinariness of days at the farm. Perhaps it would have been better if they had left me at Stóra-Borg. I might have starved to death. I would be mud-slick, stuffed to the guts with cold and hopelessness, and my body might know it was doomed and give up on its own. That would be better than idly winding wool on a snowy day, waiting for someone to kill me.

Perhaps next Sunday I could ask to go with Margrét to church. What else is God good for other than a distraction from the mire we're all stranded in? We're all shipwrecked. All beached in a peat bog of poverty. When was the last time I even attended church? Not while I was at Illugastadir. It must have been at Geitaskard, with the other servants. We rode there and changed into our best behind the church wall, feeling the nip of the morning breeze on our bare legs as we struggled into our better clothes, free from horsehair. I miss the stuffy warmth from too many bodies in one place, and the sniffing and coughing and the babies whimpering. I want to let the sound of a priest's voice wash over me, just to hear the music of it. Like when I was small, hired out to backwater farms to wipe infants' backsides clean of shit, and wash the laundry with ashes and fat; escaping to church to feel part of something. Pure.

Perhaps things would have been different if Natan had let me go to church at Tjörn. I might have made friends there. I might have met a family to turn to when it all became twisted. Other farmers I could have worked for. But he didn't let me go, and there was no other friend, no light to head towards in that wintered landscape.

Perhaps Rósa and I might have been friends if we'd met in another way. Natan always said we were as alike as a swan to a raven, but he was wrong. We both loved him, for one. And no matter what I tell the Reverend, Rósa's poetry kindled the shavings of my soul, and lit me up from within. Natan never stopped loving her. How could he? Her poetry made lamps out of people.

We never reached an understanding, although that was her fault as much as mine. As soon as Rósa met me, she made it clear we were on a battleground. She appeared in the badstofa at Illugastadir one summer night, like a ghost. No one heard her coming, or heard the door open. She just appeared, holding her little girl in her arms. She was dressed in black, and the sombre colour set off her skin so that she seemed to glow. Sigga always said that Rósa looked like an angel. But that night I thought she looked tired, world-weary.

I knew more about Rósa than she knew of me. 'She is a wonderful woman,' Natan said once, and a little hook of jealousy ripped at the fibre of my lungs. 'She is a fine midwife, a great poet.' He was the father of her child! That daughter of hers had his sharp way of looking, never missing anything. But he reassured me. 'She suffocated me,' he said. 'She wanted me to live forever with her and her husband. But I needed to create a life of my own. And here I have it. My own farm. My independence.'

He convinced me that he had sent her letters saying he no longer wanted her. That his love for me had eclipsed that which he'd had for her. He liked the fact that I was a bastard, a pauper, a servant. 'You have had to fight for everything,' he said. 'You take life by the teeth, Agnes. You are not like Rósa.'

Then that summer evening she stood in the doorway with their daughter, and Natan's face lit up.

Rósa didn't say anything. Her glance landed on me and her eyes narrowed. She might as well have raised a gun to my face.

'You must be Agnes Magnúsdóttir. The Rose of Kidjaskard. The Rose of the valley lands.'

Her hand, released from its mitten, was frigid in my own.

'Poet-Rósa. I'm pleased to finally meet you.'

Rósa looked over at Sigga, then raised her eyebrows at Natan. 'I'm glad to see you've made yourself a pretty little household.'

I did not miss the accusation in her voice. I knew what I was doing when I stood next to Natan. He is mine now.

'This must be Thóranna,' I said. The child smiled at the sound of her name.

Rósa took her back into her arms. 'Yes. Mine and Natan's child.'

'Come now, girls.' Natan seemed amused. 'Let us be friendly. Sigga, fetch us all some coffee. Rósa, take off your outer things.'

'No, thank you.' Rósa put Thóranna in a corner, away from me. 'I only came to bring her here.'

'What?' Natan hadn't told me Rósa's daughter was coming to stay. I whispered to Natan, asking why he hadn't told me this before. Why he hadn't warned me Rósa would visit. I hadn't known they still spoke together.

'It is the least I can do for Rósa,' he said. 'Thóranna was with us last winter as well. She is my daughter and it is only right that she come live with us for part of the year.'

Rósa's words were sharp. 'I did not realise you consulted with her on everything, Natan? I didn't know you were so far under her thumb. It's clear she doesn't want our child in her home.'

Natan was laughing. 'Her home? Rósa, Agnes is my servant.'

'Only your servant, is that right?' She raised her eyebrows. 'I don't want her to watch over our daughter.'

'I am happy to look after Thóranna,' I said. I was lying.

'What makes you happy does not concern me, Agnes.'

Natan must not have liked to see his past and present lovers collide. 'Come, Rósa. Let's all have some coffee together.'

Her laugh was shrill. 'Oh yes, you'd like that! All your whores supping together under your roof! No, thank you.' Rósa wrenched her arm from his grip and turned to leave. But she said something to me before she walked out the door.

'Please be good to Thóranna. Please.' I nodded, and Rósa suddenly leant in closer. I felt her hand light upon my arm. '*Brennt barn forðast eldinn.*' Her voice was soft, careful. 'The burnt child fears the fire.' She left without turning back.

The little girl began to wail for her mamma and Sigga comforted her. Natan stared at the doorway, as though Rósa might return.

'What have you told her about us?' I whispered to Natan.

'I haven't told Rósa anything.'

'What was that about the Rose of Kidjaskard? What was that about all your whores?'

He shrugged. 'Rósa has a way of naming people. I expect she thinks you're beautiful.'

'It did not seem a compliment.'

Natan ignored me. 'I'll be in my workshop.'

'Sigga is going to make coffee for us.'

'Damn you, Agnes! Just leave it for once.'

'Are you going after Rósa?'

He left without answering.

ONE NIGHT, IN A FEVER, Tóti saw Agnes appear in the doorway of the badstofa. 'They've let her come here,' he said to his father, who was bent over the bed, silently swaddling his shaking son in blankets.

'Come in,' Tóti said. His arms fought their way out of the bedding and reached for her in the stuffy air of the room. 'Come here. See how our lives are entwined? God has willed it so.'

Then she was kneeling by his bed, whispering. He felt her long dark hair brush against his ear and a shiver of longing passed through him. 'It's so hot in here,' he said, and she leant forward to kiss the sweat off his skin, but her tongue was rough and her hands were reaching around his throat, her fingertips clenching against his skin.

'Agnes. Agnes!' He fought her off, wheezing with the effort. Strong hands reached for his own and pressed them back into the blankets at his side. 'Don't struggle,' she said. 'Stop it.'

Tóti groaned. Flames were licking at his skin, smoke pouring into his mouth. He coughed, his chest rising and falling under the weight of Agnes as she climbed on top of him, lifting her knife.

✝

'I DON'T BELIEVE IT,' STEINA argued, sweeping the badstofa so that the dust flew from the floorboards and floated in the air.

'Steina! You're making it messier than it was before.'

Steina continued sweeping furiously. 'It's a cruel story, and it wouldn't surprise me if Róslín made it up herself.'

'But she's not the only person who has heard it.' Lauga sneezed. 'See, you're making it worse.'

'Fine, you do it then.' Steina shoved the broom at her sister and sat down on the bed.

'What are you two bickering about?' Margrét entered the room and looked down in dismay at the floor. 'Who did this?'

'Steina,' Lauga said reproachfully.

'It's not my fault the roof is falling down! Look, it's everywhere.' Steina stood up again. 'And the wet is getting in. It's dripping in the corner.' She shivered.

'You're in a mood,' said Margrét, dismissively. She turned to Lauga. 'What's she upset about?'

Lauga rolled her eyes. 'There's a story about Agnes that I've heard. Steina doesn't believe it's true.'

'Oh?' Margrét coughed and waved the dust away from her face. 'What story is that?'

'Folk remember her when she was little, and there's some that say there was a travelling man who prophesied that an axe would fall on her head.'

Margrét wrinkled her nose. 'Have you heard this from Róslín?'

Lauga pulled a face. 'Not only Róslín. They say that when Agnes was young it was her chore to watch over the *tún*, and one day she discovered a traveller who had set up camp on the grass. His horse was ruining the feed, and when she told him to leave, he cursed her and shouted that she would one day be beheaded.'

Margrét snorted, and was overcome with a fit of coughing. Lauga put down the broom and gently ushered her mother to her bed. Steina stood where she was and watched obstinately.

'There, there, Mamma. You'll be all right.' Lauga rubbed her mother's back, stifling a cry as a bright clot of blood fell out of her mouth.

'Mamma! You're bleeding!' Steina rushed forward, tripping over the broom.

Lauga pushed her sister away. 'Let her breathe!'

They watched, anxious, as Margrét continued to hack.

'Have you tried a jelly of lichen?' Agnes was standing in the doorway, looking at Lauga.

'I feel quite well,' croaked Margrét, bringing a hand to her chest.

'It eases the lungs.'

Lauga turned towards the doorway, her face pinched. 'Leave us, would you?'

Agnes ignored her. 'Have you tried such a jelly?'

'We don't have need for your potions,' Lauga snapped.

Agnes shook her head. 'I think you do.'

Margrét stopped coughing and looked sharply at her.

'What do you mean by that?' Lauga whispered.

Agnes took a deep breath. 'Boil some chopped moss in water for a time. A very long time. When the stock cools it will form a grey jelly.

The taste is not pleasant, but it may stop you from bleeding in the lungs.'

There was a moment of silence as Margrét and Lauga stared at Agnes.

Steina sat down on the bed again. 'Did Natan Ketilsson teach you that?' she asked in a quiet voice.

'They say it helps,' Agnes repeated. 'I can make it for you.'

Margrét slowly wiped her mouth on a corner of her apron and nodded. 'Do that,' she said. Agnes hesitated, then turned on her heel, walking quickly down the corridor.

Lauga turned to her mother. 'Mamma, I'm not sure you should take whatever she –'

'Enough, Lauga,' interrupted Margrét. 'Enough.'

THE REVEREND STILL DOES NOT come. But winter has. Autumn has been pushed aside by a wind driving flurries of snow up against the croft, and the air is as thin as paper. Each breath hangs in front of me like a ghost, and mists drop down from the mountains to swarm on the frozen ground. The dark comes; it has settled down in these parts like a bruise in the flesh of the earth, but the Reverend does not.

Why doesn't he come?

If the Reverend came tonight, would I tell him that Natan and I were as husband and wife? Then I could tell him about what began to change between us. Perhaps he guesses at it anyway.

The salt came. The darkling wind rose and the black sand began to sting. The way down. The cold path down to colder water. The salt came.

What would I say to Tóti?

Reverend, Natan began to leave Illugastadir at the close of summer, and each time he returned, it was as though he became more of a stranger to me. He'd catch me alone in the dairy, take the scrubbing brush out of my hand and draw me to him, only to ask me if I had kept Daníel warm in his bed while he was out, scraping together a living by luring death out of the bowels of his countrymen. He even accused me of loving Fridrik! That lug of a boy, swinging his fists about and stinking of unwashed wool. Natan's accusations seemed comical to me. Couldn't he see how much I missed him? How different he was from any other man I had known?

I imagine Tóti's face blushing. I imagine him wiping his sweaty palms against the material of his trousers. His slow nod. The light from the candle in the badstofa flickering over his face as he watches me, wide-eyed.

Reverend, I would say, I told Natan that Daníel was nothing to me. That Fridrik was enamoured with Sigga. I told him that I was his for as long as he'd have me, that I'd be his wife if he wished it.

It was those moods of his that took him away. I'd find Natan in the workshop measuring broths, skimming the dirty froth off boiling roots. I'd offer my help, as I helped him when I first came. He began to push me out of his way. He didn't want me, he said. Did he mean he didn't want my help, or my presence? He'd direct me towards the door.

'Go. I don't want you here. I'm busy.'

Sometimes I'd go to the outhouse and hammer the dried cod heads with a cow thighbone. Just to beat and rail against something. He is falling out of love with you, I told myself. And I began to wonder whether he ever loved me.

But there were still hours when he found me alone by the shore, collecting eiderdown. He would take me beside the birds' nests, his hands in my hair, his look as desperate as a drowning man's.

He needed me like he needed air. I felt it in his gaze, in the way he grappled for my body like a buoy in the water.

Reverend Tóti, draw your stool nearer. I'll tell you what it was really like.

I hated being his servant. One night I would be his lover, with the hard rhythm of his breath matching my own. And then, the next, I was Agnes the workmaid. Not even the housekeeper! And his cool commands began to seem like reprimands.

'Call the sheep home from pasture. Milk the cow. Milk the sheep. Fetch water. Collect the ashes and spread them upon the soil. Feed Thóranna. Make her stop crying. Make her stop crying! This pot is still dirty. Ask Sigga to show you how to wash the beakers properly.'

Do you understand what I am saying, Reverend? Or is love constant for you? Have you ever loved a woman? A person you love as much as you hate the hold they have on you?

I hated the way my mind would turn to Natan throughout the day, until I was sick with the pattern of my thoughts. I hated the nausea that came at the suggestion he did not care for me. I hated the way I kept tripping up over those rocks to his workshop, again and again, to bring him things he no longer required.

It took Daníel to tell me how it really was.

The farmhand was waiting for me one day when Natan was not at home. I stepped out of the workshop, locked the door, and saw Daníel standing on the shore, his scythe in one hand, his hat in the other.

'What were you doing in there?' he asked me.

'None of your business.'

'We're not allowed in there,' he said. 'Where did you find the key?'

'Natan gave it to me. He trusts me.'

'Oh yes,' Daníel said, 'I forgot you maids get special treatment.'

'And what do you mean by that?'

Daníel laughed. 'Where are *my* sealskin shoes? Where are *my* new clothes?'

Natan was generous when the mood took him. 'You haven't been here long,' I pointed out to Daníel. 'I'm sure you'll receive a present when Natan returns.'

'I don't want something from Natan.'

'No? You were just complaining about our special treatment.'

'I want something from you.'

Daníel's tone changed then. His voice became softer. 'Agnes, you must know that I am fond of you.'

I laughed. 'Fond of me? You told everyone at Geitaskard we were engaged!'

'I was hopeful, Agnes. I am hopeful. You won't be Natan's forever, Agnes.'

His words stopped me cold. A sudden dizziness spun through me. 'What did you say?'

'Don't think we don't know. Sigga, me, Fridrik. We all know. Everyone at Geitaskard. They knew you were sneaking off to the storeroom at night.' He smirked.

'If you spent less of your time spreading gossip, and more time spreading grass, we'd all be better off. Go do as you're meant to, Daníel.'

His face screwed up in anger. 'You think you're better than us because you've found another farmer who lets you share his bed?'

'Don't be vulgar.'

'Don't be fooled. Just because you play at being a wife, does not make you a married woman, Agnes.'

'I am his housemistress, that's all.'

Daníel laughed. 'Oh yes, his mistress, certainly.'

My temper broke then. I snatched the scythe from his hand and shoved it back into his chest. 'And what are you, Daníel? A workman who speaks ill of his master? Who insults the woman he would like to claim as his own? You disgust me.'

Would I tell the Reverend this, if he were here? Perhaps he has drawn his own conclusions. Perhaps that is why he does not come.

I could tell him of another day, the day of the death waves. Sigga had sent me outside to fetch stones to mend the wall of the hearth, and it was while I was out there that I heard the splash of the oar against the water. It was a still day, the kind of day where the world is holding its breath. The sea was coiled.

Daníel and Natan had gone fishing, but it was too early in the morning for them to return. I could see Daníel rowing, and Natan sitting still and upright in the boat. As they came closer I could see that Natan's face was set in a grim line, his hands clutching the wooden boat as though he were about to be sick.

As soon as they reached the shoreline, Natan threw himself out of the boat and began stomping through the shallows. He scuffed the shore with his boots so that pebbles flew in a spray about him.

I had been living with Natan long enough by then to know that nothing could assuage the black moods that overtook him, so when I saw him thunder up the beach, the water dripping from his clothes, I remained silent. He didn't look at me as he passed, but marched towards the farm.

When Daníel had pulled the boat onto the shore, I walked down to ask him what had happened. Had they fought? Had they lost a net?

Daníel seemed amused at his master's display of temper. He started to haul nets from the boat, and gave me some to carry back up to Illugastadir.

'Natan thinks we were hit with death waves,' he said. Salt clung to his beard. He said that he hadn't pegged Natan for being such a superstitious bastard.

They had been dragging the nets when out of nowhere they were hit by three large waves. Daníel said they were lucky that the boat didn't overturn. He had scrambled to save the line, and fortunately prevented it all from going overboard, but when he looked up Natan was white as a ghost. When Daníel asked him what the matter was, Natan looked at him as though he had lost his mind. 'Those were death waves, Daníel.'

Daníel told Natan that death waves were an old wives' tale, and he didn't think a learned man like him would be fooled by such a thing. Then Daníel said Natan had snapped, grabbed him by the sleeve and told him that he wouldn't be laughing when he was buried at the bottom of the ocean.

Daníel said that he'd thrown off Natan's grip, and offered to bail the water the waves had brought into the boat, but that Natan had only said: 'Damn you, Daníel. Do you think I'm going to sit here and wait for another wave to drown me? We're going back.'

Daníel thought it wouldn't be beyond Natan to drown him in a temper, just to show the truth of the superstition, so he rowed them to shore.

After Daníel had told me all of this, I decided to speak with Natan, even though Daníel told me to leave him be. He said that Natan had got it into his head that he was doomed, and that we should let him come to his senses in his own good time. But I followed Natan to the croft, where I found him shouting at Sigga. She was trying to undress him from his wet clothes, and the soaked shirt had caught about his face.

Seeing that Sigga was upset by his harsh words, I told her to leave and began to undress Natan myself, but he pushed me away and called Sigga back. 'You forget your place, Agnes,' he said.

Later that day I followed Natan to his workshop, carrying an unlit lamp I thought he might need. The days had shortened so rapidly over the weeks, and the light was shuddering to a close. The ocean looked uneasy.

When Natan tried the workshop door, he found it was already open. He demanded to know if I'd been in there without his permission, and I told him that he knew I had been tending the fire while he'd gone fishing. I had probably forgotten to lock the door, but he began to accuse me of meddling with his things, of trying to find his money, of taking advantage of him.

Taking advantage of *him*! My tongue got the better of me then, and I told him that he was the one who had lured me out to his lonely farm with a lie. He had told me I was his housemistress, and yet all the while it was Sigga. I asked him if he'd been paying her higher wages than me, and why he had thought to trick me in the first place, when he knew I would have followed him anyway!

Natan began to check his belongings. It hurt me that he thought I might have taken something of his. What did I want with his coins, or medicines, or whatever else he had hidden in there?

I stayed in the workshop. He could not make me leave. When he was satisfied nothing was missing he took out some sealskins that needed curing and refused to say anything more to me. But it was late in the afternoon and the sky outside was flat and grey, a poor light to be working by. I sulked by the hearth and watched him, waiting for him to turn to me, to take me in his arms, to apologise.

Perhaps Natan forgot I was there, or else he did not care, but after a time he set his knife on the ground, and wiped his hands on a rag. Then he walked outside the workshop and stood on the furthest fringe of the outcrop, staring out to sea. I followed him.

I slipped my arms about his waist to comfort him and told him I was sorry.

Natan did not pull away from my embrace, but I felt his body stiffen at my touch. I buried my face into the greasy folds of his shirt and kissed his back.

'Don't,' he muttered. His face was still turned towards the sea. I tightened my hands upon his stomach and pressed myself against him.

'Stop it, Agnes.' He grabbed my hands, and pushed me away from him. His muscles moved as he clenched and unclenched his jaw.

A gale picked up. It knocked Natan's hat from his head and carried it out to sea.

I asked him what was wrong. I asked him if someone had threatened him, and he laughed. His eyes were stony. His hair, no longer constrained by his hat, whipped about his head in a dark tangle.

He said that he saw signs of death all about him.

In the silence that followed, I took a deep breath. 'Natan, you're not going to die.'

'Explain the death waves then.' His voice was low, taut. 'Explain the premonitions. The dreams that I've been having.'

'Natan, you laugh about those dreams.' I was trying to remain calm. 'You tell everybody about them.'

'Do you see me laughing, Agnes?'

He stepped towards me and grasped my shoulders, bringing his face so close to mine that our foreheads touched.

'Every night,' he hissed, 'I dream of death. I see it everywhere. I see blood, everywhere.'

'You've been skinning animals –'

Natan gripped me harder about the shoulders. 'I see it upon the ground, in dark, sticky pools.' He licked his lips. 'I taste it, Agnes. I wake with the taste of blood in my mouth.'

'You bite your tongue in your sleep –'

He gave an unfriendly smile. 'I saw you and Daníel talking about me by the boat.'

'Let go of me, Natan.'

He ignored me.

'Let go of me!' I twisted myself out of his grasp. 'You should listen to yourself. You sound like an old woman, harping on about dreams and premonitions.'

It was cold. A great, churning cloud had moved in from the sea, snuffing all but the faintest scratchings of light from the sky. Yet even in the near darkness, I could see Natan's eyes shine. His gaze unnerved me.

'Agnes,' he said. 'I've been dreaming about you.'

I said nothing, suddenly longing to return to the croft and light the lamps. I was aware of the ocean, not two steps from our feet.

'I dream that I'm in bed and I can see blood running down the walls. It drips on my head and the drops burn my skin.'

He took a step towards me.

'I am bound to my bed, and the blood rises about me until I am covered. Then, suddenly, it's gone. I can move, and I sit up and look about me and the room is empty.'

He pressed my hand and I felt the sharp edge of his nail dig into the flesh of my palm.

'But then, I see *you*. I walk towards you. And as I draw closer I see that you're nailed to the wall by your hair.'

As he said this, a great gust of wind blew my cap from my head, and my hair was loosed. Unbraided as it was, the long tendrils were immediately lashed about by the wind. Natan quickly reached out and grabbed a handful, using it to pull me closer.

'Natan! You're hurting me!'

But Natan was distracted. 'What's that?' he whispered.

On the wind I could suddenly smell the heavy stench of rot, dark and putrid.

'It's the seaweed. Or a dead seal. Let go of my hair.'

'Shh!'

I was sick of his temper. 'No one is out to get you, Natan. You're not so important as that.'

I wrenched my hair out of his grasp and turned to walk back up to the croft, but Natan grabbed me by the sleeve of my blouse, twisted me and struck me full on the face.

I gasped and immediately brought my hand to my cheek, but Natan seized my fingers and held them tightly in his own, forcing me to crouch close to him. Even against the chill of the wind I could feel the blood rush to where he had hit me.

'Never speak to me like that again.' Natan's mouth pressed against my ear. His voice was low and hard. 'I shouldn't have asked you here.'

He held me for a moment longer, twisting my fingers until I cried out from the pain, and then he released his grip and shoved me away from him.

I stumbled along the outcrop and up the hill to the croft in the low light, tripping over my skirts, the wind aching in my ears. I was crying, yet even over the sound of the wind, and my own ragged breathing, I heard Natan shout to me from where he stood on the knoll by the sea.

'Remember your place, Agnes!'

I waited for Natan to return to the croft that night, and kept a lamp burning in the hope that when he returned we could make up our quarrel. But the hours crept past like the guilty and midnight came and went, and still he did not come inside. Sigga and Daníel had long undressed and fallen asleep in their beds, but I remained awake and watched the flame of the lamp dance upon its wick. My head pounded. I understood that I was waiting for something bad to happen.

Several times I thought I heard footsteps outside the croft, but when I opened the door it was only to the darkness and the sound of the waves breaking against the shore. A thick fog had come down and I could not tell if Natan had a light burning in his workshop. I returned to my cooling bed and continued to wait.

I must have fallen asleep. I woke in shadows; the lamp had extinguished itself, but I knew that Natan had not yet come to bed. Then I recognised his footfall sounding in the corridor – the rattle of the door latch must have woken me. I held my breath and hoped I would feel his warm hands drawing back the blankets of my bed. I would feel his body as he eased it in next to mine, and in my ear his soft voice would murmur, full of apology.

But Natan did not come to my bed. Out of slitted eyes I saw him sit upon a stool and take off his boots. He pulled down his trousers and slowly lifted his shirt above his head. His clothes lay scattered on the floor. He stood up again, and for a moment I thought I saw him move in my direction. But then he took two soft steps towards the window, and in the poor light I saw him draw back the covers of Sigga's bed.

I knew then what Rósa meant when she had called us his whores. My body was stiff with the effort of not calling out, of not giving myself away, when I heard his whispered words and Sigga's muffled response. I bit down on the flesh of my hand as a gauze of nausea wrapped about my stomach. My heart stopped. I choked on its missed beats.

I could hear him grunt as he thrust inside her. I closed my eyes and held my breath because I knew that if I exhaled it would come in a wail, and I screwed my fingernails into the flesh of my arm until I felt a slipperiness and knew there was blood.

I waited until Natan climbed out of Sigga's bed and turned into his own. I waited until Sigga's breath grew calm and even, and Natan began to snore. I waited until I knew they were asleep before I sat up and gazed at the blankets before me. My throat closed up with pain, and something else, something hard and inciting and as black as tar. I did not let myself cry. Rage flooded through me until my hands and back grew stiff with it. I could have quietly gathered my belongings and left before it grew light, but where would I have gone? I knew only the valley of Vatnsdalur; knew where it was scabbed with rock, knew the white-headed mountains and the lake alive with swans, and the wrinkled skins of turf by the river. And the ravens, the constant, circling ravens. But Illugastadir was different. I had no friends. I didn't understand the landscape. Only the outlying tongues of rock scarred the perfect kiss of sea and sky – there was no one and nothing else. There was nowhere else to go.

CHAPTER ELEVEN

THERE, STANDING IN FRONT OF THE court on the 19th of
April, was Bjarni Sigurdsson again, Fridrik's brother from
Katadalur, a ten-year-old boy who looked to be clever and
intelligent. After a long time of questioning he still gave no
information, until at last he said that Fridrik had slit the
throats of two milk-giving sheep and one lamb last autumn,
when his father was not home. Bjarni Sigurdsson remembered
that these sheep were Natan's. His mother, he said, had, for a
long time, told him he should say he didn't know about this,
and told him not to talk about it when it came to the trial.
However we tried then, both with toughness and gentleness,
we could not get any more information out of him.

Anonymous clerk, 1828.

MARGRÉT WOKE TO THE SOUND of whimpering. She peered through the darkness to where her daughters lay. They were asleep.

Agnes.

Margrét put her head down on the pillow next to her husband's and listened. Yes, the criminal was crying; a thin, tight wail that made Margrét's throat close up. Should she go to her? Perhaps it was a trick. Margrét wished she could see better in the gloom. The cries stopped, and then broke out anew. She sounded like a child.

Margrét carefully got out of bed and felt her way to the doorway, turning down the corridor, until she could see the glow coming from the dying coals in the kitchen hearth. Taking a candle from its bracket, she kindled a flame from the embers and lit the wick. Before she left the warmth of the kitchen, Margrét paused. She could still hear the plaintive cry. She realised she was scared without understanding why.

The candlelight danced over the walls and rafters of the badstofa. Everyone was asleep, their heads tucked under blankets to ward off the December cold that had left frost on the walls. Margrét placed a hand around the flame to protect it from draughts, and slowly walked towards Agnes. The woman was asleep, but her eyes darted under her lids, and the blankets had been pushed to the end of the bed. Agnes was shivering, her elbows tightly tucked to her sides, her hands bunched into fists as though she was about to fight, bare-knuckled.

'Agnes?'

The woman groaned. Margrét reached down for the blankets with her spare hand, and started to draw them up over the woman's exposed body, but as she pulled them over her chest, Agnes grabbed hold of Margrét's wrist.

Margrét opened her mouth to scream, but no sound came out. She froze at the sudden grip of Agnes's cold fingers.

'What are you doing?' Agnes's voice was as unfriendly as her grasp. The candlelight sputtered.

'Nothing. You were shivering.'

'You were watching me.'

Margrét coughed and tasted blood. She swallowed it, reluctant to set the candle down. 'I wasn't watching you. You woke me. You were crying.'

Agnes regarded Margrét for a moment, then dropped her hand. Margrét watched as Agnes examined the tears she wiped from her cheeks.

'I was crying?'

Margrét nodded. 'You woke me.'

'I was dreaming.' Agnes stared at the rafters.

Margrét coughed again, but this time too suddenly to bring a hand to her mouth. Both of the women looked down at the blankets and saw the small spot of blood. Agnes looked from the stain to Margrét.

'Do you want to sit down?' She drew up her legs and Margrét eased herself onto the edge of the bed.

'Two dying women,' Agnes murmured.

At any other time Margrét knew she might have been insulted, but sitting across from Agnes she saw the truth of this.

'Jón worries for me,' Margrét admitted. 'He says nothing, but when you're so long married to a man, there's not much need for speaking.'

'Did you tell him about the lichen jelly?'

'He knows you have a hand with herbs. He heard about Róslín and her baby.'

Agnes was thoughtful. 'He doesn't mind it?'

Margrét shook her head. 'You mustn't think he's a bad man, my Jón.' She looked down at the floor. 'He does his best to live a quiet Christian life. We all do. He wouldn't wish harm to any soul, only with you here …' She opened her mouth as if to say more, but stopped herself. 'There's a deal on his mind, is all. But we'll carry on, for as long as we're able.'

'But he knows your sickness is worsening?'

Margrét felt the heaviness on her lungs and shrugged. 'What were you dreaming about?' she asked, after a moment's silence.

Agnes drew the blankets up about her neck. 'Katadalur.'

'Fridrik's farm?'

Agnes nodded.

'A nightmare?'

The younger woman's gaze slipped to the bloodstain on the blankets between them. She seemed to be studying it. 'I was staying there in the days before Natan died.'

'I thought you were living at Illugastadir?' Margrét shivered, and Agnes reached for her shawl, which lay draped across the headboard. She handed it to Margrét.

'I stayed at Illugastadir until Natan threw me out. I didn't have anywhere to go so I went to Fridrik's family in Katadalur.'

'You said you weren't friends.'

'We weren't.' Agnes looked up at Margrét. 'Why haven't you asked me about the murders?'

The question took Margrét by surprise. 'I thought that was between you and the Reverend.'

Agnes shook her head.

Margrét's mouth had gone dry. She looked across to where her husband lay. He was snoring. 'Would you like to come to the kitchen with me?' she asked. 'I need to warm my bones or I'll be dead by morning.'

Agnes sat on a stool brought from the dairy, and watched as Margrét broke open the embers in the hearth, prising flames from them with pieces of dried dung. She coughed in the smoke and wiped her eyes.

'Are you thirsty?'

Agnes nodded, and Margrét set a small pot of milk on the hook. She sat down on the stool next to Agnes and together they watched the flames begin to crowd the kindling.

'My mother would never let the hearth die in her home,' Margrét said. She felt Agnes turn to look at her, but didn't meet her gaze. 'She believed that as long as a light burned in the house, the Devil couldn't get in. Not even during the witching hour.'

Agnes was quiet. 'What do you believe?' she asked eventually.

Margrét extended her hands towards the flames. 'I think a fire is a useful thing to keep a body warm,' she said.

Agnes nodded. The fire crackled and flared in front of them. 'When I worked at Gafl, the fire went out during winter. It was my fault. We were snowed in and the children were starving, and I was so busy trying to get the youngest to take a little whey from a rag that I forgot to check the kitchen. We went three days without a light, without a fire, before the weather cleared and we could get help from the next farm. I thought our neighbours would find us dead and blue in our beds.'

'It happens,' Margrét conceded. 'There's more than one way a body can die.'

The two women fell silent. The milk began to tremble, and Margrét got up to pour it off. She handed a steaming cup to Agnes and sat down again.

'Your family is lucky to have enough supplies,' Agnes said.

'We had a little extra money this year,' Margrét replied. 'District Commissioner Blöndal has given us some compensation.' She regretted her words as soon as she spoke, but Agnes did not react.

'I hadn't thought of that,' she said eventually.

'Not much, mind you,' Margrét added.

'No, I'm not worth much,' Agnes remarked bitterly. Margrét glanced at her. She sipped her milk, feeling the hot liquid fill her stomach and begin to spread its warmth through her body.

'The Reverend has not come recently,' Margrét said, changing the subject.

'No.' Agnes's face was still puffy from sleep, and the older woman suddenly felt an impulse to put an arm around her. It is because she looks like a child, Margrét thought. She tightened her hands about her cup.

'I didn't mean to wake you before,' Agnes said.

Margrét shrugged. 'I often wake at night. When my girls were small I used to wake to check that they were still breathing.'

'Is that why you're awake now?'

Margrét looked at Agnes sharply. 'No. That's not it at all.'

'I'm sorry you have been afraid for them,' Agnes said. 'With me here, I mean.'

'A mother is always afraid for her children,' Margrét said.

'I've never been a mother.'

'No, but you have one.'

Agnes shook her head. 'My mother left me when I was small. I haven't had a mother since.'

'It doesn't matter,' Margrét said eventually. 'Wherever she is, she thinks of you.'

'I don't think so.'

Margrét paused. 'A mother always thinks of her children,' she repeated. 'Your mother, Fridrik's mother, Sigga's mother. All mothers.'

'Sigga's mother is dead,' Agnes said bluntly. 'And Fridrik's mother is going to be sent to Copenhagen.'

'Why?'

Agnes glanced cautiously at Margrét. 'Thórbjörg had an inkling of what Fridrik planned. She knew about some sheep Fridrik stole. She lied to the courtroom.'

'I see,' Margrét said. She took another sip of milk.

'Thórbjörg saved my life,' Agnes added after a moment's pause. 'She found me on her doorstep after Natan threw me out. I would have died had she not brought me inside and let me stay there.'

Margrét nodded. 'No one is all bad.'

'When Thórbjörg was young and a servant, she set fire to her mistress's bed and killed her master's dog with an axe. They brought it up in the trial.'

'Good Lord.'

'It did not help my case,' Agnes said quickly. 'She said we were friends. She told them Natan and I had fought, and that I had sought her advice.'

'But you hadn't?'

'She never told me to burn down Illugastadir, as they claimed. I never went to Katadalur to ask for Thórbjörg's assistance or to conspire with Fridrik. They made it seem that I had gone to Katadalur on purpose. To plan murder.' Agnes sipped her milk, spluttering as she swallowed. 'I went to Katadalur because Natan would not let me stay at Illugastadir and I had nowhere else to go.'

Margrét was silent. She stared into the fire and imagined Agnes creeping about Kornsá at night, lighting a torch in the kitchen and setting the farm ablaze while they slept. Would she smell the smoke and wake?

'It was Fridrik who burned Illugastadir down, wasn't it, Agnes?' Margrét tried to keep the concern from her voice.

'At the trial I said that the fire spread from the kitchen,' Agnes said firmly. 'I said that Natan had set a pot of herbs to boil. It spread from there.'

Margrét said nothing for a moment. 'I heard it was Fridrik.'

'It wasn't,' Agnes said.

Margrét coughed again, and spat into the fire. The moisture bubbled upon the live embers. 'If you are protecting your friend –'

'Fridrik is *not* my friend!' Agnes interrupted. She shook her head and set her milk on the ground. 'He's not my friend.'

'I thought you two spent a deal of time together,' Margrét explained.

Agnes frowned at her, and then returned her gaze to the hearth. 'No. But at Illugastadir . . .' Agnes sighed. 'Natan was not often home. Loneliness . . .' She struggled for words. 'Loneliness threatened to *bite* you at every turn. I took what company presented itself.'

'So Fridrik would visit Illugastadir.'

Agnes nodded. 'It's not far from Katadalur. Fridrik had a little romance with Sigga.'

'I have heard of Sigga.' Margrét got up to set some more dung on the fire.

'People are fond of her. She's pretty.'

'And simple, I have heard.'

Agnes looked at Margrét carefully. 'Yes, well, Fridrik thought otherwise. When Natan was away Fridrik would come from Katadalur on some small errand, or carrying some false message from his parents or the priest, and then he'd feign thirst or hunger. Sigga would fetch a sup of milk or a bite to eat, and they'd laugh and chatter, and by autumn it was not unusual for me to find them sitting together on Sigga's bed, cooing over each other like birds.'

'It's hard to be alone in winter,' Margrét agreed.

Agnes nodded. 'It was worse at Illugastadir. It wasn't like it is here, in the valley. The days crept along as weary as they come, and I had no friends or neighbours. Only Sigga, and Daníel – the manservant Natan hired from Geitaskard – and sometimes Fridrik.'

'The dark can make a body lonely,' Margrét said thoughtfully. 'It's not good for people to be kept too much to themselves.' She offered Agnes more milk.

'Natan never liked winter. He went his whole life without getting used to the darkness.'

'I wonder at him buying Illugastadir then, and not some other farm where folks might keep a body company.'

'He went away a lot,' Agnes conceded. 'To Geitaskard, mainly. He said it was for work, but I think it was to be with friends. Or to avoid me,' she added. 'It would have been better if he was home. We needed him there. But each month he seemed to stay away for longer and longer at a time, and when he did come back he wasn't pleased to see us. He didn't even seem happy to see Thóranna, his daughter. He left her with us.'

'I suppose it was hard-hearted of him to begrudge you a visitor, with you three so lonesome and penned up amongst yourselves.'

Agnes gave a thin smile. 'His problem was perhaps not the fact of a visitor, but the fact of it being Fridrik.'

'I see.'

'Fridrik and Natan had a fraught friendship at the best of times. They were always suspicious of each other. And then they had a fight. It was when the whale was beached at Hindisvík, that autumn.'

'I remember. We bought some whale oil from folk up north of the valley. They went to get what they could.'

'It was a stroke of luck for us. It rained a lot that harvest and we were worried the hay would rot or burst into flames, and we'd find all our animals dead and ourselves no more than skeletons come spring. Natan was home when he heard of the whale, and went to go buy some meat from the family who owned that part of the shoreline.

'Natan was gone all day and didn't come home till evening. When I met him at the door he was covered in mud. It was in his hair, on his face; there wasn't a clean patch on his clothes. When I asked him what had happened, Natan told me that he had been slicing his share from the whale, already bought and paid for, when Fridrik appeared and began to help himself. When Natan told Fridrik to get a knife and pay for his own, Fridrik shoved him to the ground and attacked him. Later, the family at Stapar, the farm next to Illugastadir, told me a different story. They said that Natan had shouted at Fridrik and pushed him in the back, and Fridrik had swung at him, knocking Natan to the ground. Fridrik then beat him, and dragged Natan in the mud. But at the time all I knew was that Natan had come back home in a mess, and a mood to match.'

'How unpleasant for you,' Margrét murmured.

Agnes shook her head. 'It was worse for Sigga. When I was pickling the whale meat I could hear Natan washing in front of the fire, and Sigga trying to soothe him. Natan was shouting that Fridrik was crazy, that he'd kill someone before he turned twenty. Fridrik was Sigga's sweetheart and she took it badly. Of course, she didn't dare say anything to Natan, but when we had gone to bed later that night I heard her crying.'

Margrét didn't say anything. She badly wanted to look at Agnes, but she thought that if she turned in her direction, she would stop talking and things would be as before. She chose her next words carefully.

'It must have been hard for you at Illugastadir.'

'It grew worse after the whale. Natan spent less and less time at home. When he did come back he spent hours telling Sigga and me that he was not paying us to be idle. He found fault with everything we did. The butter was too wet, the badstofa was dirty, someone had been in his workshop and upset his vials. No matter that neither of us dared go inside his workshop when he wasn't there. The wind would stir some object of his, or the yard would be disturbed after one of us had hauled driftwood up to the house, and he'd think that we'd been digging holes, trying to find his money. Neither one of us even knew he buried it out there until he said that.

'Then everything took another turn for the worse. Natan met Fridrik coming from Illugastadir on his return from the south. At first they seemed civil enough, but Sigga, Daníel and I soon heard them shouting at each other across the pass. Natan was threatening blows and the District Commissioner should Fridrik ever step foot on his farm. They went on for some time, before Fridrik left and went home.

'Natan was raging that night. He dragged Sigga outside and I could hear him accusing her of betraying his trust, of lying to him. He threatened to throw her to the winds, and I could hear Sigga pleading with him. She had nowhere to go. No one would hire a servant at this time of year. It was snowing, she would die from cold. Eventually Natan lowered his voice, and I could not hear what he was saying. Neither of them returned indoors for over an hour, but when they did come inside Sigga's eyes were red, and she went straight to bed. Then Natan ordered me to get up and follow him.

'It was as black as pitch. He walked me down to the sea's edge, and told me that Fridrik had asked him for permission to marry Sigga. He said that he had known Sigga had been carrying on with Fridrik behind his back, but he did not think it would lead to this. He thought it had been an idle flirtation.

'When I told Natan that I thought it was a harmless sentiment between two innocents, he laughed, and said that neither of them were what he would call innocent. Then he reached into his pocket and showed me three silver coins, and said the boy had offered him money for his permission to marry Sigga. I asked him why he had taken the money if he seemed so set against it, and Natan laughed and said that only a fool refuses money freely offered. Then he asked me why I'd let Sigga and Fridrik carry on when I knew he didn't want the boy on his property in his absence. I told him that I didn't like Fridrik, but that I was used to farms full of servants and folk about the place, and the days at Illugastadir were the longest I had ever known.'

Agnes took a final draught of her milk and threw the dregs on the fire. Margrét flinched at the hiss.

'I won't sleep again now,' Agnes said.

Margrét nodded. 'No, I don't suppose I will either.' She hesitated. 'I didn't know that Fridrik and Sigga were wedded.'

Agnes gave a short laugh. 'They never married,' she said. 'Although Fridrik did offer her his hand. He came back the very next day. Natan had gone to Geitaskard. Sigga was in a sulk, and slipping about the place like a shadow, and when I cornered her in the kitchen and asked her what Natan had said the night before, she burst into tears and wouldn't say a word. I asked her if she'd told Natan she loved Fridrik and she shook her head. Then I told her about Fridrik's money, how he had paid Natan for her hand in marriage, and this shocked her out of her tears. She gaped at me and mumbled that she couldn't believe Natan had agreed. He had said she ought not to marry such a man. She was too young, and besides, she was *his* servant and would remain so until he saw fit to let her go.

'Daniel saw Fridrik coming that day and told him that he was better off turning tail if he cared to see summer, but Fridrik ignored him and asked me where Sigga was. I hadn't the stomach to follow him indoors and see what passed, so I went down to the shore and waited. And sure enough, Fridrik came out holding Sigga's hand, and told me and Daníel that they were engaged to be wed.'

'What did you do?' Margrét asked.

Agnes sighed. 'What was there to do? I trudged up the slope and poured us all a capful of brandy. Fridrik was beaming, but Sigga was anxious. After a few nips Daníel began to sing songs to the couple and I slipped outside for some fresh air and walked down to the ocean.'

The fire crackled before them. A clump of burning dung broke apart and sent a flurry of sparks towards the rafters.

Eventually Agnes spoke again. 'Do you ever visit the sea?'

Margrét shook her head and huddled into her shawl. 'When I was younger I spent some time working by it. Around Langidalur.'

'The sea is different up around Vatnsnes. Sometimes the water in the fjord is like a looking glass. Something you want to run your tongue across. "As glazed as a dead man's eye," as Natan used to say.' She shifted closer to the fire. 'One time I saw two icebergs grinding against each other. The wind had blown them together. When they came closer I saw that both boulders had gathered driftwood upon their shelves, and after some time I heard a terrible cracking and saw the driftwood erupt into flames.'

'It sounds like something out of the sagas,' Margrét remarked.

'It was eerie,' Agnes agreed. 'I couldn't help but watch. Even when night fell I could still see small flames burning out to sea.'

For a few moments the two women gazed at the fire. The flames were now dying in a red glow that spread over the women's faces. Outside a low moan signalled the onset of more winter winds.

†

AFTER FRIDRIK PROPOSED TO SIGGA it snowed hard enough to bury a highwayman. There was no riding home for Fridrik, and I made him bunk with Daníel. The brandy slipped them into sleep like a shoehorn.

I remained wakeful. Thoughts of Natan and Sigga wormed through my brain, interrupting my dreams. I knew why Natan hated Fridrik. It wasn't because the boy had taken a shine to his wealth and valuables, although that was part of it. No, it was because of Sigga. I decided that he wanted Sigga as much as he didn't want me.

I must have eventually fallen into an uneasy sleep. The badstofa was empty when I woke, and the snow had finally stopped falling. The world outside was white, except for the oily grey of the ocean. There was a noise out by the home field, and when I went out to see what it was, I saw Fridrik kicking a dead sheep. His aggression made my stomach turn.

'What are you doing?' My voice rang out clear and strong in the still air. Fridrik didn't hear me. He kept kicking, grunting. His boots sent up a spray of bloody snow.

'Fridrik!' I called again. 'What are you doing?'

He stopped and turned around. I saw him rub his face on his sleeve and he began to haul his boots through the heavy drifts towards me. As he came closer I saw that he was in a mood.

'Hello, Agnes,' he said, breathing heavily.

'Why are you kicking that animal?'

Fridrik was panting. His breath issued from his mouth in a puff of fog. 'It was already dead.'

'But why were you kicking it?'

'What does it matter?' Fridrik squinted up at the heavy sky. 'More snow's coming, I'm thinking. Best not get caught in it.' He sniffed and wiped his nose on his glove, leaving a shiny smear upon the wool.

'Natan will kill you.' I gestured towards the stain of blood and dirt surrounding the sheep. 'You've ruined the meat. And the skin.'

Fridrik laughed. I wanted to slap him for kicking the sheep, but I had no power over him, and he knew it.

'It was already dead, Agnes. It died this morning.' He wiped a melting fleck of bloody snow from his cheek, and heaved his boot out of the drift to walk past me. 'Don't worry, it will still be good to eat.'

'You've trampled it.'

He rolled his eyes.

'You'll catch your death,' he called out, his back to me. I watched the snow clouds descend upon the mountain and let the chill air prickle at my ribs until I shuddered with the cold.

Seeing Fridrik hack at the sheep with his boots unsettled something within me. It was portentous: the rapid limbs, dark against the snow, colliding with the soft corpse until a fine mist of blood floated above.

Snow began to fall. I turned around to follow Fridrik back to the farm, and saw a raven descend upon the sheep. It gave a mournful caw and then plunged its beak into the innards. Snowflakes landed on its black feathers.

I interrupted Fridrik and Sigga sitting together on her bed, whispering in low voices. Sigga looked as though she had been crying.

'There are two sheep missing,' I said.

'Well, one of them is dead. You saw it yourself.' Fridrik yawned.

'Not the one you were kicking. There are another two besides.'

Fridrik gave a nasty smile and I knew at once what had happened.

'You killed them.' Sigga let out a sob, and Fridrik stood up. He walked over to me and bent close. I could smell his sweat.

'Agnes. You might like to know that Sigga and I have been talking this morning.' His voice cracked with anger. 'Natan has been taking advantage of her.'

I waited until I could speak calmly.

'I already knew.'

Sigga burst into tears. 'I'm sorry, Agnes! I wanted to tell you so bad!'

Fridrik paused. 'You knew?'

'I thought she'd agreed to it.' My voice was brittle.

'He's been raping her!' He began pacing the floor. I noticed that he held Sigga's green silk nightdress in his hand, a present from Natan. 'I'm going to kill him.'

I rolled my eyes. 'Go ahead. A lot of difference that will make now.' I turned to Sigga. 'Did he force you?'

'Of course he forced her!' Fridrik sat down again next to Sigga and punched the mattress. Sigga gave a start.

'I don't know,' she whispered.

I thought back to the night I heard him moving inside her. The night after the death waves. The hurried breathing. A quick, light moan. There had not been a struggle.

'It's against God,' Fridrik said.

I couldn't help but laugh. 'I don't think any of this has much to do with God.'

Sigga looked panicked. 'Agnes? Are you very disappointed in me?'

'Why would I be disappointed?' My voice was as smooth as the ocean.

Fridrik glared, looking down at the nightdress. 'He's a bastard. I'll kill him.'

'I don't want Natan to die.' The simper in Sigga's voice made me want to slap her.

I laughed. 'Fridrik's not going to kill anyone.'

'Yes I am.' He stood up again, his hands in meaty fists.

'No, you're not,' I said. 'Anyway, what does it matter? You're still going to marry her.'

Fridrik sneered. 'I wouldn't expect a woman like you to understand.'

I felt my mouth grow dry.

'Sigga said Natan's been having his way with you as well. Only we seem to think that you enjoy it a sight more than Sigga!'

I stepped towards Sigga and saw her flinch. 'I'm not going to hit you,' I said. But I could have. I wanted to.

Daníel came in and Fridrik fell quiet. I was shaking with anger. I hated Fridrik. I hated his pimpled skin, flushed red by the cold. Hated his blue eyes and their sticky rim of blond lashes. I hated his high voice, his smell of horseshit, his constant visits.

'Go home, Fridrik.' It was Daníel who spoke first.

'There's a snowstorm coming.'

'Then go get caught in it.' I was suddenly grateful for Daníel's presence.

'I'm not going anywhere,' Fridrik said, and he sat down again next to Sigga, putting an arm around her protectively.

'It's true, isn't it?' Daníel asked, whispering. 'It's true about Natan sharing a bed with the both of you.' He shook his head. 'It's unholy.'

'Fridrik has killed some sheep.'

'What? Here?'

'I think he took at least two to Katadalur last night, or early this morning, and killed them there.'

'Natan will murder Fridrik!'

'Not if Fridrik kills Natan first,' I said. 'He's in a temper.'

Daníel ran his hands through his hair, and looked over at the couple on the bed. 'He's a fool and a thug,' he sighed. 'I'll talk to him once his blood cools.'

Natan returned to Illugastadir three days later. Fridrik was not there when he came home. I cannot imagine what would have happened if he had been. As it was, Natan wasn't overjoyed to hear the news of Sigga and Fridrik's engagement. I told him. Sigga slipped out to the storeroom at the sound of his arrival in the yard.

'I can't leave you alone without some disaster befalling the lot of us.'

'It's hardly a disaster, Natan. You accepted Fridrik's money for her; you should have known this was coming.'

'I suppose you're happy about this,' he grunted.

'Me? What has any of this got to do with me?'

'You've been playing matchmaker all autumn long.'

I held out my hands for the bridle as he unsaddled his horse. 'I have been doing no such thing.'

'I suppose you have all been celebrating.'

'No. Even Sigga seems confused about what has happened.'

He turned around to face me properly, raising an eyebrow. 'Is that so?'

I nodded. 'Fridrik's leaping out of his pants for joy, but Sigga doesn't seem so thrilled.'

Natan smiled then, and shook his head. 'A couple of young idiots, the both of them.' He gently took the bridle and saddlecloth out of my hand and placed them on the snow. His face was sober. 'Agnes. My Agnes, I owe you an apology. I shouldn't have hit you.'

I didn't say anything, but I didn't resist when he took up my hand.

'I have been talking with Worm, and he thinks I am distracted. Travelling too much in the damp. The dreams, they ...' His voice trailed off. 'We've all behaved badly towards one another. I have not been myself.'

He released my hand and picked up the bridle and cloth. 'Here,' he said, giving them to me. 'Put these away and I'll see you inside.'

I turned to leave, but he held onto me. 'Agnes,' he said, gently. 'I'm glad to see you.'

That night we shook with the same desires that possessed us as before. And when we woke in the wintered darkness, my body flushed with happiness at the knowledge that he slept beside me. If Sigga or Daníel woke and saw us lying there together they said nothing. I stripped his bed of blankets and placed them at the foot of my own.

MARGRÉT RETURNED FROM THE DAIRY with another pan of milk. Outside the wind blew so hard that a hollow moaning could be heard.

Agnes leaned over and prodded the coals of the fire. 'Shall I use peat or dung?' she asked.

Margrét pointed to the dung. 'Go on. We may as well keep the fire burning for as long as we sit here.'

'Where was I?'

'You were saying that Fridrik proposed to Sigga.' Margrét gently poured more milk into the pot. It hissed as it touched the hot metal.

'Sigga was terrified to see Natan after she'd agreed to marry Fridrik. Natan found her hiding in the storeroom. She told me later that he said he'd been unreasonable, and let his own grievances with Fridrik blind him. He'd given her his blessing, and said that if she wanted to marry a boy with neither a coin nor a name to be proud of, then that was her choice. He told me he was not going to stop two puppies from playing with one another.

'I thought perhaps he'd realised that if Sigga married Fridrik, he wouldn't have to see the boy's face again. Wouldn't have to worry about his money, hidden about the place.

'The days of Yuletide flew past, and we did little to mark them. Natan sent Daníel back to Geitaskard, and I thought it would be like the old days when it was just Sigga and me. I wanted to clean the croft and prepare skate for St Thorlak's Mass, but she'd lost interest in talking to me since her engagement to Fridrik. She'd become moody, lax with her work and forever gazing out the window. She'd jump when spoken to. Avoid eye contact. Natan had told her she might invite Fridrik to Illugastadir for a drink to mark Yuletide, but he hadn't come. Perhaps Sigga didn't trust Natan's sudden goodwill towards Fridrik. I believe she was anxious to keep the two men apart.'

LATE ONE NIGHT I DECIDED to tell him.

'Natan, I know that you have had Sigga.'

He had been dozing, but his eyes opened at this.

'I know, Natan. I forgive you.'

He looked at me, and then suddenly laughed. 'You forgive me?'

I reached for his hand in the darkness. 'I'm not talking about this to argue. But I want you to know that I know.'

His fingers lay in mine like a dead weight. He was thinking.

'I knew you saw us,' he said.

His words hit me like a blow to the stomach. My mouth opened and shut with no sound escaping. I got out of bed and brought back a lamp. I could not talk to him without seeing his face. I could not trust his words in the dark.

The lamplight flared over his bare skin. He regarded me coolly, turning away only to glance in Sigga's direction, to see if she was awake.

'Natan.'

My voice sounded old. I looked down and saw myself, naked, and for the first time I guessed how he saw me.

'You've been playing with me.'

Natan shielded his eyes with a hand. 'Put the lamp out, Agnes.'

I grabbed hold of the bedpost to steady myself. 'You're cruel.'

'I don't want to talk about this.'

'You were never going to give me the housekeeping position, were you?'

'Put the lamp out, and let's go to sleep. Your eyes look like two piss-holes in the snow.'

'Go to sleep?!' I stared at him, waiting until I knew I could speak without crying. 'How did you know I knew?'

He smiled at this. Said nothing.

'Do you love me?'

'You're being ridiculous.'

'Answer me.'

He reached for the lamp. 'Put it out!'

'Natan.' I was beseeching him. The whine in my voice horrified me. 'Would I have asked you here if I didn't want you here?'

'Yes, as your *workmaid*.'

'You're more than a servant, Agnes.'

'Am I?'

'Put the lamp out.'

'No!' I snatched it out of his grasp. 'You can't treat me like this!'

His eyes flashed. 'You're a nag, Agnes.'

I exploded.

'A nag? Go to hell! I've always let you do what you want. Do I stop you leaving all the time? Do I stop you climbing on top of Sigga in the next bed when you think I'm asleep? She's fifteen! You're a fucking dog.'

He leaned back on his elbows. 'What makes you think I wait until you're asleep?'

The look on Natan's face was not of derision, but of scornful amusement. An immediate weight of despair and loss pressed on me until I was suddenly, unalterably, concave with grief.

'I hate you.' The words seemed stupid, childish.

'And do you think I love you?' Natan shook his head. 'You, Agnes?' He narrowed his eyes and stood up, his breath hot in my face. 'You're a cheap sort of woman. I was wrong about you.'

'If I am cheap it is because you have made me so!'

'Yes, go on. You're pure and holy, and everyone else is to blame.'

'No, you are to blame!'

'Forgive me, I thought you wanted this.' He grabbed me and pulled me roughly to him. 'I thought you wanted to get out of the valley. But you just want what you can't have.'

'I wanted you! I wanted to leave the valley because I wanted to be with you.' I felt sick with anger. 'I can't stand it here.'

'Then go!' He took a step back and grabbed me by my wrist. 'Get out! You've done nothing but cause trouble!' He started to pull me out of the badstofa. I was aware of Sigga sitting up in bed, watching us. Thóranna had begun to cry.

'Let go of me!'

'I'm just giving you what you want. You hate me? You want to leave? Good! Here is the door.'

As small as he was, Natan was strong. He dragged me down the corridor and pushed me over the doorstep. I tripped on the ledge and went sprawling into the snow, naked. By the time I got to my knees, he had slammed the door in my face.

It was dark and snowing heavily outside, but I was so light-headed with anger and grief that I felt nothing. I wanted to hammer down the door, to go to the window and scream for Sigga to let me back inside, but I also wanted to punish him. I wrapped my bare arms about my body and wondered where I should go. The cold needled through my skin. I thought about killing myself, about walking down to the shore and pushing my limbs into the frigid water. The cold would kill me; I wouldn't have to drown. I imagined Natan finding me dead, washed up amongst the seaweed.

I went to the cowshed.

It was too cold to sleep. I crouched down next to the cow and pressed my bare skin against her warm bulk, and pulled down a saddlecloth to cover myself with. I pushed my freezing toes into a cowpat so they would not suffer.

At some time in the night someone entered the cowshed.

'Natan?' My voice was thin and pathetic.

It was Sigga. She had brought me my clothes and shoes. Her eyes were puffy from crying.

'He won't let you back inside,' she said.

I dressed slowly, my fingers stiff with cold. 'And what if I die out here?'

She turned to leave, but I grabbed her shoulder.

'Talk some sense into him, Sigga. He's actually gone mad this time.'

She looked at me, her eyes filling with tears. 'I'm so sick of living here,' she whispered.

The next morning I woke, and for a few moments I didn't know where I was. Then my memory of the night came back to me, and anger tightened my stomach, invigorating me. I leaned against the cow, warming my cold nose and fingers, thinking of what I should do. I wanted to leave before Natan came out to feed the stock.

TÓTI WOKE IN THE SHADOWED badstofa of Breidabólstadur and saw his father at the end of his bed, slumped against the wall. His grizzled head lolled on his chest. He was asleep.

'Pabbi?' His voice was no more than a whisper. The effort seared his throat.

He tried to move his foot to nudge his father awake, but his limbs were heavier than he had ever known them to be. 'Pabbi?' he tried again.

Reverend Jón stirred, and suddenly opened his eyes. 'Son!' He wiped his beard and leaned forward. 'You're awake. Thank God.'

Tóti tried to lift his arm and realised that it was bound to his side. He was swaddled in blankets.

'You've been suffering yet another fever,' his father explained. 'I've had to sweat it out.' He pressed a calloused hand against Tóti's forehead.

'I need to go to Kornsá,' Tóti murmured. His tongue was dry. 'Agnes.'

His father shook his head. 'It's the care of her that's done this to you.'

Tóti looked distressed. 'I have forgotten the month.'

'December.'

He tried to sit up, but Reverend Jón gently pushed his head back down on the pillow. 'You'll pay her no heed until God restores you.'

'She has no one,' Tóti argued, trying again to lift himself. His muscles barely responded.

'And for good reason,' his father said, his voice suddenly loud in the small room. He held his son down on the bed, his face grey in the unlit badstofa. 'She's not worth the time you give her.'

MARGRÉT WAS SILENT A MOMENT. The milk had cooled in her cup. 'He threw you into the snow?'

Agnes nodded, watching the older woman carefully.

Margrét shook her head. 'You could have frozen to death.'

'He wasn't in his right mind.' Agnes drew her shawl more tightly about her shoulders. 'Natan had wanted Sigga for himself. He finally understood that she preferred Fridrik.'

Margrét sniffed and nudged a burning ember back against the hearth wall with a poker. 'As you say, then.' She stole a glance at Agnes, who was staring into the fire. 'Go on,' she said quietly.

Agnes sighed and unfolded her arms. 'I went to Fridrik's family's home at Katadalur. I had not been there before, but I knew where it lay beyond the mountain, and the day grew clear enough for me to walk there without falling victim to the weather. It took me hours though, and by the time I entered the mouth of the valley where Katadalur stood, I was delirious with fatigue. Fridrik's mother found me on my knees on her doorstop.

'Katadalur is a horrible place. All slumped and squat, with the roof threatening to fall in, and the inside of the farm as miserable as its outside. Smoke from dung fires on the walls of the kitchen and the badstofa as cheerless as they come. When I entered there was a group of children, all of them Fridrik's siblings, huddled together on one bed, just trying to stay warm. Fridrik was sitting next to his father and uncle on another bed, sharpening knives.

'The first thing Fridrik said to me was, "What has he done now?" He asked me if Natan had decided to marry Sigga.

'I shook my head and explained that he'd thrown me out. I told him I'd spent the night in the cowshed. Fridrik was not sympathetic. He asked me what I'd done to cause it, and I told him I'd fought with Natan, saying I couldn't abide him treating Sigga the way he was.

'That's when Fridrik's mother interrupted. She'd been listening quietly to us, and all of a sudden she gripped Fridrik's arm and said: "He means to deprive you of your wife."

'I thought I saw Fridrik glance down to the knife on the bed covers and I became fearful.

'I suggested that Fridrik speak to the priest at Tjörn, that maybe they could go to a District Officer. But Thórbjörg, Fridrik's mother, interrupted me again. She stood up and gripped Fridrik about the shoulders, and looked him in the eye. She said: "You will not have Sigga while Natan is alive." Then they all sat down, and while I slept, they must have decided to kill him.'

Margrét was still. The fire had died. Only a thin glowing crust of live ember flickered amid the ashes. The wind had not stopped wailing. Margrét slowly exhaled. She felt weary. 'Perhaps we ought to return to bed.'

Agnes turned to her. 'Don't you want to hear the rest?'

CHAPTER TWELVE

OVER AT LAUGAR, IN SÆLINGSDALE, Gudrún rose early
as soon as the sun was up. She went to the room where her
brothers were sleeping, and shook Ospak. Ospak and his
brothers woke up at once; and when he saw it was his sister he
asked her what she wanted, to be up so early in the morning.
Gudrún said she wanted to know what they were planning to
do that day. Ospak said they would be having a quiet day – 'for
there isn't much work to be done just now.'

Gudrún said, 'You would have had just the right temper
if you had been peasants' daughters – you do nothing about
anything, whether good or bad. Despite all the disgrace
and dishonour that Kjartan has done you, you lose no sleep
over it even when he rides past your door with only a single
companion. It's obviously futile to hope that you will ever dare
to attack Kjartan at home if you haven't the nerve to face him
now when he is travelling with only one or two companions.
You just sit at home pretending to be men, and there are
always too many of you about.'

Ospak said she was making too much of this, but admitted
that it was difficult to argue against her. He jumped out of bed
at once and dressed, as did all the brothers one after another;
then they made ready to lay an ambush for Kjartan.

Laxdæla Saga

NATAN WAS NOT HOME WHEN Fridrik and I arrived at Illugastadir. I'm not sure what would have happened if he had been. It took several minutes of knocking before Sigga opened the door to let us in. She carried Natan's daughter on her hip.

'He told me to refuse you if you came back,' she said, but she let us in anyway.

I accepted the coffee she gave us. 'Where is Natan?' I asked.

'A messenger from Geitaskard arrived. Worm's not well. Natan left early this morning.'

'How has he been?'

Sigga gave me a look. 'He's been in a bad temper.'

'Has he forced you again?' Fridrik was examining Natan's shelf by his bed. Sigga watched anxiously as he picked up a few boxes and rattled them.

'What are you looking for?'

'Compensation,' Fridrik muttered. He peered out the window at the snow outside. 'I bet I was right. I bet he's buried it all in the yard.'

I looked at Sigga. 'Has he said anything about me?'

Sigga shook her head.

I attempted a grim smile. 'Nothing you'd like to repeat to my face.'

Fridrik dusted the snow off his shoulders and sat down next to Sigga, drawing her onto his lap. 'My little bird,' he said. 'My wife.'

Sigga resisted his caresses and sat back down on the bed. 'Don't call me that,' she said.

Fridrik flushed red. 'Why not? You're mine.'

'Natan told me he's changed his mind. He won't allow it.' Her voice broke into a sob. 'Not ever.'

'Goddamn Natan!'

Despite the sombre mood of our gathering, it was hard not to smile at Fridrik's dramatic cry. 'I'm sure Natan will get over it,' I said.

Sigga wiped her eyes and shook her head. 'He says he will be the one to marry me if anyone does.'

My stomach dropped, and I noticed Fridrik turn pale. 'What?'

'That's what he said,' Sigga sniffed.

'What did you say?' My voice sounded thin and shaky.

Sigga burst into a fresh bout of sobbing.

'You didn't say yes, did you?' Fridrik placed an arm around her, and Sigga pushed her face into his neck. She howled.

We three spent the next two days together at Illugastadir, making plans to leave. Sigga thought that she might be able to return to Stóra-Borg, and I offered to take her with me back to the valley as soon as the weather allowed. Fridrik suggested that I go to Ásbjarnarstadir to ask for work until winter's end. He said the farmer there did not like Natan; he might take me on out of sympathy.

We were talking in this way one afternoon when we saw travellers coming down the mountain pass. We'd been so wrapped up in our plans to escape that we hadn't seen them appear. We were outside in the yard, taking some air in the finer weather, and it was too late for us to hide. They would have seen us.

'Agnes!' Sigga hissed. 'It's Natan. He'll tan me when he sees you.'

My heart was beating like a battle drum, but I dared not show it. 'He's not alone, Sigga. He won't do anything with company about.'

We three stood waiting for the pair of riders. When they came close enough, I was surprised to see Sheepkiller-Pétur riding with Natan.

'Look, Pétur,' Natan said. 'Three little foxes sneaking about the place.' He smiled, but his eyes were cold. I thought he might attack Fridrik, but instead he dismounted and walked up to me.

'What is she doing here?' His smile vanished. I flushed red, and stole a glance at Pétur. He seemed taken aback.

'Please let her come back, just until winter is over,' Sigga protested.

'I've had enough of you, Agnes.'

'What have I even done?' I was pretending to be calm.

'You said you wanted to go, so go!' He took another step towards me. 'Leave!'

Sigga looked anxious. 'She's got no place to stay, Natan. It's going to snow.'

Natan laughed. 'You never mean what you say, Agnes. You say one thing, and a different meaning lurks beneath it. You want to leave? Leave!'

I wanted to tell Natan that I wanted him; that I wanted him to love me back. But I said nothing. There was nothing I could have said.

It was Fridrik who broke the silence.

'You're not going to marry her,' he announced through gritted teeth.

Natan laughed. 'Not this again.' He turned to Pétur. 'See what happens when you live with children? They draw you into their little games.'

Pétur gave a thin smile.

'Fine.' Natan started to lead his horse towards the field. 'Agnes can stay, but not in the badstofa. Pétur and I are going to sleep here tonight, and then we're going to Geitaskard again in the morning. If you're still here when we return, I'm handing you over to the District

Commissioner as a trespasser. Fridrik, leave before I get Pétur to slit your throat.' He laughed, but Pétur looked at the ground.

I slept in the cowshed again that night. It wasn't so cold as when Natan first threw me out, and Sigga helped me make up a little bed before returning inside. It stank of shit, and the floor was alive with lice, but eventually I fell asleep.

When I woke, it was dark. I stood up and went to the doorway, and saw light still issuing from the window in the croft. I felt clear-headed after my rest, and was about to walk back to the farm to see if I couldn't make it up with Natan when I heard footsteps in the snow behind the cowshed.

'Sigga?'

The footsteps stopped, then I heard their soft crunch again. They were coming towards me. I retreated into the darkness of the shed and pressed my back against the wall.

I heard a low whisper. 'Agnes?'

It was Fridrik.

He slipped inside the entrance.

'What the hell are you doing here?'

He was breathing hard. I couldn't see him in the shadows, but I could smell his sweat. Something clinked.

'Did you walk here from Katadalur?'

He coughed and spat. 'Yes.'

'Natan's going to kill you if he sees you.'

'I'll wait until he's asleep.'

'To do what? If he wakes up and catches you and Sigga whispering sweet nothings in the bed next to his he'll have you hung and quartered before day breaks.'

I heard Fridrik sniff.

'I've not come for that.'

There was something in his tone that gave me pause.

'Fridrik. What have you come for?'

'I'm going to sort this out once and for all. I've come for what's mine.'

Behind us the cow gave a low groan. I heard the scrape of hooves on the earthen floor.

'Fridrik?'

'Admit it. You want this too, Agnes.'

At that point the moon slipped out from its shield of clouds, and I saw what Fridrik held in his hands. It was a hammer and a knife.

WHAT DO I REMEMBER? I didn't believe him. I went back to my bed on the floor of the cowshed, suddenly weary. I wanted nothing to do with him.

What happened?

I woke up from a fitful sleep and went outside. The light from the croft window had gone out. Fridrik was nowhere to be seen.

I went to go find him. I was suddenly scared. The night sky was clear and the farm was lit with moonlight. The sting of stars. Snow squeaked under my shoes. I fumbled at the latch but the door creaked open anyway.

Sigga was crouched against the wall of the corridor, clutching Rósa's little girl. They were whimpering.

'Sigga?'

It took her a moment before she could respond. 'The badstofa,' she whispered. I could hardly hear her.

I walked down that long passageway. Somehow I knew to take a light from the kitchen. My heart was in my throat.

What happened?

I was shaking, my hands fumbled, and I dropped the lamp in the dark. There was the sudden smell of a snuffed wick, and a sound in the corner. A creaking board and someone panting, hard and fast, and more sounds, dull, like a child punching a pillow. A groan, the sound of something wet, and then a voice whispering: 'Agnes?'

My heart skipped a beat. I thought Natan was there.

But it was Fridrik.

'Agnes,' he was saying, 'Agnes, where are you?' His voice was thin.

'I'm here,' I said. I bent down and felt in the murk for the lamp. 'I dropped the light.'

I heard Fridrik take a step towards the direction of my voice. 'Agnes, I don't know if he's dead.' His voice caught on the last word. 'I can't tell if he's dead.'

My heart stopped still. My fingers would not move. I was pushing them across the gritty boards, trying to find the lamp, but my knuckles had seized and would not bend. He hasn't killed him. He's a boy. He hasn't killed him.

Somehow I found the lamp. I scooped it up, my hand grazing against the splinters of the floor.

'Agnes?'

'I'm here!' I snapped back. The tone of my voice surprised me. I did not sound as frightened as I was. 'I need to light the lamp.'

'Hurry then,' Fridrik said.

I felt my way to the corridor, where a single candle stood alight in a wall bracket. I lit the lamp, and then turned back towards the badstofa. My hands were trembling and the light of the lamp flickered uneasily over the rough walls, towards the black mouth of the badstofa. When I reached the room I felt my throat close from fear. I didn't want to go in there. But I needed to see what Fridrik had done.

At first I thought he'd tricked me. When I extended the lamp towards Natan's bed, I saw his blankets, and his sleeping face. Nothing seemed wrong. Then Fridrik said: 'Here, Agnes, bring the lamp here,' and as the light crept across the bed I saw that Pétur's head was crushed. Blood darkened the pillow. Something glistened on the wall, and when I looked I saw several drops of blood slowly running down the planks.

'Oh God,' I said. 'Oh God. Oh God.'

I looked at the hammer he held in his hands, and there was something stuck to it – it was hair. I was sick then, on the floor.

Fridrik helped me to my feet. He was still gripping the hammer, holding it out at the ready. 'Have you hurt Natan?' I asked, and Fridrik told me to bring the lamp closer to the bed. Natan was bleeding also. One side of his face looked strange, as though his cheekbone had been flattened, and what I thought was Pétur's blood was pooling in the cavity of his neck.

A scream erupted from my chest and strength left me. I dropped the lamp again, and fell to the floor in the darkness that erupted over us.

Fridrik must have fetched the candle from the corridor. I saw his face shine as he entered the room. Then, we both heard a voice.

'What was that?' Fridrik quickly walked over to my side and pulled me to my feet. We were trembling. The sound came again. A groan.

'Natan?' I grabbed the candle from Fridrik and lurched towards the bed, holding it close to Natan's face. I saw his eyelids twitch in the bright flare, and he tried to stir on the bed.

'What did you do to him?' Fridrik was as white as a corpse, his pupils so dilated they looked black.

'The hammer ...' he mumbled.

Natan groaned again, and this time Fridrik bent close, listening.

'He said "Worm".'

'Worm Beck?'

'Maybe he's dreaming.'

We stood still, watching Natan for more signs of life. The silence was deadening. Then Natan slowly opened one of his eyes, and looked right at me.

'Agnes?' he murmured.

'I'm here,' I said. A rush of relief went through me. 'Natan, I'm here.'

His eye moved from me to Fridrik. Then, he swivelled his head and saw Pétur's staved-in skull. I saw that he knew what had happened.

'No,' he croaked. 'No, no no no.'

Fridrik stepped backwards from me. I wasn't going to let him leave.

'Look what you've done!' I whispered. 'Look at your work.'

'I didn't mean to! Natan, I swear.' Fridrik began to pant, staring at the bloody hammer by our feet.

Natan cried out again. He was trying to get up from his bed, but screamed when he put weight on his arm. Fridrik had crushed it.

'You wanted him dead!' I cried, facing Fridrik. 'What are you going to do now?'

There was a thump and we both looked down and saw Natan on the ground. He had dragged himself out of the bed with his good arm, but could go no further.

'Help me lift him,' I said to Fridrik, setting the candle on the floor, but the boy wouldn't touch him. I bent down and tried to drag Natan upright, so that he could rest his head against the beam, but he was too heavy, and when I saw the way his skull had swollen, the blood that had poured down his back, I lost all my strength: my limbs turned to water. I cradled his head in my lap and I saw that he would not survive the night.

'Fridrik,' Natan was repeating over and over. 'Fridrik, I will pay you, I will pay you.'

'He wants to talk to you, Fridrik,' I said, but Fridrik had turned his face away, and would not look at us. 'Turn around,' I screamed. 'The least you could do is speak to the man you have killed!'

Natan stopped murmuring. I felt his body stiffen, and he looked up at me, his head lolling slightly. 'Agnes …'

'Yes, it's me, Agnes. I'm here, Natan. I'm here.'

His mouth gaped open. I thought he was trying to say something, but all that came out was a gargling. I looked up at Fridrik and he was standing there, his face white-pale and his hair in his eyes and red at one side where the blood had burst and hit him. His eyes were wide and scared.

'Why is he doing that?' he asked. Natan was choking, blood spilling out onto his chin, onto my skirt.

'Why is he doing that?!' Fridrik screamed. 'Make him stop!'

I reached over and picked the knife up from the floor. 'Do it then, finish what you've begun!'

Fridrik shook his head. His face was ashen and he stared at me in horror.

'Do it!' I said. 'Will you leave him to slowly die?'

Fridrik kept shaking his head. He flinched as a little stream of blood erupted anew from Natan's head wound. 'No,' he said. 'I can't. I can't.'

Natan looked up at me: his teeth were red from blood. His lips moved silently, and I understood what he was trying to say.

The knife went in easily. It pierced Natan's shirt with neat rips, sounding like an ill-practised kiss – I couldn't have stopped if I'd wanted to. My fist jerked, until I felt sudden, close warmth over my wrist and realised that his blood covered my hand. The warmth of it was noticeable against the chill of the night. I released the handle, and pushed Natan away from me, looking down at the knife. It stuck out from his belly, and his shirt was dark and wetly puckered around the blade. For a moment we stared at each other. The light from the candle caught the edge of his forehead, his eyelashes, and I was suddenly overwhelmed with gratitude – he regarded me clearly. It seemed like forgiveness.

'Agnes.' Fridrik was behind me, his hands on his head, the hammer on the floor. 'Agnes, you've killed him.'

I wanted to cry. I wanted to kneel over his body and wail. But there was no time.

I hated Fridrik. He had crumbled, had shrunk to the floor and begun to sob, heaving huge lungfuls of air in a panic that never seemed to cease. Eventually he got up, his breath shuddering, and pulled the knife out of Natan's belly.

'What are you doing?' I asked him. I did not have the energy to scream.

'That's my knife,' Fridrik said. He wiped it on his trousers and began to walk outside.

'Wait!' I called.

Fridrik turned and shrugged.

'You'll be hanged for this,' I croaked. Fridrik paused. I saw his fingers clench around the knife's sticky handle.

'If I am hanged,' he said slowly, sniffing back a breath of snot, 'you will be burnt alive.'

I looked down and saw the blood on my hands. On my neck, soaking my dress. I saw the candle flame flicker in an unseen draught, and wondered at what the room would look like in the grey light of day.

That's when I remembered the whale fat that Natan had bought at Hindisvík.

CHAPTER THIRTEEN

22nd of December 1829

*Promemoria: To Björn Blöndal, District Commissioner of
Húnavatn*

Here I am presenting to Your Honour the following:

*1. The original copy of the Supreme Court's ruling from
the 25th of June of this year in the case and prosecution
against Fridrik Sigurdsson, Agnes Magnúsdóttir and Sigrídur
Gudmundsdóttir from Húnavatn District for murder, arson and
theft, among other crimes. The Supreme Court sentence arrived
here on the 20th of this month with an extra mail delivery from
Reykjavík.*

*2. Confirmed copy of His Majesty the King's letter: To the
District Governor on the 26th of August, in regard to Sigrídur
Gudmundsdóttir, the aforementioned is by the King's grace and
mercy pardoned from the punishment of death as sentenced
by the aforementioned Supreme Court in Copenhagen. She
will instead, by His Majesty the King's decree, be moved to
Copenhagen to work in a prison for the term of her natural*

life under strict surveillance. It has also been decided that the Supreme Court's sentencing in regards to the convicts Fridrik Sigurdsson and Agnes Magnúsdóttir will stand.

3. Confirmed copy of the document from the Royal Secretarial Office of Denmark to the District Governor from the 29th of August concerning this case, where the Secretary to the Royal Sovereign has published the opinion that it would be best for the penalty to be fulfilled where the crime was committed, or as close to it as possible, and only then if it will not cause riot or unpredictable events. The District Governor must be in absolute agreeance with this.

4. The sanction, which has been made ready today, for Gudmundur Ketilsson, the farmer at Illugastadir, to execute the convicts Fridrik Sigurdsson and Agnes Magnúsdóttir according to the Supreme Court ruling, which, according to the secretarial letters, I must now request you, Your Honour, to manage in a proper manner. Your Honour must ensure that the death sentences, in consideration of the changes that are outlined in the aforementioned Royal letter from His Majesty the King, are carried out in a legal manner and fulfilled without delay. Your Honour is requested to send confirmation when the death sentences have been fulfilled. My most Honourable Sir, as the local District Commissioner you are trusted to prepare and execute the convicts in a proper manner, and to arrange all things according to the intricacies of this situation. However, I must insist that you heed the following details:

a. If it has not already been done, Your Honour must immediately arrange for priests to visit the guilty persons,

Fridrik Sigurdsson and Agnes Magnúsdóttir, every day. The priests must be supervised, and must address to the prisoners religious lectures of meaning, must comfort them and prepare them to walk towards their destiny. The priests should follow the prisoners to their execution place.

b. It has been agreed that Your Honour may decide if the execution will take place close to Illugastadir, or at a good site in the so-called Thingi, or upon a hill at some place (but not too high), where others may see it in all directions.

c. Instead of a wooden platform, Your Honour may give directions for a good turf platform with a handrail to be built. Your Honour must arrange for a block with a chin-groove to be placed on top of this platform, and to see that it is covered with a red cloth of cotton or plain-woven wool.

d. The selected executioner shall, at Your Honour's home and with secrecy and encouragement, be trained for the mission that he has been entrusted with. This will be done to ensure, as much as possible, that he, at this important moment, will not lose faith or control. The beheading must be carried out in one blow without any pain for the convicted. Gudmundur Ketilsson must only drink a very little dose of spirits.

e. Your Honour is requested to summon as many men from the neighbouring farms as needed to build two or three rings around the platform. These farmers are all obligated to attend without accepting any payment thereof.

f.   No unauthorised person is permitted to go inside the rings.

g.   The one who will be executed later is not permitted to witness the execution of the first, and should be kept aside at a place where they do not have a direct view of the platform.

h.   The dead bodies that remain behind following the execution must be buried on the spot without ceremony, in white untreated wood. It is absolutely vital that Your Honour and Most Respected Person be present at the execution site to read out the verdict of the Supreme Court and His Majesty the King, to organise and control the execution procedure, and to record the execution in the book of the office. Your Honour may register the executions in Danish or Icelandic, but it must be done well and a translation of the record must be sent to my office. Your Honour's record must include a perfect and detailed description of the events and how it concluded. Also, you must record that Gudmundur Ketilsson was promised for the job, and specify how he has decided to use the money awarded to him for his services, for what purpose and so on. And at last I want to thank you for Your Honour's letter on the 20th of August. In response, I tell you here that the axe must be returned to Copenhagen after the execution and that the payment for it must be paid as with the other costs of this case.

G. Johnson
SECRETARY TO HIS ROYAL MAJESTY
COPENHAGEN, DENMARK

To the District Officers of Svínavatn,
Thorkelshóll and Thverá Districts

After receiving the Right Honourable Supreme Court sentence
from the 25th of June, and His Majesty the King's most gracious
Royal Letter from the 26th of August, I hereby confirm that
the criminals, Fridrik Sigurdsson and Agnes Magnúsdóttir
will be executed on Tuesday the 12th of January, on a little hill
close to the cottage of Ránhóla, between the farms Hólabak and
Sveinsstadir.

   After the description provided to the District Governor from
the 22nd of December, I must ask you to order the farmers in
the District of Svínavatn, whom you yourself select, to attend the
execution with you at this certain place on this day, at the latest
time of noon. This must be done as soon as possible. According
to Chapter Seven of Jónsbok, titled Mannhelgisbalk, and Chapter
Two, titled Thjófnadarbalk, these farmers are obligated to attend,
and if they don't obey your directions they will be penalised. It
is recommended that you warn the men who will have the most
difficulties leaving their farms, or travelling, about this. Please
also note that you, yourselves, must be present at this event.

   If it is such that that the executions are not possible to carry
out on this day due to weather, the next day possible will then be
selected, and all the people who have been ordered to attend must
do so, as stated above. It will be necessary for each and every one
of the men to arrange food and sustenance for themselves, as it is

quite possible their journey there and back will incur delays due to the weather at this time of year.

DISTRICT COMMISSIONER
Björn Blöndal

Thursday, 7th of January 1830

Most respected and deeply beloved friend and brother (B. Blöndal).

For what you have done for me, for our many meetings and for your instruction and delivery this morning, I thank you with love and passion, and confirm here that this morning I will meet the people in Vídidalur and warn them about being early enough on Tuesday next. I have told Sigrídur about the conditions of her pardon, and she is praying to God and thanking the King for her kind treatment. Sorry about the hastiness, God be with you and yours, wishing you all well in this new beginning year, as with all coming time, both in this life and in the next one. So say I, your truthful, loving friend,

Br. P. Pétursson of Midhóp

The Icelandic Burial Hymn

I think upon my Saviour,
I trust His power to keep,
His mighty arm enfolds me
Awaking and in sleep.
Christ is my rock, my courage;
Christ is my soul's true life;
And Christ (my still heart knows it)
Will bear me through the strife.

Thus in Christ's name I'm living;
Thus in Christ's name I'll die;
I'll fear not though life's vigour,
From Death's cold shadow fly.
O Grave, where is thy triumph?
O Death, where is thy sting?
'Come when thou wilt, and welcome!'
Secure in Christ I sing.

ON THE SIXTH DAY OF January, a sharp rapping on the cottage door woke Tóti. He opened one eye and saw the weak light in the room: he had slept late. The knocking continued. Reluctantly, he dragged his stockinged feet to the floor and got out of bed, wrapping his blankets about him to ward off the sharp bite of cold. His legs trembled, he walked to the front door, one hand against the wall to steady himself.

The visitor was a messenger from Hvammur, blowing on his hands and stamping his boots in the frigid morning air. He nodded and handed Tóti a small folded letter. It was marked with the red seal of Blöndal, looking like a drop of blood against the pale paper.

'Assistant Reverend Thorvardur Jónsson?'

'Yes.'

The man's nose was pink from cold. 'Sorry about the delay. The weather has been so bad, I haven't been able to come any sooner.'

Tóti wearily invited the man in for a cup of coffee, but the servant looked out towards the northern pass anxiously. 'If you don't mind, Reverend, I'll be on my way again. There's more snow coming and I don't have a mind to get caught in it.'

Tóti heaved the door to and staggered into the kitchen to stir up the coals. Where was his father? He set a kettle of water upon the hearth to bring to the boil, and slowly dragged a stool over to the fire. After the dizziness had passed, he broke the seal and opened the letter.

Tóti read the letter three times, then let it rest on his knee as he stared at the fire. It could not be happening. Not like this. Not with so much unsaid and undone, and him not even by her side. He suddenly rose, the blankets slipping off his shoulders, and walked unsteadily into the badstofa. He was opening his trunk, pulling out clothes and dressing, and stuffing a few more into a sack, when his father came in to the croft.

'Tóti? What has happened? Why are you dressing? You're not yet recovered.'

Tóti let the lid of his trunk slam shut and shook his head. 'It's Agnes. She is to be killed in six days' time. I only received the letter now.' He fell onto his bed and tried to force his foot into a boot.

'You're not fit to go.'

'It is too sudden, Father. I've failed her.'

The old man sat down alongside his son. 'You're not well enough,' he said sternly. 'The cold will kill you. It's snowing outside.'

Tóti's head pounded. 'I have to get to Kornsá. If I leave now I might miss the storm.'

Reverend Jón placed a heavy hand on his son's shoulder. 'Tóti, you can hardly dress yourself. Do not kill yourself for the sake of this murderess.'

Tóti glared at his father, his eyes lit with anger. 'And what of the Son of God? Did He die only for the righteous?'

'You are not the Son of God. If you go you will kill yourself.'

'I'm leaving.'

'I forbid it.'

'It is God's will.'

The old Reverend shook his head. 'It is suicide. It is against God.'

Tóti stood unsteadily and looked down at his father. 'God will forgive me.'

The church was bitterly cold. Tóti lurched towards the altar and collapsed onto his knees. He was aware of his hands trembling, his skin burning under the layers of clothes. The ceiling swam above him.

'Lord God ...' His voice cracked. 'Pity her,' he continued. 'Pity us all.'

†

MARGRÉT WAS WRAPPING A SHAWL about her head, preparing to fetch some dried dung from the storeroom, when she heard the sound of someone scraping snow from the front door. She waited. The door creaked open.

'Good heavens, is that you, Gudmundur?' she said, hurrying out of the badstofa only to meet Tóti coming up the hallway, his face as white as milk, drops of sweat pebbled across his skin. 'Good Lord, Reverend! You look like death! How thin you have become!'

'Margrét, is your husband in?' His voice was urgent.

Margrét nodded and invited Tóti into the badstofa. 'Take a seat in the parlour,' she said, drawing aside the curtain. 'You ought not to be travelling in weather like this. Good Lord, how you are shaking! No, come into the kitchen and warm your bones. Whatever has happened?'

'I have been unwell.' Tóti's voice was a croak. 'Fevers, and a swelling of the throat and neck until I thought I might suffocate.' He sat down heavily. 'That is why I have not come until now.' He paused, wheezing a little. 'I could not help it.'

Margrét stared at him. 'I'll fetch Jón for you.' She quietly summoned Lauga to come and help the Reverend out of his ice-covered coat.

After a few short minutes, Margrét and Jón returned to the kitchen.

'Reverend,' Jón said warmly, giving Tóti his hand. 'It is good to see you. My wife tells me that you are not in good health?'

'Where is Agnes?' Tóti interrupted.

Margrét and Jón glanced at each other. 'With Kristín and Steina. Shall I get her?' Margrét asked.

'No, not yet,' Tóti said. He pulled off his glove with effort and rummaged about his shirt. 'Here.' He offered Jón the District Commissioner's letter, swallowing hard.

'What is this?' Jón asked.

'From Blöndal. It announces the date of Agnes's execution.'

There was a gasp from Lauga.

'When is it?' Jón asked quietly.

'The twelfth day of January. And today is the sixth. You haven't heard about it then?' Tóti asked.

Jón shook his head. 'No. The weather has been so bad, it's hard to go out.'

Tóti nodded grimly. 'Well, now you know.'

Lauga looked from the priest to her father. 'Are you going to tell her?'

Margrét reached across the table and took up Tóti's bare hand. She glanced up at him. 'Your skin is so hot. I'll go get her,' she said. 'She would want to hear it from you.'

THE REVEREND IS TALKING TO me, but I can't hear what he is saying, it is as though we are all underwater, the light keeps flickering overhead and I can see the Reverend's hands wave in front of me, he takes hold of my wrists and lets go, he looks like a drowning man trying to catch hold of something to bring him up to the surface. He looks like a skeleton. Where has all the water come from? I don't think I can breathe.

Agnes, he is saying. Agnes, I will be there with you.

Agnes, the Reverend says.

He is so kind, he is reaching around me, he is pulling my body closer to his, but I don't want him near. His mouth is opening and shutting like a fish, the bones of his face like knives under his skin, but I cannot help him, I don't know what he wants. Those who are not being dragged to their deaths cannot understand how the heart grows hard and sharp, until it is a nest of rocks with only an empty egg in it. I am barren; nothing will grow from me any more. I am the dead fish drying in the cold air. I am the dead bird on the shore. I am dry, I am not certain I will bleed when they drag me out to meet the axe. No, I am still warm, my blood still howls in my veins like the wind itself, and it shakes the empty nest and asks where all the birds have gone, where have they gone?

'AGNES? AGNES? I AM HERE. I am with you.' Tóti looked at Agnes anxiously. The woman was staring at the floor, breathing hard and rocking, making her stool creak. He felt the prick of tears at the back of his throat, but he was aware of Margrét, Jón, Steina and Lauga behind him, and the servants, waiting in the doorway to the kitchen, watching.

'I think she needs some water,' Steina said.

'No,' Jón said. He turned around to where the farmhands waited. 'Bjarni! Go get some brandy, would you?'

The bottle was fetched and Margrét brought it to Agnes's lips. 'There,' she said, as Agnes spluttered on the mouthful, spilling most of it on her shawl. 'That will make you feel better.'

'How many days?' Agnes croaked. Tóti noticed that she was digging her fingernails into the flesh of her arm.

'Six days,' Tóti said gently. He reached across and took up her hands in his own. 'But I'm here, I won't let go.'

'Reverend Tóti?'

'Yes, Agnes?'

'Perhaps I could beg them, perhaps if I go to Blöndal he will change his mind and we can appeal. Can you talk to him for me, Reverend? If you go and talk to him and explain I think he would listen to you. Reverend, they can't ...'

Tóti put his trembling hand on the woman's shoulder. 'I am here for you, Agnes. I am here.'

'No!' She pushed him away. 'No! We have to talk to them! You have to make them listen!'

Tóti heard Margrét click her tongue. 'It's not right,' she was muttering. 'It wasn't her fault.'

'What?' Tóti turned to her. 'Did she talk to you?' Someone was crying behind him, one of the daughters.

Margrét nodded, her eyes welling up. 'One night. We stayed up late. It's not right,' she repeated. 'Oh, Lord. Is there something we can do? Tóti? What can we do for her?' Before he could respond, Margrét gasped and shuffled out of the room, her hands to her eyes. Jón followed her.

Agnes was shaking, staring at her hands.

'I can't move them,' she said quietly. She looked up at him with wide eyes. 'I can't move them.'

Tóti took her stiff hands into his own again. He didn't know who was trembling more.

'I am here for you, Agnes.' It was the only thing he could say.

I DO NOT CRUMBLE, I think of the small things. I concentrate my mind on the feeling of linen next to my skin.

I breathe in as deeply and as silently as I am able.

Now comes the darkening sky and a cold wind that passes right through you, as though you are not there, it passes through you as though it does not care whether you are alive or dead, for you will be gone and the wind will still be there, licking the grass flat upon the ground, not caring whether the soil is at a freeze or thaw, for it will freeze and thaw again, and soon your bones, now hot with blood and thick-juicy with marrow, will be dry and brittle and flake and freeze and thaw with the weight of the dirt upon you, and the last moisture of your body will be drawn up to the surface by the grass, and the wind will come and knock it down and push you back against the rocks, or it will scrape you up under its nails and take you out to sea in a wild screaming of snow.

REVEREND TÓTI STAYED UP WITH Agnes well into the night, until finally the woman fell asleep. Margrét watched the Reverend anxiously from the corner of the badstofa. He, too, had fallen asleep, and sat slumped upright against the bedpost, shivering violently under the blanket she had carefully pulled over him. Margrét considered waking him and moving him to a spare bed, but decided against it. She didn't believe he would be easily moved.

Margrét finally laid down her knitting. She was reminded of when Hjördis died. She hadn't given so much as a thought to that dead woman since the first days of Agnes's arrival. But this – the sombre expectation of death, the light burning too late into the night, the weeping into exhaustion. This reminded her. Margrét looked out over the rest of the sleeping household. Lauga, she noticed, was missing from her bed.

Margrét eased herself up off the chair to find her daughter, and almost immediately fell into a fit of coughing that pushed her to her knees. She hacked at the floorboards until a thick clot of blood was expelled from her lungs. It left her feeble, and she waited there on all fours, breathing hard, until she felt strong enough to rise.

It took Margrét several minutes to find Lauga. She was not by the warmth of the hearth in the kitchen, nor in the dairy. Margrét shuffled into the darkness of the pantry, holding a candle aloft.

'Lauga?'

There was a faint noise from the corner where the barrels stood together.

'Lauga, is that you?'

The candlelight threw shadows over the walls, before lighting on someone behind a half-filled sack of meal.

'Mamma?'

'What are you doing in here, Lauga?' Margrét stepped forward and brought the candle closer to her daughter's face.

Lauga squinted in the light and hurriedly stood up. Her eyes were red. 'Nothing at all.'

'Are you upset?'

Lauga blinked and quickly rubbed her eyes. 'No, Mamma.'

Margrét studied her daughter. 'I've been trying to find you,' she said.

'I only wanted a minute to myself.'

They regarded each other for a moment in the ragged light of the guttering candle.

'To bed, then,' Margrét finally suggested. She handed Lauga the candle and silently followed her out of the room.

THERE WAS NO PURSE. FRIDRIK never found the money he wanted. Agnes, Agnes, where did he bury it, is it in the trunk? But it was too late, my fingers were slippery-thick with the whale fat all rubbed into the wood and mingled with the blood on the floor and the lamp was already dashed on the boards and Sigga had already screamed at the sound of glass breaking.

They try to make me eat, but, Tóti, I cannot do it. Don't feed me or I will bite you, I will bite the hand that feeds me, that refuses to love me, that leaves me. Where is my stone? You don't understand! I have nothing to say to you, where are the ravens? Jóas has sent them all away, they never speak to me, it's not fair. See what I do for them? I eat stones, I shatter my teeth, and still they will not speak to me. Only the wind. Only the wind speaks and it will not talk sense, it screams like the widow of the world and will not wait for a reply.

You will be lost. There is no final home, there is no burial, there is only a constant scattering, a thwarted journey that takes you everywhere without offering you a way home, for there is no home, there is only this cold island and your dark self spread thinly upon it until you take up the wind's howl and mimic its loneliness you are not going home you are gone silence will claim you, suck your life down into its black waters and churn out stars that might remember you, but if they do they will not say, they will not say, and if no one will say your name you are forgotten I am forgotten.

THE NIGHT BEFORE THE EXECUTION, the family of Kornsá sat together in the badstofa. Steina, tear-streaked, had gathered as many lamps as she could find, lighting them and placing them about the room to dispel the shadows that lingered in the corners. The servants sat on their beds with their backs against the wall, dumbly watching Tóti and Agnes as they huddled together on her bed. They were holding hands, the Reverend whispering quietly to her. She gazed at the floor, shivering.

Jón came in from feeding the stock, and eased himself down on the bed next to Margrét, bending down slowly to untie his boots. Margrét took the knitting out of her lap and stood to help him out of his jacket, and then hovered there, holding the frayed coat out from her.

'Mamma?' Steina got up from her place beside Lauga, who was staring impassively at the dancing wick of the lamp at her side. 'Mamma, let me take that.'

Margrét pressed her lips together and silently handed Steina the wet coat. Then she slowly got down on her knees and, stifling a cough, shuffled closer to her bed. Her daughter watched as she reached beneath the bunk. 'Steina?'

Steina bent down and helped Margrét pull out a painted trunk. 'Put it on the bed there, next to Jón.' With some difficulty, Steina heaved the wooden trunk onto the blankets. Dust rose into the air. She watched as Margrét undid the iron latch. Inside the trunk were clothes.

Margrét cast a glance at Agnes shaking against the Reverend's side, reached into the trunk and took out a fine woollen shawl. Without a word she walked to her bed and, nodding to Tóti, leant down and wrapped it about Agnes's shoulders.

Tóti looked up at Margrét's face in the dim light and gave a tight smile, his face wan.

The rest of the family watched as Margrét continued to rifle through the trunk, her lips pressed together firmly. She took out a dark skirt with an embroidered pattern about the hem and laid it carefully on the blankets beside her. Then she did the same with a white cotton shirt, an embroidered bodice, and finally a striped apron. She smoothed the wrinkles out of the folds of material with both hands.

'What are you doing, Mamma?' Steina asked.

'It's the least we can do,' Margrét replied. She looked around the room, as if waiting for someone to object, then she snapped the lid of the trunk closed and motioned for Steina to put it back under the bed.

For a moment Margrét stood still, looking across the room to where Lauga sat on her bed. Then, in a few quick strides, she crossed the badstofa and held out her hand.

'Your brooch,' she said. Lauga looked up, her mouth falling open. Then, after a moment's hesitation, she got off the bed and bent to the floor. She slowly handed her mother the clasp and sat back down, blinking away tears. Margrét turned, placed the silver brooch on the bodice spread out over the bed, and picked up her knitting.

THE WORLD HAS STOPPED SNOWING, stopped moving; the clouds hang still in the air like dead bodies. The only things that move are the ravens, and the family of Kornsá, but I cannot tell which is which: they are all in black, jerking in circles around me, waiting to be fed. Where did time go? It left with summer. I am beyond time. Where is the Reverend? Waiting by the river at Gönguskörd. Looking for a skeleton amongst the moss, amongst the lava, amongst the ashes.

Margrét is reaching out to me and she takes my hand in hers, clasps my fingers so tightly that it hurts, it hurts.

'You are not a monster,' she says. Her face is flushed and she bites her lip, she bites down. Her fingers, entwined with my own, are hot and greasy.

'They're going to kill me.' Who said that? Did I say that?

'We'll remember you, Agnes.' She presses my fingers more tightly, until I almost cry out from the pain, and then I am crying. I don't want to be remembered, I want to be here!

'Margrét!'

'I am right here, Agnes. You'll be all right, my girl. My girl.'

I am crying and my mouth is open and filled with something, it is choking me and I spit it out. On the ground is a stone, and I look back at Margrét, and see that she did not notice. 'The stone was in my mouth,' I say, and her face creases because she does not understand. There is no time to explain, she has passed my hands on to Steina, as though I am a token, or a piece of bread and they are all taking communion of me, and Steina's fingers are cold. She lets go of my hands and wraps her arms around my neck. The sound of her sobbing is loud in my ear, but I cling to her because her body is warm and I cannot remember when someone last held me like this, when someone last cared enough to lay their cheek next to mine.

'I'm so sorry,' I hear myself say. 'I am so sorry.' But I don't know what I am sorry for. Everyone is speaking in bubbles of air and it is taking everything not to cry, my spine is cramped from not crying, but I am, the tears are here on my face, I don't know, perhaps they are Steina's. Everything is wet. It is the ocean.

'Will they drown me?' I ask, and someone shakes her head. It is Lauga. 'Agnes,' she says, and I say, 'That is the first time you have called me by my name,' and that is it, she collapses as though I have stabbed her in the stomach.

'I think we should go,' Tóti is saying, and I want to turn to him, but I can't because we are all underwater and I cannot swim.

'Here.' A hand takes my arm and I am lifted into the air. The sky comes closer and for a moment I am going to collide with the clouds, but then I see, they have put me on a horse, and like a corpse they are going to take me to the grave, like a dead woman they will bury me in the earth, pocket me like a stone. There are ravens in the sky, but what bird flies underwater? What bird can sing without stones beneath him to listen?

Natan would know. I must remember to ask him.

✝

SNOW LAY OVER THE VALLEY like linen, like a shroud waiting for the dead body of sky that slumped overhead.

It's all over, Tóti thought. He nudged his horse onwards and brought it next to Agnes's. Holding the reins in one hand, he pulled off a glove and reached across to put his hand on her leg. As he did, he smelt the hot stench of urine. Agnes looked at him, her eyes wide. Her mouth was chattering uncontrollably.

'I'm sorry,' she mouthed.

Tóti squeezed her leg. He tried to hold her gaze, but her eyes were darting all over the valley. 'Agnes,' he murmured. 'Agnes, look at me.'

She glanced at him, and he thought the light blue of her eyes had faded to almost white. 'I'm here,' he said, and squeezed her leg again.

Next to him, District Officer Jón rode with his mouth in a determined line. Tóti was surprised to see that several other men had joined them, all dressed in black, scarves pulled up high about their mouths to ward off the freezing air. They rode in a loose pack, their horses champing at their bridles, snorting stiff clouds of steam.

'Reverend!' There was a call from behind. As Tóti turned, he saw a large man with long blond hair ride up from the rear. As he pulled closer, the man reached into his coat and took out a small flask. He handed it to Tóti without a word. Tóti nodded. He leaned over, and took Agnes's hand, and pressed the flask into it.

'Drink, Agnes.'

The woman looked down at the flask, and then at Tóti, who nodded. After pulling out the corked stopper, she brought the flask up to her trembling mouth with both hands and took a sip that left her spluttering and coughing. Tóti reassured her with soft words.

'Take another, Agnes,' he insisted. 'It will help.'

The next sip went down more easily, and Tóti noticed that her teeth stopped chattering quite so violently.

'Drink it all, Agnes,' the blond-haired man said. 'I brought it for you.'

Agnes swivelled in her saddle to try and see the man who spoke. She pushed her long, dark hair out of her face to regard him better.

'Thank you,' she murmured.

After some time the riders had climbed the ridge leading up out of the valley, and saw the first hills of Vatnsdalshólar. The strange mounds looked eerie in the blue light, and Tóti shuddered at the sight.

Agnes had pushed her chin down into the scarves around her neck, and her hair had fallen over her face. Tóti wondered whether the brandy had sent her to sleep. But as he wondered this, the horses came to a halt, and Agnes jerked her face upwards. She looked down towards the valley's entrance and began to shake.

'Have we arrived?' she whispered to Tóti. The Reverend dismounted and quickly handed his reins to another rider. He shook his head clear of the nausea that swamped him and stepped through the snow, the squeak of his footsteps resounding through the frosted air. He reached up for Agnes.

'Let me help you down.'

Jón and another man helped him take Agnes out of the saddle. As they set her feet upon the ground, she teetered, and fell.

'Agnes! Here, take my hand.'

Agnes looked up at Tóti with tears in her eyes. 'I can't move my legs,' she croaked. 'I can't move my legs.'

Tóti bent down and put her arm around his shoulders. As he tried to lift her up his knees buckled and they fell into the snow drifts again.

'Reverend!' Jón darted forward to help them.

'No!' The word came out as a scream. Tóti stared up at the circle of men standing over them. Agnes clutched at his arm. 'No,' he said again. 'Please let me lift her. I need to lift her.'

The men stood back as he crawled onto his knees, then slowly pushed himself upwards. He stumbled, then righted himself, closing his eyes and taking a deep breath until he wasn't so light-headed. Do not falter, he told himself. He bent down and offered his hand to Agnes. 'Take it,' he said. 'Take my hand.'

Agnes opened her eyes and grasped it, her nails gripping his skin. 'Don't let go,' she whimpered. 'Don't let go of me.'

'I won't let go of you, Agnes. I'm right here.'

Clenching his teeth, he hauled her out of the snow, wrapping her arm about his neck to lift her higher. 'There you go,' he said gently, holding her fast about the waist. He ignored the smell of shit. 'I've got you.'

Around them the farmers of the District started walking towards the three hills that stood together in a clump. Already over forty men stood around the middle hill, all dressed in black. They look like birds of prey surrounding their kill, Tóti thought.

'Do we have to go with them?' Agnes asked, her voice cracking.

'No, Agnes.' Tóti reached over and brushed her hair out of her eyes with his free hand. 'No, we have to walk just a little way, and then wait. Fridrik is walking out first.'

Agnes nodded, and clung to Tóti as he slowly stumbled through the drifts to a tussock, lifting her as best as he could. Breathing heavily, he gently lowered her onto the snowy ground and sank down next to her. Jón squatted beside them and picked up the flask that had slipped from his gloved hand. Tóti watched as the older man took a quick sip and winced.

The minutes staggered past. Tóti tried to ignore the deadening needles of cold that wormed into his bones. He held Agnes's hands in his own, her head was on his shoulder.

'Why don't we pray, Agnes?'

The woman opened her eyes and stared into the distance. 'I can hear singing.'

Tóti turned his face to where the sound was coming from. He recognised the burial hymn, 'Just like the flower'. Agnes was listening intently, shivering on the ground.

'Let's listen together then,' he whispered. He put his arm about her as the verses lifted over the snowy field and fell about them like a mist.

On Tóti's left, Jón was bent on his knees, his hands clasped before him, his lips muttering the Lord's Prayer. 'Dear Lord, forgive us all our trespasses.' Tóti gripped Agnes's hand more tightly, and she gave a small gasp.

'Tóti,' she said in a panicked voice. 'Tóti, I don't think I'm ready. I don't think they can do it. Can you make them wait? They have to wait.'

Tóti pulled Agnes closer to him and squeezed her hand.

'I won't let go of you. God is all around us, Agnes. I won't ever let go.'

The woman looked up into the blank sky. The sudden sound of the first axe fall echoed throughout the valley.

EPILOGUE

The criminals Fridrik Sigurdsson and Agnes Magnúsdóttir
were today moved out of custody to the place of execution, and
following them to the execution site were the priests Reverend
Magnús Árnason, Reverend Gísli Gíslason, Reverend Jóhann
Tómasson and Reverend Thorvardur Jónsson, an assistant
priest. The criminals had wished that the latter two help them
prepare for their deaths. After the priest Jóhann Tómasson
completed a speech of admonition to the convict Fridrik
Sigurdsson, Fridrik's head was taken off with one blow of
the axe. The farmer Gudmundur Ketilsson, who had been
ordered to be executioner, committed the work that he had
been asked to do with dexterity and fearlessness. The criminal
Agnes Magnúsdóttir, who, while this was taking place, had
been kept at a remote station where she could not see the site
of execution, was then fetched. After the Assistant Reverend
Thorvardur Jónsson had appropriately prepared her for death,
the same executioner cut off her head, and with the same
craftsmanship as before. The lifeless heads were then set upon
two stakes at the site of execution, and their bodies put in two
coffins of untreated boards, and buried before the men were
dismissed. While the deed took place, and there until it was
finished, everything was appropriately quiet and well-ordered,

and it was concluded by a short address by Reverend Magnús
Árnason to those that were there.

Actum ut supra.
B. Blöndal, R. Olsen, A. Árnason
From the Magistrate's Book of Húnavatn District, 1830

AUTHOR'S NOTE

WHILE THIS NOVEL IS A work of fiction, it is based on real events. Agnes Magnúsdóttir was the last person to be executed in Iceland, convicted for her role in the murders of Natan Ketilsson and Pétur Jónsson on the night between the 13th and 14th of March 1828, at Illugastadir (Illugastaðir), on the Vatnsnes Peninsula, North Iceland. In 1934, Agnes and Fridrik Sigurdsson's (Friðrik Sigurðsson's) remains were removed from Thrístapar (Þrístapar) to the churchyard at Tjörn, where they share a grave. Natan Ketilsson's grave in the same churchyard is no longer marked. Sigrídur Gudmundsdóttir (Sigríður Guðmundsdóttir) was sent to a Copenhagen textile prison, where she is believed to have died after a few years. There was, for some time, a popular local myth that claimed she was rescued from the prison by a wealthy man and went on to live a long life. While this is untrue, it is indicative of public sympathy towards her in the years after these events.

My interpretation of the Illugastaðir murders and executions is informed by many years of research, during which I have accessed ministerial records, parish archives, censuses, local histories and publications, and have spoken with many Icelanders. While some historical characters have been invented, omitted, or had their names altered out of necessity, most, including Björn Blöndal, Assistant Reverend Thorvardur (Þorvarður) Jónsson, most members of the family at Kornsá, and Agnes's parents and siblings, are taken from historical records.

No offence is intended towards living relatives of any character whose name I have borrowed in the service of telling Agnes's story.

Many of the letters, documents and extracts presented at the beginning of each chapter have been translated and adapted from original sources. The ruins of Natan's workshop still stand at Illugastaðir today, and a stone plaque marks the site of execution at Þrístapar. All place names used in this novel are true to life, and many of the farms referenced by Agnes and other characters remain working farms to this day.

Many known and established facts about Agnes's life and the murders have been reproduced in this novel, and events have either been drawn directly from the record, or are the result of speculation; they are fictional likelihoods. The family at the farm of Kornsá did hold Agnes in custody after she was held at Stóra-Borg, and Agnes chose Assistant Reverend Þorvarður Jónsson to act as her priest in her last days. The nature of their relationship, including their first mysterious meeting and Agnes's dream, is drawn from local accounts and histories of the area. The high level of literacy shown by the characters is historically accurate. Icelanders have had almost universal literacy rates since the end of the eighteenth century.

I am indebted to the research of scholars such as Gísli Ágúst Gunnlaugsson, Ólöf Garðarsdóttir, Loftur Guttormson, Gunnar Thorvaldsen, Sören Edvinsson, Richard Tomasson, and Sigurður Magnússon, who have published extensively on subjects such as foster children and paupers, infant mortality, illegitimacy and kinship networks in nineteenth-century Iceland. I have also drawn on many nineteenth-century journals by foreign travellers to Iceland, including those of Ebenezer Henderson, John Barrow, Alexander Bryson, Arthur Dillon, William Hooker, Niels Horrebow, Sir

George Mackenzie and Uno Von Troil. *Húnavetningur, Sagnaþættir úr Húnaþing*, and *Hunavatnsþing Brandsstaðaannáll* also proved to be invaluable publications.

Several noteworthy books and articles have been written about the Illugastaðir murders, and the life (and death) of Natan Ketilsson, including *Enginn Má Undan Líta* by Guðlaugur Guðmundsson, *Yfirvaldið* by Þorgeir Þorgeirsson, *Dauði Natans Ketilssonar* by Gunnar S. Þorleifsson, *Dauði Natans Ketilssonar* by Guðbrandur Jónsson, *Dauði Natans Ketilssonar* by Eline Hoffman (translated into Icelandic by Halldór Friðjónsson), *Friðþæging* by Tómas Guðmundsson and *Agnes of Friðrik fyrir og eftir dauðann* by Sigrún Huld Þorgrímsdóttir. While wonderfully useful, some of these publications contradict one another, and some hold a common view of Agnes as 'an inhumane witch, stirring up murder'. This novel has been written to supply a more ambiguous portrayal of this woman.

ACKNOWLEDGEMENTS

I AM INDEBTED TO MANY people who have assisted me with the research and writing of this book. My sincere thanks to Knútur Óskarsson and his mother for your generosity and coffee, assistance with translation and all the late night conversations at Ósar. Meeting you both remains a singular moment of synchronicity and good fortune. Thank you to Jón Torfason and your fellow archivists at Þjóðskjalasafn Íslands for your assistance and enthusiasm, and for finding me the original letters from the trial. Thank you to Guðmundur Jóhannsson for your vastly useful letter. To the librarians and staff at the Þjóðminjasafn, Árni Magnússon Institute for Icelandic Studies, Kringlan Library, Árbæjarsafn and Glumbær, thank you for your patience and assistance.

To my 'Icelandic family' – *þakka þér kærlega fyrir*. Without you this novel could never have been written. My love and gratitude to dear Pétur Björnsson, Regína Gunnarsdóttir, Hera Birgisdóttir, Halldór Sigurðsson, Sylvía Dögg Gunnarsdóttir and María Reynisdóttir, for your kindness, spare beds and generosity. I am also grateful to the many other Icelanders I have met who have contributed to this novel in strange and various ways. I hope you see this novel as the dark love letter to Iceland I intend it to be.

Thanks to those at Flinders University, especially Ruth Starke, who has supported me since the very beginning. Thank you to my early readers, Kylie Cardell and Kalinda Ashton, and to Kate Douglas, David Sornig and Bec Starford for your friendship and the opportunities you have given me.

To Geraldine Brooks, for your sage observations and mentorship – thank you so much. To the Writing Australia Unpublished Manuscript Award, the SA Writers' Centre and to Peter Bishop, Valerie Parv, Patrick Allington and Mark Macleod for your generous comments: thank you.

I'm ever so grateful to the marvellous Pippa Masson and dear Annabel Blay at Curtis Brown Australia. Thank you to Gordon Wise, Kate Cooper and colleagues at Curtis Brown UK, and to Dan Lazar at Writers House. To Emma Rafferty, Sophie Jonathan, Amanda Brower and Jo Jarrah for your keen eyes and considered suggestions – thank you. To my wonderful publishers, Alex Craig and Paul Baggaley at Picador, and Judy Clain at Little, Brown, thank you for believing in this book.

Finally, my most heartfelt thanks go to Pam, Alan and Briony for your love and constancy, and for caring about Agnes Magnúsdóttir as much as I do. And last, but never least: thank you to Angharad, for never doubting, and for fortifying me every day, every hour.